Fanny Fern, the first weekly newspaper columnist in America, was born Sara Payson Willis on July 9, 1811, in Portland, Maine, the daughter of Nathaniel and Hannah Parker Willis. Her father founded the *Boston Recorder*, the first religious newspaper in the United States, and later the *Youth's Companion*, the first children's newspaper. Sara's older brother, Nathaniel P. Willis, was a poet and editor of the *New York Mirror* and later the *Home Journal*. Educated at Catharine Beecher's Female Seminary in Hartford, Connecticut, Sara Willis was a good student who was particularly adept at writing compositions. On May 4, 1837, she married Charles Harrington Eldredge, a cashier at a Boston bank. When Eldredge died of typhoid fever in 1846, Sara and her two small daughters were left nearly penniless. Receiving only grudging support from her father and father-in-law, Sara tried unsuccessfully to find work as a teacher and as a seamstress. In 1849, under pressure from her father, she married Samuel P. Farrington, a cruel and jealous man, whom Sara left after two years. Farrington obtained a divorce on the grounds of desertion in 1852.

Determined to make a living for herself and her children, Sara decided to follow in the family tradition of journalism. After months of effort, she sold her first story to the *Olive Branch*, which published "The Model Husband" on June 28, 1851. Soon Sara was writing articles and reviews for both the *Olive Branch* and the *True Flag*; by the fall of 1851 her work was appearing under the name of "Fanny Fern" and was quickly becoming famous. In September 1852, she entered into an agreement to write a weekly article for the *Musical World and Times*. Her first collection of articles, *Fern Leaves from Fanny's Portfolio*, was published in June 1853 and sold 70,000 copies in the first year. *Little Ferns for Fanny's Little Friends*, a collection of essays for children, appeared later that year, and *Fern Leaves from Fanny's Portfolio*, Second Series, followed in 1854.

Fern, now a highly successful journalist, moved to New York with her children. There, she wrote for a variety of papers and, in 1855, she published *Ruth Hall,* her autobiographical account of her difficult life. Her other two works of fiction followed shortly: "Fanny Ford," a serialized novel which appeared in the *New York Ledger;* and *Rose Clark* (1856). That year she also married James Parton, a writer and biographer, signing a prenuptial agreement guaranteeing that the income Fern made from her writing was her own. Beginning on January 5, 1856, Fern published a weekly column in the *Ledger* for which she wrote exclusively until her death. Her other published works included stories and articles for children and collections of her newspaper articles, *Fresh Leaves* (1857); *Folly as It Flies* (1868); *Ginger Snaps* (1870); and *CaperSauce* (1872). At her death from cancer in New York on October 10, 1872, Fanny Fern was among the most famous women in America.

Susan Belasco is professor of English at the University of Nebraska, Lincoln. The author of articles and reviews on nineteenth-century American women writers and American periodical literature, she is the editor of Margaret Fuller's *Summer on the Lakes, in 1843* and a contributing editor for *The Walt Whitman Archive.* She is the co-editor of *"These Sad but Glorious Days": Dispatches from Europe, 1846–1850 by Margaret Fuller; Periodical Literature in Nineteenth-Century America;* and *Approaches to Teaching Uncle Tom's Cabin.*

RUTH HALL

A Domestic Tale of the Present Time

———

FANNY FERN

INTRODUCTION AND NOTES BY
SUSAN BELASCO

PENGUIN BOOKS

PENGUIN BOOKS

Published by the Penguin Group
Penguin Group (USA) Inc., 375 Hudson Street,
New York, New York 10014, USA
Penguin Group (Canada), 90 Eglinton Avenue East, Suite 700, Toronto,
Ontario M4P 2Y3, Canada (a division of Pearson Penguin Canada Inc.)
Penguin Books Ltd., 80 Strand, London WC2R 0RL, England
Penguin Ireland, 25 St. Stephen's Green, Dublin 2,
Ireland (a division of Penguin Books Ltd.)
Penguin Group (Australia), 250 Camberwell Road, Camberwell, Victoria 3124,
Australia (a division of Pearson Australia Group Pty. Ltd.)
Penguin Books India Pvt. Ltd., 11 Community Centre, Panchsheel Park,
New Delhi - 110 017, India
Penguin Group (NZ), 67 Apollo Drive, Mairangi Bay,
Auckland 1311, New Zealand (a division of Pearson New Zealand Ltd.)
Penguin Books (South Africa) (Pty.) Ltd., 24 Sturdee Avenue,
Rosebank, Johannesburg 2196, South Africa

Penguin Books Ltd., Registered Offices:
80 Strand, London WC2R 0RL, England

First published in the United States of America by Mason Brothers 1855
This edition with an introduction and notes by Susan Belasco
published in Penguin Books 1997

13   15   17   19   20   18   16   14   12

Introduction and notes copyright © Susan Belasco, 1997
All rights reserved

LIBRARY OF CONGRESS CATALOGING IN PUBLICATION DATA
Fern, Fanny, 1811–1872.
Ruth Hall: a domestic tale of the present time/Fanny Fern;
introduction by Susan Belasco Smith.
p.   cm.—(Penguin classics)
Includes bibliographical references (p.   ).
ISBN 0 14 01.8952 1 (pbk.)
I. Title.   II. Series.
PS2523.P9R8   1997
813'.3—dc20   96-28158

Printed in the United States of America
Set in Bembo

ACKNOWLEDGMENTS

I am grateful to my former colleagues at the University of Tulsa for a Faculty Development Fellowship in the summer of 1995 that provided time and resources for the study and preparation of the initial printing of this edition. I am grateful to Joyce W. Warren, whose books and articles first introduced me to Fanny Fern. Students in my American literature classes at Tulsa in 1995–96 provided lively discussion of *Ruth Hall* and suggested many of the notes for the text; I am thankful to Jennifer Johnson, Glenda Mims, Alexis Whitney, and Marja Willis. Since 2000, students at the University of Nebraska, Lincoln, have helped me consider new ways of thinking about this novel, and I am especially grateful to the students in a recent graduate seminar, "Nineteenth-Century American Women Writers and Reform," for their insights. James G. Watson and John Seelye provided close readings and helpful suggestions on an early draft of the introduction. Once again, I am indebted to Linck C. Johnson for illuminating conversation, expert editorial advice, and warm companionship.

CONTENTS

Introduction by Susan Belasco   xv

Suggestions for Further Reading   xlvii

A Note on the Text   lii

RUTH HALL

PREFACE
To the Reader   1

CHAPTER I
The Eve Before the Bridal—Ruth's Little Room—
A Retrospective Reverie   3

CHAPTER II
The Wedding—A Glimpse of the Character of Ruth's Brother
Hyacinth   9

CHAPTER III
The New Home—Soliloquy of the Mother-in-Law   10

CHAPTER IV
The First Interview with the Mother-in-Law   12

CHAPTER V
Ruth's Reflections on the Interview   15

CHAPTER VI
A Bit of Family History   16

CHAPTER VII
The First-born   19

CHAPTER VIII
The Nurse   20

CHAPTER IX
Further Developments of the Mother-in-Law's Character   22

CHAPTER X
Ruth's Country Home   24

CHAPTER XI
Ruth and Daisy   26

CHAPTER XII
The Old Folks Follow the Young Couple—
An Entertaining Dialogue   27

CHAPTER XIII
The Old Lady's Surreptitious Visit to Ruth's, and Her Encounter
with Dinah   29

CHAPTER XIV
The Old Lady Searches the House—What She Finds   32

CHAPTER XV
The Old Doctor Meddles with Harry's Farming Arrangements   35

CHAPTER XVI
Little Daisy's Reverie—Her Strange Playfellow   37

CHAPTER XVII
"Pat" Mutinies   38

CHAPTER XVIII
A Growl from the Old Lady   39

CHAPTER XIX
Daisy's Glee at the First Sleigh-ride   41

CHAPTER XX
Daisy's Illness—The Old Doctor Refuses to Come   42

CHAPTER XXI
Dinah's Warning—Harry Goes Again for the Doctor   45

CHAPTER XXII
The Old Doctor Arrives Too Late   47

CHAPTER XXIII
"The Glen" Deserted—The Old Doctor's and His Wife's Version
of the Cause of Daisy's Death—Mrs. Jones Gives Her Opinion   50

CHAPTER XXIV
Anniversary of Daisy's Death—Ruth's Reverie—
Little Katy's Request   53

CHAPTER XXV
Hotel Life—A New Friend   55

CHAPTER XXVI
The Fall of the Leaf—Harry's Illness—The Lonely Watcher   58

CONTENTS

CHAPTER XXVII
Arrival of the Old Doctor and His Wife   61

CHAPTER XXVIII
The Old Doctor's Announcement—Harry's Death   63

CHAPTER XXIX
Hyacinth's Sensibilities Shocked   66

CHAPTER XXX
Miss Skinlin   69

CHAPTER XXXI
Harry's Funeral   73

CHAPTER XXXII
A Servant's Devotion   75

CHAPTER XXXIII
Bickerings of the Father and Father-in-Law—Dispute About the
Support of the Children   77

CHAPTER XXXIV
Ruth Receives a Visit from Her Father—He Insists on Her Giving
Up Her Children to the Old Doctor—Ruth's Refusal   79

CHAPTER XXXV
The Old Lady, Enraged, Proposes a Compromise—Mr. Ellet Is
Forced to Accede   82

CHAPTER XXXVI
Ruth's New Lodgings—Speculations of the Boarders   87

CHAPTER XXXVII
Mr. Develin's Counting-House—The Old Doctor's Letter   89

CHAPTER XXXVIII
Little Katy Mourns for Her Papa   92

CHAPTER XXXIX
Mr. Develin Demands Harry's Clothes of Ruth—
The Wedding Vest   94

CHAPTER XL
Ruth's Application for Needle-work   96

CHAPTER XLI
Disgust of Ruth's Fashionable Friends   99

CHAPTER XLII
Conversation in Mrs. Millet's Kitchen   101

CHAPTER XLIII
The Bouquet   103

CHAPTER XLIV
Mrs. Millet and the Wooden Man   105

CHAPTER XLV
Little Katy Visits Her Grandpa and Meets with a Characteristic
Reception—The Strange Gentleman   107

CHAPTER XLVI
A Peep from Ruth's Chamber Window—Katy's Return   111

CHAPTER XLVII
Boarding-House Revolution—Mrs. Skiddy's Flight—
Mr. Skiddy in the Capacity of Dry Nurse   114

CHAPTER XLVIII
A New Idea—The Millets Exhibit Their Friendship
and Delicacy   119

CHAPTER XLIX
Ruth Resolves to Become a Teacher   122

CHAPTER L
Ruth Applies for a Primary School   124

CHAPTER LI
The Examination by the School Committee   126

CHAPTER LII
Mrs. Skiddy's Unexpected Return   130

CHAPTER LIII
Skiddy's Intercepted Hegira—His Incarceration—
His Final Escape   134

CHAPTER LIV
The Lunatic Asylum   138

CHAPTER LV
Ruth's New Landlady   142

CHAPTER LVI
The Strange Lodger—Ruth Resolves to Resort to Her Pen to
Obtain a Subsistence—She Applies to her Brother Hyacinth for
Advice and Assistance—His Characteristic Reply   145

CHAPTER LVII
The Old Lady Resorts to Stratagem, and Carries Her Point   148

CHAPTER LVIII
Mr. Ellet Exhibits His Usual Fatherly Interest in Ruth's Affairs   151

CHAPTER LIX
Ruth Applies for Employment at Newspaper Offices   153

CHAPTER LX
The Bread of Life   156

CHAPTER LXI
A Chapter Which May Be Instructive   158

CHAPTER LXII
Ruth Obtains Employment—Illness of Nettie—
The Strange Lodger Proves Useful   160

CHAPTER LXIII
A Peep into the Old Doctor's Cottage   164

CHAPTER LXIV
A Glimpse of Coming Success   167

CHAPTER LXV
Little Nettie's Sorrows—Cheering Letters   172

CHAPTER LXVI
Katy's First Day at School—The Town-Pump Controversy—
Cruelty of Katy's Grandparents   176

CHAPTER LXVII
Mr. John Walter   180

CHAPTER LXVIII
A Letter from Mr. Walter, and Its Effect   183

CHAPTER LXIX
Ruth Engages to Write Solely for the Household Messenger   187

CHAPTER LXX
What Mr. Lescom Said   189

CHAPTER LXXI
A Sharp Correspondence   193

CHAPTER LXXII
Offers of Marriage and Offers to Publish   197

CHAPTER LXXIII
What Mr. Tibbetts Said About Ruth's Writing for the
Household Messenger   201

CHAPTER LXXIV
Soliloquy of a Sub-Editor   204

CHAPTER LXXV
Mr. Walter's Visit   209

CHAPTER LXXVI
The Phrenological Examination   215

CHAPTER LXXVII
Publication Day Comes at Last   223

CHAPTER LXXVIII
Hyacinth Cornered   226

CHAPTER LXXIX
Mr. Lewis Enlightened   229

CHAPTER LXXX
More Letters   232

CHAPTER LXXXI
Freshet in the Doctor's Cellar—"Hams" in Danger of a Total
Wreck—Sudden Appearance of Ruth—Rescue of Little Katy   236

CHAPTER LXXXII
Arrival of Katy with Her Mother, Mr. Walter, and Mr. Grey, at
New Lodgings; Dinner and Letters—Conversations Between the
Children   240

CHAPTER LXXXIII
The Little Family Alone at Their New Quarters—Nettie in the
Confession Box—Katy's Mirth   249

CHAPTER LXXXIV
Katy and Nettie Compare Notes—Ruth Dreams—Midnight
Conflagration—Rescue of the Little Family by Johnny Galt   253

CHAPTER LXXXV
Tea-Table Talk Between "The Wooden Man" and His Spouse—
Letter from "Our John" 257

CHAPTER LXXXVI
The Old Lady Extinguished in a Conversation with Her Neighbors,
Who Announce the Astonishing Fact That "Floy" Is Ruth 260

CHAPTER LXXXVII
Conversation Between Ruth's Father and Mr. Jones Regarding
Ruth's Literary Debut 264

CHAPTER LXXXVIII
Interview Between the Literary Bookseller and Mr. Walter 266

CHAPTER LXXXIX
Arrival of Mr. Walter—Bank Stock and Bank Certificate 268

CHAPTER XC
The Last Visit to Harry's Grave 271

Explanatory Notes 273

INTRODUCTION

Until recently, antebellum American literature was defined in terms of a handful of "classic" texts, such as Ralph Waldo Emerson's *Representative Men* (1850); Nathaniel Hawthorne's *The Scarlet Letter* (1850); Herman Melville's *Moby-Dick* (1851); Henry David Thoreau's *Walden* (1854); and Walt Whitman's *Leaves of Grass* (1855). At the time, however, those texts were overshadowed by a series of enormously popular novels written by women, including Susan Warner's *The Wide, Wide World* (1850); Harriet Beecher Stowe's *Uncle Tom's Cabin* (1852); Maria Susanna Cummins's *The Lamplighter* (1854); and *Ruth Hall: A Domestic Tale of the Present Time* (1855). Indeed, in 1855 few writers, male or female, were as famous as Fanny Fern. In contrast to other contemporary writers of fiction, however, her fame was the result of Fern's phenomenal success as a journalist, which provided both the foreground and the subject matter of *Ruth Hall*. Fern's unconventional; and intensely autobiographical novel is the story of a woman who perseveres despite the rigid social expectations and cultural pressures for women in her time. It is also a first-hand account of the development of the profession of writing and the conditions in the expanding literary marketplace of mid-nineteenth-century America, a marketplace few understood so well or exploited so triumphantly as Fanny Fern.

I

On December 29, 1855, an arresting notice appeared on the front page of a popular weekly publication, the *New York Ledger*. Accustomed to a steady supply of family-oriented short stories, serials, articles, and poems written by celebrated writers, readers would not have been surprised to learn about the latest *Ledger* acquisition:

> A new agreement with FANNY FERN for a new series of her spirited, lively, dashing unrivalled sketches. We will have a complete Sketch from her brilliant and popular pen every week during the entire year. Her efforts will be devoted exclusively to the LEDGER, *as she will write for no other paper!*

This announcement indicated that Robert J. Bonner, the innovative editor and owner of this flourishing family newspaper, had successfully negotiated an unprecedented arrangement with Fanny Fern, a rising star as a journalist and author of the bestselling novel *Ruth Hall.* In June, Bonner had, with considerable fanfare and advertising acumen, published Fern's "Fanny Ford," a novella in ten parts, for which he had paid $100 for each installment, an unparalleled sum of money for newspaper writing in 1855. Following the success of this serial, Bonner contracted with Fern to write a signed, weekly column exclusively for the *Ledger.* Overnight, Fanny Fern became one of the most highly paid writers in the country—male or female. Her spirited, witty articles of social criticism and commentary appeared weekly from January 5, 1856, until October 12, 1872, two days after her death from cancer at age sixty-one.

In concluding this arrangement, Bonner made Fanny Fern the first celebrity journalist and his successful newspaper a hit. Bonner, an Irish immigrant who served a printing apprenticeship for the *Hartford Courant,* left New England for New York in 1844 and took a job as a printer for a faltering publication devoted to mercantile affairs for country businessmen, unimaginatively entitled the *Merchants' Ledger and Statistical Review.* Determined to publish a different kind of periodical, Bonner managed to save enough money to purchase the weekly outright and promptly changed the name to the *New York Ledger*. He set about the business of printing a variety of literary materials, placing less and less emphasis on news reports and accounts of commercial activities. Although he wished to establish a readership for a family paper that could be used for weekly entertainment within the home, Bonner had no interest in dull, conventional material. He sought out lively and informative works; he recruited the best writers he could afford and determined (as he had printed on the masthead) to devote the *Ledger* to "choice literature, romance, the news, and commerce." He first invited Lydia Sigourney, a well-known and popular poet, to write exclusively for the paper; later, when Fanny Fern was becoming a household name, he secured her work as well. Unlike many other editors of the day who paid little or nothing for irregular contributions from both known and unknown writers, Bonner developed a system of exclusive contracts for regular contributors and paid them fixed salaries, enabling them to support themselves as professional authors. By the end of 1855, when Bonner announced that Fanny Fern would become an exclusive writer for the *Ledger*, the circulation stood at 100,000 subscribers, up from 2,500 in 1851, when he had first bought the original *Merchants' Ledger*. During the first year of Fanny Fern's exclusive contract with the *Ledger*, the circulation grew to 180,000. By 1860, the circulation topped 400,000—including 50,000 copies sent by mail, some to cities as far away as St. Louis—a successful venture by any measure. While Bonner had a penchant for clever advertisement and flashy promotion in the style of his contemporary, P. T. Barnum, he took care to maintain high standards for the quality of the contributions for his paper. The combination made Bonner an innovative leader in developing a major new market for literature; he also led the way in placing the emerging profession of authorship on a much firmer economic basis.

In becoming a part of Bonner's enterprise, Fanny Fern joined an impressive group who wrote for the *Ledger*, one that would eventually include many of the most influential writers of the day: Lydia Sigourney, E.D.E.N. Southworth, Sylvanus Cobb, Jr., Henry Ward Beecher, John Greenleaf Whittier, Henry Wadsworth Longfellow, Edward Everett, Louisa May Alcott, James Parton, Harriet Beecher Stowe, George Bancroft, William Cullen Bryant, Alice and Phoebe Cary, Sara Jane Lippincott (Grace Greenwood), and even such British luminaries as Tennyson and Charles Dickens, to whom Bonner paid $5,000 for a three-part serial, "Hunted Down," published on August 20, 27, and September 3, 1859. And these writers were part of the larger literary establishment who wrote for the periodical press, including Herman Melville, Edgar Allan Poe, Nathaniel Hawthorne, Walt Whitman, Margaret Fuller, Frances E. W. Harper, Frederick Douglass, Lydia Maria Child, Ralph Waldo Emerson, Henry David Thoreau, and Elizabeth Barstow Stoddard, all of whom wrote poems, stories, serialized fiction, or articles and essays which appeared in papers such as the abolitionist *Liberator,* the monthly women's magazine *Godey's Lady's Book,* Horace Greeley's *New York Tribune,* or in one of the high-powered literary journals, like *Putnam's Magazine* and the *Atlantic Monthly.*

For Fanny Fern, the *Ledger* announcement—with all the implications of success, stature, a nd recognition—surely represented the triumphant end of a long, lonely, and often bitter struggle to create a place for herself in the periodical press. In December 1855, she could look back to a series of remarkable professional accomplishments. A frequent contributor to the Boston *Olive Branch* and *True Flag,* the New York *Musical World and Times,* and the Philadelphia *Saturday Evening Post,* she was also the author of four books: *Fern Leaves from Fanny's Portfolio* (1853), a collection of her newspaper articles; *Little Ferns for Fanny's Little Friends* (1853), a book of short articles and stories for children; *Fern Leaves from Fanny's Portfolio, Second Series* (1854), an additional collection of her newspaper articles and short pieces; and her first novel, *Ruth Hall* (1855). The exclusive arrangement with the *Ledger* must have seemed a well-earned reward for her hard work and tenacity. Four and a half years before, on June 28, 1851, she had published her first article, "The Model Husband," in Reverend Thomas F. Norris's *Olive Branch*. It is a short, satiric account of what an ideal married man should be, the humor of which belied the trying circumstances under which the author—who had known both a painful widowhood and a bitter divorce—labored. The piece is pointedly funny but also clearly indicative of the resolute character of the impoverished single mother who had sold this article for fifty cents by walking the streets of Boston from editor's door to editor's door, determined to sell her unknown work. Those days of quiet desperation were now firmly behind her.

II

The woman later known as "Fanny Fern" was born Sara Payson Willis on July 9, 1811, in Portland, Maine, to a family who for three generations had been closely associated with the rise of periodical literature and the profession of authorship in the United States. Nathaniel Willis, Jr., Sara's father, was the son of a pioneering journalist, Nathaniel Willis, who published his *Independent Chronicle* in a Boston building where Benjamin Franklin had once worked as a printer. In 1784, Willis sold his interest in the *Chronicle* and established newspapers in Virginia and Ohio. Nathaniel Willis, Jr., worked with his father in Virginia and later at the *Independent Chronicle* in Boston with the new owner in 1795. In 1803, he married Hannah Parker and worked first as a printer and then as the editor of the *Eastern Argus* in Portland, Maine, a paper supported by the Jeffersonians, a political party that favored states' rights, limited government, and strict construction of the Constitution. After experiencing a religious conversion in 1807, Willis began to print an increasing number of essays on religious topics instead of partisan articles in support of the politicians who had helped establish the paper.

Willis's sponsors, understandably annoyed, pressured him to sell the paper to his partner. At this time Sara was born, and the now unemployed Willis tried and failed to run a grocery store. Admitting defeat, he moved his family to his native Boston and returned to journalism. Staunchly opposed to the Unitarian incursions on his strict Calvinist beliefs, he became a deacon of the Park Street Congregational Church and earned a living by publishing tracts and devotional books. In 1816, he founded the *Boston Recorder*, which Willis described as the first religious newspaper in America. In 1827, he developed the *Youth's Companion* from the children's section of the *Recorder*, turning it into a religious newspaper designed to provide instruction as well as amusements for children. Willis edited the increasingly successful *Youth's Companion* until 1862. (Among the more long lived periodicals established in the nineteenth century, the *Youth's Companion* continued publication until 1929, when it merged with the *American Boy*.)

While the publication of newspapers was a significant aspect of the Willis family life, it was not an unusual feature of the lives of many people who lived in the first half of the nineteenth century. The production and distribution of periodical literature had a profound impact on the culture and society of this period. The various successes and failures that Willis experienced reflected the boom and bust cycles of an emerging enterprise. Beginning in the decade of the 1820s, there was rapid development of periodicals in the United States, some of which was a consequence of the completion of the Erie Canal in 1825. This link from New York to Buffalo changed the nature of routes to the west and consequently drew the northeast and the west closer together both economically and politically, as well as providing for relatively easy and cheaper distribution of printed materials. The election in 1829 of the first populist president, Andrew

Jackson, marked important changes in the nature of the presidency, signaling the growing political power of the common man, which continued during the next twenty years.

By 1850, the era was marked by the spirit of enlargement and extension, by significant growth in the population as well as a rise in literacy. In that year, for example, the population of New York was over 500,000, while the population of Boston was 136,000. According to the census of 1850, the literacy rate for white adults was over 90 percent. The growth in the number and scope of periodicals reflected the mood of the country and made it possible for newspapers like Willis's *Boston Recorder* and his *Youth's Companion* to succeed, but it also resulted in the failure of numerous ventures, as editors and publishers slowly learned what would sell and what would not. In the 1830s a variety of technological developments in papermaking and the development and use of the cylinder press further altered the nature of publication. Cheaper postal routes contributed to wider distribution and a larger potential audience for printed materials. In addition, railroads were connecting various parts of the country—by 1840, there were 9,000 miles of track; by the beginning of the Civil War, the figure had reached more than 30,000. Not only did the railroads provide more efficient transportation for goods and mail, they also provided opportunities for travel, as well as a new outlet for selling portable reading materials. Periodical publication soared as demand increased. But there were economic downturns as well. The Panic of 1837 and the depression that lasted into the early 1840s caused numerous bankruptcies and many periodicals to fail; publishers and editors had to be determined, resourseful, and willing to take some significant risks. By 1833, there were approximately 1,300 ongoing periodicals of various kinds in the country; by the beginning of the Civil War, there would be 4,000.

The periodical quickly came to play a central role in communication, information, and entertainment. William Kirkland, a contemporary critic and reviewer for *Godey's Lady's Book*, observed in 1845 that periodicals were rapidly becoming the pervasive reading material of the day: "A large percentage of books published scarce find a purchaser; numbers of those purchased are never read and many that *are* read, are read by one or two persons, while with periodicals the *un*read are the exception. One has but to look into circulating libraries, reading-rooms and the like places to see that an extensive class of readers finds time or inclination for little else." Not everyone, of course, agreed that the rise of the periodicals and the expansion of the publication industry in general was a positive cultural advancement. Margaret Fuller published some of Henry David Thoreau's work when she edited the *Dial* from 1840 to 1842, but Thoreau was not ultimately successful in obtaining the interest of the general periodical audience. Although some of his work did appear in the *Boston Miscellany*, *Graham's Magazine*, and the *United States Magazine and Democratic Review*, he felt some bitterness about his numerous rejections, and in *Walden* (1854) he was specifically critical of the kind of papers that the Reverend Thomas F. Norris and Robert Bonner published: "If we will read newspapers, why not skip the gossip of Boston and take the best newspaper in the world at once?—not be sucking the pap of 'neutral family' papers, or browsing 'Olive Branches' here in New England. Let the reports of all the learned societies come to us, and we will see if they know any thing." Despite Thoreau's reservations about the quality of the literary marketplace, the newspaper—in all its many nineteenth-century forms and formats—had become a central feature of the American literary landscape. For four generations, the Willis family participated in the growth, development, and exploitation of the periodical press.

By the time Sara was born, Nathaniel Willis was deeply affected by his commitment to his conservative religious beliefs and engaged almost solely in the religious mission of the newspapers he produced and edited. As a child, Sara was well acquainted with her father's work. She helped read proof and even wrote short pieces for her father's publications as she grew older. In addition to providing early training at home, Willis and his wife, Hannah Parker Willis, were vitally engaged in the general literacy of their nine children and sent them away to schools and seminaries designed to combine religious and educational instruction. Nathaniel P. Willis, Sara's older brother, was sent to Boston Latin School, Andover Academy, and then to Yale, where he began as a precocious undergraduate his career as a poet, writer, and editor. Although such preparatory schools and universities were closed to women, Sara Willis was a student at good boarding schools, including the Ladies' Seminary, the school of Ralph Waldo Emerson's second cousin, the Reverend Joseph Emerson, and later Catharine Beecher's Hartford Female Seminary, among the best schools for women at the time.

During the years she attended the Hartford Seminary (1828–1831), Sara Willis met many of Beecher's friends and family members who attended events and paid visits to the seminary. She had the chance to become acquainted with Lydia Sigourney, already a well-known poet who was to be her future colleague at the *Ledger.* She also knew Beecher's sister, Harriet (later Harriet Beecher Stowe), and her brother, Henry Ward Beecher, whom she occasionally accompanied on horseback rides. On a summer visit to a sister, she met Catharine Maria Sedgwick, the successful author of *A New-England Tale* (1822), *Redwood* (1824), *Hope Leslie* (1827), and *Clarence* (1830), as well as a frequent contributor to a variety of magazines and annuals. At the seminary, Sara developed her talent for writing, especially satiric, humorous pieces, and at the invitaiton of the editor occaisonally contributed short pieces to the Hartford newspaper. Athough her father had taken pains to ensure what he considered a proper religious education, the young Sara Willis seemed resistant to the efforts of Beecher and other teachers who would have her more committed to a religious life. Sara later wrote about the importance of understanding individual diferences in a *Ledger* column in 1858, "The Child Whom Nobody Can Do Anything With," when she observed that she would not have

> parents or teachers stretch or dwarf children of all sorts, sizes and capacities, on the same narrow Procrustean bed of scholastic or parental rule. No farmer plants his celery and potatoes in the same spot, and expects it to bear good fruit. Some vegetables he shields from the rude touch, the rough wind, the blazing sun; he knows that each requires different and appropriate nurture, according to its capacities. Should they who have the care of the immortal be less wise?

The biblical echoes notwithstanding, Fern's point is that the blind adherence to convention is not healthy for children. Indeed, from an early age, Fern seems to have been particularly resistant to all efforts to enforce conformity of behavior and belief, especially as prescribed by what she clearly considered to be the arid Calvinism of her father. In *Ruth Hall*, Fern describes at length the hypocrisy and cruelty of the outwardly devout elder Halls, who amid the disharmony of their domestic life remind each other of their "Calvinist church obligations to keep the peace." And in her columns for the *Ledger*, she often commented on the strictly social motivations—a "fashion exchange," as she said in 1865—of church attendance in New York. But, despite a certain waywardness and eagerness to challenge the rules and regulations of the seminary, the young Sara Willis became a favorite of both Catharine Beecher and Harriet Beecher Stowe, with whom she was friends in their later middle age.

While Sara Willis was in school at Hartford, her brother Nathaniel P. Willis was already a well-known poet, having published his first volume, *Sketches*, in 1827, the year he graduated from Yale. For a time, he wrote poetry, drama, short fiction, and miscellaneous prose, establishing himself as one of the best-known male writers of his day. Following in the tradition of the

Willis family, he also became an editor and a journalist. In Boston, he founded the *American Monthly Magazine* in 1829 as a vehicle for reviews of current books, light verse and articles, travel letters, and stylish commentary on fads and fashionable life. He enjoyed his social life with such enthusiasm that the church to which he belonged canceled his membership, and he developed an increasingly notorious reputation as a sophisticated man-about-town. Finding Boston confining and realizing that his magazine was too much in debt to continue, he ended its publication in 1831 and left Boston for New York. George Pope Morris, a journalist and poet, invited him to join the *New York Mirror* as his co-editor, specifically responsible for the literary side of the paper. A periodical designed to provide literary pieces written for what he and Morris agreed would be "instruction and agreeable amusement" appealed to Willis, and the *Mirror* began to reflect his own taste for fashion and society. Judging that the American readership would find accounts of foreign travel amusing and interesting, Willis arranged to become a foreign correspondent. For the next five years, he lived mostly in Europe and sent sketches and essays back to New York for publication in the *Mirror*. Emulating the very successful career of Washington Irving, he collected his travel sketches in two collections, *Pencillings by the Way* (1835) and *Loiterings of Travel* (1840). He also published a book of poetry in England, *Melanie and Other Poems* (1835). In addition, Willis wrote for a variety of periodicals, including *Godey's Lady's Book* and *Graham's Magazine*.

After the *New York Mirror* ceased publication in 1842, Willis and Morris established a series of other ventures, the *New Mirror*, the *Weekly Mirror*, and the *Evening Mirror*. Recognizing the talent of Edgar Allan Poe, Willis and Morris hired the poet and short-story writer as a staff literary critic from 1844 to 1845, and "The Raven" appeared in the *Evening Mirror* in January 1845. The next year, Willis and Morris left the *Weekly* and *Evening Mirror* to establish the popular weekly magazine of society news, essay, and verse, the *Home Journal* (1846–1901), which survives today as the elegant magazine of high society, *Town and Country*. By the early 1840s, Nathaniel P. Willis was a powerful figure in the New York Literary marketplace who had published several books and a series of periodicals that appealed to the fashionable and to those who wished to be so. Willis shrewdly capitalized on the large number of women readers of his periodicals and sought out both well-known and unknown women contributors whom he judged would provide additional appeal. For example, he published the poetry of Lydia Sygourney and Elizabeth F. Ellet; he also helped promote the careers of two women who would become very popular: Emily Chubbock Judson, who wrote as Fanny Forrester, and Sara Jane Clarke Lippincott, who wrote as Grace Greenwood.

In the meantime, Sara Willis returned to her family home in Boston in 1831 to "learn the arts of bread-making and buttonhole stitching," as she recalled in a column in the *Ledger* in 1870. During the years that her brother was living mostly in Europe, writing his travel sketches and becoming increasingly famous as a writer and an editor, Sara Willis was living at home, helping her father by writing occasional pieces for the *Youth's Companion* and attending a continual round of parties and other social engagements. But the family's main intention for Sara was that she would learn domestic skills, her education now being complete and of limited relevance to her true mission in life: to be a wife and mother. Such notions, even about women who had been as unusually well educated as Sara Willis had been, were commonplace. And later, the famous Fanny Fern wrote often of her domestic accomplishments. In her articles in the *Ledger,* she commented frequently on being adept at a variety of household chores, such as making puddings and cakes, trimming bonnets, and mending stockings, but there is often a satiric edge to her pride in these accomplishments, and she clearly had ambivalent feelings about the activities in which she was expected to excel.

In due course, however, she learned her domestic lessons and followed the plan set for her by social convention. In 1837, she met and married Charles Harrington Eldredge, a bank cashier in Boston. By all accounts, the marriage was a happy one, and Sara Willis Eldredge gave birth to three daughters, in 1838, 1841, and 1844. But the Eldredges' happiness was cut short by a series of tragedies. Sara's younger sister, Ellen, and their mother, Hannah, died within six weeks of one another in 1844. Early in 1845, the Eldredges' first child died, and in 1846, Charles Eldredge died of typhoid fever shortly after losing a lawsuit, leaving Sara with many debts and virtually no financial resources. Sara's father, Nathaniel, reluctantly agreed to provide a small allowance, and the Eldredges grudgingly agreed to do the same. Neither set of parents was interested in providing sustained support for Sara and her two daughters, and Sara's father urged her to marry again. Griefstricken and unable to make a living as a seamstress or secure a position as a teacher, Sara agreed to a marriage with an acquaintance of her father's, Samuel P. Farrington, a widower with two daughters.

Sara married Farrington on January 17, 1849. From the beginning, the marriage was obviously a mistake for both. Sara had married for social and financial security, without love or even affection for her new husband. Farrington was an almost obsessively jealous man who found his wife's attention to others, including his own children, intolerable. Two years later, in January 1851, Sara took the unprecedented step of leaving her husband with no intention of returning. Farrington took his revenge by spreading stories about her supposed infidelities and even had her followed in a desperate, misguided effort to find evidence by which he might divorce her on the grounds of adultery. Refusing to support her, Farrington left Boston and later obtained a divorce in Chicago in 1853 on the grounds of desertion. The Willis and Eldredge families were shocked and mortified by the vicious rumors that Farrington had circulated and by what they saw as Sara's unconventional, unacceptable behavior of leaving her husband. They refused further financial assistance, and Sara felt herself friendless and alone in the world with her two daughters. Throughout the winter and spring of 1851, Sara determined to earn a living by writing. She was, after all, the granddaughter, daughter, and sister of successful editors and writers. Moreover, recalling the schoolgirl compositions that had been published in the Hartford paper, she felt she had some talent and ability. She also had determination, and she knew full well that the periodical press provided important new vocational opportunities for women.

Certainly there were numerous and well-known examples. Lydia Maria Child, author of *Hobomok* (1824), founded and edited the first children's magazine, the *Juvenile Miscellany*, from 1826 to 1833. She later edited the *National Anti-Slavery Standard* from 1841 to 1843, a paper that published letters from Frances E. W. Harper, a free black woman who was gaining a considerable reputation as a brilliant abolitionist orator. Often the sole supporter of her husband and herself, Child successfully broadened the readership of the *Standard* and made an important contribution to the abolitionist movement. Sarah Josepha Hale, a widow left with little money and five children, supported her family by assuming editorship of the Boston *Ladies' Magazine* in 1827 and later merged this magazine with *Godey's Lady's Book*, which she edited from 1837 to 1877. The highly visible and successful *Godey's* maintained a list of 70,000 subscribers by 1851 and 150,000 just before the Civil War. Although Hale envisioned a primarily female audience and actively promoted women writers in the pages of her magazine, her contributors included Edgar Allan Poe, Nathaniel Hawthorne, and even Nathaniel P. Willis. Margaret Fuller, former editor of the *Dial*, and author of *Summer on the Lakes* (1844) and *Woman in the Nineteenth Century* (1845), was a literary editor and writer for the *New York*

Tribune. She became the first woman foreign correspondent for an American newspaper when Greeley contracted with her to write a series of dispatches from Europe, beginning in 1846. Also the victim of the economic disaster imposed upon her family when her father died unexpectedly and left little money or means for livelihood, Fuller found journalism more satisfying than the traditional option of teaching as an opportunity for women to make their own independent lives.

Sara was also personally acquainted with women who were making money from their writing. She knew Harriet Beecher Stowe from her days at the Hartford Seminary; Stowe had helped her husband, Calvin, a professor, by supplementing the family income with her articles and stories, which were appearing regularly in the *Evangelist*, the *Independent*, and Gamaliel Bailey's anti-slavery newspaper, the *National Era*. In the same month that Sara sold her first article to the *Olive Branch*, the first installment of Stowe's novel *Uncle Tom's Cabin, or, Life Among the Lowly* appeared in the *Era* and ran from June 5, 1851, to April 1, 1852. When John P. Jewett published *Uncle Tom's Cabin* in book form just before the serialization ended, he claimed that it sold 10,000 copies in two weeks. Eventually it would become a best-selling novel of the nineteenth century and occupy a central position in the debate that led to the Civil War. When Fanny Fern became a regular contributor for the *Olive Branch*, she reviewed the famous novel on May 28, 1853, defending it against the charge that it was "too graphic" to have been "written by a woman."

There were other careers for Sara to contemplate, women writers to whom her brother, Nathaniel P. Willis, was showing a helpful interest. Sara Jane Clarke, one of Willis's protégés, named herself Grace Greenwood in 1842 and wrote a variety of articles and short pieces for several periodicals, some of which were published in a collection, *Greenwood Leaves*, in 1850. Greenwood also served as a junior editor for *Godey's* until she was fired for publishing anti-slavery articles in the *National Era*. In 1852, she went to England and published an entertaining book of her travels, *Haps and Mishaps of a Tour in Europe* (1854). And later, when she married Leander K. Lippincott, she founded a new magazine for children, *Little Pilgrim*. Emily Chubbuck Judson, "Fanny Forrester," began her career by publishing a variety of sketches for the *New Mirror*. Upon Willis's recommendation, she also published her work in *Graham's Magazine* and in *Godey's Lady's Book,* becoming very popular for her light, chatty sketches. She had also published a successful novel, *Allen Lucas, the Self-Made Man* (1847).

All of these women were taking advantage of the emerging vocational opportunities in publishing for women: as editors of new periodicals for a vareity of audiences, writers of articles, reviewers of cultural events and books, as well as novelists. That Sara wished to join is not surprising, especially in view of her familial connections and her acute economic needs. But the plight in which Sara found herself was complex. As Ann Douglas, Mary Kelley, Susan Coultrap-McQuinn, Nicole Tonkovich, Joyce Warren, and other scholars have suggested about women writers in the nineteenth century, the impulses for self-expression, economic survival, and the maintenance of traditional domestic roles for women were in deep and often painful conflict. At the same time that women were succeeding as shrewd participants in the periodical press, they were well aware of the social and cultural imperatives that made the domestic sphere primary for women and demonstrated the perils of moving outside it. While dire economic necessity motivated many women, most were careful to maintain a clear domestic base both literally and figuratively. They worked at home and, in addition, brought the home into the literary marketplace, writing articles, poems, and novels of domestic life and manners. While Elizabeth Barstow Stoddard's position with the *Alta California* (1854–1858) was primarily to report on the cultural scene in New York for the benefit of transplanted northeasterners in California, she always included witty commentary about domestic problems, such as traveling with a baby or maintaining a wardrobe on a small income. The effect was to bring the details of the home onto the front pages of the main organ for reporting on the details of the larger world. By the early 1850s, there was no doubt about the success of the combination.

Encouraged by the publication of "The Model Husband" in June 1851 and by the fact that another paper immediately copied and published it, as was customary in the days before copyright laws, Sara collected several articles during the summer and sent them to her brother Nathaniel. She obviously hoped that he might help her by publishing some of her work in the *Home Journal*, just as he had launched the careers of Fanny Forrester and Grace Greenwood. Willis's response about the literary opportunities available was pointedly discouraging. "New York is the most over-stocked market in the country, for writers," he wrote to his sister, "as we get a dozen applications a day from authors who merely wish to have the privilege of seeing themselves in print—writing for vanity only. Besides all the country flock & send here for fame etc. I have tried to find employment for dozens of starving writers, in vain. The Home Journal pays for no contributions." Even worse, Willis offered little in the way of constructive criticism: "Your writings show talent, but they are in a style that would only do in Boston. You overstrain the pathetic, and your humor runs into dreadful vulgarity sometimes. I am sorry that any editor knows that a sister of mine wrote some of these which you sent me. In one or two cases they trench very close on indecency." Why Willis refused to help his sister is not clear. The family was deeply embarrassed by her separation from Farrington, and it is likely that Willis did not find his sister's writing suitable for publication in his magazine. The sharp and occasionally brusque style was not to his taste and not, he undoubtedly imagined, to the taste of the fashionable readership he was trying to cultivate in New York. Certainly the other writers he employed did not write as his sister did. (When Grace Greenwood read *Ruth Hall*, she was shocked by what she saw as the single-minded determination of the heroine and referred to the novel as "Ruthless Hall.") Furthermore, Willis felt he had a reputation to uphold. On December 21, 1850, the *New York Tribune* had said, "On topics related to manners, taste and fashion, the *Home Journal* is justly an oracle." To him, perhaps, his sister lacked the social standing he wished to preserve for himself and his magazine. For whatever complicated reasons, Willis refused to help his sister. When Fanny Fern began to enjoy some success, she took an opportunity for some revenge in print and published "Apollo Hyacinth" in the *Musical World and Times* (June 18, 1853). In this brief and sarcastic column, she commented bitterly on this early refusal to help:

> Apollo never says an uncivil thing—never; he prides himself on that, as well as on his perfect knowledge of human nature; therefore, his sins are all sins of omission. His tastes are very exquisite, and his nature peculiarly sensitive; consequently, he cannot bear trouble. He will tell you, in his elegant way, that trouble "annoys" him, that it "bores" him; in short that it unfits him for life—for business; so, should you hear that a friend or relative of his, even a brother or a sister, was in distress, or persecuted in any manner, you could not do Apollo a greater injury (in his estimation) than to inform him of the fact.

Not surprisingly, Sara and her brother were estranged for years.

Sara, the determined writer, did not allow herself to be deterred by her brother's lack of interest. By the fall of 1851, she was writing for both the *Olive Branch* and William U. Moulton's *True Flag*, eking out a tiny income. During this time, she adopted the pseudonym "Fanny Fern." Writing under another name was common for women, but Sara probably had several reasons: to protect her identity and her privacy, to solve the problem of her multiple names, and probably, as her biographer Joyce Warren has suggested, to parody the names of Fanny Forrester and Grace Greenwood, who wrote in the style of which her brother approved. During the next year, Oliver Dyer, editor of the New York *Musical World and Times*, offered Fanny Fern an exclusive contract to write an article a week for his paper, much to the disappointment of her editors Thomas Norris and especially William Moulton, who evidently threatened to damage her reputation in retaliation for her decision. Soon Fern's work was being read everywhere, even in the pages of Willis's *Home Journal*. Without his knowledge, James Parton, a new editor, began to reprint Fanny Fern's works. When Willis discovered that these essays were his sister's, he insisted that Parton stop publishing them; Parton, who would later befriend and then marry Fern, promptly resigned. The publisher James Derby wrote to Fern proposing the publication of a collection of her newspaper articles, and *Fern Leaves from Fanny's Portfolio* was published in 1853. In less than a year, 29,000 copies were sold in England and 70,000 in the United States, including one that enlivened evening entertainment for Emily Dickinson, her sister, and her father, all fans of the witty and acerbic new figure on the literary scene. As her brother had before her, Fanny Fern then decided to leave Boston for the larger opportunities of New York and moved there in June to make a home for herself and her two daughters. By the fall of 1853, Fanny Fern was a successful and popular author who was making a very good living exclusively by her writing.

III

In November 1853, Fern contracted with the Philadelphia *Saturday Evening Post*, a paper devoted to literature, news, and entertainment for families, to write a series of sketches and articles. When that series concluded in the spring, Fern ceased writing and publishing for newspapers because she had signed another contract, this time with the publishing house of Mason Brothers, to write a novel. Her contract with them stipulated that she would write and prepare the novel for publication "as soon as circumstances will permit" and not engage in any other projects that would take away her time and attention. The Mason Brothers wished to capitalize on Fern's popularity and bring the book out quickly; they were committed to a major advertising campaign and furthermore agreed to royalties of fifteen cents for each book sold. Fern, a disciplined writer, completed *Ruth Hall: A Domestic Tale of the Present Time* in nine months. The book was published in mid-December of 1854, and the Mason Brothers launched their extensive advertising campaign. It was hugely successful; in January 1855, the Mason Brothers claimed that *Ruth Hall* was the most successful American book and had sold more copies than any other. Sales figures of books published in the mid-nineteenth century are difficult to determine exactly, but *Ruth Hall* reportedly sold 70,000 copies in the first year of publication.

Although *Ruth Hall* was undoubtedly a best-seller, it did not sell more than Maria Cummins's *The Lamplighter* (1854), which sold 40,000 copies during the first two months of its publication. And certainly, *Ruth Hall* was no match for *Uncle Tom's Cabin,* the blockbuster that sold 310,000 copies in 1852. By comparison, Nathaniel Hawthorne's *The Scarlet Letter,* published in 1850, enjoyed more modest sales of just over 10,000. In a famous exchange of letters in early 1855 with his publisher, William Ticknor, Hawthorne complained that "America is now wholly given over to a d——d mob of scribbling women, and I should have no chance of success while the public is occupied with their trash—and should be ashamed of myself if I did succeed. What is the mystery of these innumerable editions of the Lamplighter, and other books neither better nor worse?—worse they could not be, and better they need not be, when they sell by the 100,000." While it is true that women writers were largely re-

sponsible for the best-sellers of the mid-nineteenth century,
Hawthorne exaggerated the sales figures and objected to books
that he saw as repetitive and unoriginal. In February of 1855, he
wrote again to Ticknor, making an important exception to his
earlier comments:

> In my last, I recollect, I bestowed some vituperation on female
> authors. I have been reading *Ruth Hall* and I must say I enjoyed
> it a good deal. The woman writes as if the devil was in her; and
> that is the only condition under which a woman ever writes
> anything worth reading. Generally women write like emasculated
> men, and are only to be distinguished from male authors by
> greater feebleness and folly; but when they throw off the re-
> straints of decency, and come before the public stark naked, as
> it were—then their books are sure to possess character and value.
> Can you tell me anything about this Fanny Fern? If you meet
> her, I wish you would let her know how much I admire her.

Hawthorne's remarkable commentary reveals how much he understood the departure from conventional novels that Fern was
making in writing *Ruth Hall*. Highly autobiographical, narra-
tively structured in a series of short scenes, and opposing the
usual romantic plotline, the novel is pointedly critical of rigid
and constricting social roles for women. It was indeed an
achievement that the author of *The Scarlet Letter* could admire.

In writing *Ruth Hall*, Fanny Fern drew heavily on the details
and experiences of her own life. Consciously challenging the "set
rules for novel-writing," Fern subtitles her book "A Domestic
Tale of the Present Time" and tells us in her preface that it is a
"continuous story." The novel with its formal conventions and
concomitant expectations on the part of readers is here replaced
with a more casual form—a story or a tale with a plot based on
the life of the writer. Fern used several of the central events of
her own life in her book: her marriage to Charles Eldredge, the
death of their first child, her widowhood, her estrangement from

her family, and her difficult struggle to make a living as a writer. Many of these events in *Ruth Hall* are based closely on the details of Fern's life. Like Charles Eldredge, for example, Harry Hall dies of typhoid fever and seriously in debt. Like Fanny Fern, Ruth Hall finds her family unwilling to provide much assistance, and tries to support herself as a seamstress and gradually turns to writing. Like Nathaniel P. Willis, Ruth Hall's brother is a successful editor who refuses to help her by publishing her work or even in giving her encouragement. Like Fanny Fern, Ruth Hall writes first for small periodicals, later collects her articles into a book, and begins to enjoy significant economic success. And like Fanny Fern, Ruth Hall is finally aided by a sensitive publisher and editor who helps her to a more professional position. In these similarities, *Ruth Hall* is in many ways the story of Fanny Fern's life. Certainly many contemporary readers saw it in this way, especially after William Moulton wrote a scathing article in the *True Flag* on December 30, 1854, in which he revealed the closely-guarded secret of Fanny Fern's identity as Sara Willis Eldredge Farrington and presented her as a compromised woman of questionable reputation. In 1855, an anonymous book appeared, *The Life and Beauties of Fanny Fern*, which was the work of Moulton as well. In these ways, Moulton was making good on his threat to retaliate for Fern's decision to leave the *True Flag* in 1853. If Moulton thought he would destroy Fanny Fern's career with these sensational revelations, he was quite mistaken. Although Fern was greatly pained and distressed by the exposure, sales of *Ruth Hall* soared.

And yet *Ruth Hall* is not an autobiography in the nineteenth-century sense of writing the story of one's life to demonstrate an orderly life well lived or to outline a program of self-help for others to follow. At the most literal level, two significant events in Fern's life are left out of Fern's account: her second marriage, to Samuel Farrington, and the development of her third quite happy relationship and eventual marriage to James Parton, which took place on January 5, 1856. More important, the omission of these details points toward a different conception of Fanny Fern's purpose in writing her novel. In *Ruth Hall*, Fanny Fern takes some of the events of her own life and uses them to make visible the experience of the woman who is not a wife—through no fault of her own—and to order that experience as normative. Her purpose was to show, based on some painful personal experiences, the way in which the "domestic tale" in its usual configuration could go significantly awry. Because Ruth Hall is completely dependent upon her family and her husband for her livelihood and has no separate identity, she is at a complete loss when her husband dies. Without an alternative and equally acceptable lifestyle available as a model, a woman who has the bad luck to lose her husband is left with few choices outside the well-defined social and cultural pattern of marriage. Consequently, *Ruth Hall* is not an autobiography (Fanny Fern would, of course, choose to marry again), but a continuing story about the construction of a different model. The novel concludes not with a romance, marriage, and the promise of a conventional domestic life but with Ruth Hall in possession of her fatherless children, a successful career as a journalist, a comfortable income, and a formidable bank account. As Ruth's editor, John Walter, says to her, ". . . imagine yourself, if you can, in that dismal attic one year ago, a bank stock holder! Now confess that you are proud of yourself!" Although triumphant pride is not quite the tone of the final scene in the novel, Ruth is content and willing to accept without comment the benediction of Mr. Walter that "Life has much of harmony yet in store for you."

Even as *Ruth Hall* departs from autobiography, it is also at odds with the conventions of the nineteenth-century romantic novel. As Nina Baym has described it, there was a general plotline that many novelists followed: a young woman, generally orphaned or alone in the world, overcomes significant hardships and struggles, and is rewarded in the end by marriage and a

family of her own. If the outlines of such an overplot sound like
Jane Eyre (1847), it is because this very successful novel established what is a continuing tradition of an increasingly impoverished romantic plot that survives today in countless books,
movies, and television programs. In its own day, *Jane Eyre*
(published with the subtitle "An Autobiography") was an enormously influential and widely read book in both England and
America. In fact, on January 5, 1850, James Parton, later a distinguished biographer and Fern's husband, published his first article in Nathaniel P. Willis's *Home Journal* on the identity of
"Currer Bell," the pseudonym under which Charlotte Brontë
published her novel. Like Brontë's popular and influential novel
(also entitled with the name of the central character), *Ruth Hall*
begins with a female figure sitting at a window. Unlike the orphaned Jane who has retreated to a window seat to avoid the
snubs and petty tyrannies of her unkind cousins, however, Ruth
is a young woman contemplating her wedding, to take place the
next day. Ruth and Jane both encounter acts of cruelty and
insensitivity; both of them, for example, watch friends (Helen
Burns and Mary Leon) die of neglect. But *Ruth Hall* opposes
Jane Eyre in fundamental ways. Jane, who reluctantly becomes a
teacher and a governess, spends most of the novel searching for
the family that she desperately wants and needs. The novel ends
with Jane duly rewarded and established as Mr. Rochester's wife.
For all Jane's intelligence and spirit, *Jane Eyre* is a profoundly
conservative book and finally quite unlike Fanny Fern's counter-
version of a strong central character who seeks independence and
a career in order to take care of herself and her children in her
own way. In a sense, *Ruth Hall* begins where *Jane Eyre* ends,
offering a sequel that does not end quite so neatly or happily. In
fact, *Ruth Hall* offers a very different version of a domestic tale
and presents an alternative vision: a woman who is economically
independent, in charge of her own life and professional career.

The difference is, of course, that the second story was a long way from being acceptable, much less normative.

For example, most of the action of *Ruth Hall* does not take place in a conventional domestic setting at all. Although Ruth and Charles enjoy brief happiness in a household of their own, they later live in a hotel, and then Ruth lives in a series of boardinghouses, each one more unhomelike than the last, suggesting yet another way in which the fabric of the domestic tale can unravel. The tension between the domestic model presented by society on the one hand and by Ruth Hall's experience of it on the other is partially revealed by a question from Ruth's child. When Nettie asks her mother if she too will write books when she is a woman, Ruth tells her without hesitation: "God forbid . . . No happy woman ever writes," suggesting her final satiric commentary on the domestic tale that Ruth now perceives to be a fantasy. A few years, later, on May 16, 1857, Fanny Fern published "Soliloquy of a Literary Housekeeper" in the *Ledger*, an article bemoaning the necessity of spring cleaning, asking cheerfully instead: "Give me good health—the morning for writing and no interruptions, plenty of fresh air afterwards, and an old gown to enjoy it in. . . ." And several years later, she exhorted her *Ledger* readers to:

> Write! Rescue a part of each week at least for reading, and putting down on paper, for your own private benefit, your thoughts and feelings. Not for the *world's* eye unless you choose, but to lift yourselves out of the dead-level of your lives; to keep off inanition; to lessen the number who are yearly added to our lunatic asylums from the ranks of misappreciated, unhappy womanhood, narrowed by lives made up of details. Fight it! Oppose it, for your own sakes and your children's! (August 10, 1867)

The message by this time is that happy women do indeed write and write often; Fern clearly suggests that, whether one writes for a public audience or not, the act of writing is an important way out of the tedium of the actual details of domestic life as well as a potential independent occupation for women. By the end of *Ruth Hall*, readers are presented with a new model for a woman's happiness: the writing profession has provided Ruth independence and stability of her own making.

In several respects, the structure and style of *Ruth Hall* also reflects another difference between Fern's novel and other novels of the mid-nineteenth century. As she explains in the preface, Fern deliberately chose to avoid "long introductions and descriptions" and enters "unceremoniously and unannounced, into people's houses, without stopping to ring the bell." In the main, the book is a collection of vignettes, scenes, and snatches of overheard dialogues, with limited narrative exposition and little character development. As such, the book often seems strikingly modern. Nonetheless, the language patterns and other literary devices remind us constantly that we are reading a nineteenth-century novel. Although there are marvelous images—the elder Halls, for instance, are "two scathed trees," and a child on her way to her frightening first day at school carries a "big orange thumping in the new satchel"—there are many examples of imagery that today's readers might find overblown. Ruth sets out to earn a "crust" and not a living, and a letter to John Walter, her editor, is mailed with the hopeful feelings that Noah had on sending out a dove from the ark for the third time. The characters are generally one-dimensional. Ruth's relatives and especially the elder Halls are presented as having no redeeming qualities whatsoever; they are cruel, grasping, and ungenerous to the last. In contrast, Ruth has no faults. She is pure, virtuous, and unwaveringly good. There are also moments where the plot is rather mechanically contrived. Near the end of the novel, Ruth and her daughters are saved from a house fire by their old friend, Johnny Galt, who mysteriously and coincidentally arrives on the scene just in time for a dramatic rescue. The standard elements of nineteenth-century fiction are also in operation. There are three lengthy deathbed scenes (Daisy, Harry Hall, and Mary Leon) and an ongoing series of comic moments with Ruth's boardinghouse landlords, Mr. and Mrs. Skiddy, characters of whom Charles Dickens would have been justly proud. And yet, despite these conventional features, *Ruth Hall* is innovative and unusual in Fanny Fern's explicit challenge to the novel form. In using her self-described "primitive mode," the presentation of short scenes with little introduction and context, she contends that the novel—in its present form—is out of step with the actual realities of a "domestic tale of the present time."

Instead of a series of orderly chapters of similar lengths, *Ruth Hall* is composed of ninety numbered chapters which are described in brief phrases in the table of contents. Some are little more than a page in length, and many of them are about the same length as the newspaper columns Fern wrote. Often these short chapters are dialogues of overheard conversation. In chapter 36, for example, two fellow boarders of Ruth's in the establishment of a "loud-voiced landlady" sit smoking "cheap" cigars. Jim, described as "low-browed, pig-faced," and "thick-lipped," and his companion, Sam, discuss Ruth, the pretty, young widow, as easy prey. Readers are left to their own conclusions, but the grim details and the flat exchange between the two men are completely convincing. Ruth is unprotected and vulnerable. Her position is heightened further by the next chapter, a scene in the bookstore of Tom Develin, who receives a letter from Ruth's father-in-law, asking him to collect his dead son's clothes and belongings from the home of his widow. The message is clear: Ruth can depend on neither friend nor family member for help. Fern uses longer, more discursive chapters sparingly. In chapter 47, for instance, Fern narrates the account of Mrs. Skiddy's surprising decision to enjoy an unannounced sabbatical from her husband and baby. Subsequent chapters that develop this subplot are similar; however, most of the story of Ruth and the obstacles she overcomes in her efforts to find a way to support herself and her children are developed by the short chapters of thematically related scenes and dialogues. The effect is unusual and modern; readers discover Ruth's story as it unfolds in the minds and conversations of others.

Such an uncommon narrative style befits the unconventional story that Fanny Fern had to tell. While students today generally find *Ruth Hall* a striking example of a feminist heroine who seeks and achieves independence through success in a professional career in journalism, contemporary readers had mixed reactions to the novel. It sold well, in part because of the revelations about the Willis family and because of the extensive advertising efforts undertaken by the Mason Brothers. But, in general, critics and reviewers reacted unfavorably. While Hawthorne praised Fern for writing "as if the devil was in her," the majority of reviewers seemed to feel as though Fern was indeed in league with the devil, and they had more reservations about the author than about the book. Most found the fact that a woman had written so negatively about her family and in such an "unfeminine" way, as the *New York Tribune* said, was a serious obstacle to appreciating anything about the novel as a novel. The reviewer for the *New York Times* (December 20, 1854) provided what was to become a fairly general view: "If Fanny Fern were a man,—a man who believed that the gratification of revenge were a proper occupation for one who has been abused, and that those who have injured us are fair game, *Ruth Hall* would be a natural and excusable book. But we confess that we cannot understand how a delicate, suffering woman can hunt down even her persecutors so remorselessly." Sarah Josepha Hale felt similarly; she refused to review it at all in *Godey's*.

Others were more impressed with the novel. In what may have been the single positive review of the book, the women's rights activist Elizabeth Cady Stanton attacked the general view of the author as unfeminine and took the opportunity to challenge what she correctly saw as a double standard for a woman writer. Writing for the *Una* in 1855, she observed that "if her pictures are not pleasing ones, it seems to me the censure more justly belongs to the living subjects," ironically adding, "If you [gentlemen] do not wish us to paint you wolves, get into lambs' clothing quickly as possible." Finally, Stanton admonished her readers that "The great lesson taught in *Ruth Hall* is that God has given to woman sufficient brain and muscle to work out her own destiny unaided and alone." Moreover, many newspaper reviewers had to admit that it was a compelling story. The *Hartford Union* called it a "fresh racy volume," while the *Tiffin Tribune* in Ohio observed that "every page glitters with some gem of intellect, some bright truth." Certainly the reviewer for the *New Orleans Bulletin* was correct when he or she said that "No novel has created such a sensation." No reviewer seems to have considered *Ruth Hall* a novel about the American story of individual success translated into a woman's terms. Furthermore, no reviewer seems to have commented on the significance of the new professional career of a newspaper columnist that Ruth Hall and her editor invented for a woman.

After the publication of *Ruth Hall*, Fanny Fern published a serialized novella, "Fanny Ford," in the *Ledger* during the summer of 1855; her only other work of fiction was her novel *Rose Clark*, which appeared in December 1855. In many ways, both the novella and the book are responses to the criticism she received about *Ruth Hall*. The novella, although at face value a rather conventional story, portrays the plight of seamstresses and suggests the necessity for prison reform. The complicated plot of *Rose Clark* is also conventional, as Fern's preface clearly indicated. "Readers," she began, "When the frost curtains the windows, when the wind whistles fiercely at the key-hole, when the bright fire glows, and the tea-tray is removed, and father in his slippered feet lolls in his arm-chair; and mother with her nimble needle 'makes auld claes look amast as well as new,' and grandmamma draws closer to the chimney-corner, and Tommy with this plate of chestnuts nestles contentedly at her feet; then let my unpretending story be read. For such an hour, for such an audience, was it written." Appealing to the domestic family circle, Fern then tells the story of Rose Clark, an orphan who undergoes numerous trials and tribulations, including a long stint at an orphanage which rivals Jane Eyre's Lowood Institution in its chilly atmosphere. Rose also endures (but eventually overcomes) the charge that she is an unwed mother, a shocking circumstance for a nineteenth-century heroine. In the end, Rose finds happiness and is reunited with her husband and daughter. Full of improbable coincidences, settings as diverse as New Orleans and a New England village, cruel women and weak men, *Rose Clark* is a mixed success as a novel. Nonetheless, Fern directs some pointed criticisms against editors and reviewers. Rose, unlike Ruth Hall, is not able to find an occupation and thinks for a time that she will write books. Her friend, the artist Gertrude Dean, teases her by composing aloud a series of the kind of reviews she could expect: "We have perused this book; it is unnecessary to state in its title-page that it was written by a *female* hand. The plot is feeble and inartistic. . . . We advise the authoress of 'Gore House' to choose some other escape-valve for her restless femininity; petticoat literature has become a drug in the market." And another: "We have read 'Gore House.' We do not hesitate it to pronounce it a *bad* book, unfit to lie on the table of any *religious* family. . . . It can not fail to have a most pernicious influence on the minds of the young." Readers of *Ruth Hall* would have noticed some striking similarities between Gertrude's satiric improvisations and the tone and spirit of the actual reviews.

Ultimately, for Fanny Fern the novel was not the genre in which she would make her major literary contribution. Instead, Fern saw the potential of the newspaper, a literary vehicle under construction in the nineteenth century, as providing more possibilities for a woman determined to find a new vocational opportunity. Through the use of painful experiences in her own life, Fern tried to present in *Ruth Hall* a fictional account of a woman who found and examined the fissures in the edifice of the domestic sphere. At the same time, the novel is a close examination of the potential of the periodical as a literary marketplace for women writers. But it was clear that the larger reading public was not quite prepared for the implications of either, and Fanny Fern was finally not as interested in fiction as she was in more direct commentary about the injustices and deficiencies of contemporary life and culture. She returned to writing her columns for the *Ledger*, and, like Ruth Hall, created a successful and happy life for herself through a vehicle—the newspaper column—by which she could effectively send her frank and intelligent messages of social critique.

SUGGESTIONS FOR FURTHER READING

The only contemporary edition of some of Fanny Fern's works is *Ruth Hall and Other Writings,* edited by Joyce W. Warren (New Brunswick: Rutgers University Press, 1986), which provides the text of *Ruth Hall* as well as over a hundred of the short newspaper articles and reviews that Fern wrote, mostly for the *New York Ledger.* There is no edition of her correspondence, nor are any of her other published works currently in print. The invaluable guide to Fern's life and work is Joyce W. Warren, *Fanny Fern: An Independent Woman* (New Brunswick: Rutgers University Press, 1992).

BIOGRAPHIES OF FERN:

Adams, Florence Bannard. *Fanny Fern, or a Pair of Flaming Shoes.* West Trenton, N.J.: Hermitage, 1966.

Walker, Nancy A. *Fanny Fern.* New York: Twayne, 1993.

Warren, Joyce W. *Fanny Fern: An Independent Woman.* New Brunswick: Rutgers University Press, 1992.

ESSAYS ON FERN:

Askeland, Lori. " 'Has a Mother a Right to Her Chidren?': Fanny Fern's Urban Domesticity and the 'Birth' of Foster Care and Adoption in Mid-Nineteenth-Century America." *A/B: Auto/Biography Studies* (2003): 171–95.

Berlant, Lauren. "The Female Woman: Fanny Fern and the Form of Sentiment." *American Literary History* 3 (1991): 429–54.

Easton, Alison M. J. "My Banker and I Can Afford to Laugh! Class and Gender in Fanny Fern and Nathaniel Hawthorne." In *Soft Canons: American Women Writers and Masculine Tradition.* Edited by Karen L. Kilcup. Iowa City: University of Iowa Press, 1999.

Grasso, Linda. "Anger in the House: Fanny Fern's *Ruth Hall* and the Redrawing of Emotional Boundaries in Mid-19th Century America." *Studies in the American Renaissance* (1995): 251–61.

Hamilton, Kristie. "The Politics of Survival: Sara Parton's *Ruth Hall* and the Literature of Labor." In *Redefining the Political Novel: American Women Writers, 1797–1901.* Edited by Sharon M. Harris. Knoxville: University of Tennessee Press, 1995.

Harker, Jaime, " 'Pious Cant' and Blasphemy: Fanny Fern's Radicalized Sentiment." *Legacy: A Journal of American Women Writers* 18 (2001): 52–64.

Hartnett, Stephen. "Fanny Fern's 1855 *Ruth Hall,* the Cheerful Brutality of Capitalism, and the Irony of Sentimental Rhetoric." *Quarterly Journal of Speech* 88 (2002): 1–18.

Homestead, Melissa J. " 'Every Body Sees the Theft': Fanny Fern and Literary Proprietorship in Antebellum America." *New England Quarterly* 74 (2001): 210–237.

Laffrado, Laura " 'I Thought from the Way You Writ, That You Were a Great Six-Footer of a Woman': Gender and the Public Voice in Fanny Fern's Newspaper Essays." *In Her Own Voice: Nineteenth-Century American Women Essayists.* Edited by Sherry Lee Linkon. New York: Garland, 1997.

Marzolf, Marion. "Sara Payson Willis Parton (Fanny Fern)." In *American Newspaper Journalists, 1690–1872.* Vol. 43 of *Dictionary of Literary Biography.* Edited by Perry J. Ashley. Detroit: Gale Research, 1985: 358–62.

Pettengill, Claire C. "Against Novels: Fanny Fern's Newspaper Fictions and the Reform of Print Culture." *American Periodicals* 6 (1996): 81–96.

Sánchez, María C. "Re-Possessing Individualism in Fanny Fern's *Ruth Hall.*" *Arizona Quarterly* 56 (2000): 25–56.

Temple, Gale. "A Purchase on Goodness: Fanny Fern, Ruth Hall, and Fraught Individualism." *Studies in American Fiction* (2003): 131–63.

Warren, Joyce W. "Domesticity and the Economics of Independence: Resistance and Revolution in the Work of Fanny Fern." In *The (Other) American Traditions: Nineteenth-Century Women Writers.* Edited by Joyce W. Warren. New Brunswick: Rutgers University Press, 1993.

———. "Fanny Fern (Sara Payson Willis Parton) (1811–1872)." In *Nineteenth-Century American Women Writers: A Bio-Bibliographical Critical Sourcebook.* Edited by Denise D. Knight. Westport, CT: Greenwood, 1997: 123–30.

———. Fanny Fern, Performative Incivilities and Rap." *Studies in American Humor* 3 (1999): 17–36.

———. Introduction. *Ruth Hall and Other Writings,* edited by Joyce W. Warren. New Brunswick: Rutgers University Press, 1986.

———. "Profile of Fanny Fern." *Legacy: A Journal of American Women Writers* 2 (1985): 54–60.

———. "Text and Context in Fanny Fern's *Ruth Hall:* From Widowhood to Independence." In *Joinings and Disjoinings: The Significance of Marital Status in Literature.* Edited by Jo Anna Stephens Mink and Janet Daubler Ward. Bowling Green: Bowling Green State University Press, 1991.

———. "Uncommon Discourse: Fanny Fern and the *New York Ledger.*" In *Periodical Literature in Nineteenth-Century America.* Edited by Kenneth M. Price and Susan Belasco Smith. Charlottesville: University Press of Virginia, 1995. 51–68.

Wood, Ann Douglas. "The Scribbling Women and Fanny Fern: Why Women Wrote." *American Quarterly* 23 (1971): 3–14.

Wright, Elizabethada A. " 'Joking Isn't Safe': Fanny Fern, Irony, and Signifyin(g) Author(s)." *Rhetoric Society Quarterly* 31 (2001): 91–111.

Yu, Ning. "Fanny Fern and Sui Sin Far: The Beginning of an Asian American Voice." *Women and Language* 19 (1996): 44–47.

HISTORICAL AND CULTURAL STUDIES:

Admari, Ralph. "Bonner and 'The Ledger.' " *The American Book Collector* 6 (1935): 176–93.

Auser, Cortland P. *Nathaniel P. Willis.* New York: Twayne, 1969.

Baym, Nina. *Women's Fiction: A Guide to Novels by and about Women in America, 1820–1870.* Ithaca: Cornell University Press, 1978.

Coultrap-McQuinn, Susan. *Doing Literary Business: American Woman Writers in the Nineteenth Century.* Chapel Hill: University of North Carolina Press, 1990.

Douglas, Ann. *The Feminization of American Culture.* New York: Alfred A. Knopf, 1977.

Geary, Susan. "The Domestic Novel as a Commercial Commodity: Making a Best Seller in the 1850s." *Papers of the Bibliographic Society of America* 70 (1976): 365–93.

Harris, Susan K. *Nineteenth-Century American Women's Novels: Interpretive Strategies.* New York: Cambridge University Press, 1990.

Homestead, Melissa J. *American Women Authors and Literary Property, 1822–1869*. New York: Cambridge University Press, 2005.

Johnson, Linck C. "*Walden* and the Construction of the American Renaissance." In *Approaches to Teaching Thoreau's Walden and Other Works.* Edited by Richard J. Schneider. New York: MLA, 1996.

Kelley, Mary. *Private Women, Public Stage: Literary Domesticity in Nineteenth-Century America*. New York: Oxford University Press, 1984.

Tonkovich, Nicole. *Domesticity with a Difference: The Nonfiction of Catharine Beecher, Sarah J. Hale, Fanny Fern, and Margaret Fuller*. Jackson: University Press of Mississippi, 1997.

Tompkins, Jane. *Sensational Designs: The Cultural Work of American Fiction, 1790–1860*. New York: Oxford University Press, 1985.

Warner, Charles Dudley. *American Men of Letters: Nathaniel Parker Willis*. Boston: Houghton, Mifflin, 1892.

Weber, Ronald. *Hired Pens: Professional Writers in America's Golden Age of Print*. Athens: Ohio University Press, 1997.

A NOTE ON THE TEXT

The text of *Ruth Hall: A Domestic Tale of the Present Time* is taken from the original edition published in 1855 by Mason Brothers of New York. Typographical errors have been silently corrected, and the system of open contractions has been retained.

PREFACE

I PRESENT you with my first continuous story. I do not dignify it by the name of "A novel." I am aware that it is entirely at variance with all set rules for novel-writing. There is no intricate plot; there are no startling developments, no hair-breadth escapes. I have compressed into one volume what I might have expanded into two or three. I have avoided long introductions and descriptions, and have entered unceremoniously and unannounced, into people's houses, without stopping to ring the bell. Whether you will fancy this primitive mode of calling, whether you will like the company to which it introduces you, or— whether you will like the book at all, I cannot tell. Still, I cherish the hope that, somewhere in the length and breadth of the land, it may fan into a flame, in some tried heart, the fading embers of hope, well-nigh extinguished by wintry fortune and summer friends.

FANNY FERN

CHAPTER I

THE old church clock rang solemnly out on the midnight air. Ruth started. For hours she had sat there, leaning her cheek upon her hand, and gazing through the open space between the rows of brick walls, upon the sparkling waters of the bay, glancing and quivering 'neath the moon-beams. The city's busy hum had long since died away; myriad restless eyes had closed in peaceful slumber; Ruth could not sleep. This was the last time she would sit at that little window. The morrow would find her in a home of her own. On the morrow Ruth would be a bride.

Ruth was not sighing because she was about to leave her father's roof, (for her childhood had been anything but happy,) but she was vainly trying to look into a future, which God has mercifully veiled from curious eyes. Had that craving heart of hers at length found its ark of refuge? Would clouds or sunshine, joy or sorrow, tears or smiles, predominate in her future? Who could tell? The silent stars returned her no answer. Would a harsh word ever fall from lips which now breathed only love? Would the step whose lightest footfall now made her heart leap, ever sound in her ear like a death-knell? As time, with its ceaseless changes, rolled on, would love flee affrighted from the bent form, and silver locks, and faltering footstep? Was there no talisman to keep him?

"Strange questions," were they, "for a young girl!" Ah, but Ruth could remember when she was no taller than a rosebush, how cravingly her little heart cried out for love! How a careless word, powerless to wound one less sensitive, would send her, weeping, to that little room for hours; and, young as she was, life's pains seemed already more to her than life's pleasures.

Would it *always* be so? Would she find more thorns than roses in her *future* pathway?

Then, Ruth remembered how she used to wish she were beautiful,—not that she might be admired, but that she might be loved. But Ruth was "very plain,"—so her brother Hyacinth told her, and "awkward," too; she had heard that ever since she could remember; and the recollection of it dyed her cheek with blushes, whenever a stranger made his appearance in the home circle.

So, Ruth was fonder of being alone by herself; and then, they called her "odd," and "queer," and wondered if she would "ever make anything;" and Ruth used to wonder, too; and sometimes she asked herself why a sweet strain of music, or a fine passage in a poem, made her heart thrill, and her whole frame quiver with emotion?

The world smiled on her brother Hyacinth. He was handsome, and gifted. He could win fame, and what was better, love. Ruth wished he would love her a little. She often used to steal into his room and "right" his papers, when the stupid housemaid had displaced them; and often she would prepare him a tempting little lunch, and carry it to his room, on his return from his morning walk; but Hyacinth would only say, "Oh, it is you, Ruth, is it? I thought it was Bridget;" and go on reading his newspaper.

Ruth's mother was dead. Ruth did not remember a great deal about her—only that she always looked uneasy about the time her father was expected home; and when his step was heard in the hall, she would say in a whisper, to Hyacinth and herself, "Hush! hush! your father is coming;" and then Hyacinth would immediately stop whistling, or humming, and Ruth would run up into her little room, for fear she should, in some unexpected way, get into disgrace.

Ruth, also, remembered when her father came home and

found company to tea, how he frowned and complained of headache, although he always ate as heartily as any of the company; and how after tea he would stretch himself out upon the sofa and say, "I think I 'll take a nap;" and then, he would close his eyes, and if the company commenced talking, he would start up and say to Ruth, who was sitting very still in the corner, "*Ruth,* don't make such a noise;" and when Ruth's mother would whisper gently in his ear, "Would n't it be better, dear, if you laid down up stairs? it is quite comfortable and quiet there," her father would say, aloud, "Oh yes, oh yes, you want to get rid of me, do you?" And then her mother would say, turning to the company, "How very fond Mr. Ellet is of a joke!" But Ruth remembered that her mother often blushed when she said so, and that her laugh did not sound natural.

After her mother's death, Ruth was sent to boarding-school, where she shared a room with four strange girls, who lay awake all night, telling the most extraordinary stories, and ridiculing Ruth for being such an old maid that she could not see "where the laugh came in." Equally astonishing to the unsophisticated Ruth, was the demureness with which they would bend over their books when the pale, meek-eyed widow, employed as du-enna, went the rounds after tea, to see if each inmate was preparing the next day's lessons, and the coolness with which they would jump up, on her departure, put on their bonnets and shawls, and slip out at the side-street door to meet expectant lovers; and when the pale widow went the rounds again at nine o'clock, she would find them demurely seated, just where she left them, apparently busily conning their lessons! Ruth wondered if *all* girls were as mischievous, and if fathers and mothers ever stopped to think what companions their daughters would have for room-mates and bed-fellows, when they sent them away from home. As to the Principal, Madame Moreau, she contented herself with sweeping her flounces, once a day, through the recitation rooms; so it was not a difficult matter, in so large an establishment, to pass muster with the sub-teachers at recitations.

Composition day was the general bugbear. Ruth's madcap room-mates were struck with the most unqualified amazement and admiration at the facility with which "the old maid" executed this frightful task. They soon learned to put her services in requisition; first, to help them out of this slough of despond; next, to save them the necessity of wading in at all, by writing their compositions for them.

In the all-absorbing love affairs which were constantly going on between the young ladies of Madame Moreau's school and their respective admirers, Ruth took no interest; and on the occasion of the unexpected reception of a bouquet, from a smitten swain, accompanied by a copy of amatory verses, Ruth crimsoned to her temples and burst into tears, that any one could be found so heartless as to burlesque the "awkward" Ruth. Simple child! She was unconscious that, in the freedom of that atmosphere where a "prophet out of his own country is honored," her lithe form had rounded into symmetry and grace, her slow step had become light and elastic, her eye bright, her smile winning, and her voice soft and melodious. Other bouquets, other notes, and glances of involuntary admiration from passers-by, at length opened her eyes to the fact, that she was "plain, awkward Ruth" no longer. Eureka! She had arrived at the first epoch in a young girl's life,—she had found out her power! Her manners became assured and self-possessed. *She,* Ruth, could inspire love! Life became dear to her. There was something worth living for—something to look forward to. She had a motive—an aim; she should *some* day make somebody's heart glad,—somebody's hearthstone bright; somebody should be proud of her; and oh, how she *could* love that somebody! History, astronomy, mathematics, the languages, were all pastime now. Life wore a new aspect; the skies were bluer, the earth greener, the flowers more fragrant;—her twin-soul existed somewhere.

When Ruth had been a year at school, her elegant brother Hyacinth came to see her. Ruth dashed down her books, and bounded down three stairs at a time, to meet him; for she loved him, poor child, just as well as if he were worth loving. Hyacinth drew languidly back a dozen paces, and holding up his hands, drawled out imploringly, "kiss me if you insist on it, Ruth, but for heaven's sake, don't tumble my dickey." He also remarked, that her shoes were too large for her feet, and that her little French apron was "slightly askew;" and told her, whatever else she omitted, to be sure to learn "to waltz." He was then introduced to Madame Moreau, who remarked to Madame Chicchi, her Italian teacher, what a very *distingué* looking person he was; after which he yawned several times, then touched his hat gracefully, praised "the very superior air of the establishment," brushed an imperceptible atom of dust from his beaver, kissed the tips of his fingers to his demonstrative sister, and tiptoed Terpsichoreally over the academic threshold.

In addition to this, Ruth's father wrote occasionally when a term-bill became due, or when his tradesmen's bills came in, on the first of January; on which occasion an annual fit of poverty seized him, an almshouse loomed up in perspective, he reduced the wages of his cook two shillings, and advised Ruth either to get married or teach school.

Three years had passed under Madame Moreau's roof, Ruth's schoolmates wondering the while why she took so much pains to bother her head with those stupid books, when she was every day growing prettier, and all the world knew that it was quite unnecessary for a pretty woman to be clever. When Ruth once more crossed the paternal threshold, Hyacinth leveled his eye-glass at her, and exclaimed, " 'Pon honor, Ruth, you 've positively had a narrow escape from being handsome." Whether old

Mr. Ellet was satisfied with her physical and mental progress, Ruth had no means of knowing.

And now, as we have said before, it is the night before Ruth's bridal; and there she sits, though the old church bell has long since chimed the midnight hour, gazing at the moon, as she cuts a shining path through the waters; and trembling, while she questions the dim, uncertain future. Tears, Ruth? Have phantom shapes of terror glided before those gentle prophet eyes? Has death's dark wing even now fanned those girlish temples?

CHAPTER II

IT was so odd in Ruth to have no one but the family at the wedding. It was just one of her queer freaks! Where was the use of her white satin dress and orange wreath? what the use of her looking handsomer than she ever did before, when there was nobody there to see her?

"Nobody to see her?" Mark that manly form at her side; see his dark eye glisten, and his chiseled lip quiver, as he bends an earnest gaze on her who realizes all his boyhood dreams. Mistaken ones! it is not admiration which that young beating heart craves; it is love.

"A very fine-looking, presentable fellow," said Hyacinth, as the carriage rolled away with his new brother-in-law. "Really, love is a great beautifier. Ruth looked quite handsome to-night. Lord bless me! how immensely tiresome it must be to sit opposite the same face three times a day, three hundred and sixty-five days in a year! I should weary of Venus herself. I 'm glad my handsome brother-in-law is in such good circumstances. Duns *are* a bore. I must keep on the right side of him. Tom, was that tailor here again yesterday? Did you tell him I was out of town? Right, Tom."

CHAPTER III

"WELL, I *hope* Harry will be happy," said Ruth's mother-in-law, old Mrs. Hall, as she untied her cap-strings, and seated herself in the newly-furnished parlor, to await the coming of the bride and bridegroom. "I can't say, though, that I see the need of his being married. I always mended his socks. He has sixteen bran new shirts, eight linen and eight cotton. I made them myself out of the Hamilton long-cloth. Hamilton long-cloth is good cotton, too; strong, firm, and wears well. Eight cotton and eight linen shirts! Can anybody tell what he got married for? *I* don't know. If he tired of his boarding-house, of course he could always come home. As to Ruth, I don't know anything about her. Of course she is perfect in *his* eyes. I remember the time when he used to think *me* perfect. I suppose I shall be laid on the shelf now. Well, what beauty he can find in that pale, golden hair, and those blue-gray eyes, I don't know. I can't say I fancy the family either. Proud as Lucifer, all of 'em. Nothing to be proud of, either. The father next to nothing when he began life. The son, a conceited jackanapes, who divides his time between writing rhymes and inventing new ties for his cravat. Well, well, we shall see; but I doubt if this bride is anything but a well-dressed doll. I 've been peeping into her bureau drawers to-day. What is the use of all those ruffles on her under-clothes, I 'd like to know? Who 's going to wash and iron them? *Presents* to her! Well, why don't people make *sensible* presents, —a dozen of dish towels, some crash rollers, a ball of wick-yarn, or the like of that?"

"O-o-oh d-e-a-r! there 's the carriage! Now, for one month to come, to say the least, I shall be made perfectly sick with their billing and cooing. I should n't be surprised if Harry did n't speak

to me oftener than once a day. Had he married a practical
woman I would n't have cared—somebody who looked as if
God made her for something; but that little yellow-haired
simpleton—umph!"

Poor Ruth, in happy ignorance of the state of her new
mother-in-law's feelings, moved about her apartments in a sort
of blissful dream. How odd it seemed, this new freedom, this
being one's own mistress. How odd to see that shaving-brush
and those razors lying on *her* toilet table! then that saucy looking
smoking-cap, those slippers and that dressing-gown, those fancy
neckties, too, and vests and coats, in unrebuked proximity to her
muslins, laces, silks and de laines!

Ruth liked it.

CHAPTER IV

"GOOD morning, Ruth; *Mrs. Hall* I suppose I *should* call you, only that I can't get used to being shoved one side quite so suddenly," said the old lady, with a faint attempt at a laugh.

"Oh, pray don't say Mrs. Hall to *me,*" said Ruth, handing her a chair; "call me any name that best pleases you; I shall be quite satisfied."

"I suppose you feel quite lonesome when Harry is away, attending to business, and as if you hardly knew what to do with yourself; don't you?"

"Oh, no," said Ruth, with a glad smile, "not at all. I was just thinking whether I was not glad to have him gone a little while, so that I could sit down and think how much I love him."

The old lady moved uneasily in her chair. "I suppose you understand all about housekeeping, Ruth?"

Ruth blushed. "No," said she, "I have but just returned from boarding-school. I asked Harry to wait till I had learned house-keeping matters, but he was not willing."

The old lady untied her cap-strings, and patted the floor restlessly with her foot.

"It is a great pity you were not brought up properly," said she. "I learned all that a girl should learn, before I married. Harry has his fortune yet to make, you know. Young people, now-a-days, seem to think that money comes in showers, whenever it is wanted; that 's a mistake; a penny at a time—that 's the way we got ours; that 's the way Harry and you will have to get yours. Harry has been brought up sensibly. He has been taught economy; he is, like me, naturally of a very generous turn; he will occasionally offer you pin-money. In those cases, it will be best for you to pass it over to me to keep; of course you can always have it again, by telling me how you wish to spend it. I would advise you, too, to lay by all your handsome clothes. As to the silk stockings you were married in, of course you will never be so extravagant as to wear them again. I never had a pair of silk stockings in my life; they have a very silly, frivolous look. Do you know how to iron, Ruth?"

"Yes," said Ruth; "I have sometimes clear-starched my own muslins and laces."

"Glad to hear it; did you ever seat a pair of pantaloons?"

"No," said Ruth, repressing a laugh, and yet half inclined to cry; "you forget that I am just home from boarding-school."

"Can you make bread? When I say *bread* I *mean* bread—old fashioned, yeast riz bread; none of your sal-soda, salæratus, sal-volatile poisonous mixtures, that must be eaten as quick as baked, lest it should dry up; *yeast* bread—do you know how to make it?"

"No," said Ruth, with a growing sense of her utter good-for-nothingness; "people in the city always buy baker's bread; my father did."

"Your father! land's sake, child, you must n't quote your father now you 're married; you have n't any father."

I never had, thought Ruth.

"To be sure; what does the Bible say? 'Forsaking father and mother, cleave to your wife,' (or husband, which amounts to the same thing, I take it;) and speaking of that, I hope you won't be always running home, or running anywhere in fact. Wives should be keepers at home. Ruth," continued the old lady after a short pause, "do you know I should like your looks better, if you did n't curl your hair?"

"I don't curl it," said Ruth, "it curls naturally."

"That 's a pity," said the old lady, "you should avoid everything that looks frivolous; you must try and pomatum it down. And Ruth, if you should feel the need of exercise, don't gad in the streets. Remember there is nothing like a broom and a dust-pan to make the blood circulate."

"You keep a rag bag, I suppose," said the old lady; "many 's the glass dish I 've peddled away my scissors-clippings for. 'Waste not, want not.' I 've got that framed somewhere. I 'll hunt it up, and put it on your wall. It won't do you any harm to read it now and then."

"I hope," continued the old lady, "that you don't read novels and such trash. I have a very select little library, when you feel inclined to read, consisting of a treatise on 'The Complaints of Women,' an excellent sermon on Predestination, by our old minister, Dr. Diggs. and Seven Reasons why John Rogers, the martyr, must have had *ten* children instead of *nine* (as is *generally* supposed); any time that you stand in need of *rational* reading come to me;" and the old lady, smoothing a wrinkle in her black silk apron, took a dignified leave.

CHAPTER V

POOR Ruth! her sky so soon overcast! As the door closed on the prim, retreating figure of her mother-in-law, she burst into tears. But she was too sensible a girl to weep long. She wiped her eyes, and began to consider what was to be done. It would never do to complain to Harry—dear Harry. He would have to take sides; oh no, that would never do; she could never complain to him of his *own* mother. But why did he bring them together? knowing, as he must have known, how little likely they were to assimilate. This thought she smothered quickly, but not before it had given birth to a sigh, close upon the heels of which love framed this apology: It was so long since Harry had lived under the same roof with his mother he had probably forgotten her eccentricities; and then she was so dotingly fond of him, that probably no points of collision ever came up between the two.

In the course of an hour, what with cold bathing and philosophy, Ruth's eyes and equanimity were placed beyond the suspicion even of a newly-made husband, and when she held up her lips to him so temptingly, on his return, he little dreamed of the self-conquest she had so tearfully achieved for his sake.

CHAPTER VI

HARRY'S father began life on a farm in Vermont. Between handling ploughs, hoes, and harrows, he had managed to pick up sufficient knowledge to establish himself as a country doctor; well contented to ride six miles on horseback of a stormy night, to extract a tooth for some distracted wretch, for twenty-five cents. Naturally loquacious, and equally fond of administering jalap and gossip, he soon became a great favorite with the "women folks," which every aspiring Esculapius, who reads this, knows to be half the battle. They soon began to trust him, not only in drawing teeth, but in cases involving the increase of the village census. Several successes in this line, which he took no pains to conceal, put him behind a gig of his own, and enabled his practice to overtake his fame as far as the next village.

Like many other persons, who revolve all their life in a peck measure, the doctor's views of the world in general, and its denizens in particular, were somewhat circumscribed. Added to this, he was as persevering as a fly in the dog-days, and as immovable as the old rusty weather-cock on the village meeting-house, which for twenty years had never been blown about by any whisking wind of doctrine. "When he opened his mouth, no dog must bark;" and any dissent from his opinion, however circumspectly worded, he considered a personal insult. As his wife entertained the same liberal views, occasional conjugal collisions, on this narrow track, were the consequence; the interest of which was intensified by each reminding the other of their Calvinistic church obligations to keep the peace. They had, however, one common ground of undisputed territory—their *"Son Harry,"* who was as infallible as the Pope, and (until he got married) never did a foolish thing since he was born. On this last point, their "Son Harry" did not exactly agree with them, as he considered it decidedly the most delightful negotiation he had ever made, and one which he could not even think of without a sudden acceleration of pulse.

Time wore on, the young couple occupying their own suite of apartments, while the old people kept house. The doctor, who had saved enough to lay his saddle-bags with his medical books on the shelf, busied himself, after he had been to market in the morning, in speculating on what Ruth was about, or in peeping over the balustrade, to see who called when the bell rang; or, in counting the wood-pile, to see how many sticks the cook had taken to make the pot boil for dinner. The second girl (a supernumerary of the bridal week) had long since been dismissed; and the doctor and his wife spent their evenings with the cook, to save the expense of burning an extra lamp. Consequently, Betty soon began to consider herself one of the family, and surprised Ruth one day by modestly requesting the loan of her bridal veil "to wear to a little party;" not to speak of sundry naps to which she treated herself in Ruth's absence, in her damask rocking chair, which was redolent, for some time after, of a strong odor of dish-water.

Still, Ruth kept her wise little mouth shut; moving, amid these discordant elements, as if she were deaf, dumb, and blind.

Oh, love! that thy silken reins could so curb the spirit and bridle the tongue, that thy uplifted finger of warning could calm that bounding pulse, still that throbbing heart, and send those rebellious tears, unnoticed, back to their source.

Ah! could we lay bare the secret history of many a wife's heart, what martyrs would be found, over whose uncomplaining lips the grave sets its unbroken seal of silence.

But was Harry blind and deaf? Had the bridegroom of a few months grown careless and unobservant? Was he, to whom every hair of that sunny head was dear, blind to the inward struggles, marked only by fits of feverish gayety? Did he never see the

se to hide the tell-tale blush, or starting tear? Did it
notice, that Ruth would start, like a guilty thing, if a
sudden impulse of tenderness betrayed her into laying her hand
upon his forehead, or leaning her head upon his shoulder, or
throwing her arms about his neck, when the jealous mother was
by? Did not his soul bend the silent knee of homage to that
youthful self-control that could repress its own warm emotions,
and stifle its own sorrows, lest *he* should know a heart-pang?

Yes; Ruth read it in the magnetic glance of the loving eye as
it lingeringly rested on her, and in the low, thrilling tone of the
whispered, "God bless you, my wife;" and many an hour, when
alone in his counting room, was Harry, forgetful of business,
revolving plans for a separate home for himself and Ruth.

This was rendered every day more necessary, by the increased
encroachments of the old people, who insisted that no visitors
should remain in the house after the old-fashioned hour of nine;
at which time the fire should be taken apart, the chairs set up,
the lights extinguished, and a solemn silence brood until the next
morning's cock-crowing. It was also suggested to the young couple, that the wear and tear of the front entry carpet might be
saved by their entering the house by the back gate, instead of
the front door.

Meals were very solemn occasions; the old people frowning,
at such times, on all attempts at conversation, save when the
doctor narrated the market prices he paid for each article of food
upon the table. And so time wore on. The old couple, like two
scathed trees, dry, harsh, and uninviting, presenting only rough
surfaces to the clinging ivy, which fain would clothe with bright-
est verdure their leafless branches.

CHAPTER VII

HARK! to that tiny wail! Ruth knows that most blessed of all hours. Ruth is a *mother!* Joy to thee, Ruth! Another outlet for thy womanly heart; a mirror, in which thy smiles and tears shall be reflected back; a fair page, on which thou, God-commissioned, mayst write what thou wilt; a heart that will throb back to thine, love for love.

But Ruth thinks not of all this now, as she lies pale and motionless upon the pillow, while Harry's grateful tears bedew his first-born's face. She cannot even welcome the little stranger. Harry thought her dear to him before; but now, as she lies there, so like death's counterpart, a whole life of devotion would seem too little to prove his appreciation of all her sacrifices.

The advent of the little stranger was viewed through very different spectacles by different members of the family. The doctor regarded it as a little automaton, for pleasant Æsculapian experiments in his idle hours; the old lady viewed it as another barrier between herself and Harry, and another tie to cement his already too strong attachment for Ruth; and Betty groaned, when she thought of the puny interloper, in connection with washing and ironing days; and had already made up her mind that the first time its nurse used her new saucepan to make gruel, she would strike for higher wages.

Poor, little, unconscious "Daisy," with thy velvet cheek nestled up to as velvet a bosom, sleep on; thou art too near heaven to know a taint of earth.

CHAPTER VIII

R UTH'S nurse, Mrs. Jiff, was fat, elephantine, and unctuous. Nursing agreed with her. She had "tasted" too many bowls of wine-whey on the stairs, tipped up too many bottles of porter in the closet, slid down too many slippery oysters before handing them to "her lady," not to do credit to her pantry devotions. Mrs. Jiff wore an uncommonly stiff gingham gown, which sounded, every time she moved, like the rustle of a footfall among the withered leaves of autumn. Her shoes were new, thick, and creaky, and she had a wheezy, dilapidated-bellowsy way of breathing, consequent upon the consumption of the above-mentioned port and oysters, which was intensely cruci-fying to a sick ear.

Mrs. Jiff always "forgot to bring" her own comb and hair brush. She had a way, too, of opening drawers and closets "by mistake," thereby throwing her helpless victim into a state of profuse perspiration. Then she would go to sleep between the andirons, with the new baby on the edge of her knee, in alarming proximity to the coals; would take a pinch of snuff over the bowl of gruel in the corner, and knock down the shovel, poker, and tongs, every time she went near the fire; whisper-ing—sh—sh—sh—at the top of her lungs, as she glanced in the direction of the bed, as if its demented occupant were the guilty cause of the accident.

Mrs. Jiff had not nursed five-and-twenty years for nothing. She particularly affected taking care of young mothers, with their first babies; knowing very well that her chain shortened, with every after addition to maternal experience: she considered her-self, therefore, quite lucky in being called upon to superintend little Daisy's advent.

It *did* occasionally cross Ruth's mind as she lay, almost faintly with exhaustion, on the pillow, while the ravenous little Daisy cried, "give, give," whether it took Mrs. Jiff two hours to make *one* cup of tea, and brown *one* slice of toast; Mrs. Jiff solacing herself, meanwhile, over an omelette in the kitchen, with Betty, and pouring into her ready ears whole histories of "gen'lemen as was n't gen'lemen, whose ladies she nursed," and how "nobody but herself knew how late they *did* come home when their wives were sick, though, to be sure, she 'd scorn to tell of it!" Sometimes, also, Ruth innocently wondered if it was necessary for the nurse to occupy the same bed with "her lady;" particularly when her circumference was as Behemoth-ish, and her nose as musical as Mrs. Jiff's; and whether there would be any impropriety in her asking her to take the babe and keep it quiet *part* of the night, that she might occasionally get a nap. Sometimes, too, she considered the feasibility of requesting Mrs. Jiff not to select the time when she (Ruth) was sipping her chocolate, to comb out her "false front," and polish up her artificial teeth; and sometimes she marveled why, when Mrs. Jiff paid such endless visits to the kitchen, she was always as fixed as the North Star, whenever dear Harry came in to her chamber to have a conjugal chat with her.

CHAPTER IX

"HOW do you do this morning, Ruth?" said the old lady, lowering herself gradually into a softly-cushioned arm chair. "How your sickness *has* altered you! You look like a ghost? I should n't wonder if you lost all your hair; it is no uncommon thing in sickness; or your teeth either. How 's the baby? She don't favor our side of the house at all. She is quite a plain child, in fact. Has she any symptoms, yet, of a sore mouth? I hope not, because she will communicate it to your breast, and then you 'll have a time of it. I knew a poor, feeble thing once, who died of it. Of course, you intend, when Mrs. Jiff leaves, to take care of the baby yourself; a nursery girl would be very expensive."

"I believe Harry has already engaged one," said Ruth.

"I don't think he has," said the old lady, sitting up very straight, "because it was only this morning that the doctor and I figured up the expense it would be to you, and we unanimously came to the conclusion to tell Harry that you 'd better take care of the child yourself. I always took care of my babies. You ought n't to have mentioned a nursery girl, at all, to Harry."

"He proposed it himself," replied Ruth; "he said I was too feeble to have the care of the child."

"Pooh! pshaw! stuff! no such thing. You are well enough, or will be, before long. Now, there 's a girl's board to begin with. Servant girls eat like boa-constrictors. Then, there 's the soap and oil she 'll waste;—oh, the thing is n't to be thought of; it is perfectly ruinous. If you had n't made a fool of Harry, he never could have dreamed of it. You ought to have sense enough to check him, when he would go into such extravagances for you, but some people *have n't* any sense. Where would all the sugar, and starch, and soap, go to, I 'd like to know, if we were to have a second girl in the house? How long would the wood-pile, or pitch-kindlings, or our new copper-boiler last? And who is to keep the back gate bolted, with such a chit flying in and out?"

"Will you please hand me that camphor bottle?" said Ruth, laying her hand upon her throbbing forehead.

"How's my little snow-drop to-day?" said Harry, entering Ruth's room as his mother swept out; "what ails your eyes, Ruth?" said her husband, removing the little hands which hid them.

"A sudden pain," said Ruth, laughing gayly; "it has gone now; the camphor was too strong."

Good Ruth! brave Ruth! Was Harry deceived? Something ails *his* eyes, now; but Ruth has too much tact to notice it.

Oh Love! thou skillful teacher! learned beyond all the wisdom of the schools.

CHAPTER X

"YOU will be happy here, dear Ruth," said Harry; "you will be your own mistress."

Ruth danced about, from room to room, with the careless glee of a happy child, quite forgetful that she was a wife and a mother; quite unable to repress the flow of spirits consequent upon her new-found freedom.

Ruth's new house was about five miles from the city. The approach to it was through a lovely winding lane, a little off the main road, skirted on either side by a thick grove of linden and elms, where the wild grapevine leaped, clinging from branch to branch, festooning its ample clusters in prodigal profusion of fruitage, and forming a dense shade, impervious to the most garish noon-day heat; while beneath, the wild brier-rose unfolded its perfumed leaves in the hedges, till the bees and humming-birds went reeling away, with their honeyed treasures.

You can scarce see the house, for the drooping elms, half a century old, whose long branches, at every wind-gust, swept across the velvet lawn. The house is very old, but Ruth says, "All the better for that." Little patches of moss tuft the sloping roof, and swallows and martens twitter round the old chimney. It has nice old-fashioned beams, running across the ceiling, which threaten to bump Harry's curly head. The doorways, too, are low, with honeysuckle, red and white, wreathed around the porches; and back of the house there is a high hill (which Ruth says must be terraced off for a garden), surmounted by a gray rock, crowned by a tumble-down old summer-house, where you have as fine a prospect of hill and valley, rock and river, as ever a sunset flooded with rainbow tints.

It was blessed to see the love-light in Ruth's gentle eyes; to see the rose chase the lily from her cheek; to see the old spring come back to her step; to follow her from room to room, while she draped the pretty white curtains, and beautified, unconsciously, everything her fingers touched.

She could give an order without having it countermanded; she could kiss little Daisy, without being called "silly;" she could pull out her comb, and let her curls flow about her face, without being considered "frivolous;" and, better than all, she could fly into her husband's arms, when he came home, and kiss him, without feeling that she had broken any penal statute. Yes; she was free as the golden orioles, whose hanging nests swayed to and fro amid the glossy green leaves beneath her window.

But not as thoughtless.

Ruth had a strong, earnest nature; she could not look upon this wealth of sea, sky, leaf, bud, and blossom; she could not listen to the little birds, nor inhale the perfumed breath of morning, without a filling eye and brimming heart, to the bounteous Giver. Should she revel in all this loveliness,—should her heart be filled to its fullest capacity for earthly happiness, and no grateful incense go up from its altar to Heaven?

And the babe? Its wondering eyes had already begun to seek its mother's; its little lip to quiver at a harsh or discordant sound. An unpracticed hand must sweep that harp of a thousand strings; trembling fingers must inscribe, indelibly, on that blank page, characters to be read by the light of eternity: the maternal eye must never sleep at its post, lest the enemy rifle the casket of its gems. And so, by her child's cradle, Ruth first learned to pray. The weight her slender shoulders could not bear, she rolled at the foot of the cross; and, with the baptism of holy tears, mother and child were consecrated.

CHAPTER XI

TIME flew on; seasons came and went; and still peace brooded, like a dove, under the roof of Harry and Ruth. Each bright summer morning, Ruth and the little Daisy, (who already partook of her mother's love for nature,) rambled, hand in hand, through the woods and fields, with a wholesome disregard of those city bugbears, sun, dew, bogs, fences, briers, and cattle. Wherever a flower opened its blue eye in the rock cleft; wherever the little stream ran, babbling and sparkling, through the emerald meadow; where the golden moss piled up its velvet cushion in the cool woods; where the pretty clematis threw the graceful arms of youth round the gnarled trunk of decay; where the bearded grain, swaying to and fro, tempted to its death the reaper; where the red and white clover dotted the meadow grass; or where, in the damp marsh, the whip-poor-will moaned, and the crimson lobelia nodded its regal crown; or where the valley smiled in its beauty 'neath the lofty hills, nestling 'mid its foliage the snow-white cottages; or where the cattle dozed under the broad, green branches, or bent to the glassy lake to drink; or where, on the breezy hill-tops, the voices of childhood came up, sweet and clear, as the far-off hymning of angels,—there, Ruth and her soul's child loved to linger.

It was beautiful, yet fearful, to mark the kindling eye of the child; to see the delicate flush come and go on her marble cheek, and to feel the silent pressure of her little hand, when this alone could tell the rapture she had no words to express.

Ah, Ruth! gaze not so dotingly on those earnest eyes, Know'st thou not,

> The rose that sweetest doth awake,
> Will soonest go to rest?

CHAPTER XII

"WELL," said the doctor, taking his spectacles from his nose, and folding them up carefully in their leathern case; "I hope you 'll be easy, Mis. Hall, now that we 've toted out here, bag and baggage, to please you, when I supposed I was settled for the rest of my life."

"*Fathers* can't be expected to have as much natural affection, or to be as self-sacrificing as *mothers,*" said the old lady. "Of course, it was some trouble to move out here; but, for Harry's sake, I was willing to do it. What does Ruth know about house-keeping, I 'd like to know? A pretty muss she 'll make of it, if *I 'm* not around to oversee things."

"It strikes me," retorted the doctor, "that you won't get any thanks for it—from *one* side of the house, at least. Ruth never *says* anything when you vex her, but there 's a look in her eye which—well, Mis. Hall, it tells the whole story."

"I 've seen it," said the old lady, while her very cap-strings fluttered with indignation, "and it has provoked me a thousand times more than if she had thrown a brick-bat at my head. That girl is no fool, doctor. She knows very well what she is about: but diamond cut diamond, *I* say. Doctor, doctor, there are the hens in the garden. I want that garden kept nice. I suppose Ruth thinks that nobody can have flowers but herself. Wait till my china-asters and sweet peas come up. I 'm going over to-day to take a peep round her house; I wonder what it looks like? Stuck full of gimcracks, of all sorts, I 'll warrant. Well, I shan't furnish my best parlor till I see what she has got. I 've laid by a little money, and—"

"Better give it to the missionaries, Mis. Hall," growled the doctor; "I tell you Ruth don't care a pin what you have in your parlor."

27

"Don't you believe it," said the old lady.

"Well, anyhow," muttered the doctor, "you can't get the upper hand of *her* in that line; i. e., if she has a mind that you shall not. Harry is doing a very good business; and you know very well, it is no use to try to blind your eyes to it, that if she wanted Queen Victoria's scepter, he 'd manage to get it for her."

"That 's more than I can say of *you*," exclaimed the old lady, fanning herself violently, "for all that I used to mend your old saddle-bags, and once made, with my own hands, a pair of leather small-clothes to ride horseback in. Forty years, doctor, I 've spent in your service. I don't look much as I did when you married me. I was said then to have 'woman's seven beauties,' including the 'dimple in the chin,' which I see still remains;" and the old lady pointed to a slight indentation in her wrinkled face. "I might have had him that was Squire Smith, or Pete Packer, or Jim Jessup. There was n't one of 'em who had not rather do the chores on *our* farm, than on any other in the village."

"Pooh, pooh," said the doctor, "don't be an old fool; that was because your father kept good cider."

Mrs. Hall's cap-strings were seen flying the next minute through the sitting-room door; and the doctor was heard to mutter, as she banged the door behind her, "*that* tells the whole story!"

CHAPTER XIII

"A SUMMER house, hey!" said the old lady, as with stealthy, cat-like steps, she crossed a small piece of woods, between her house and Ruth's; "a summer house! that 's the way the money goes, is it? What have we here? a book;" (picking up a volume which lay half hidden in the moss at her feet;) "poetry, I declare! the most frivolous of all reading; all pencil marked;— and here 's something in Ruth's own hand-writing—*that 's* poetry, too: worse and worse."

"Well, we 'll see how the *kitchen* of this poetess looks. I will go into the house the back way, and take them by surprise; that 's the way to find people out. None of your company faces for me." And the old lady peered curiously through her spectacles, on either side, as she passed along towards the kitchen door, and exclaimed, as her eye fell on the shining row, "*six* milkpans!—wonder if they *buy* their milk, or keep a cow. If they buy it, it must cost them something; if they keep a cow, I 've no question the milk is half wasted."

The old lady passed her skinny forefinger across one of the pans, examining her finger very minutely after the operation; and then applied the tip of her nose to the interior of it. There was no fault to be found with that milkpan, if it was Ruth's; so, scrutinizing two or three dish towels, which were hanging on a line to dry, she stepped cautiously up to the kitchen door. A tidy, respectable-looking black woman met her on the threshold; her woolly locks bound with a gay-striped bandanna, and her ebony face shining with irresistible good humor.

"Is Ruth in?" said the old lady.

"Who, Missis?" said Dinah.

"Ruth."

"Missis Hall lives *here,*" answered Dinah, with a puzzled look.

"Exactly," said the old lady; "she is my son's wife."

"Oh! I beg your pardon, Missis," said Dinah, courtesying respectfully. "I never heard her name called Ruth afore: massa calls her 'bird,' and 'sunbeam.' "

The old lady frowned.

"Is she at home?" she repeated, with stately dignity.

"No," said Dinah, "Missis is gone rambling off in the woods with little Daisy. She 's powerful fond of flowers, and things. She climbs fences like a squir'l! it makes this chil' laf' to see the ol' farmers stare at her."

"You must have a great deal to do, here;" said the old lady, frowning; "Ruth is n't much of a hand at house-work."

"Plenty to do, Missis, and willin' hands to do it. Dinah don't care how hard she works, if she don't work to the tune of a lash; and Missis Hall goes singing about the house so that it makes time fly."

"She don't ever *help* you any, does she?" said the persevering old lady.

"Lor' bless you! yes, Missis. She comes right in and makes a pie for Massa Harry, or cooks a steak jess' as easy as she pulls off a flower; and when Dinah's cooking anything new, she asks more questions how it 's done than this chil' kin answer."

"You have a great deal of company, I suppose; that must make you extra trouble, I should think; people riding out from the city to supper, when you are all through and cleared away: don't it tire you?"

"No; Missis Hall takes it easy. She laf's merry, and says to the company, 'you get *tea* enough in the city, so I sha n't give you any; we had tea long ago; but here 's some fresh milk, and some raspberries and cake; and if you can't eat *that,* you ought to go hungry.' "

"She irons Harry's shirts, I suppose?" said the old lady.

"She? s'pose dis chil' let her? when she 's so careful, too, of ol' Dinah's bones?"

"Well," said the old lady, foiled at all points, "I 'll walk over the house a bit, I guess; I won't trouble you to wait on me, Dinah;" and the old lady started on her exploring tour.

CHAPTER XIV

"THIS is the parlor, hey?" soliloquized old Mrs. Hall, as she seated herself on the sofa. "A few dollars laid out here, I guess."

Not so fast, my dear madam. Examine closely. Those long, white curtains, looped up so prettily from the open windows, are plain, cheap muslin; but no artist could have disposed their folds more gracefully. The chairs and sofas, also, Ruth covered with her own nimble fingers: the room has the fragrance of a green-house, to be sure; but if you examine the flowers, which are scattered so profusedly round, you will find they are *wild* flowers, which Ruth, basket in hand, climbs many a stone fence every morning to gather; and not a country boy in the village knows their hiding-places as well as she. See how skillfully they are arranged! with what an eye to the blending of colors! How dainty is that little tulip-shaped vase, with those half opened wild-rose buds! see that little gilt saucer, containing only a few tiny green leaves; yet, mark their exquisite shape and finish. And there are some wood anemones; some white, with a faint blush of pink at the petals; and others blue as little Daisy's eyes; and see that velvet moss, with its gold-star blossoms!

"Must take a deal of time to gather and fix 'em," muttered the old lady.

Yes, my dear madam; but, better pay the shoe-maker's than the doctor's bill; better seek health in hunting live flowers, than ruin it by manufacturing those German worsted abortions.

You should see your son Harry, as he ushers a visitor in through the low door-way, and stands back to mark the surprised delight with which he gazes upon Ruth's little fairy room. You should see how Harry's eyes glisten, as they pass from one flower vase to another, saying, "Who but Ruth would ever have spied out *that* tiny little blossom?"

And little Daisy has caught the flower mania, too; and every day she must have *her* vase in the collection; now withdrawing a rose and replacing it with a violet, and then stepping a pace or two back and looking at it with her little head on one side, as knowingly as an artist looks at the finishing touches to a favorite picture.

But, my dear old lady, we beg pardon; we are keeping you too long from that china closet, which you are so anxious to inspect; hoping to find a flaw, either in crockery or cake. Not a bit! You may draw those prying fingers across the shelves till you are tired, and not a particle of dust will adhere to them. Neither cups, saucers, tumblers, nor plates, stick to your hands; the sugar-bowl is covered; the cake, in that tin pail, is fresh and light; the preserves, in those glass jars, tied down with brandy papers, are clear as amber; and the silver might serve for a looking-glass, in which you could read your own vexation.

Never mind! A great many people keep the *first* floor spick and span; mayhap you 'll find something wrong *up* stairs. Walk in; 'tis the "best chamber." A gilt arrow is fastened to the wall, and pretty white lace curtains are thrown (tent fashion) over it; there is a snow-white quilt and a pair of plump, tempting pillows; the furniture and carpet are of a light cream color; and there is a vase of honeysuckle on the little light-stand. Nothing could be more faultless, you see.

Now, step into the nursery; the floor is strewed with playthings; thank God, there 's a child in the house! There is a broken doll; a torn picture-book; a little wreath of oak leaves; a dandelion chain; some willow tassels; a few acorns; a little red shoe, full of particolored pebbles; the wing of a little blue-bird; two little, speckled eggs, on a tuft of moss; and a little orphan chicken, nestling in a basket of cotton wool, in the corner. Then, there is a work-basket of Ruth's with a little dress of Daisy's, partly finished, and a dicky of Harry's, with the needle still sticking in it, which the little gypsey wife intends finishing when she comes back from her wood ramble.

The old lady begins to think she must give it up; when, luckily, her eye falls on a crouching "Venus," in the corner. Saints and angels! why, she has never been to the dress-makers! There 's a text, now! What a pity there is no appreciative audience to see the glow of indignation with which those half averted eyes regard the undraped goddess!

"Oh, Harry! is this the end of all my teachings? Well, it is all *Ruth's* doings—*all* Ruth's doings. Harry is to be pitied, not blamed;" and the old lady takes up, at length, her *triumphant* march for home.

CHAPTER XV

"HALLO! what are you doing there?" exclaimed the doctor, looking over the fence at a laborer, at work in one of Harry's fields.

"Ploughing this bit o' ground, sir. Mr. Hall told me to be sure and get it finished before he came home from the city this afthernoon."

"Nonsense!" replied the doctor, "I was born sometime before my son Harry; put up your plough, and lay that bit of stone wall yonder; that needs to be done first."

"I 'm thinking Masther Hall won't be afther liking it if I do, sir," said Pat; "I had my orders for the day's work before masther went to the city, sir, this morning."

"Pooh, pooh," said the old man, unchaining the horse from the plough, and turning him loose in the pasture; "young folks *think* old folks are fools; old folks *know* young folks to be so."

Pat eyed the doctor, scratched his head, and began slowly to lay the stone wall.

"What 's *that* fellow doing over yonder?" said the doctor to Pat.

"Planting corn, yer honor."

"Corn? ha! ha! city farming! Good. Corn? That 's just the spot for potatoes. H-a-l-l-o there! Don't plant any more corn in that spot, John; it never 'll come to anything—never."

"But, Mr. Hall?" said John, hesitatingly, leaning on his hoe-handle.

"Harry, Oh, never mind him. He has seen more ledgers than corn. Corn? Ha! that 's good. You can go cart that load of gravel up the hill. What a fortunate thing for Harry, that I am here to oversee things. This amateur farming is pretty play enough; but the way it sinks the money is more curious than profitable. I wonder, now, if that tree is grafted right. I 'll take off the ligatures and see. That hedge won't grow, I 'm certain; the down-east cedars thrive the best for hedges. I may as well pull these up, and tell Harry to get some of the other kind;" and the doctor pulled them up by the roots, and threw them over the fence.

CHAPTER XVI

"TIME for papa to come," said little Daisy, seating herself on the low door-step; "the sun has crept way round to the big apple-tree;" and Daisy shook back her hair, and settling her little elbows on her knees, sat with her chin in her palms, dreamily watching the shifting clouds. A butterfly alights on a blade of grass near her: Daisy springs up, her long hair floating like a veil about her shoulders, and her tiny feet scarce bending the clover blossoms, and tiptoes carefully along in pursuit.

He 's gone, Daisy, but never mind; like many other coveted treasures, he would lose his brilliancy if caught. Daisy has found something else; she closes her hand over it, and returns to her old watch-post on the door-step. She seats herself again, and loosing her tiny hold, out creeps a great, bushy, yellow caterpillar. Daisy places him carefully on the back of her little, blue-veined hand, and he commences his travels up the polished arm, to the little round shoulder. When he reaches the lace sleeve, Daisy's laugh rings out like a robin's carol; then she puts him back, to retravel the same smooth road again.

"Oh, Daisy! Daisy!" said Ruth, stepping up behind her, "what an *ugly* playfellow; put him down, do darling; I cannot bear to see him on your arm."

"Why—*God* made him," said little Daisy, with sweet, upturned eyes of wonder.

"True, darling," said Ruth, in a hushed whisper, kissing the child's brow, with a strange feeling of awe. "Keep him, Daisy, dear, if you like."

CHAPTER XVII

"PLEASE, sir, I 'll be afther leaving the night," said John, scraping out his hind foot, as Harry drew rein on Romeo, and halted under a large apple-tree.

"Leave?" exclaimed Harry, patting Romeo's neck; "you seemed a contented fellow enough when I left for the city this morning. Don't your wages suit? What's in the wind now? out with it, man."

John scratched his head, kicked away a pebble with the toe of his brogan, looked up, and looked down, and finally said, (lowering his voice to a confidential whisper, as he glanced in the direction of the doctor's cottage;) "It 's the ould gintleman, sir, savin' yer presence. It is not *two* masthers Pat would be afther having;" and Pat narrated the affair of the plough.

Harry bit his lip, and struck Romeo a little quick cut with his riding-whip. Harry was one of the most dutiful of sons, and never treated his father with disrespect; he had chosen a separate home, that he might be master of it; and this old annoyance in a new shape was very provoking. "Pat," said he at length, "there is only one master here; when *I* give you an order, you are to stick to it, till you get a different one from me. D' ye understand?"

"By the Holy Mother I 'll do it," said Pat delightedly, resuming his hoe with fresh vigor.

CHAPTER XVIII

"THAT 's the fourth gig that has been tied to Harry's fence, since dinner," said the old lady. "I hope Harry's business will continue to prosper. Company, company, company. And there 's Ruth, as I live, romping round that meadow, without a bit of a bonnet. Now she 's climbing a cherry-tree. A *married woman* climbing a cherry-tree! Doctor, do you hear that?"

"Shoot 'em down," said the doctor, abstractedly, without lifting his eyes from the Almanac.

"Shoot *who* down?" said the old lady, shaking him by the shoulder. "I said that romp of a Ruth was up in a cherry-tree."

"Oh, I thought you were talking of those thievish robins stealing the cherries," said the doctor; "as to Ruth I 've given her up long ago; *she* never will settle down to anything. Yesterday, as I was taking a walk over Harry's farm to see if things were not all going to the dogs, I saw her down in the meadow yonder, with her shoes and stockings off, wading through a little brook to get at some flowers, which grew on the other side. Half an hour after she came loitering up the road, with her bonnet hanging on the back of her neck, and her apron crammed full of grasses, and herbs, and branches and all sorts of green trash. Just then the minister came along. I was glad of it. Good enough for her, thinks I to myself; she 'll blush for once. Well, what do you think she did, Mis. Hall?"

"*What?*" said the old lady, in a sepulchral whisper, dropping her knitting-needles and drawing her rocking-chair within kissing distance of the doctor.

"Why, she burst out a-laughing, perched herself on top of a stone wall, took a great big leaf to fan herself, and then invited

the minister to sit down 'long side of her, *jest* as easy as if her
hair was n't all flying round her face like a wild Arab's."

"I give up now," said the old lady, dropping her hands in an
attitude of the extremest dejection; "there 's no hope of her after
that; and what is worse, it is no use talking to Harry; she 's got
him so bewitched that he imagines everything she does is right.
How she did it, passes me. I 'm sure she has no beauty. I 've no
patience to see Harry twisting those yellow curls of hers round
his fingers, and calling them 'threads of gold;' threads of fiddle-
sticks! She 'd look a deal more proper like, if she 'd wear her
hair smooth behind her ears, as I do."

"But your hair is false," said the literal doctor.

"Doctor," said the old lady, snapping her eyes, "I never can
argue with you but you are sure to get off the track, sooner or
later; there is no need of your telling all, you know. Suppose I
was always alluding to your wig, how would you like it?"

CHAPTER XIX

WINTER had set in. The snow in soft, white piles, barred up the cottage door, and hung shelving over the barn-roof and fences; while every tiny twig and branch bent heavily, with its soft fleecy burthen. "Papa," was to go to the city that morning in a sleigh. Daisy had already heard the bells tinkling at the barn-door, as Pat necklaced Romeo, who stood pawing and snorting, as if it were fine fun to plough five miles of un-broken road into the city. Daisy had turned Papa's over-coat sleeves inside out, and warmed them thoroughly at the fire; she had tied on his moccasins, and had thrown his fur collar round his neck; and now she stood holding his warm cap and furred gloves, while he and mamma were saying their usual good-bye.

"Take care of that cough, Daisy," said Harry; "don't come to the door, darling, to breathe in this keen air. Kiss your hand to papa, from the window;" and Harry scratched the frost away with his finger nails from the window-pane, that Daisy might see him start.

"Oh, how pretty!" exclaimed the child, as Pat tossed the bright, scarlet-lined buffalo robe into the sleigh, and tucked the corners snugly over his master's feet, and Romeo, inspirited by the merry tinkle of the bells and the keen frosty air, stood on his hind legs and playfully held up his fore feet; "Oh, how pretty!" Harry turned his head as he gathered the reins in his hand; his cap was crowded down so snugly over his forehead, and his fur collar turned up so closely about his chin, that only a glimpse of his dark eye and fine Roman nose was visible. One wave of the hand, and the light, feathery snow flew, on either side, from under Romeo's flying heels—and Papa was out of sight.

CHAPTER XX

"WHY in the world, Ruth, are you wandering about there, like a ghost, in the moonlight?" said Harry, rubbing open his sleepy eyes.

"Hist, Harry! listen to Daisy's breathing; it sounds as if it came through a brazen tube. She must be ill."

"Little wife, don't torment yourself, She has only a bad cold, which, of course, appears worse at night. Her breathing is irregular, because her head is too low. Give her this pillow: there; now she 's comfortable. What a frightened little puss you are! Your hand trembles as if you had the palsy; now go to sleep; it must be near two o'clock; you 'll be sick yourself to-morrow:" and Harry, wearied out with an annoying day of business, was soon fast asleep.

Only the eye of God watches like a mother's. Ruth could not sleep. She was soon again at Daisy's side, with her fingers upon her wrist, and her eye fixed upon the child's face; marking every contortion of feature, noting every change of posture.

"What is it, darling?" asked her mother, as Daisy grasped her throat with both hands.

"It hurts," said the child.

Ruth glanced at Harry. He was so weary, it were a pity to wake him needlessly. Perhaps her fears were groundless, and she was over-anxious; and then, perhaps, Daisy really needed *immediate* medical aid.

Ruth's fears preponderated.

"Dear Harry," said she, laying her hand softly on his forehead, "do call up Pat, and send for the doctor."

"Certainly, if you think best," said Harry, springing up; "but it is a cold night for the old man to come out; and really, Ruth, Daisy has only a stuffed cold."

"*Please* let Pat go," said Ruth, pleadingly; "I shall feel happier, Harry."

It was a venturous undertaking to rouse Pat suddenly, as his bump of destructiveness generally woke first; and a fight seemed always with him a necessary preliminary to a better understanding of things.

"Hold! hold!" said Harry, seizing his brawny, belligerent fists; "not quite so fast man; open your eyes, and see who I am."

"Did I sthrike yer honor?" said Pat; "I hope yer 'll forgive me; but you see, I was jist born with my fists doubled up."

"All right," said his master, laughing; "but get on your clothes as soon as possible; harness Romeo, and bring the old gentleman up here. Mrs. Hall feels very uneasy about Daisy, and wants him to prescribe for her."

"I 'll bring him back in a flash," said Pat; "but what 'll I do if he won't come?"

"Who 's there? what do you want? Speak quick, if you 've anything to say, for I 'm catching the rheumatiz' in my head;" said the doctor, as he poked his bald poll out the cottage window, into the frosty night air. Who are you? and what on earth do you want?"

"It 's me," said Pat.

"Who 's me?" said the Doctor.

"Botheration," growled Pat; "don't the ould owl know the voice of me?—It 's Pat Donahue; the childer is sick, and Misthress Ruth wants you to come wid me, and give her something to betther her."

"Pooh! pooh! is that all you woke me up for? The child was well enough this noon, except a slight cold. Ruth is full of notions. Go home and take that bottle, and tell her to give Daisy half a teaspoonful once in two hours; and I 'll come over in the morning. She 's always a-fussing with that child, and thinking, if she sneezes, that she is going to die. It 's a wonder if I don't die myself, routed out of a warm bed, without my wig, this time of night. There—there—go along, and mind you shut the gate after you. Ten to one he 'll leave it open," soliloquized the doctor, slamming down the window with a jerk. "I hate an Irishman as I do a rattlesnake. An Irishman is an incomplete biped—a human tower of Babel; he was finished up to a certain point, and there he was left.

"Mis. Hall! Mis. Hall! if you 've no objection, I should like you to stop snoring. I should like to sleep, if the village of Glenville will let me. Dear, dear, what a thing it is to be a doctor!"

CHAPTER XXI

"I F de las' day *has* come, dis chil' ought to know it," said Dinah, springing to her feet and peering out, as she scratched away the frost from the window; "has de debbel broke loose? or only de horse? Any way, 'tis about de same ting;" and she glanced in the direction of the barn. "Massy sakes! dere's Pat stealing off in de night wid Romeo; no he aint neider—he 's putting him up in de barn. Where you s'pose he 's been dis time o' night? *Courting* p'r'aps! Well, dis chil' dunno. And dere's a bright light shining on de snow, from Massa Harry's window. Dinah can't sleep till she knows what 's to pay, dat 's a fac';" and tying a handkerchief over her woolly head, and throwing on a shawl, she tramped down stairs. "Massy sakes!" said she, stopping on the landing, as Daisy's shrill cough fell on her ear; "Massy! jes' hear dat!" and opening the chamber-door, Dinah stood staring at the child, with distended eye-balls, then looking from Harry to Ruth, as if she thought them both under the influence of night-mare. "For de *Lord's* sake, Massa Harry, send for de doctor," said Dinah, clasping her hands.

"We have," said Harry, trying to coax Daisy to swallow another spoonful of the medicine, "and he said he 'd be here in the morning."

"She won't," said Dinah, in a low, hoarse whisper to Harry, as she pointed to Daisy. "Don't you *know,* Massa, it 's de croup! de croup; de *wu'st* way, Massa! *Oh* Lor'!"

Harry was harnessing Romeo in an instant, and on his way to the doctor's cottage. In vain he knocked, and rang, and thumped. The old man, comfortably tucked up between the blankets, was far away in the land of dreams.

"What is to be done?" said Harry; "I must tie Romeo to the post and climb in at the kitchen-window."

"Father! father!" said he, shaking the old gentleman by the shoulders, "Daisy is worse, and I want you to go right home with me."

"Don't believe it," said the old man; "you are only frightened; its an awful cold night to go out."

"I know it," said Harry; "but I brought two buffaloes; hurry, father. Daisy is *very* sick."

The old doctor groaned; took his wig from the bed post, and put it on his head; tied a woollen muffler, with distressing deliberation, over his unbelieving ears, and, returning four times to tell "Mis. Hall to be sure and bolt the front door after him," climbed into the sleigh. "I shall be glad if I don't get a sick spell myself," said the doctor, "coming out this freezing night. Ruth has frightened you to death, I s'pose. Ten to one when I get up there, nothing will ail the child. Come, come, don't drive so fast; my bones are old, and I don't believe in these gay horses of yours, who never make any use of their fore-legs, except to hold them up in the air. Whoa, I say—Romeo, whoa!"

"Get out de way, Pat!" said Dinah; "your Paddy fingers are all thumbs. Here, put some more water in dat kettle dere; now stir dat mustard paste; now run quick wid dat goose-grease up to Missus, and tell her to rub de chil's troat wid it; 't aint no use, though. Oh, Lor'! dis nigger knew she would n't live, ever since she said dat 'bout de caterpillar. De Lord wants de chil', dat 's a fac'; she nebber played enough to suit Dinah."

CHAPTER XXII

STAMPING the snow from his feet, the doctor slowly untied his woolen muffler, took off his hat, settled his wig, hung his overcoat on a nail in the entry, drew from his pocket a huge red handkerchief, and announcing his arrival by a blast, loud enough to arouse the seven sleepers, followed Harry up stairs to the sick chamber.

The strong fire-light fell upon Ruth's white figure, as she sat, pale and motionless, in the corner, with Daisy on her lap, whose laborious breathing could be distinctly heard in the next room. A dark circle had settled round the child's mouth and eyes, and its little hands hung helplessly at its side. Dinah was kneeling at the hearth, stirring a fresh mustard paste, with an air which seemed to say, "it is no use, but I must keep on doing something."

The doctor advanced, drew his spectacles from their leathern case, perched them astride the end of his nose, and gazed steadily at Daisy without speaking.

"Help her," said Ruth, imploringly.

"Nothing to be done," said the doctor, in an unmoved tone, staring at Daisy.

"Why did n't you come afore, den?" said Dinah, springing to her feet and confronting the doctor. "Don't you see you 've murdered *two* of 'em?" and she pointed to Ruth, whose head had dropped upon her breast.

"I tell you, Harry, it 's no use to call another doctor," said his father, shaking off his grasp; "the child is struck with death; let her drop off quietly; what 's the sense of tormenting her?"

Harry shuddered, and drew his father again to Daisy's side.

"Help her," said Ruth; "don't talk; try *something*."

47

"Well, I can put on these leeches, if you insist," said the old man, uncorking a bottle; "but I tell you, it is only tormenting the dying."

Dinah cut open the child's night dress, and bared the fair, round chest, to which the leeches clung eagerly; Daisy, meanwhile, remaining motionless, and seemingly quite insensible to the disagreeable pricking sensation they caused.

"The other doctor is below," whispered Pat, thrusting his head in at the door.

"Bring him up," said the old gentleman.

An expression of pain passed over the young man's features as his eye fell upon the child. As yet, he had not become so professionally hardened, as to be able to look unmoved upon the group before him, whose imploring eyes asked vainly of him the help no mortal hand could give.

A few questions he asked to avoid being questioned himself; a few remedies he tried, to appease the mother's heart, whose mournful eyes were on him like a spell.

"Water," said Daisy, faintly, as she languidly opened her eyes.

"God be thanked," said Ruth, overcome by the sound of that blessed little voice, which she never expected to hear again, "God be thanked."

The young doctor returned no answering smile, as Ruth and Harry grasped his hand; but he walked to the little window and looked out upon the gray dawn, with a heavy sigh, as the first faint streak of light ushered in the new-born day.

Still the fire-light flashed and flickered—now upon the old doctor, who had fallen asleep in his arm chair; now upon Ruth's bowed head; now upon Daisy, who lay motionless in her mother's lap, (the deadly paleness of her countenance rendered still more fearful by the dark blood-stains on her night dress;) then upon Harry, who, kneeling at Daisy's side, and stifling his own strong heart, gazed alternately at mother and child; then upon

Dinah, who, with folded arms, stood like some grim sentinel, in the shadow of the farther corner; the little mantel clock, meanwhile, ticking, ticking on—numbering the passing moments with startling distinctness.

Oh, in such an hour, when wave after wave of anguish dashes over us, where are the infidel's boasted doubts, as the tortured heart cries out, instinctively, "save, Lord; or we perish!"

Slowly the night waned, and the stars paled. Up the gray east the golden sun slowly glided. One beam penetrated the little window, hovering like a halo over Daisy's sunny head. A quick, convulsive start, and with one wild cry (as the little throat filled to suffocation), the fair white arms were tossed aloft, then dropped powerless upon the bed of Death!

CHAPTER XXIII

"THERE can be no sorrow greater than this sorrow," sobbed Ruth, as the heavy sod fell on Daisy's little breast.

In after years, when bitterer cups had been drained to the dregs, Ruth remembered these, her murmuring words. Ah! mourning mother! He who seeth the end from the beginning, even in this blow "remembered mercy."

"Your daughter-in-law is quite crushed by her affliction, I hear," said a neighbor to old Mrs. Hall.

"Yes, Mrs. Jones, I think she is," said the old lady complacently. "It has taken right hold of her."

"It died of croup, I believe," said Mrs. Jones.

"Well, they *say* so," said the old lady. "It is *my* opinion the child's death was owing to the thriftlessness of the mother. I don't mourn for it, because I believe the poor thing is better off."

"You surprise me," said Mrs. Jones. "I always had the impression that young Mrs. Hall was a pattern mother."

"People differ," said the old lady, raising her eyebrows, compressing her lips, and looking mysteriously at the ceiling, as if she *could* tell a tale, were she not too charitable.

"Well, the amount of it is," said the garrulous old doctor, emerging from the corner; "the amount of it is, that the mother always thought she knew better than anybody else how to manage that child. Now, you know, Mis. Jones, I 'm a physician, and *ought* to know something about the laws that govern the human body, but you 'll be astonished to hear that she frequently acted directly contrary to my advice, and this is the result, tells the whole story. However, as Mis. Hall says, the child is better off; and as to Ruth, why the Lord generally sends afflictions where they are *needed;*" and the doctor returned to his corner.

"It looks very lonely at the Glen since they moved away," remarked Mrs. Jones. "I suppose they don't think of coming back."

"How?" replied the doctor, re-appearing from his corner.

"I suppose your son and his wife have no idea of returning to the Glen," said Mrs. Jones.

"No—no. Ruth is one of the uneasy kind; it 's coming and going—coming and going with her. She fancied everything in doors and out reminded her of Daisy, and kept wandering round, trying to be rid of herself. Now that proves she did n't make a sanctifying use of her trouble. It 's no use trying to dodge what the Lord sends. We 've just got to stand and take it; if we don't, he 'll be sending something else. Them 's my sentiments, and I consider 'em scripteral. I should n't be surprised if *Harry* was taken away from her;—a poor, miserable thing she 'd be to take care of herself, if he was. She could n't earn the salt to her porridge. Thriftless, Mis. Jones, thriftless—come of a bad stock —can't expect good fruit off a wild apple tree, at least, not without grace is grafted on; that tells the whole story."

"Well; my heart aches for her," said the kind Mrs. Jones. "Mrs. Hall is very delicately organized,—one of those persons capable of compressing the happiness or misery of a lifetime into a few moments."

"Stuff," said the doctor, "stuff; don't believe it. *I* 'm an example to the contrary. I 've been through everything, and just look at me;" and the doctor advanced a pace or two to give Mrs. Jones a better view of his full-blown peony face, and aldermanic proportions; "don't believe it, Mis. Jones; stuff! Fashion to be sentimental; nerves a modern invention. Ridiculous!"

"But," said the persistent Mrs. Jones, "don't you think, doctor that—"

"Don't think anything *about* it," said the doctor. "Don't want to *hear* anything about it. Have no patience with any woman who 'd let a husband sell a farm at such a sacrifice as Harry's was sold, merely because there was a remote chance she would become insane if she staid there. Now, I 've enough to do—plenty to do, but, still, I was willing to superintend that farm a little, as my doing so was such a help to Harry. Well, well; they 'll both go to the dogs, that 's the amount of it. A rolling stone gathers no moss. Harry was good for something before he married Ruth; had a mind of his own. Ruth aint the wife for him."

"He did not appear to think so," replied the obstinate Mrs. Jones. "Everybody in the village says, 'what a happy couple they are.' "

"*O-o-h*—my!" hissed the old lady, "did you *ever,* doctor? Of course, Mrs. Jones, you don't suppose Harry would be such a fool as to tell people how miserable he was; but *mothers,* Mrs. Jones, *mothers* are keen sighted; can't throw dust in a *mother's* eyes."

"Nor in mine," retorted the independent Mrs. Jones, with a mock courtesy to the old lady, as she walked out the door, muttering as she went down the road, "Sally Jones will tell her the truth if nobody else will."

"Mis. Hall," said the doctor, drawing himself up so straight as to snap off his waist-band button, "this is the last time that woman ever crosses *my* threshold. I shall tell Deacon Smith that I consider her a proper subject for church discipline; she 's what the Bible calls 'a busy body in other men's matters;' a character which both you and I despise and abominate, Mis. Hall."

CHAPTER XXIV

THE *first-born!* Oh, other tiny feet may trip lightly at the hearth-stone; other rosy faces may greet us round the board; with tender love we soothe their childish pains and share their childish sports; but "Benjamin is not," is written in the secret chamber of many a bereaved mother's heart, where never more the echo of a childish voice may ring out such liquid music as death hath hushed.

Spring had garlanded the earth with flowers, and Autumn had withered them with his frosty breath. Many a Summer's sun, and many a Winter's snow, had rested on Daisy's grave, since the date of our last chapter.

At the window of a large hotel in one of those seaport towns, the resort alike of the invalid and pleasure-seeker, sat Ruth; the fresh sea-breeze lifting her hair from temples thinner and paler than of yore, but stamped with a holier beauty. From the window might be seen the blue waters of the bay leaping to the bright sunlight; while many a vessel outward and inward bound, spread its sails, like some joyous white-winged sea bird. But Ruth was not thinking of the sapphire sky, though it were passing fair; nor of the blue sea, decked with its snowy sails; for in her lap lay a little half-worn shoe, with the impress of a tiny foot, upon which her tears were falling fast.

A little half-worn shoe! And yet no magician could conjure up such blissful visions; no artist could trace such vivid pictures; no harp of sweetest sounds could so fill the ear with music.

Eight years since the little Daisy withered! And yet, to the mother's eye, she still blossomed fair as Paradise. The soft, golden hair still waved over the blue-veined temples; the sweet, earnest eyes still beamed with their loving light; the little fragile hand

53

was still outstretched for maternal guidance, and in the wood and by the stream they still lingered. Still, the little hymn was chanted at dawn, the little prayer lisped at dew-fall; still, that gentle breathing mingled with the happy mother's star-lit dreams.

A little, bright-eyed creature, crept to Ruth's side, and lifting a long, wavy, golden ringlet from a box on the table near her, laid it beside her own brown curls.

"Daisy 's in heaven," said little Katy, musingly. "Why do you cry, mamma? Don't you like to have God keep her for you?"

A tear was the only answer.

"*I* should like to die, and have you love my curls as you do Daisy's, mother."

Ruth started, and looked at the child; the rosy flush had faded away from little Katy's cheek, and a tear stole slowly from beneath her long lashes.

Taking her upon her lap, she severed one tress of her brown hair, and laid it beside little Daisy's golden ringlet.

A bright, glad smile lit up little Katy's face, and she was just throwing her arms about her mother's neck, to express her thanks, when, stopping suddenly, she drew from her dimpled foot one little shoe, and laid it in her mother's palm.

'Mid smiles and tears Ruth complied with the mute request; and the little sister shoes lay with the twin ringlets, lovingly side by side.

Blessed childhood! the pupil and yet the teacher; half infant, half sage, and whole angel! what a desert were earth without thee!

CHAPTER XXV

HOTEL life is about the same in every latitude. At Beach Cliff there was the usual number of vapid, fashionable mothers; dressy, brainless daughters; half-fledged wine-bibbing sons; impudent, whisker-dyed roués; bachelors, anxious to give their bashfulness an airing; bronchial clergymen, in search of health and a text; waning virgins, languishing by candle-light; gouty uncles, dyspeptic aunts, whist-playing old ladies, flirting nursery maids and neglected children.

Then there were "hops" in the hall, and sails upon the lake; there were nine-pin alleys, and a gymnasium; there were bathing parties, and horse-back parties; there were billiard rooms, and smoking rooms; reading rooms, flirtation rooms,—room for everything but—thought.

There could be little or nothing in such an artificial atmosphere congenial with a nature like Ruth's. In all this motley crowd there was but one person who interested her, a Mrs. Leon, upon whose queenly figure all eyes were bent as she passed; and who received the homage paid her, with an indifference which (whether real or assumed) became her passing well. Her husband was a tall, prim, proper-looking person, who dyed his hair and whiskers every Saturday, was extremely punctilious in all points of etiquette, very particular in his stated inquiries as to his wife's and his horse's health, very fastidious in regard to the brand of his wine, and the quality of his venison; maintaining, under all circumstances, the same rigidity of feature, the same immobility of the cold, stony, gray eye, the same studied, stereotyped conventionalism of manner.

Ruth, although shunning society, found herself drawn to Mrs. Leon by an unaccountable magnetism. Little Katy, too, with that

instinct with which childhood selects from the crowd,
fish and loving nature, had already made rapid advances
toward acquaintance. What road to a mother's heart so direct,
as through the heart of her children? With Katy for a "medium,"
the two ladies soon found themselves in frequent conversation.
Ruth had always shrunk from female friendship. It might be that
her boarding-school experience had something to do in effecting
this wholesale disgust of the commodity. Be that as it may, she
had never found any woman who had not misunderstood and
misinterpreted her. For the common female employments and
recreations, she had an unqualified disgust. Satin patchwork, the
manufacture of German worsted animals, bead-netting, crochet-
stitching, long discussions with milliners, dress-makers, and mo-
distes, long forenoons spent in shopping, or leaving bits of
paste-board, party-giving, party-going, prinking and coquetting,
all these were her aversion. Equally with herself, Mrs. Leon
seemed to despise these air bubbles. Ruth was sure that, under
that faultless, marble exterior, a glowing, living, loving heart lay
slumbering; waiting only the enchanter's touch to wake it into
life. The more she looked into those dark eyes, the deeper
seemed their depths. Ruth longed, she scarce knew why, to
make her life happy. Oh, if she *had* a soul!

Ruth thought of *Mr.* Leon and shuddered.

Mrs. Leon was often subject to severe and prostrating attacks
of nervous headache. On these occasions, Ruth's magnetic touch
seemed to woo coy slumber, like a spell; and the fair sufferer
would lie peacefully for hours, while Ruth's fingers strayed over
her temples, or her musical voice, like David's harp, exorcised
the demon Pain.

"You are better now," said Ruth, as Mrs. Leon slowly opened
her eyes, and looked about her; "you have had such a nice sleep,
I think you will be able to join us at the tea table to-night. I
will brush these long disheveled locks, and robe these dainty
limbs; though, to my eye, you look lovelier just as you are. You

are very beautiful, Mary. I heard a couple of young ladies discussing you, in the drawing-room, the other evening, envying
your beauty and your jewels, and the magnificence of your
wardrobe."

"Did they envy me my *husband?*" asked Mary, in a slow,
measured tone.

"That would have been useless," said Ruth, averting her eyes;
"but they said he denied you nothing in the way of dress,
equipage, or ornament."

"Yes," said Mary; "I have all those pretty toys to satisfy my
heart-cravings; they, equally with myself, are necessary append-
ages to Mr. Leon's establishment. Oh, Ruth!" and the tears
streamed through her jeweled fingers—"love me—pity me; you
who are so blessed. I too *could* love; that is the drop of poison
in my cup. When *your* daughters stand at the altar, Ruth, never
compel them to say words to which the heart yields no response.
The chain is none the less galling, because its links are golden.
God bless you, Ruth; 'tis long since I have shed such tears. You
have touched the rock; forget that the waters have gushed forth."

CHAPTER XXVI

OCTOBER had come! coy and chill in the morning, warm and winning at noon, veiling her coat of many colors in a fleecy mist at evening, yet lovely still in all her changeful moods. The gay butterflies of fashion had already spread their shriveled wings for the warmer atmosphere of the city. Harry and Ruth still lingered;—there was beauty for them in the hill-side's rainbow dyes, in the crimson barberry clusters, drooping from the wayside hedges; in the wild grape-vine that threw off its frost-bitten leaves, to tempt the rustic's hand with its purple clusters; in the piles of apples, that lay gathered in parti-colored heaps beneath the orchard trees; in the yellow ears of Indian corn, that lay scattered on the seedy floor of the breezy barn; in the festoons of dried apples, and mammoth squashes, and pumpkins, that lay ripening round the thrifty farmers' doors; and in the circling leaves, that came eddying down in brilliant showers on the Indian summer's soft but treacherous breath.

"You are ill, Harry," said Ruth, laying her hand upon his forehead.

"Slightly so," replied Harry languidly; "a pain in my head, and—"

A strong ague chill prevented Harry from finishing the sentence.

Ruth, who had never witnessed an attack of this kind, grew pale as his teeth chattered, and his powerful frame shook violently from head to foot.

"Have you suffered much in this way?" asked the physician who was summoned.

"I had the fever and ague very badly, some years since, at the west," said Harry. "It is an unpleasant visitor, doctor; you must rid me of it as soon as you can, for the sake of my little wife, who, though she can endure pain herself like a martyr, is an arrant little coward whenever it attacks me. Don't look so sober, Ruth, I shall be better to-morrow. I cannot afford time to be sick long, for I have a world of business on hand. I had an important appointment this very day, which it is a thousand pities to postpone; but never mind, I shall certainly be better to-morrow."

But Harry was not "better to-morrow;" nor the next day; nor the next; the doctor pronouncing his case to be one of decided typhus fever.

Very reluctantly the active man postponed his half formed plans, and business speculations, and allowed himself to be placed on the sick list. With a sigh of impatience, he saw his hat, and coat, and boots, put out of sight; and watched the different phials, as they came in from the apothecary; and counted the stroke of the clock, as it told the tedious hours; and marveled at the patience with which (he now recollected) Ruth bore a long bed-ridden eight-weeks' martyrdom, without a groan or complaint. But soon, other thoughts and images mixed confusedly in his brain, like the shifting colors of a kaleidoscope. He was floating—drifting—sinking—soaring, by turns;—the hot blood coursed through his veins like molten lava; his eye glared deliriously, and the hand, never raised but in blessing, fell, with fevered strength, upon the unresisting form of the loving wife.

"You must have a nurse," said the doctor to Ruth; "it is dangerous for you to watch with your husband alone. He might injure you seriously, in one of these paroxysms."

"But Harry has an unconquerable dislike to a hired nurse," said Ruth; "his reason may return at any moment, and the sight of one will trouble him. I am not afraid," replied Ruth, between a tear and a smile.

"But you will wear yourself out; you must remember that you owe a duty to your children."

"My *husband* has the *first* claim," said Ruth, resuming her place by the bed-side; and during the long hours of day and night, regardless of the lapse of time—regardless of hunger, thirst or weariness, she glided noiselessly about the room, arranged the pillows, mixed the healing draught, or watched with a silent prayer at the sufferer's bed-side; while Harry lay tossing from side to side, his white teeth glittering through his unshorn beard, raving constantly of her prolonged absence, and imploring her in heart-rending tones to come to his side, and "bring Daisy from the Glen."

Many a friendly voice whispered at the door, "How is he?" The Irish waiters crossed themselves and stept softly through the hall, as they went on their hasty errands; and many a consultation was held among warm-hearted gentlemen friends, (who had made Harry's acquaintance at the hotel, during the pleasant summer,) to decide which should first prove their friendship by watching with him.

Ruth declined all these offers to fill her place. "I will never leave him," she said; "his reason may return, and his eye seek vainly for me. No—no; I thank you all. Watch *with* me, if you will, but do not ask me to leave him."

In the still midnight, when the lids of the kind but weary watchers drooped heavily with slumber, rang mournfully in Ruth's ear the sad plaint of Gethsemane's Lord, "Could ye not watch with me one hour?" and pressing her lips to the hot and fevered hand before her, she murmured, "I will never leave thee, nor forsake thee."

CHAPTER XXVII

"HAVE you got the carpet-bag, doctor? and the little brown bundle? and the russet-trunk? and the umberil? and the demi-john, and the red band-box, with my best cap in it? one —two—three—four; yes—that 's all right. Now, mind those thievish porters. Goodness, how they charge here for carriage hire! I never knew, before, how much money it took to journey. Oh dear! I wonder if Harry *is* worse? There now, doctor, you 've put your foot right straight through that band-box. Now, where, for the land's sake, are my spectacles? 'Tis n't possible you 've left them behind? I put them in the case, as you stood there in the chayna closet, drinking your brandy and water, and asked you to put them in your side-pocket, because my bag was full of orange-peels, scissors, camphor, peppermint-drops, and seed-cakes. I would n't have left 'em for any money. Such a sight of trouble as it was to get them focussed right to my eyes. How *could* you, doctor, be so blundering? I declare it is enough to provoke a saint."

"If that 's the case, there 's no immediate call for *you* to get vexed," said the doctor, tartly.

"Is that the house?" asked the old lady, her curiosity getting the better of her indignation; "what a big hotel! I wonder if Harry *is* worse? Mercy me, I 'm all of a quiver. I wonder if they will take us right into the drawing-room? I wonder if there 's many ladies in it—my bonnet is awfully jammed: beside, I 'm so powdered with dust, that I look as if I had had an ash barrel sifted over me. Doctor! doctor! don't go on so far ahead. It looks awk'ard, as if I had no protector."

★ ★ ★

"How 's Harry?" said the doctor, to a white-jacketed waiter, who stood gossiping on the piazza steps with a comrade.

"Funny old chap!" said the waiter, without noticing the doctor's query; "I say, Bill, look how his hair is cut!"

" 'Taint hair," said Tom, "it is a wig."

"Bless my eyes! so it is; and a red one, too! Bad symptoms; red wigs are the cheapest; no extra fees to be got out of *that* customer, for blacking boots and bringing hot beefsteaks. Besides, just look at his baggage; you can always judge of a traveler, Bill, by his trunks; it never fails. Now, *I* like to see a trunk thickly studded with brass nails, and covered with a linen overall; then I know, if it is a lady's, that there 's diamond rings inside, and plenty of cash; if 'tis a gentleman's, that he knows how to order sherry-cobblers in the forenoon, and a bottle of old wine or two with his dinner; and how to fee the poor fellow who brings it, too, who lives on a small salary, with large expectations."

"How 's Harry?" thundered the doctor again, (after waiting what he considered a reasonable time for an answer,) "or if *you* are too lazy to tell, you whiskered jackanapes, go call your employer."

The word "employer" recalled the rambling waiter to his senses, and great was his consternation on finding that "the old chap with the red wig" was the father of young Mr. Hall, who was beloved by everything in the establishment, down to old Neptune the house-dog.

"I told you so," said the doctor, turning to his wife; "Harry 's no better—consultation this morning—very little hope of him; —so much for *my* not being here to prescribe for him. Ruth shouldered a great responsibility when she brought him away out of reach of *my* practice. You go into that room, there, Mis. Hall, No. 20, with your traps and things, and take off your bonnet and keep quiet, while I go up and see him."

CHAPTER XXVIII

"HUMPH!" said the doctor, "humph!" as Ruth drew aside the curtain, and the light fell full upon Harry's face. "Humph! it is all up with *him;* he 's in the last stage of the complaint; won't live two days;" and stepping to the table, the doctor uncorked the different phials, applied them to the end of his nose, examined the labels, and then returned to the bed-side, where Ruth stood bending over Harry, so pallid, so tearless, that one involuntarily prayed that death, when he aimed his dart, might strike down both together.

"Humph!" said the doctor again! "when did he have his reason last?"

"A few moments, day before yesterday," said Ruth, without removing her eyes from Harry.

"Well; he has been *murdered,*—yes murdered, just as much as if you had seen the knife put to his throat. That tells the whole story, and I don't care who knows it. I have been looking at those phials,—wrong course of treatment altogether for typhoid fever; fatal mistake. His death will lie heavy at *somebody's* door," and he glanced at Ruth.

"Hush! he is coming to himself," said Ruth, whose eyes had never once moved from her husband.

"Then I must tell him that his hours are numbered," said the doctor, thrusting his hands in his pockets, and pompously walking round the bed.

"No, no," whispered Ruth, grasping his arm with both hands; "you will kill him. The doctor said it might destroy the last chance for his life. *Don't* tell him. You know he is not afraid *to die;* but oh, spare him the parting with me! it will be so hard; he loves me, father."

"Pshaw!" said the doctor, shaking her off; "he ought to settle up his affairs while he can. I don't know how he wants things fixed. Harry! Harry!" said he, touching his shoulder, "I 've come to see you; do you know me?"

"Father!" said Harry, languidly, "yes, I 'm—I 'm sick. I shall be better soon; don't worry about me. Where 's my wife? where 's Ruth?"

"You 'll *never* be better, Harry," said the doctor, bluntly, stepping between him and Ruth; "you may not live the day out. If you have got anything to say, you 'd better say it now, before your mind wanders. You are a dead man, Harry; and you know that when I say *that,* I know what I 'm talking about."

The sick man gazed at the speaker, as if he were in a dream; then slowly, and with a great effort, raising his head, he looked about the room for Ruth. She was kneeling at the bedside, with her face buried in her hands. Harry reached out his emaciated hand, and placed it upon her bowed head.

"Ruth? wife?"

Her arm was about his neck in an instant—her lips to his; but her eyes were tearless, and her whole frame shook convulsively.

"Oh, how *can* I leave you? who will care for you? Oh God, in mercy spare me to her;" and Harry fell back on his pillow.

The shock was too sudden; reason again wandered; he heard the shrill whistle of the cars, recalling him to the city's whirl of business; he had stocks to negotiate; he had notes to pay; he had dividends due. Then the scene changed;—he could not be carried on a hearse through the street, surrounded by a gaping crowd. Ruth must go alone with him, by night;—why *must* he die at all? He would take anything. Where was the doctor? Why did they waste time in talking? Why not do something more for him? How cruel of Ruth to let him lie there and die?

"We will try this new remedy," said one of the consulting physicians to Harry's father; "it is the only thing that remains to be done, and I confess I have no faith in its efficacy in this case."

"He rallies again!" said Ruth, clasping her hands.

"The children!" said Harry; "bring me the children."

"Presently," said the new physician; "try and swallow this first;" and he raised his head tenderly.

They were brought him. Little Nettie came first,—her dimpled arms and rosy face in strange contrast to the pallid lips she bent, in childish glee, to kiss. Then little Katy, shrinking with a strange awe from the dear papa she loved so much, and sobbing, she scarce knew why, at his whispered words, "Be kind to your mother, Katy."

Again Harry's eyes sought Ruth. She was there, but a film— a mist had come between them; he could not see her, though he felt her warm breath.

And now, that powerful frame collected all its remaining energies for the last dread contest with death. So fearful—so terrible was the struggle, that friends stood by, with suppressed breath and averted eyes, while Ruth alone, with a fearful calmness, hour after hour, wiped the death damp from his brow, and the oozing foam from his pallid lips.

"He is gone," said the old doctor, laying Harry's hand down upon the coverlid.

"No; he breathes again."

"Ah; that 's his last!"

"Take her away," said the doctor, as Ruth fell heavily across her husband's body; and the unresisting form of the insensible wife was borne into the next room.

Strange hands closed Harry's eyes, parted his damp locks, straightened his manly limbs, and folded the marble hands over as noble a heart as ever lay cold and still beneath a shroud.

CHAPTER XXIX

"IT is really quite dreadful to see her in this way," said Hyacinth, as they chafed Ruth's hands and bathed her temples; "it is really quite dreadful. Somebody ought to tell her, when she comes to, that her hair is parted unevenly and needs brushing sadly. Harry's finely-chiseled features look quite beautiful in repose. It is a pity the barber should have been allowed to shave off his beard after death; it looked quite oriental and picturesque. But the sight of Ruth, in this way, is really dreadful; it quite unnerves me. I shall look ten years older by to-morrow. I must go down and take a turn or two on the piazza." And Hyacinth paced up and down, thinking—not of the bereaved sister, who lay mercifully insensible to her loss, nor yet of the young girl whose heart was to throb trustfully at the altar, by his side, on the morrow,—but of her broad lands and full coffers, with which he intended to keep at bay the haunting creditors, who were impertinent enough to spoil his daily digestion by asking for their just dues.

One o'clock! The effect of the sleeping potion administered to Ruth had passed away. Slowly she unclosed her eyes and gazed about her. The weary nurse, forgetful of her charge, had sunk into heavy slumber.

Where was Harry?

Ruth presses her hands to her temples. Oh God! the consciousness that *would* come! the frantic out-reaching of the arms to clasp—a vain shadow!

Where had they laid him?

She crossed the hall to Harry's sick room; the key was in the lock; she turned it with trembling fingers. Oh God! the dreadful stillness of that outlined form! the calm majesty of that marble brow, on which the moonbeams fell as sweetly as if that peaceful sleep was but to restore him to her widowed arms. That half-filled glass, from which his dying lips had turned away;—those useless phials;—that watch—*his* watch—moving—and *he* so still!—the utter helplessness of human aid;—the dreadful might of Omnipotence!

"Harry!"

Oh, when was he ever deaf before to the music of that voice? Oh, how could Ruth (God forgive her!) look upon those dumb lips and say, "Thy will be done!"

"Horrible!" muttered Hyacinth, as the undertaker passed him on the stairs with Harry's coffin. "These business details are very shocking to a sensitive person. I beg your pardon; did you address me?" said he, to a gentleman who raised his hat as he passed.

"I wished to do so, though an entire stranger to you," said the gentleman, with a sympathizing glance, which was quite thrown away on Hyacinth. "I have had the pleasure of living under the same roof, this summer, with your afflicted sister and her noble husband, and have become warmly attached to both. In common with several warm friends of your brother-in-law, I am pained to learn that, owing to the failure of parties for whom he had become responsible, there will be little or nothing for the widow and her children, when his affairs are settled. It is our wish to make up a purse, and request her acceptance of it, through you, as a slight token of the estimation in which we held her husband's many virtues. I understand you are to leave before the funeral, which must be my apology for intruding upon you at so unseasonable an hour."

With the courtliest of bows, in the blandest of tones, Hyacinth assured, while he thanked Mr. Kendall, that himself, his father, and, indeed, all the members of the family, were abundantly able, and most solicitous, to supply every want, and anticipate every wish of Ruth and her children; and that it was quite impossible she should ever suffer for anything, or be obliged in any way, at any future time, to exert herself for her own, or their support; all of which good news for Ruth highly gratified Mr. Kendall, who grasped the velvet palm of Hyacinth, and dashed away a grateful tear, that the promise to the widow and fatherless was remembered in heaven.

CHAPTER XXX

"THEY are very attentive to us here," remarked the doctor, as one after another of Harry's personal friends paid their respects, for his sake, to the old couple at No. 20. "Very attentive, and yet, Mis. Hall, I only practiced physic in this town six months, five years ago. It is really astonishing how long a good physician will be remembered," and the doctor crossed his legs comfortably, and tapped on his snuff-box.

"Ruth's brother, Hyacinth, leaves before the funeral, doctor," said the old lady. "I suppose you see through *that*. He intends to be off and out of the way, before the time comes to decide where Ruth shall put her head, after Harry is buried; and there 's her father, just like him; he has been as uneasy as an eel in a frying-pan, ever since he came, and this morning *he* went off, without asking a question about Harry's affairs. I suppose he thinks it is *our* business, and he owning bank stock. I tell you, doctor, that Ruth may go a-begging, for all the help she 'll get from *her* folks."

"Or from me, either," said the doctor, thrusting his thumbs into the arm-holes of his vest, and striding across the room. "She has been a spoiled baby long enough; she will find earning her living a different thing from sitting with her hands folded, with Harry chained to her feet.

"What did you do with that bottle of old wine, Mis. Hall, which I told you to bring out of Harry's room? He never drank but one glass of it, after that gentleman sent it to him, and we might as well have it as to let those lazy waiters drink it up. There were two or three bunches of grapes, too, he did n't eat; you had better take them, too, while you are about it."

"Well, it don't seem, after all, as if Harry was dead," said the

asingly; "but the Lord's will be done. Here comes your
er, Mis. Hall."

"Good afternoon, ma'am, good afternoon, sir," said Miss Skinlin, with a doleful whine, drawing down the corners of her
mouth and eyes to suit the occasion. "Sad affliction you 've met
with. As our minister says, 'man is like the herb of the field;
blooming to-day, withered to-morrow.' Life is short: will you
have your dress gathered or biased, ma'am?"

"Quite immaterial," said the old lady, anxious to appear indifferent; "though you may as well, I suppose, do it the way
which is worn the most."

"Well, some likes it one way, and then again, some likes it
another. The doctor's wife in the big, white house yonder—do
you know the doctor's wife, ma'am?"

"No," said the old lady.

"Nice folks, ma'am; open-handed; never mind my giving 'em
back the change, when they pay me. *She* was a Skefflit. Do you
know the Skefflits? Possible? why they are our first folks. Well,
la, where was I? Oh! the doctor's wife has *her* gowns biased; but
then she 's getting fat, and wants to look slender. I 'd advise you
to have yourn gathered. Dreadful affliction you 've met with,
ma'am. Beautiful corpse your son is. I always look at corpses to
remind me of my latter end. Some corpses keep much longer
than others; don't you think so, ma'am? They tell me your son's
wife is most crazy, because they doted on one another so."

The doctor and his wife exchanged meaning looks.

"Do tell?" said Miss Skinlin, dropping her shears, "Well, I
never! 'How desaitful the heart is,' as our minister says. Why,
everybody about here took 'em for regular turtle-doves."

" 'All is not gold that glitters,' " remarked the old lady.
"There is many a heart-ache that nobody knows anything about,
but He who made the heart. In my opinion our son was not
anxious to continue in this world of trial longer."

"You don't?" said Miss Skinlin. "Pious?"

"Certainly," said the doctor. "Was he not *our* son? Though, since his marriage, his wife's influence was very worldly."

"Pity," whined Miss Skinlin; "professors should let their light shine. *I* always try to drop a word in season, wherever business calls *me*. Will you have a cross-way fold on your sleeve, ma'am? I don't think it would be out of place, even on this mournful occasion. Mrs. Tufts wore one when her eldest child died, and she was dreadful grief-stricken. I remember she gave me (poor dear!) a five-dollar note, instead of a two; but that was a thing I had n't the heart to harass her about at such a time. I respected her grief too much, ma'am. Did I understand you that I was to put the cross-way folds on your sleeve, ma'am?"

"You may do as you like," whined the old lady; "people *do* dress more at hotels."

"Yes," said Miss Skinlin; "and I often feel reproved for aiding and abetting such foolish vanities; and yet, if I refused, from conscientious scruples, to trim dresses, I suppose somebody else *would;* so you see, it would n't do any good. Your daughter-in-law is left rich, I suppose. I always think that 's a great consolation to a bereaved widow."

"You need n't *suppose* any such thing," said the doctor, facing Miss Skinlin; "she has n't the first red cent."

"Dreadful!" shrieked Miss Skinlin. "What *is* she going to do?"

"That tells the whole story," said the doctor; "sure enough, what *is* she going to do?"

"I suppose she 'll live with *you,*" said Miss Skinlin, suggestively.

"You need n't suppose *that,* either," retorted the doctor. "It is n't every person, Miss Skinlin, who is agreeable enough to be taken into one's house; besides, she has got folks of her own."

"Oh,—ah!"—said Miss Skinlin; "rich?"

"Yes, very," said the doctor; "unless some of their poor relatives turn up, in which case, they are always dreadfully out of pocket."

"I un-der-stand," said Miss Skinlin, with a significant nod. "Well; I don't see anything left for her to do, but to earn her living, like some other folks."

"P-r-e-c-i-s-e-l-y," said the doctor.

"Oh—ah,"—said Miss Skinlin, who had at last possessed herself of "the whole story."

"I forgot to ask you how wide a hem I should allow on your black crape veil," said Miss Skinlin, tying on her bonnet to go. "Half a yard width is not considered too much for the *deepest* affliction. Your daughter, the widow, will probably have that width," said the crafty dress-maker.

"In my opinion, Ruth is in no deeper affliction than we are," said the doctor, growing very red in the face; "although she makes more fuss about it; so you may just make the hem of Mis. Hall's veil half-yard deep too, and send the bill into No. 20, where it will be footed by Doctor Zekiel Hall, who is not in the habit of ordering what he can't pay for. *That* tells the whole story."

"Good morning," said Miss Skinlin, with another doleful whine. "May the Lord be your support, and let the light of His countenance shine upon you, as our minister says."

CHAPTER XXXI

SLOWLY the funeral procession wound along. The gray-haired gate-keeper of the cemetery stepped aside, and gazed into the first carriage as it passed in. He saw only a pale woman veiled in sable, and two little wondering, rosy faces gazing curiously out the carriage window. All about, on either side, were graves; some freshly sodded, others green with many a summer's verdure, and all treasuring sacred ashes, while the mourners went about the streets.

"Dust to dust."

Harry's coffin was lifted from the hearse, and laid upon the green sward by the side of little Daisy. Over him waved leafy trees, of his own planting; while through the branches the shifting shadows came and went, lending a mocking glow to the dead man's face. Little Katy came forward, and gazed into the yawning grave till her golden curls fell like a veil over her wondering eyes. Ruth leaned upon the arm of her cousin, a dry, flinty, ossified man of business; a man of angles—a man of forms—a man with veins of ice, who looked the Almighty in the face complacently, "thanking God he was not as other men are;" who gazed with stony eyes upon the open grave, and the orphan babes, and the bowed form at his side, which swayed to and fro like the young tree before the tempest blast.

"Dust to dust!"

Ruth shrinks trembling back, then leans eagerly forward; now she takes the last lingering look at features graven on her memory with lines of fire; and now, as the earth falls with a hard, hollow sound upon the coffin, a lightning thought comes with stunning force to little Katy, and she sobs out, "Oh, they are covering my papa up; I can't ever see papa any more."

"Dust to dust!"

The sexton smooths the moist earth carefully with his reversed spade; Ruth's eyes follow his movements with a strange fascination. Now the carriages roll away one after another, and the wooden man turns to Ruth and says, "Come." She looks into his stony face, then at the new-made mound, utters a low, stifled cry, and staggers forth with her crushing sorrow.

Oh, Earth! Earth! with thy mocking skies of blue, thy placid silver streams, thy myriad, memory-haunting odorous flowers, thy wheels of triumph rolling—rolling on, over breaking hearts and prostrate forms—maimed, tortured, crushed, yet not destroyed. Oh, mocking Earth! snatching from our frenzied grasp the life-long coveted treasure! Most treacherous Earth! are these thy unkept promises?

Oh, hadst thou no Gethsemane—no Calvary—no guarded tomb—no risen Lord!

CHAPTER XXXII

"AND is it because Biddy M'Pherson don't suit yer, that ye 'd be afther sending her away?" said Ruth's nursery maid.

"No, Biddy," replied Ruth; "you have been respectful to me, and kind and faithful to the children, but I cannot afford to keep you now since—" and Ruth's voice faltered.

"If that is all, my leddy," said Biddy, brightening up, "then I 'll not be afther laving, sure."

"Thank you," said Ruth, quite moved by her devotion; "but you must not work for me without wages. Besides, Biddy, I could not even pay your board."

"And the tears not dry on your cheek; and the father of him and you with plenty of the siller. May the divil fly away wid 'em! Why, Nettie is but a babby yet, and Masther used to say you must walk every day, to keep off the bad headaches; and it 's coming could weather, and you can't take Nettie out, and you can't lave her with Katy; and anyhow it is n't Biddy M'Pherson that 'll be going away intirely."

The allusion to Harry's tender care of Ruth's health opened the wound afresh, and she wept convulsively.

"I say it 's a shame," said Biddy, becoming more excited at the sight of her tears; "and you can't do it, my leddy; you are as white as a sheet of paper."

"I *must*," said Ruth, controlling herself with a violent effort; "say no more, Biddy. I don't know where I am going; but wherever it may be I shall always be glad to see you. Katy and Nettie shall not forget their kind nurse; now, go and pack your trunk," said Ruth, assuming a composure she was far from feeling. "I thank you for your kind offer, though I cannot accept it."

"May the sowls of 'em niver get out of purgatory; that 's Biddy's last word to 'em," said the impetuous Irish girl; "and if the priest himself should say that St. Peter would n't open the gate for your leddyship, I would n't believe him." And unclasping little Nettie's clinging arms from her neck, and giving a hurried kiss to little Katy, Biddy went sobbing through the door, with her check apron over her broad Irish face.

CHAPTER XXXIII

"WHO 's that coming up the garden-walk, doctor?" said the old lady; "Ruth's father, as true as the world. Ah! I understand, we shall see what we shall see; mind you keep a stiff upper lip, doctor."

"Good morning, doctor," said Mr. Ellet.

"Good morning, sir," said the doctor, stiffly.

"Fine place you have here, doctor."

"Very," replied the doctor.

"I have just come from a visit to Ruth," said Mr. Ellet.

The imperturbable doctor slightly nodded to his visitor, as he took a pinch of snuff.

"She seems to take her husband's death very hard."

"Does she?" replied the doctor.

"I 'm sorry to hear," remarked Mr. Ellet, fidgeting in his chair, "that there is nothing left for the support of the family."

"So am I," said the doctor.

"I suppose the world will talk about us, if nothing is done for her," said the non-committal Mr. Ellet.

"Very likely," replied the doctor.

"Harry was *your* child," said Mr. Ellet, suggestively.

"Ruth is yours," said the doctor.

"Yes, I know," said Mr. Ellet; "but you are better off than I am, doctor."

"I deny it—I deny it," retorted the doctor, fairly roused; "you own the house you live in, and have a handsome income, or *ought* to have," said he, sneeringly, "at the rate you live. If you have brought up your daughter in extravagance, so much the worse for *her;* you and Ruth must settle that between you. I wash *my* hands of her. I have no objection to take Harry's *children,* and try to bring them up in a sensible manner; but, in that case, I 'll have none of the mother's interference. Then her hands will be free to earn her own living, and she's none too good for it, either. I don't believe in your doll-baby women; she's proud, you are all proud, all your family—that tells the whole story."

This was rather plain Saxon, as the increased redness of Mr. Ellet's ears testified; but pecuniary considerations helped him to swallow the bitter pill without making a wry face.

"I don't suppose Ruth could be induced to part with her children," said Mr. Ellet, meditatively.

"Let her try to support them then, till she gets starved out," replied the doctor. "I suppose you know, if the mother's inability to maintain them is proved the law obliges each of the grand-parents to take one."

This was a new view of the case, and one which immediately put to flight any reluctance Mr. Ellet might have had to force Ruth to part with her children; and remarking that he thought upon reflection, that the children *would* be better off with the doctor, Mr. Ellet took his leave.

"I thought that stroke would tell," said the doctor, laughing, as Mr. Ellet closed the door.

"Yes, you hit the right nail on the head that time," remarked the old lady; "but those children will be a sight of trouble. They never sat still five minutes at a time, since they were born; but I 'll soon cure them of that. I 'm determined Ruth shan't have them, if they fret me to fiddling-strings; but what an avaricious old man Mr. Ellet is. We ought to be thankful we have more of the gospel spirit. But the clock has struck nine, doctor. It is time to have prayers, and go to bed."

CHAPTER XXXIV

THE day was dark and gloomy. Incessant weeping and fasting had brought on one of Ruth's most violent attacks of nervous headache. Ah! where was the hand which had so lately charmed that pain away? where was the form that, with uplifted finger and tiptoe tread, hushed the slightest sound, excluded the torturing light, changed the heated pillow, and bathed the aching temples? Poor Ruth! nature had been tasked its utmost with sad memories and weary vigils, and she sank fainting to the floor.

Well might the frightened children huddle breathless in the farther corner. The coffin, the shroud, and the grave, were all too fresh in their childish memory. Well might the tearful prayer go up to the only Friend they knew,—"Please God, don't take away our mamma, too."

Ruth heard it not; well had she *never* woke, but the bitter cup was not yet drained.

"Good morning, Ruth," said her father, (a few hours after,) frowning slightly as Ruth's pale face, and the swollen eyes of her children, met his view. "Sick?"

"One of my bad headaches," replied Ruth, with a quivering lip.

"Well, that comes of excitement; you should n't get excited. I never allow myself to worry about what can't be helped; this is the hand of God, and you ought to see it. I came to bring you good news. The doctor has very generously offered to take both your children and support them. It will be a great burden off your hands; all he asks in return is, that he shall have the entire control of them, and that you keep away. It is a great thing, Ruth, and what I did n't expect of the doctor, knowing his avaricious habits. Now you 'll have something pleasant to think about, getting their things ready to go; the sooner you do it the better. How soon, think?"

"I can *never* part with my children," replied Ruth, in a voice which, though low, was perfectly clear and distinct.

"Perfect madness," said her father, rising and pacing the floor; "they will have a good home, *enough* to eat, drink, and wear, and be taught—"

"To disrespect their mother," said Ruth, in the same clear, low tone.

"Pshaw," said her father impatiently; "do you mean to let such a trifle as that stand in the way of their bread and butter? I 'm poor, Ruth, or at least I *may* be tomorrow, who knows? so you must not depend on me; I want you to consider that, before you refuse. Perhaps you expect to support them yourself; you can't do it, that 's clear, and if you should refuse the doctor's offer, and then die and leave them, he would n't take them."

"Their *Father in Heaven* will," said Ruth. "He says, 'Leave thy fatherless children with me.' "

"Perversion of Scripture, perversion of Scripture," said Mr. Ellet, foiled with his own weapons.

Ruth replied only with her tears, and a kiss on each little head, which had nestled up to her with an indistinct idea that she needed sympathy.

"It is of no use getting up a scene, it won't move me, Ruth," said Mr. Ellet, irritated by the sight of the weeping group before him, and the faint twinges of his own conscience; "the doctor *must* take the children, there 's nothing else left."

"Father," said Ruth, rising from her couch and standing before him; "my children are all I have left to love; in pity do not distress me by urging what I can never grant."

"As you make your bed, so lie in it," said Mr. Ellet buttoning up his coat, and turning his back upon his daughter.

It was a sight to move the stoutest heart to see Ruth that night, kneeling by the side of those sleeping children, with upturned eyes, and clasped hands of entreaty, and lips from which no sound issued, though her heart was quivering with agony; and yet a pitying Eye looked down upon those orphaned sleepers, a pitying Ear bent low to list to the widow's voiceless prayer.

CHAPTER XXXV

"WELL, Mis. Hall, you have got your answer. Ruth won't part with the children," said the doctor, as he refolded Mr. Ellet's letter.

"I believe you have lived with me forty years, come last January, have n't you, doctor?" said his amiable spouse.

"What of that? I don't see where that remark is going to fetch up, Mis. Hall," said the doctor. "You are not as young as you might be, to be sure, but I 'm no boy myself."

"There you go again, off the track. I did n't make any allusion to my age. It 's a thing I *never* do. It 's a thing I never wish *you* to do. I repeat, that I have lived with you these forty years; well, did you ever know me back out of anything I undertook? Did you ever see me foiled? That letter makes no difference with me; Harry's children I 'm determined to have, sooner or later. What can't be had by force, must be had by stratagem. I propose, therefore, a compromise, (*pro-tem.*) You and Mr. Ellet had better agree to furnish a certain sum for awhile, for the support of Ruth and her children, giving her to understand that it is discretionary, and may stop at any minute. That will conciliate Ruth, and will *look* better, too.

"The fact is, Miss Taffety told me yesterday that she heard some hard talking about us down in the village, between Mrs. Rice and Deacon Gray (whose child Ruth watched so many nights with, when it had the scarlet fever). Yes, it will have a better look, doctor, and we can withdraw the allowance whenever the 'nine days' wonder' is over. These people have something else to do than to keep track of poor widows."

"I never supposed a useless, fine lady, like Ruth, would rather work to support her children than to give them up; but I don't give her any credit for it now, for I 'm quite sure it 's all sheer obstinacy, and only to spite us," continued the old lady.

"Doctor!" and the old lady cocked her head on one side, and crossed her two forefingers, "whenever—you—see—a—blue-eyed—soft-voiced—gentle—woman,—look—out—for—a—hurricane. I tell you that placid Ruth is a smouldering volcano."

"That tells the whole story," said the doctor. "And speaking of volcanoes, it won't be so easy to make Mr. Ellet subscribe anything for Ruth's support; he thinks more of one cent than of any child he ever had. I am expecting him every moment, Mis. Hall, to talk over our proposal about Ruth. Perhaps you had better leave us alone; you know you have a kind of irritating way if anything comes across you, and you might upset the whole business. As to my paying anything towards Ruth's board unless he does his full share, you need n't fear."

"Of course not; well, I 'll leave you," said the old lady, with a sly glance at the china closet, "though I doubt if *you* understand managing him alone. Now I could wind him round my little finger in five minutes if I chose, but I hate to stoop to it, I so detest the whole family."

"I 'll shake hands with you there," said the doctor; "but that puppy of a Hyacinth is my *especial* aversion, though Ruth is bad enough in her way; a mincing, conceited, tip-toeing, be-curled, be-perfumed popinjay—faugh! Do you suppose, Mis. Hall, there *can* be anything in a man who wears fancy neck-ties, a seal ring on his little finger, and changes his coat and vest a dozen times a day? No; he 's a sensuous fop, that tells the whole story; ought to be picked up with a pair of sugar-tongs, and laid carefully on a rose-leaf. Ineffable puppy!"

"They made a great fuss about his writings," said the old lady.

"*Who* made a fuss? Fudge—there 's that piece of his about 'The Saviour'; he describes him as he would a Broadway dandy.

That fellow is all surface, I tell you; there 's no depth in him.
How should there be? Is n't he an Ellet? but look, here comes
his father."

"Good day, doctor. My time is rather limited this morning,"
said Ruth's father nervously; "was it of Ruth you wished to
speak to me?"

"Yes," said the doctor; "she seems to feel so badly about
letting the children go, that it quite touched my feelings, and I
thought of allowing her something for awhile, towards their
support."

"Very generous of you," said Mr. Ellet, infinitely relieved;
"very."

"Yes," continued the doctor, "I heard yesterday that Deacon
Gray and Mrs. Rice, two very influential church members, were
talking hard of you and me about this matter; yes, as you remarked, Mr. Ellet, I *am* generous, and I am *willing* to give Ruth
a small sum, for an unspecified time, provided you will give her
the same amount."

"*Me?*" said Mr. Ellet; "*me?*—I am a poor man, doctor;
should n't be surprised any day, if I had to mortgage the house
I live in: you would n't have me die in the almshouse, would
you?"

"No; and I suppose you would n't be willing that Ruth
should?" said the doctor, who could take her part when it suited
him to carry a point.

"Money is tight, money is tight," said old Mr. Ellet, frowning; "when a man marries his children, they ought to be considered off his hands. I don't know why I should be called upon.
Ruth went out of my family, and went into yours, and there
she was when her trouble came. Money is tight, though, of
course, *you* don't feel it, doctor, living here on your income
with your hands folded."

"Yes, yes," retorted the doctor, getting vexed in his turn;

"that all sounds very well; but the question is, what *is* my 'income'? Beside, when a man has earned his money by riding six miles of a cold night, to pull a tooth for twenty-five cents, he don't feel like throwing it away on other folks' children."

"Are not those children as much your grand-children as they are mine?" said Mr. Ellet, sharply, as he peered over his spectacles.

"Well, I don't know about that," said the doctor, taking an Æsculapian view of the case; "should n't think they were—blue eyes—sanguine temperament, like their mother's—not much Hall blood in 'em I fancy; more 's the pity."

"It is no use being uncivil," said Mr. Ellet, reddening. "*I* never am uncivil. I came here because I thought you had something to say; if you have not, I 'll go; my time is precious."

"You have not answered my question yet," said the doctor; "I asked you, if you would give the same that I would to Ruth for a time, only a *short* time?"

"The fact is, Mr. Ellet," continued the doctor, forced to fall back at last upon his reserved argument; "we are both church members; and the churches to which we belong have a way (which I think is a wrong way, but that 's neither here nor there) of meddling in these little family matters. It would not be very pleasant for you or me to be catechised, or disciplined by a church committee; and it 's my advice to you to avoid such a disagreeable alternative: they say hard things about us. We have a Christian reputation to sustain, brother Ellet," and the doctor grew pietistic and pathetic.

Mr. Ellet looked anxious. If there was anything he particularly prided himself upon, it was his reputation for devoted piety. Here was a desperate struggle—mammon pulling one way, the church the other. The doctor saw his advantage, and followed it.

"Come, Mr. Ellet, what will you give? here 's a piece of paper; put it down in black and white," said the vigilant doctor.

"Never put anything on paper, never put anything on paper," said Mr. Ellet, in a solemn tone, with a ludicrously frightened air; "parchments, lawyers, witnesses, and things, make me nervous."

"Ha! ha!" chuckled the old lady from her hiding-place in the china-closet.

"Well, then, if you won't put it on paper, *tell* me what you will give," said the persistent doctor.

"I 'll *think* about it," said the frenzied Mr. Ellet, seizing his hat, as if instant escape were his only safety.

The doctor followed him into the hall.

"Did you make him do it?" asked the old lady, in a hoarse whisper, as the doctor entered.

"Yes; but it was like drawing teeth," replied the doctor. "It is astonishing how avaricious he is; he may not stick to his promise now, for he would not put it on paper, and there was no witness."

"Was n't there though?" said the old lady, chuckling. "Trust me for that."

CHAPTER XXXVI

IN a dark, narrow street, in one of those heterogeneous boarding-houses abounding in the city, where clerks, market-boys, apprentices, and sewing-girls, bolt their meals with railroad velocity; where the maid-of-all-work, with red arms, frowzy head, and leathern lungs, screams in the entry for any boarder who happens to be inquired for at the door; where one plate suffices for fish, flesh, fowl, and dessert; where soiled table-cloths, sticky crockery, oily cookery, and bad grammar, predominate; where greasy cards are shuffled, and bad cigars smoked of an evening, you might have found Ruth and her children.

"Jim, what do you think of her?" said a low-browed, pig-faced, thick-lipped fellow, with a flashy neck-tie and vest, over which several yards of gilt watch-chain were festooned ostentatiously; "prettyish, is n't she?"

"Deuced nice form," said Jim, lighting a cheap cigar, and hitching his heels to the mantel, as he took the first whiff; "I should n't mind kissing her."

"*You?*" said Sam, glancing in an opposite mirror; "I flatter myself you would stand a poor chance when your humble servant was round. If I had not made myself scarce, out of friendship, you would not have made such headway with black-eyed Sue, the little milliner."

"Pooh," said Jim, "Susan Gill was delf, this little widow is porcelain; I say it is a deuced pity she should stay up stairs, crying her eyes out, the way she does."

"Want to marry her, hey?" said Sam, with a sneer.

"Not I; none of your ready-made families for me; pretty foot, has n't she? I always put on my coat in the front entry, about

87

the time she goes up stairs, to get a peep at it. It is a confounded pretty foot, Sam, bless me if it is n't; I should like to drive the owner of it out to the race-course, some pleasant afternoon. I must say, Sam, I like widows. I don't know any occupation more interesting than helping to dry up their tears; and then the little dears are so grateful for any little attention. Wonder if my swallow-tailed coat won't be done to-day? that rascally tailor ought to be snipped with his own shears."

"Well, now, I wonder when you gentlemen intend taking your-selves off, and quitting the drawing-room," said the loud-voiced landlady, perching a cap over her disheveled tresses; "this parlor is the only place I have to dress in; can't you do your talking and smoking in your own rooms? Come now—here 's a lot of newspapers, just take them and be off, and give a woman a chance to make herself beautiful."

"Beautiful!" exclaimed Sam, "the old dragon! she would make a good scarecrow for a corn-field, or a figure-head for a piratical cruiser; beautiful!" and the speaker smoothed a wrinkle out of his flashy yellow vest; "it is my opinion that the uglier a woman is, the more beautiful she thinks herself; also, that any of the sex may be bought with a yard of ribbon, or a breastpin."

"Certainly," said Jim, "you need n't have lived to this time of life to have made that discovery; and speaking of that, reminds me that the little widow is as poor as Job's turkey. My wash-erwoman, confound her for ironing off my shirt-buttons, says that she wears her clothes rough-dry, because she can't afford to pay for both washing and ironing."

"She does?" replied Sam; "she 'll get tired of that after awhile. I shall request 'the dragon,' to-morrow, to let me sit next her at the table. I 'll begin by helping the children, offering to cut up their victuals, and all that sort of thing—that will please the mother, you know, hey? But, by Jove! it 's three o'clock, and I engaged to drive a gen'leman down to the steamboat landing; now some other hackney coach will get the job. Confound it!"

CHAPTER XXXVII

COUNTING houses, like all other spots beyond the pale of female jurisdiction, are comfortless looking places. The counting-room of Mr. Tom Develin was no exception to the above rule; though we will do him the justice to give in our affidavit, that the ink-stand, for seven consecutive years, had stood precisely in the same spot, bounded on the north by a box of letter stamps, on the south by a package of brown business envelopes, on the east by a pen wiper, made originally in the form of a butterfly, but which frequent ink dabs had transmuted into a speckled caterpillar, on the west by half sheets of blank paper, rescued economically from business letters, to save too prodigal consumption of foolscap.

It is unnecessary to add that Mr. Tom Develin was a bachelor; perpendicular as a ram-rod, moving over *terra firma* as if fearful his joints would unhinge, or his spinal column slip into his boots; carrying his *arms* with military precision; supporting his ears with a collar, never known by 'the oldest inhabitant' to be limpsey; and stepping circumspectly in boots of mirror-like brightness, never defiled with the mud of the world.

Perched on his apple-sized head, over plastered wind-proof locks, was the shiniest of hats, its wearer turning neither to the right nor the left; and, although possessed of a looking-glass, laboring under the hallucination that *he,* of all masculine moderns, was most dangerous to the female heart.

Mr. Develin's book store was on the west side of Literary Row. His windows were adorned with placards of new theological publications of the blue-school order, and engravings of departed saints, who with their last breath had, with mock humility, requested brother somebody to write their obituaries.

There was, also, to be seen there an occasional oil painting "for sale," selected by Mr. Develin himself, with a peculiar eye to the greenness of the trees, the blueness of the sky, and the moral "tone" of the picture.

Mr. Develin congratulated himself on his extensive acquaintance with clergymen, professors of colleges, students, scholars, and the literati generally. By dint of patient listening to their desultory conversations, he had picked up threads of information on literary subjects, which he carefully wound around his memory, to be woven into his own tête-à-têtes, where such information would "tell;" always, of course, omitting quotation marks, to which some writers, as well as conversationists, have a constitutional aversion. It is not surprising, therefore, that his tête-à-têtes should be on the *mosaic* order; the listener's interest being heightened by the fact, that he had not, when in a state of pinafore, cultivated Lindley Murray too assiduously.

Mr. Develin had fostered his bump of caution with a truly praiseworthy care. He meddled very gingerly with new publications; in fact, transacted business on the old fogy, stage-coach, rub-a-dub principle; standing back with distended eyes, and suppressed breath, in holy horror of the whistle, whiz-rush and steam of modern publishing houses. "A penny saved, is a penny gained," said this eminent financier and stationer, as he used *half a wafer* to seal his business letters.

"Any letters this morning?" said Mr. Develin to his clerk, as he deposited his umbrella in the northwest corner of his counting-room, and re-smoothed his unctuous, unruffled locks; "any letters?" and taking a package from the clerk's hand, he circumspectly lowered himself between his coat-tails into an arm-chair, and leisurely proceeded to their inspection.

"MR. DEVELIN:—

"Sir,—I take the liberty, knowing you to be one of the referees about our son's estate, which was left in a dreadful confusion, owing probably to his wife's thriftlessness, to request of you a small favor. When our son died, he left a great many clothes, vests, coats, pants, &c., which his wife, no doubt, urged his buying, and which, of course, can be of no use to her now, as she never had any boys, which we always regretted. I take my pen in hand to request you to send the clothes to me, as they will save my tailor's bill; please send, also, a circular broadcloth cloak, faced with velvet, his cane, hats, and our son's Bible, which Ruth, of course, never looks into—we wish to use it at family prayers. Please send them all at your earliest convenience. Hoping you are in good health, I am yours to command,

"ZEKIEL HALL."

Mr. Develin re-folded the letter, crossed his legs and mused. "The law allows the widow the husband's wearing apparel, but what can Ruth do with it? (as the doctor says, she has no boys,) and with her *peculiar notions,* it is not probable she would sell the clothes. The law is on her side, undoubtedly, but luckily she knows no more about law than a baby; she is poor, the doctor is a man of property; Ruth's husband was my friend to be sure, but a man must look out for No. 1 in this world, and consider a little what would be for his own interest. The doctor may leave me a little slice of property if I keep on the right side of him, who knows? The clothes must be sent."

CHAPTER XXXVIII

" 'T is n't a pretty place," said little Katy, as she looked out
the window upon a row of brick walls, dingy sheds, and
discolored chimneys; " 'tis n't a pretty place, mother, I want to
go home."

"Home!" Ruth started! the word struck a chord which vi-
brated—oh how painfully.

"Why *don't* we go home, mother?" continued Katy; "won't
papa ever, ever, come and take us away? there is something in
my throat which makes me want to cry all the time, mother,"
and Katy leaned her curly head wearily on her mother's
shoulder.

Ruth took the child on her lap, and averting her eyes, said
with a forced smile:

"Little sister don't cry, Katy."

"Because she is a little baby, and don't know anything," replied Katy; "she used to stay with Biddy, but papa used to take
me to walk, and toss me up to the wall when he came home,
and make rabbits with his fingers on the wall after tea, and take
me on his knee and tell me about little Red Riding Hood,
and—oh, I want papa, I want papa," said the child, with a fresh
burst of tears.

Ruth's tears fell like rain on Katy's little up-turned face. Oh,
how could she, who so much needed comfort, speak words of
cheer? How could her tear-dimmed eyes and palsied hand, 'mid
the gloom of so dark a night, see and arrest a sunbeam?

"Katy, dear, kiss me; you *loved* papa—it grieved you to see
him sick and suffering. Papa has gone to heaven, where there is
no more sickness, no more pain. Papa is happy now, Katy."

92

"Happy? without *me,* and *you,* and *Nettie?*" said Katy, with a grieved lip.

Oh, far-reaching—questioning childhood, who is sufficient for thee? How can lips, which so stammeringly repeat, 'thy will be done,' teach *thee* the lesson perfect?

CHAPTER XXXIX

"GOOD morning, Mrs. Hall," said Mr. Develin, handing Ruth the doctor's letter, and seating himself at what he considered a safe distance from a female; "I received that letter from the doctor this morning, and I think it would be well for you to attend to his request as soon as possible."

Ruth perused the letter, and handed it back with a trembling hand, saying, " 'tis true the clothes are of no use, but it is a great comfort to me, Mr. Develin, to keep everything that once belonged to Harry." Then pausing a moment, she asked, "have they a *legal* right to demand those things, Mr. Develin?"

"I am not very well versed in law," replied Mr. Develin, dodging the unexpected question; "but you know the doctor does n't bear thwarting, and your children—in fact—" Here Mr. Develin twisted his thumbs and seemed rather at a loss. "Well, the fact is, Mrs. Hall, in the present state of your affairs, you cannot afford to refuse."

"True," said Ruth, mournfully, "true."

Harry's clothes were collected from the drawers, one by one, and laid upon the sofa. Now a little penciled memorandum fluttered from the pocket; now a handkerchief dropped upon the floor, slightly odorous of cologne, or cigars; neck-ties there were, shaped by his full round throat, with the creases still in the silken folds, and there was a crimson smoking cap, Ruth's gift—the gilt tassel slightly tarnished where it had touched the moist dark locks; then his dressing-gown, which Ruth herself had often playfully thrown on, while combing her hair—each had its little history, each its tender home associations, daguerreotyping, on tortured memory, sunny pictures of the past.

"Oh, I cannot—I cannot," said Ruth, as her eye fell upon Harry's wedding-vest; "oh, Mr. Develin, I cannot."

Mr. Develin coughed, hemmed, walked to the window, drew off his gloves, and drew them on, and finally said, anxious to terminate the interview, "I can fold them up quicker than you, Mrs. Hall."

"If you please," replied Ruth, sinking into a chair; "*this* you will leave me, Mr. Develin," pointing to the white satin vest.

"Y-e-s," said Mr. Develin, with an attempt to be facetious. "The old doctor can't use that, I suppose."

The trunk was packed, the key turned in the lock, and the porter in waiting, preceded by Mr. Develin, shouldered his burden, and followed him down stairs, and out into the street.

And there sat Ruth, with the tears dropping one after another upon the wedding vest, over which her fingers strayed caressingly. Oh, where was the heart which had throbbed so tumultuously beneath it, on that happy bridal eve? With what a dirge-like echo fell upon her tortured ear those bridal words,—"till death do us part."

CHAPTER XL

"TOM Herbert, are you aware that this is the sixth spoonful of sugar you have put in that cup of tea? and what a forlorn face! I 'd as lief look at a tombstone. Now look at *me*. Did you ever see such a fit as that boot? Is not my hair as smooth and as glossy as if I expected to dine with some other gentleman than my husband? Is not this jacket a miracle of shapeliness? Look what a foil you are to all this loveliness; lack-lustre eyes—mouth drawn down at the corners: you are a dose to contemplate."

"Mary," said her husband, without noticing her raillery; "do you remember Mrs. Hall?"

"Mrs. Hall," replied Mary; "oh, Ruth Ellet? yes; I used to go to school with her. She has lost her husband, they say."

"Yes, and a fine noble fellow he was too, and very proud of his wife. I remember he used to come into the store, and say, with one of his pleasant smiles, 'Herbert, I wonder if you have anything here handsome enough for my wife to wear.' He bought all her clothes himself, even to her gloves and boots, and was as tender and careful of her as if she were an infant. Well, to-day she came into my store, dressed in deep mourning, lead-ing her two little girls by the hand, and asked to see me. And what do you think she wanted?"

"I am sure I don't know," said Mary, carelessly; "a yard of black crape, I suppose."

"She wanted to know," said Mr. Herbert, "if I could employ her to make up and trim those lace collars, caps, and under sleeves we sell at the store. I tell you, Mary, I could scarce keep the tears out of my eyes, she looked so sad. And then those poor little children, Mary! I thought of you, and how terrible it would be if you and our little Sue and Charley were left so destitute."

"Destitute?" replied Mary; "why her father is a man of property; her brother is in prosperous circumstances; and her cousin lives in one of the most fashionable squares in the city."

"Yes, wife, I know it; and that makes it all the harder for Mrs. Hall to get employment; because, people knowing this, take it for granted that her relatives help her, or *ought* to, and prefer to give employment to others whom they imagine need it more. This is natural, and perhaps I should have thought so too, had it been anybody but Harry Hall's wife; but all I could think of was, what Harry (poor fellow!) *would* have said, had he ever thought his little pet of a wife would have come begging to me for employment."

"What did you tell her?" said Mary.

"Why—you know the kind of work she wished, is done by forty hands, in a room directly over the store, under the superintendence of Betsy Norris; of course, they would *all* prefer doing the work at home, to coming down there to do it; but that is against our rules. I told her this, and also that if I made an exception in her favor, the forewoman would know it, because she had to prepare the work, and that would cause dissatisfaction among my hands. What do you think she said? she offered to come and sit down among those girls, and work *with* them. My God, Mary! Harry Hall's wife!

"Of course that was out of the question, wife, for she could not bring her two children there, and she had no one to leave them with, and so she went away; and I looked after her, and those little bits of children, till they were out of sight, trying to devise some way to get her employment. Cannot you think of anything, Mary? Are there no ladies you know, who would give her nice needlework?"

"I don't know anybody but Mrs. Slade," replied Mary, "who puts out work of any consequence, and she told me the other day that she never employed any of those persons who 'had seen better days;' that somehow she could n't drive as good a bargain

with them as she could with a common person, who was ig-
norant of the value of their labor."

"God help poor Mrs. Hall, then," exclaimed Harry, "if *all*
the sex are as heartless! *We* must contrive some way to help her,
Mary—help her to *employment,* I mean, for I know her well
enough to be sure that she would accept of assistance in no
other way."

CHAPTER XLI

"Is this the house?" said one of two ladies, pausing before Ruth's lodgings.

"I suppose so," replied the other lady; "they said it was No. 50 —— street, but it can't be, either; Ruth Hall could n't live in such a place as this. Just look at that red-faced Irish girl leaning out the front window on her elbows, and see those vulgar red bar-room curtains; I declare, Mary, if Ruth Hall has got down hill so far as this, *I* can't keep up her acquaintance; just see how they stare at us here! if you choose to call you may—faugh! just smell that odor of cabbage issuing from the first entry. Come, come, Mary, take your hand off the knocker; I would n't be seen in that vulgar house for a kingdom."

"It seems *heartless,* though," said the other lady, blushing slightly, as she gathered up her six flounces in her delicately gloved-hand; "do you remember the afternoon we rode out to their pretty country-seat, and had that delicious supper of straw-berries and cream, under those old trees? and do you remember how handsome and picturesque her husband looked in that broad Panama hat, raking up the hay when the thunder-shower came up? and how happy Ruth looked, and her children? 'Tis a dreadful change for her, I declare; if it were me, I believe I should cut my throat."

"That is probably just what her relatives would like to have her do," replied Mary, laughing; "they are as much mortified at her being here, as you and I are to be seen in such a quarter of the city."

"Why don't they provide for her, then," said the other lady, "at least till she can turn round? that youngest child is only a baby yet."

"Oh, that 's *their* affair," answered Mary, "don't bother about it. Hyacinth has just married a rich, fashionable wife, and of course he cannot lose caste by associating with Ruth now; you cannot blame him."

"Well, that don't prevent him from *helping* her, does it?"

"Good gracious, Gertrude, do stop! if there 's anything I hate, it is an argument. It is clearly none of our business to take her up, if her own people don't do it. Come, go to La Temps' with me, and get an ice. What a love of a collar you have on; it is handsomer than mine, which I gave fifty dollars for, but what is fifty dollars, when one fancies a thing? If I did n't make my husband's money fly, his second wife would; so I will save her ladyship that trouble;" and with an arch toss of her plumed head, the speaker and her companion entered the famous saloon of La Temps, where might be seen any sunny day, between the hours of twelve and three, the disgusting spectacle of scores of ladies devouring, *ad infinitum,* brandy-drops, Roman punch, Charlotte Russe, pies, cakes, and ices; and sipping "parfait amour," till their flushed cheeks and emancipated tongues prepared them to listen and reply to any amount of questionable nonsense from their attendant roué cavaliers.

CHAPTER XLII

"SOME folks' pride runs in queer streaks," said Betty, as she turned a beefsteak on the gridiron; "if I lived in such a grand house as this, and had so many fine clothes, I would n't let my poor cousin stand every Monday in my kitchen, bending over the wash-tub, and rubbing out her clothes and her children's, with my servants, till the blood started from her knuckles."

"Do you know what dis chil' would do, if she were Missis Ruth Hall?" asked Gatty. "Well, she 'd jess go right up on dat shed fronting de street, wid 'em, and hang 'em right out straight before all de grand neighbors, and shame Missus Millet; dat 's what *dis* chil' would do."

"Poor Mrs. Ruth, she knows too much for that," replied Betty; "she shoulders that great big basket of damp clothes and climbs up one, two, three, four flights of stairs to hang them to dry in the garret. Did you see her sit down on the stairs last Monday, looking so pale about the mouth, and holding on to her side, as if she never would move again?"

"Yes, yes," said Gatty, "and here now, jess look at de fust peaches of de season, sent in for dessert; de Lor' he only knows what dey cost, but niggers must n't see noffing, not dey, if dey wants to keep dere place. But white folks *is* stony-hearted, Betty."

"Turn that steak over," said Betty; "now get the pepper; work and talk too, that 's *my* motto. Yes, Gatty, I remember when Mrs. Ruth's husband used to ride up to the door of a fine morning, and toss me a large bouquet for Mrs. Millet, which Mrs. Ruth had tied up for her, or hand me a box of big strawberries, or a basket of plums, or pears, and how all our folks here would go out there and stay as long as they liked, and use the horses, and pick the fruit, and the like of that."

"Whar's her brudder, Massa Hyacinth? Wonder if *he* knows how tings is gwyin on?" asked Gatty.

"He knows fast enough, only he *don't* know," replied Betty, with a sly wink. "I was setting the table the other day, when Mrs. Millet read a letter from him to her husband. It seems he's got a fine place in the country, where he lives with his new bride. Poor thing, I hope he won't break her heart, as he did his first wife's. Well, he told how beautiful his place was, and how much money he had laid out on his garden, and hot-house, and things, and invited Mrs. Millet to come and see him; and then he said, he 'sposed Mrs. Ruth was getting on; he did n't know anything about her."

"Know about de debbel!" exclaimed Gatty, throwing down the pepper castor; "wonder whose fault dat is, Betty? 'Spose all dese folks of ours, up stairs, will go to de bressed place? When I heard Massa Millet have prayers dis morning, I jess wanted to ask him dat. You 'member what our minister, Mr. Snowball, said las' Sunday, 'bout de parabola of Dives and Lazarus, hey?"

"Parable," said Betty contemptuously; "Gatty, you are as ig-norant as a hippopotamus. Come, see that steak now, done to a crisp; won't you catch it when you take it into breakfast. It is lucky I can cook and talk too."

CHAPTER XLIII

"SOMETHING for you, ma'am," said the maid-of-all-work to Ruth, omitting the ceremony of a premonitory knock, as she opened the door. "A bunch of flowers! handsome enough for Queen Victory; and a basket of apples all done up in green leaves. It takes widders to get presents," said the girl, stowing away her tongue in her left cheek, as she partially closed the door.

"Oh, how pretty!" exclaimed little Nettie, to whom those flowers were as fair as Eve's first view of Paradise. "Give me *one* posy, mamma, only *one;*" and the little chubby hands were outstretched for a tempting rosebud.

"But, Nettie, dear, they are not for me," said Ruth; "there must be some mistake."

"Not a bit, ma'am," said the girl, thrusting her head into the half-open door; "the boy said they were 'for Mrs. Ruth Hall,' as plain as the nose on my face; and that 's plain enough, for I reckon I should have got married long ago, if it had n't been for my big nose. He was a country boy like, with a ploughman's frock on, and was as spotted in the face as a tiger-lily."

"Oh! I know," replied Ruth, with a ray of her old sunshiny smile flitting over her face; "it was Johnny Galt; he comes into market every day with vegetables. Don't you remember him, Katy? He used to drive our old Brindle to pasture, and milk her every night. You know dear papa gave him a suit of clothes on the Fourth of July, and a new hat, and leave to go to Plymouth to see his mother? Don't you remember, Katy, he used to catch butterflies for you in the meadow, and pick you nosegays of buttercups, and let you ride the pony to water, and show you where the little minnies lived in the brook? Have you forgotten

103

the white chicken he brought you in his hat, which cried
'peep—peep,' and the cunning little speckled eggs he found for
you in the woods, and the bright scarlet partridge berries he
strung for a necklace for your throat, and the glossy green-oak-
leaf-wreath he made for your hat?"

"Tell more—tell more," said Katy, with eyes brimming with
joy; "smile more, mamma."

Aye, "Smile more, mamma." Earth has its bright spots; there
must have been sunshine to make a shadow. All hearts are not
calloused by selfishness; from the lips of the honest little donor
goeth up each night and morning a prayer, sincere and earnest,
for "the widow and the fatherless." The noisome, flaunting
weeds of earth have not wholly choked the modest flower of
gratitude. "Smile more, mamma!"

How cheap a thing is happiness! Golconda's mines were dross
to that simple bunch of flowers! They lit the widow's gloomy
room with a celestial brightness. Upon the dingy carpet Ruth
placed the little vase, and dimpled limbs hovered about their
brilliant petals; poising themselves daintily as the epicurean butterfly who circles, in dreamy delight, over the rose's heart, long-
ing, yet delaying to sip its sweets.

A simple bunch of flowers, yet oh, the tale they told with
their fragrant breath! "Smile, mamma!" for those gleeful children's sake; send back to the source that starting tear, ere like a
lowering cloud it o'ercasts the sunshine of those beaming faces.

CHAPTER XLIV

"MY dear," said Mrs. Millet, as the servant withdrew with the dessert, "Walter has an invitation to the Hon. David Greene's to-night."

No response from Mr. Millet, "the wooden man," one of whose pleasant peculiarities it was never to answer a question till the next day after it was addressed to him.

Mrs. Millet, quite broken in to this little conjugal eccentricity, proceeded; "It will be a good thing for John, Mr. Millet; I am anxious that all his acquaintances should be of the right sort. Hyacinth has often told me how much it made or marred a boy's fortune, the set he associated with. Herbert Greene has the air of a thorough-bred man already. You see now, Mr. Millet, the importance of Hyacinth's advice to us about five years ago, to move into a more fashionable neighborhood; to be sure rents are rather high here, but I am very sure young Snyder would never have thought of offering himself to Leila had not we lived at the court-end of the town. Hyacinth considers it a great catch in point of family, and I have no doubt Snyder is a nice fellow. I wish before you go, Mr. Millet, you would leave the money to buy Leila a velvet jacket; it will not cost more than forty dollars (lace, trimmings, and all); it will be very becoming to Leila. What, going? oh, I forgot to tell you, that Ruth's father was here this morning, bothering me just as I was dressing my hair for dinner. It seems that he is getting tired of furnishing the allowance he promised to give Ruth, and says that it is *our* turn now to do something. He is a great deal better off than we are, and so I told him; and also, that we were obliged to live in a certain style for the dear children's sake; beside, are we *not* doing something for her? I allow Ruth to do her washing in our kitchen every week, provided she finds her own soap. Stop a minute, Mr. Millet; *do* leave the forty dollars for Leila's jacket before you go. Cicchi, the artist, wants her to sit for a Madonna,—quite a pretty tribute to Leila's beauty; he only charges three hundred dollars; his study is No. 1, Clive street."

"S-t-u-d-i-o," said Mr. Millet, (slowly and oracularly, who, being on several school committees, thought it his duty to make an extra exertion, when the king's English was misapplied;) "s-t-u-d-i-o, Mrs. Millet;" and buttoning the eighth button of his overcoat, he moved slowly out the front door, and down the street to his counting-room, getting over the ground with about as much flexibility and grace of motion as the wooden horses on the stage.

headaches

"COME here, Katy," said Ruth, "do you think you could go *alone* to your grandfather Ellet's for once? My board bill is due to-day, and my head is so giddy with this pain, that I can hardly lift it from the pillow. Don't you think you can go without me, dear? Mrs. Skiddy is very particular about being paid the moment she sends in her bill."

"I 'll try, mamma," replied little Katy, unwilling to disoblige her mother.

"Then bring your bonnet, dear, and let me tie it; be very, very careful crossing the streets, and don't loiter on the way. I have been hoping every moment to be better, but I cannot go."

"Never mind, mother," said Katy, struggling bravely with her reluctance, as she kissed her mother's cheek, and smiled a goodbye; but when she gained the crowded street, the smile faded away from the little face, her steps were slow, and her eyes downcast; for Katy, child as she was, knew that her grandfather was never glad to see them now, and his strange, cold tone when he spoke to her, always made her shiver; so little Katy threaded her way along, with a troubled, anxious, care-worn look, never glancing in at the shopkeepers' tempting windows, and quite forgetting Johnny Galt's pretty bunch of flowers, till she stood trembling with her hand on the latch of her grandfather's counting-room door.

"That *you!*" said her grandfather gruffly, from under his bent brows; "come for money *again?* Do you think your grandfather is made of money? people have to *earn* it, did you know that? I worked hard to earn mine. Have you done any thing to earn this?"

107

"No, Sir," said Katy, with a culprit look, twisting the corner of her apron, and struggling to keep from crying.

"Why don't your mother go to work and earn something?" asked Mr. Ellet.

"She cannot get any work to do," replied Katy; "she tries very hard, grandpa."

"Well, tell her to *keep on* trying, and you must grow up quick, and earn something too; money don't grow on trees, or bushes, did you know that? What's the reason your mother did n't come after it herself, hey?"

"She is sick," said Katy.

"Seems to me she's always sick. Well, there's a dollar," said her grandfather, looking at the bill affectionately, as he parted with it; "if you keep on coming here at this rate, you will get all my money away. Do you think it is right to come and get all my money away, hey? Remember now, you and your mother must earn some, *somehow,* d' ye hear?"

"Yes, Sir," said Katy meekly, as she closed the door.

There was a great noise and bustle in the street, and Katy was jostled hither and thither by the hurrying foot passengers; but she did not heed it, she was so busy thinking of what her grandfather had said, and wondering if she could not sell matches, or shavings, or sweep the crossings, or earn some pennies somehow, that she need never go to her grandfather again. Just then a little girl her own age, came skipping and smiling along, holding her father's hand. Katy looked at her and thought of *her* father, and then she began to cry.

"What is the matter, my dear?" said a gentleman, lifting a handful of Katy's shining curls from her face; "why do you cry, my dear?"

"I want *my* papa," sobbed Katy.

"Where is he, dear? tell me, and I will take you to him, shall I?"

"If you please, Sir," said Katy, innocently, "he has gone to heaven."

"God help you," said the gentleman, with moistened eyes, "where had you been when I met you?"

"Please, Sir—I—I—I had rather not tell," replied Katy, with a crimson blush.

"Very odd, this," muttered the gentleman; "what is your name, dear?"

"Katy, Sir."

"Katy what?" asked the gentleman. "Katy-did, I think! for your voice is as sweet as a bird's."

"Katy Hall, Sir."

"Hall? Hall?" repeated the gentleman, thoughtfully; "was your father's name Harry?"

"Yes," said Katy.

"Was he tall and handsome, with black hair and whiskers?"

"Oh, *so* handsome," replied Katy, with sparkling eyes.

"Did he live at a place called 'The Glen,' just out of the city?"

"Yes," said Katy.

"My child, my poor child," said the gentleman, taking her up in his arms and pushing back her hair from her face; "yes, here is papa's brow, and his clear, blue eyes, Katy. I used to know your dear papa."

"Yes?" said Katy, with a bright, glad smile.

"I used to go to his counting-house to talk to him on business, and I learned to love him very much, too. I never saw your mamma, though I often heard him speak of her. In a few hours, dear, I am going to sail off on the great ocean, else I would go home with you and see your mamma. Where do you live, Katy?"

"In —— court," said the child. The gentleman colored and started, then putting his hand in his pocket and drawing out something that looked like paper, slipped it into little Katy's bag, saying, with delicate tact, "Tell your mamma, my dear, that is something I owed your dear papa; mind you carry it home safely; now give me a good-bye kiss, and may God forever bless you, my darling."

Little Katy stood shading her eyes with her hand till the gentleman was out of sight; it was so nice to see somebody who "loved papa;" and then she wondered why her grandfather never spoke so to her about him; and then she wished the kind gentleman were her grandpapa; and then she wondered what it was he had put in the bag for mamma; and then she recollected that her mamma told her "not to loiter;" and then she quickened her tardy little feet.

CHAPTER XLVI

K ATY had been gone now a long while. Ruth began to grow
anxious. She lifted her head from the pillow, took off the
wet bandage from her aching forehead, and taking little Nettie
upon her lap, sat down at the small window to watch for Katy.
The prospect was not one to call up cheerful fancies. Opposite
was one of those large brick tenements, let out by rapacious
landlords, a room at a time at griping rents, to poor emigrants,
and others, who were barely able to prolong their lease of life
from day to day. At one window sat a tailor, with his legs
crossed, and a torn straw hat perched awry upon his head, cutting
and making coarse garments for the small clothing-store in the
vicinity, whose Jewish owner reaped all the profits. At another,
a pale-faced woman, with a handkerchief bound round her aching face, bent over a steaming wash-tub, while a little girl of ten,
staggering under the weight of a basket of damp clothes was
stringing them on lines across the room to dry. At the next
window sat a decrepit old woman, feebly trying to soothe in her
palsied arms the wailings of a poor sick child. And there, too,
sat a young girl, from dawn till dark, scarcely lifting that pallid
face and weary eyes—stitching and thinking, thinking and stitching. God help her!

Still, tier above tier the windows rose, full of pale, anxious,
care-worn faces—never a laugh, never a song—but instead, rib-
ald curses, and the cries of neglected, half-fed children. From
window to window, outside, were strung on lines articles of
clothing, pails, baskets, pillows, feather-beds, and torn coverlets;
while up and down the door-steps, in and out, passed ever a
ragged procession of bare-footed women and children, to the
small grocery opposite, for "a pint of milk," a "loaf of bread,"

a few onions, or potatoes, a cabbage, some herrings, a sixpence worth of poor tea, a pound of musty flour, a few candles, or a peck of coal—for all of which, the poor creatures paid twice as much as if they had the means to buy by the quantity.

The only window which Ruth did not shudder to look at, was the upper one of all, inhabited by a large but thrifty German family, whose love of flowers had taken root even in that sterile soil, and whose little pot of thriving foreign shrubs, outside the window sill, showed with what tenacity the heart will cling to early associations.

Further on, at one block's remove, was a more pretentious-looking house, the blinds of which were almost always closed, save when the colored servants threw them open once a day, to give the rooms an airing. Then Ruth saw damask chairs, satin curtains, pictures, vases, books, and pianos; it was odd that people who could afford such things should live in such a neighborhood. Ruth looked and wondered. Throngs of visitors went there—carriages rolled up to the door, and rolled away; gray-haired men, business men, substantial-looking family men, and foppish-looking young men; while half-grown boys loitered about the premises, looking mysteriously into the door when it opened, or into the window when a curtain was raised, or a blind flew apart.

Now and then a woman appeared at the windows. Sometimes the face was young and fair, sometimes it was wan and haggard; but, oh God! never without the stain that the bitterest tear may fail to wash away, save in the eyes of Him whose voice of mercy whispered, "Go, and sin no more."

Ruth's tears fell fast. She knew now how it could be, when every door of hope seemed shut, by those who make long prayers and wrap themselves in morality as with a garment, and cry with closed purses and averted faces, "Be ye warmed, and filled." She knew now how, when the heart, craving sympathy, craving companionship, doubting both earth and heaven, may wreck its all in one despairing moment on that dark sea, if it lose sight of Bethlehem's guiding-star. And then, she thought, "if he who saveth a soul from death shall hide a multitude of sins," oh! where, in the great reckoning-day, shall *he* be found who, 'mid the gloom of so dark a night, pilots such struggling bark on wrecking rocks?

"Dear child, I am so glad you are home," said Ruth, as Katy opened the door; "I began to fear something had happened to you. Did you see your grandfather?"

"Oh, mother!" exclaimed Katy, "please never send me to my grandpa again; he said we 'should get away all the money he had,' and he looked so dreadful when he said it, that it made my knees tremble. Is it stealing, mamma, for us to take grandpa's money away?"

"No," replied Ruth, looking a hue more pallid, if possible, than before. "No, no, Katy, don't cry; you shall never go there again for money. But, where is your bag? Why! what 's this, Katy. Grandpa has made a mistake. You must run right back as quick as ever you can with this money, or I 'm afraid he will be angry."

"Oh, grandpa did n't give me that," said Katy; "a gentleman gave me that."

"A gentleman?" said Ruth. "Why it is *money*, Katy. How came you to take money from a gentleman? Who was he?"

"Money!" exclaimed Katy. "Money!" clapping her hands. "Oh! I 'm so glad. He did n't say it was money; he said it was something he owed papa;" and little Katy picked up a card from the floor, on which was penciled, "For the children of Harry Hall, from their father's friend."

"Hush," whispered Katy to Nettie, "mamma is praying."

CHAPTER XLVII

"WELL, I never!" said Biddy, bursting into Ruth's room in her usual thunder-clap way, and seating herself on the edge of a chair, as she polished her face with the skirt of her dress. "As sure as my name is Biddy, I don't know whether to laugh or to cry. Well, I 've been expecting it. Folks that have ears can't help hearing when folks quarrel."

"What are you talking about?" said Ruth. "Who has quarreled? It is nothing that concerns me."

"Don't it though?" replied Biddy. "I 'm thinking it *will* concern ye to pack up bag and baggage, and be off out of the house; for that 's what we are all coming to, and all for Mrs. Skiddy. You see it 's just here, ma'am. Masther has been threatnin' for a long time to go to Californy, where the gould is as plenty as blackberries. Well, misthtress told him, if ever he said the like o' that again, he 'd rue it; and you know, ma'am, it 's she that has a temper. Well, yesterday I heard high words again; and, sure enough, after dinner to-day, she went off, taking Sammy and Johnny, and laving the bit nursing baby on his hands, and the boarders and all. And it 's Biddy McFlanigan who 'll be off, ma'am, and not be made a pack-horse of, to tend that teething child, and be here, and there, and everywhere in a minute. And so I come to bid you good-bye."

"But, Biddy—"

"Don't be afther keeping me, ma'am; Pat has shouldhered me trunk, and ye see I can't be staying when things is as they is."

The incessant cries of Mrs. Skiddy's bereaved baby soon bore ample testimony to the truth of Biddy's narration, appealing to

Ruth's motherly sympathies so vehemently, that she left her room and went down to offer her assistance.

There sat Mr. John Skiddy, the forlorn widower, the ambitious Californian, in the middle of the kitchen, in his absconded wife's rocking-chair, trotting a seven months' baby on the sharp apex of his knee, alternately singing, whistling, and wiping the perspiration from his forehead, while the little Skiddy threw up its arms in the most frantic way, and held its breath with rage, at the awkward attempts of its dry nurse to restore peace to the family.

"Let me sweeten a little cream and water and feed that child for you, Mr. Skiddy," said Ruth. "I think he is hungry."

"Oh, thank you, Mrs. Hall," said Skiddy, with a man's determined aversion to owning 'checkmated.' "I am getting along famously with the little darling. Papa *will* feed him, so he *will*," said Skiddy; and, turning the maddened baby flat on his back, he poured down a whole tea-spoonful of the liquid at once; the natural consequence of which was a milky *jet d'eau* on his face, neckcloth, and vest, from the irritated baby, who resented the insult with all his mother's spirit.

Ruth adroitly looked out the window, while Mr. Skiddy wiped his face and sopped his neckcloth, after which she busied herself in picking up the ladles, spoons, forks, dredging-boxes, mortars, pestles, and other culinary implements, with which the floor was strewn, in the vain attempt to propitiate the distracted infant.

"I think I *will* spare the little dear to you a few minutes," said Skiddy, with a ghastly attempt at a smile, "while I run over to the bakery to get a loaf for tea. Mrs. Skiddy has probably been unexpectedly detained, and Biddy is so afraid of her labor in her absence, that she has taken French leave. I shall be back soon," said Skiddy, turning away in disgust from the looking-glass, as he caught sight of his limpsey dicky and collapsed shirt-bosom.

Ruth took the poor worried baby tenderly, laid it on its stomach across her lap, then loosening its frock strings, began rubbing its little fat shoulders with her velvet palm. There was a maternal magnetism in that touch; baby knew it! he stopped crying and winked his swollen eyelids with the most luxurious satisfaction, as much as to say, there, now, that 's something like!

Gently Ruth drew first one, then the other, of the magnetized baby's chubby arms from its frock sleeves, substituting a comfortable loose night-dress for the tight and heated frock; then she carefully drew off its shoe, admiring the while the beauty of the little blue veined, dimpled foot, while Katy, hush as any mouse looked on delightedly from her little cricket on the hearth, and Nettie, less philosophical, was more than half inclined to cry at what she considered an infringement of her rights.

Mr. Skiddy's reflections as he walked to the bakery were of a motley character. Upon the whole, he inclined to the opinion that it was "not good for man to be alone," especially with a nursing baby. The premeditated and unmixed malice of Mrs. Skiddy in leaving the baby, instead of Sammy or Johnny, was beyond question. Still, he could not believe that her desire for revenge would outweigh all her maternal feelings. She would return by-and-by; but where could she have gone? People cannot travel with an empty purse; but, perhaps even now, at some tantalizing point of contiguity, she was laughing at the success of her nefarious scheme; and Mr. Skiddy's face reddened at the thought, and his arms instinctively took an a-kimbo attitude.

But then, perhaps, she *never meant* to come back. What was he to do with that baby? A wet-nurse would cost him six dollars a week; and, as to bringing up little Tommy by hand, city milk would soon finish him. And, to do Mr. Skiddy justice, though no Socrates, he was a good father to his children.

And now it was nearly dark. Was he doomed to sit up all night, tired as he was, with Tommy in one hand, and a spoon

and pewter porringer in the other? Or, worse still, walk the floor
in white array, till his joints, candle, and patience gave out?
Then, there were the boarders to be seen to! He never realized
before how *many* irons Mrs. Skiddy had daily in the fire. There
was Mr. Thompson, and Mr. Johnson, on the first floor, (and
his face grew hot as he thought of it,) had seen him in the
kitchen looking so Miss-Nancy-like, as he superintended pots,
kettles, and stews. *Stews?* there was not a dry thread on him that
minute, although a cold north wind was blowing. Never mind,
he was not such a fool as to tell of his little troubles; so he entered
the bakery and bought an extra pie, and a loaf of plum-cake, for
tea, to hoodwink the boarders into the belief that Mrs. Skiddy's
presence was not at all necessary to a well-provided table.

Tea went off quite swimmingly, with Mr. John Skiddy at the
urn. The baby, thanks to Ruth's maternal management, lay
sweetly sleeping in his little wicker cradle, dreaming of a distant
land flowing with milk and honey, and *looking* as if he was destined to a protracted nap; although it was very perceptible that
Mr. Skiddy looked anxious when a door was shut hard, or a
knife or fork dropped on the table; and he had several times
been seen to close his teeth tightly over his lip, when a heavy
cart rumbled mercilessly past.

Tea being over, the boarders dispersed their various ways;
Ruth notifying Mr. Skiddy of her willingness to take the child
whenever it became unmanageable. Then Mr. Skiddy, very gingerly, and with a cat-like tread, put away the tea-things, muttering an imprecation at the lid of the tea-pot, as he went, for
falling off. Then, drawing the evening paper from his pocket,
and unfurling it, (with one eye on the cradle,) he put up his
weary legs and commenced reading the news.

Hark! a muffled noise from the cradle! Mr. Skiddy started,
and applied his toe vigorously to the rocker—it was no use. He
whistled—it did n't suit. He sang—it was a decided failure. Little

Skiddy had caught sight of the pretty bright candle, and it was his present intention to scream till he was taken up to investigate it.

Miserable Skiddy! He recollected, now, alas! too late, that Mrs. Skiddy always carefully screened the light from Tommy's eyes while sleeping. He began to be conscious of a growing respect for Mrs. Skiddy, and a growing aversion to *her* baby. Yes; in that moment of vexation, with that unread evening paper before him, he actually called it *her* baby.

How the victimized man worried through the long evening and night—how he tried to propitiate the little tempest with the castor, the salt-cellar, its mother's work-box, and last, but not least, a silver cup he had received for his valor from the Atlantic Fire Company—how the baby, all-of-a-twist, like Dickens' young hero kept asking for "more"—how he laid it on its back, and laid it on its side, and laid it on its stomach, and propped it up on one end in a house made of pillows, and placed the candle at the foot of the bed, in the vain hope that that luminary might be graciously deemed by the infant tyrant a substitute for his individual exertions—and how, regardless of all these philanthropic efforts, little Skiddy stretched out his arms imploringly, and rooted suggestively at his father's breast, in a way to move a heart of stone—and how Mr. Skiddy said several words not to be found in the catechism—and how the daylight found him as pale as a potato sprout in a cellar, with all sorts of diagonal lines tattooed over his face by enraged little fingernails—and how the little horn, that for years had curled up so gracefully toward his nose, was missing from the corner of his moustache —are they not all written in the ambitious Californian's repentant memory?

CHAPTER XLVIII

"How sweetly they sleep," said Ruth, shading the small lamp with her hand, and gazing at Katy and Nettie; "God grant *their* names be not written, widow;" and smoothing back the damp tresses from the brow of each little sleeper, she sat down to the table, and drawing from it a piece of fine work, commenced sewing. "Only fifty-cents for all this ruffling and hemming," said Ruth, as she picked up the wick of her dim lamp; "only fifty cents! and I have labored diligently too, every spare moment, for a fortnight; this will never do," and she glanced at the little bed; "*they* must be clothed, and fed, and educated. Educated?" an idea struck Ruth; "why could not she teach school? But who would be responsible for the rent of her room? There was fuel to be furnished, and benches; what capital had *she* to start with? There was Mrs. Millet, to be sure, and her father, who, though they were always saying, "get something to do," would never assist her when she tried to do anything; how easy for them to help her to obtain a few scholars, or be responsible for her rent, till she could make a little headway. Ruth resolved, at least, to mention her project to Mrs. Millet, who could then, if she felt inclined, have an opportunity to offer her assistance in this way.

The following Monday, when her washing was finished, Ruth wiped the suds from her parboiled fingers on the kitchen roller, and ascending the stairs, knocked at the door of her cousin's chamber. Mrs. Millet was just putting the finishing touches to the sleeves of a rich silk dress of Leila's, which the mantaumaker had just returned.

"How d' ye do, Ruth," said she, in a tone which implied— what on earth do you want now?

"Very well, I thank you," said Ruth, with that sudden sinking at the heart, which even the *intonation* of a voice may sometimes give; "I can only stay a few minutes; I stopped to ask you, if you thought there was any probability of success, should I attempt to get a private school?"

"There is nothing to prevent your trying," replied Mrs. Millet, carelessly; "other widows have supported themselves; there was Mrs. Snow." Ruth sighed, for she knew that Mrs. Snow's relatives had given her letters of introduction to influential families, and helped her in various ways till she could get her head above water. "Yes," continued Mrs. Millet, laying her daughter's silk dress on the bed, and stepping back a pace or two, with her head on one side, to mark the effect of the satin bow she had been arranging; "yes—other widows support themselves, though, I am sure, I don't know how they do it—I suppose there must be a way—Leila! is that bow right? seems to me the dress needs a yard or two more lace; ten dollars will not make much difference; it will be such an improvement."

"Of course not," said Leila, "it will be a very great improvement; and by the way, Ruth, don't you want to sell me that coral pin you used to wear? it would look very pretty with this green dress."

"It was *Harry's* gift," said Ruth.

"Yes," replied Leila; "but I thought you 'd be very glad to part with it for *money*."

A flush passed over Ruth's face. "Not *glad,* Leila," she replied, "for everything that once belonged to Harry is precious, though I might feel necessitated to part with it, in my present circumstances."

"Well, then," said Mrs. Millet, touching her daughter's elbow, "you 'd better have it, Leila."

"Harry gave ten dollars for it," said Ruth.

"Yes, *originally,* I dare say," replied Mrs. Millet, "but nobody expects to get much for second-hand things. Leila will give you a dollar and a quarter for it, and she would like it soon, because when this north-east storm blows over, she wants to make a few calls on Snyder's relatives, in this very becoming silk dress;" and Mrs. Millet patted Leila on the shoulder.

"Good-bye," said Ruth.

"Don't forget the brooch," said Leila.

"I wish Ruth would go off into the country, or somewhere," remarked Leila, as Ruth closed the door. "I have been expecting every day that Snyder would hear of her offering to make caps in that work-shop; he is so fastidious about such things, being connected with the Tidmarshes, and that set, you know."

"Yes," said Leila's elder brother John, a half-fledged young M.D., whose collegiate and medical education enabled him one morning to astound the family breakfast-party with the astute information, "that vinegar was an acid." "Yes, I wish she would take herself off into the country, too. I had as lief see a new doctor's sign put up next door, as to see her face of a Monday, over that wash-tub, in our kitchen. I wonder if she thinks salt an improvement in soap-suds, for the last time I saw her there she was dropping in the tears on her clothes, as she scrubbed, at a showering rate; another thing, mother, I wish you would give her a lesson or two, about those children of hers. The other day I met her Katy in the street with the shabbiest old bonnet on, and the toes of her shoes all rubbed white; and she had the impertinence to call me "*cousin* John," in the hearing of young Gerald, who has just returned from abroad, and who dined with Lord Malden, in Paris. I could have wrung the little wretch's neck."

"It *was* provoking, John. I 'll speak to her about it," said Mrs. Millet, "when she brings the coral pin."

CHAPTER XLIX

R UTH, after a sleepless night of reflection upon her new project, started in the morning in quest of pupils. She had no permission to refer either to her father, or to Mrs. Millet; and such being the case, the very fact of her requesting this favor of any one less nearly related, would be, of itself, sufficient to cast suspicion upon her. Some of the ladies upon whom she called were "out," some "engaged," some "indisposed," and all indifferent; besides, people are not apt to intrust their children with a person of whom they know nothing; Ruth keenly felt this disadvantage.

One lady on whom she called, "never sent her children where the teacher's own children were taught;" another preferred foreign teachers, "it was something to say that Alfred and Alfrida were 'finished' at Signor Vicchi's establishment;" another, after putting Ruth through the Catechism as to her private history and torturing her with the most minute inquiries as to her past, present, and future, coolly informed her that "she had no children to send."

After hours of fruitless searching, Ruth, foot-sore and heart-sore, returned to her lodgings. That day at dinner, some one of the boarders spoke of a young girl, who had been taken to the Hospital in a consumption, contracted by teaching a Primary School in —— street.

The situation was vacant; perhaps she could get it; certainly her education *ought* to qualify her to satisfy any "School Committee." Ruth inquired who they were; one was her cousin, Mr. Millet, the wooden man; one was Mr. Develin, the literary bookseller; the two others were strangers. Mr. Millet and

Mr. Develin! and both aware how earnestly she longed for employment! Ruth looked at her children; yes, for their sake she would even go to the wooden man, and Mr. Develin, and ask if it were not possible for her to obtain the vacant Primary School.

CHAPTER L

M R. MILLET sat in his counting-room, with his pen behind his ear, examining his ledger. "Do?" said he concisely, by way of salutation, as Ruth entered.

"I understand there is a vacancy in the 5th Ward Primary School," said Ruth; "can you tell me, as you are one of the Committee for that district, if there is any prospect of my obtaining it, and how I shall manage to do so."

"A-p-p-l-y," said Mr. Millet.

"When is the examination of applicants to take place?" asked Ruth.

"T-u-e-s-d-a-y," replied the statue.

"At what place?" asked Ruth.

"C-i-t-y—H-a-l-l," responded the wooden man, making an entry in his ledger.

Ruth's heroic resolutions to ask him to use his influence in her behalf, vanished into thin air, at this icy reserve; and, passing out into the street, she bent her slow steps in the direction of Mr. Develin's. On entering the door, she espied that gentleman through the glass door of his counting-room, sitting in his leathern arm-chair, with his hands folded, in an attitude of repose and meditation.

"Can I speak to you a moment?" said Ruth, lifting the latch of the door.

"Well—yes—certainly, Mrs. Hall," replied Mr. Develin, seizing a package of letters; "it is an uncommon busy time with me, but yes, certainly, if you have anything *particular* to say."

Ruth mentioned in as few words as possible, the Primary School, and her hopes of obtaining it, Mr. Develin, meanwhile, opening the letters and perusing their contents. When she had finished, he said, taking his hat to go out:

"I don't know but you 'll stand as good a chance, Mrs. Hall, as anybody else; you can apply. But you must excuse me, for I have an invoice of books to look over, immediately."

Poor Ruth! And this was human nature, which, for so many sunny years of prosperity, had turned to her only its *bright* side! She was not to be discouraged, however, and sent in her application.

CHAPTER LI

EXAMINATION day came, and Ruth bent her determined steps to the City Hall. The apartment designated was already crowded with waiting applicants, who regarded, with jealous eye, each addition to their number as so much diminution of their own individual chance for success.

Ruth's cheeks grew hot, as their scrutinizing and unfriendly glances were bent on her, and that feeling of utter desolation came over her, which was always so overwhelming whenever she presented herself as a suppliant for public favor. In truth, it was but a poor preparation for the inquisitorial torture before her.

The applicants were called out, one by one, in alphabetical order; Ruth inwardly blessing the early nativity of the letter H, for these anticipatory-shower-bath meditations were worse to her than the shock of a volley of chilling interrogations.

"Letter H."

Ruth rose with a flutter at her heart, and entered a huge, barren-looking room, at the further end of which sat, in august state, the dread committee. *Very* respectable were the gentlemen of whom that committee was composed; *respectable* was written all over them, from the crowns of their scholastic heads to the very tips of their polished boots; and correct and methodical as a revised dictionary they sat, with folded hands and spectacle-bestridden noses.

Ruth seated herself in the victim's chair, before this august body, facing a flood of light from a large bay-window, that nearly extinguished her eyes.

"What is your age?" asked the elder of the inquisitors.

Scratch went the extorted secret on the nib of the report-er's pen!

"Where was you educated?"

"Was Colburn, or Emerson, your teacher's standard for Arithmetic?"

"Did you cipher on a slate or black-board?"

"Did you learn the multiplication table, skipping, or in order?"

"Was you taught Astronomy, or Philosophy, first?"

"Are you accustomed to a quill, or a steel-pen? lines, or blank-paper, in writing?"

"Did you use Smith's, or Jones' Writing-Book?"

"Did you learn Geography by Maps, or Globes?"

"Globes?" asked Mr. Squizzle, repeating Ruth's answer; "possible?"

"They use Globes at the celebrated Jerrold Institute," re-marked Mr. Fizzle.

"Impossible!" retorted Mr. Squizzle, growing plethoric in the face; "Globes, sir, are exploded; no institution of any note uses Globes, sir. I know it."

"And I know you labor under a mistake," said Fizzle, ele-vating his chin, and folding his arms pugnaciously over his striped vest. "I am acquainted with one of the teachers in that highly-respectable school."

"And I, sir," said Squizzle, "am well acquainted with the Principal, who is a man of too much science, sir, to use globes, sir, to teach geography, sir."

At this, Mr. Fizzle settled down behind his dicky with a quenched air; and the very important question being laid on the shelf, Mr. Squizzle, handing Ruth a copy of "Pollok's Course of Time," requested her to read a marked passage, indicated by a perforation of his penknife. Poor Ruth stood about as fair a chance of proving her ability to read poetry, as would Fanny

Kemble to take up a play, hap-hazard, at one of her dramatic readings, without a previous opportunity to gather up the author's connecting thread. Our heroine, however, went through the motions. This farce concluded, Ruth was dismissed into the apartment in waiting, to make room for the other applicants, each of whom returned with red faces, moist foreheads, and a "Carry-me-back-to-Old-Virginia" air.

An hour's added suspense, and the four owners of the four pair of inquisitorial spectacles marched, in procession, into the room in waiting, and wheeling "face about," with military precision, thumped on the table, and ejaculated:

"Attention!"

Instantaneously, five-and-twenty pair of eyes, black, blue, brown, and gray, were riveted; and each owner being supplied with pen, ink, and paper, was allowed ten minutes (with the four pair of spectacles leveled full at her) to express her thoughts on the following subject: "Was Christopher Columbus standing up, or sitting down, when he discovered America?"

The four watches of the committee men being drawn out, pencils began to scratch; and the terminus of the allotted minutes, in the middle of a sentence, was the place for each inspired improvisatrice to stop.

These hasty effusions being indorsed by appending each writer's signature, new paper was furnished, and "A-t-t-e-n-t-i-o-n!" was again ejaculated by a short, pursy individual, who seemed to be struggling to get out of his coat by climbing over his shirt collar. Little armies of figures were then rattled off from the end of this gentleman's tongue, with "Peter Piper Pipkin" velocity, which the anxious pen-women in waiting were expected to arrest in flying, and have the "sum total of the hull," as one of the erudite committee observed, already added up, when the illustrious arithmetician stopped to take wind.

This being the finale, the ladies were sapiently informed that, as only *one* school mistress was needed, only *one* out of the large number of applicants could be elected, and that "the Committee would now sit on them."

At this gratifying intelligence, the ladies, favored by a plentiful shower of rain, betook themselves to their respective homes; four-and-twenty, God help them! to dream of a reprieve from starvation, which, notwithstanding the six-hours' purgatory they had passed through, was destined to elude their eager grasp.

The votes were cast. Ruth was *not* elected. She had been educated, (whether fortunately or unfortunately, let the sequel of my story decide,) at a school where "Webster" was used instead of "Worcester." The greatest gun on the Committee was a Worcesterite. Mr. Millet and Mr. Develin always followed in the wake of *great* guns. Mr. Millet and Mr. Develin voted *against* Ruth.

CHAPTER LII

IT was four o'clock in the afternoon, and very tranquil and quiet at the Skiddys'. A tidy, rosy-cheeked young woman sat rocking the deserted little Tommy to sleep, to the tune of "I 've been roaming." The hearth was neatly swept, the tin and pewter vessels hung, brightly polished, from their respective shelves. The Maltese cat lay winking in the middle of the floor, watching the play of a stray sunbeam, which had found its way over the shed and into the small window. Ruth and her children were quiet, as usual, in their gloomy back chamber. Mr. Skiddy, a few blocks off, sat perched on a high stool, in the counting-room of Messrs. Fogg & Co.

Noiselessly the front-door opened, and the veritable Mrs. Skiddy, followed by Johnny and Sammy, crept through the front entry and entered, unannounced, into the kitchen. The rosy-cheeked young woman looked at Mrs. Skiddy, Mrs. Skiddy looked at her, and Tommy looked at both of them. Mrs. Skiddy then boxed the rosy-cheeked young woman's ears, and snatching the bewildered baby from her grasp, ejected her, with lightning velocity, through the street-door, and turned the key. It was all the work of an instant. Sammy and Johnny were used to domestic whirlwinds, so they were not surprised into any little remarks or exclamations, but the cat, less philosophical, laid back her ears, and made for the ash-hole; while Mrs. Skiddy, seating herself in the rocking-chair, unhooked her traveling dress and reinstated the delighted Tommy into all his little infantile privileges.

Mr. Skiddy had now been a whole week a widower; time enough for a man in that condition to grow philosophical. In fact, Skiddy was content. He had tasted the sweets of liberty,

and he liked them. The baby, poor little soul, tired of remonstrance, had given out from sheer weariness, and took resignedly
as a little Christian to his pewter porringer. Yes, Skiddy liked it;
he could be an hour behind his time without dodging, on his
return, a rattling storm of abuse and crockery; he could spend
an evening out, without drawing a map of his travels before
starting. On the afternoon in question he felt particularly felici-
tous; first, because he had dined off fried liver and potatoes, a
dish which he particularly affected, and which, on that very account, he could seldom get in his own domicil; secondly, he
was engaged to go that very evening with his old love, Nancy
Spriggins, to see the "Panorama of Niagara;" and he had left
orders with Betty to have tea half an hour earlier in consequence,
and to be sure and iron and air his killing plaid vest by seven
o'clock.

As the afternoon waned, Skiddy grew restless; he made wrong
entries in the ledger; dipped his pen into the sand-box instead
of the inkstand, and several times said "Yes, dear," to his employer, Mr. Fogg, of Fogg Square.

Six o'clock came at last, and the emancipated Skiddy, turning
his back on business, walked towards home, in peace with himself, and in love with Nancy Spriggins. On the way he stopped
to purchase a bouquet of roses and geraniums with which to
regale that damsel's olfactories during the evening's entertainment.

Striding through the front entry, like a man who felt himself
to be master of his own house, Skiddy hastened to the kitchen
to expedite tea. If he was not prepared for Mrs. Skiddy's departure, still less was he prepared for her return, especially with that
tell-tale bouquet in his hand. But, like all other hen-pecked husbands, on the back of the scape-goat *Cunning,* he fled away from
the uplifted lash.

"My *dear* Matilda," exclaimed Skiddy, "my own wife, how
could you be so cruel? Every day since your departure, hoping

to find you here on my return from the store, I have purchased a bouquet like this to present you. My dear wife, let by-gones *be* by-gones; my love for you is imperishable."

"V-e-r-y good, Mr. Skiddy," said his wife, accepting Nancy Spriggins's bouquet, with a queenly nod; "and now let us have no more talk of *California,* if you please, Mr. Skiddy."

"Certainly not, my darling; I was a brute, a beast, a wretch, a Hottentot, a cannibal, a vampire—to distress you so. Dear little Tommy! how pleasant it seems to see him in your arms again."

"Yes," replied Mrs. Skiddy, "I was not five minutes in sending that red-faced German girl spinning through the front-door; I hope you have something decent for us to eat, Skiddy. Johnny and Sammy are pretty sharp-set; why don't you come and speak to your father, boys!"

The young gentlemen thus summoned, slowly came forward, looking altogether undecided whether it was best to notice their father or not. A ginger-cake, however, and a slice of buttered bread, plentifully powdered with sugar, wonderfully assisted them in coming to a decision. As to Nancy Spriggins, poor soul, she pulled off her gloves, and pulled them on, that evening, and looked at her watch, and looked up street and down street, and declared, as "the clock told the hour for retiring," that man was a ——, a ——, in short, that woman was born to trouble, as the sparks are—to fly away.

Mrs. Skiddy resumed her household duties with as much coolness as if there had been no interregnum, and received the boarders at tea that night, just as if she had parted with them that day at dinner. Skiddy was apparently as devoted as ever; the uninitiated boarders opened their eyes in bewildered wonder; and *triumph* sat inscribed on the arch of Mrs. Skiddy's imposing Roman nose.

The domestic horizon still continued cloudless at the next

morning's breakfast. After the boarders had left the table, the market prices of beef, veal, pork, cutlets, chops, and steaks, were discussed as usual, the bill of fare for the day was drawn up by Mrs. Skiddy, and her obedient spouse departed to execute her market orders.

CHAPTER LIII

"WELL, I hope you have been comfortable in my absence, Mrs. Hall," said Mrs. Skiddy, after dispatching her husband to market, as she seated herself in the chair nearest the door; "ha! ha! John and I may call it quits now. He is a very good fellow—John; except these little tantrums he gets into once in a while; the only way is, to put a stop to it at once, and let him see who is master. John never will set a river on fire; there's no sort of use in his trying to take the reins—the man was n't born for it. I 'm too sharp for him, that 's a fact. Ha! ha! poor Johnny! I *must* tell you what a trick I played him about two years after our marriage.

"You must know he had to go away on business for Fogg & Co., to collect bills, or something of that sort. Well, he made a great fuss about it, as husbands who like to go away from home always do; and said he should 'pine for the sight of me, and never know a happy hour till he saw me again,' and all that; and finally declared he would not go, without I would let him take my Daguerreotype. Of course, I knew that was all humbug; but I consented. The likeness was pronounced 'good,' and placed *by me* in his traveling trunk, when I packed his clothes. Well, he was gone a month, and when he came back, he told me (great fool) what a comfort my Daguerreotype was to him, and how he had looked at it twenty times a day, and kissed it as many more; whereupon I went to his trunk, and opening it, took out the case and showed it to him—*without the plate,* which I had taken care to slip out of the frame just before he started, and which he had never found out! That 's a specimen of John Skiddy!—and John Skiddy is a fair specimen of the rest of his sex, let me tell you, Mrs. Hall. Well, of course he looked sheepish enough; and now, whenever I want to take the nonsense out of him, all I have to do is to point to that Daguerreotype case, which I keep lying on the mantel on purpose. When a woman is married, Mrs. Hall, she must make up her mind either to manage, or to be managed; *I* prefer to manage," said the amiable Mrs. Skiddy; "and I flatter myself John understands it by this time. But, dear me, I can't stand here prating to you all day. I must look round and see what mischief has been done in my absence, by that lazy-looking red-faced German girl," and Mrs. Skiddy laughed heartily, as she related how she had sent her spinning through the front door the night before.

Half the forenoon was occupied by Mrs. Skiddy in counting up spoons, forks, towels, and baby's pinafores, to see if they had sustained loss or damage during her absence.

"Very odd dinner don't come," said she, consulting the kitchen clock; "it is high time that beef was on, roasting."

It *was* odd—and odder still that Skiddy had not appeared to tell her *why* the dinner did n't come. Mrs. Skiddy wasted no time in words about it. No; she seized her bonnet, and went immediately to Fogg & Co., to get some tidings of him; they were apparently quite as much at a loss as herself to account for Skiddy's non-appearance. She was just departing, when one of the sub-clerks, whom the unfortunate Skiddy had once snubbed, whispered a word in her ear, the effect of which was instantaneous. Did she let the grass grow under her feet till she tracked Skiddy to "the wharf," and boarded the "Sea-Gull," bound for California, and brought the crestfallen man triumphantly back to his domicil, amid convulsions of laughter from the amused captain and his crew? No.

"There, now," said his amiable spouse, untying her bonnet, "there 's *another* flash in the pan Skiddy. Anybody who thinks to circumvent Matilda Maria Skiddy, must get up early in the morning, and find themselves too late at that. Now hold this child," dumping the doomed baby into his lap, "while I comb

my hair. Goodness knows you were n't worth bringing back;
but when I set out to have my own way, Mr. Skiddy, Mount
Vesuvius shan't stop me."

Skiddy tended the baby without a remonstrance; he perfectly
understood, that for a probationary time he should be put "on
the limits," the street-door being the boundary line. He heaved
no sigh when his coat and hat, with the rest of his wearing
apparel, were locked up, and the key buried in the depths of his
wife's pocket. He played with Tommy, and made card-houses
for Sammy and Johnny, wound several tangled skeins of silk for
"Maria Matilda," mended a broken button on the closet door,
replaced a missing knob on one of the bureau drawers, and appeared to be in as resigned and proper a frame of mind as such
a perfidious wretch could be expected to be in.

Two or three weeks passed in this state of incarceration, during which the errand-boy of Fogg & Co. had been repeatedly
informed by Mrs. Skiddy, that the doctor hoped Mr. Skiddy
would soon be sufficiently convalescent to attend to business. As
to Skiddy, he continued at intervals to shed crocodile tears over
his past shortcomings, or rather his short-*goings!* In consequence
of this apparently submissive frame of mind, he, one fine morning, received total absolution from Mrs. Skiddy, and leave to go
to the store; which Skiddy peremptorily declined, desiring, as he
said, to test the sincerity of his repentance by a still longer period
of probation.

"Don't be a fool, Skiddy," said Maria Matilda, pointing to
the Daguerreotype case, and then crowding his beaver down
over his eyes; "don't be a fool. Make a B line for the store, now,
and tell Fogg you 've had an attack of *room-a-tism;*" and Maria
Matilda laughed at her wretched pun.

Skiddy obeyed. No Uriah Heep could have out-done him in
" 'umbleness," as he crept up the long street, until a friendly
corner hid him from the lynx eyes of Maria Matilda. Then
"Richard was himself again"! Drawing a long breath, our fly-

ing Mercury whizzed past the mile-stones, and, before sun-down of the same day, was under full sail for California.

Just one half hour our Napoleon in petticoats spent in reflection, after being satisfied that Skiddy was really "on the deep blue sea." In one day she had cleared her house of *boarders,* and re-serving one room for herself and children, filled all the other apartments with *lodgers;* who paid her good prices, and taking their meals down town, made her no trouble beyond the care of their respective rooms.

About a year after a letter came from Skiddy. He was "dis-gusted" with ill-luck at gold-digging, and ill-luck everywhere else; he had been "burnt out," and "robbed," and everything else but murdered; and " 'umbly" requested his dear Maria Ma-tilda to send him "the passage-money to return home."

Mrs. Skiddy's picture should have been taken at that moment! My pen fails! Drawing from her pocket a purse well filled with her own honest earnings, she chinked its contents at some phan-tom shape discernible to her eyes alone; while through her set teeth hissed out, like ten thousand serpents, the word

"N—e—v—e—r!"

CHAPTER LIV

"WHAT is it on the gate? Spell it, mother," said Katy, look-ing wistfully through the iron fence at the terraced banks, smoothly-rolled gravel walks, plats of flowers, and grape-trellised arbors; "what is it on the gate, mother?"

" 'Insane Hospital,' dear; a place for crazy people."

"Want to walk round, ma'am?" asked the gate-keeper, as Katy poked her little head in; "can, if you like." Little Katy's eyes pleaded eloquently; flowers were to her another name for happiness, and Ruth passed in.

"I should like to live here, mamma," said Katy.

Ruth shuddered, and pointed to a pale face pressed close against the grated window. Fair rose the building in its architec-tural proportions; the well-kept lawn was beautiful to the eye; but, alas! there was helpless age, whose only disease was too long a lease of life for greedy heirs. There, too, was the fragile wife, to whom *love* was breath—being!—forgotten by the world and him in whose service her bloom had withered, insane—only in that her love had outlived his patience.

"Poor creatures!" exclaimed Ruth, as they peered out from one window after another. "Have you had many deaths here?" asked she of the gate-keeper.

"Some, ma'am. There is one corpse in the house now; a married lady, Mrs. Leon."

"Good heavens!" exclaimed Ruth, "my friend Mary."

"Died yesterday, ma'am; her husband left her here for her health, while he went to Europe."

"Can I see the Superintendent," asked Ruth; "I must speak to him."

Ruth followed the gate-keeper up the ample steps into a wide hall, and from thence into a small parlor; after waiti[ng] seemed to her an age of time, Mr. Tibbetts, the Superin[tendent,] entered. He was a tall, handsome man, between forty and fifty, with a very imposing air and address.

"I am pained to learn," said Ruth, "that a friend of mine, Mrs. Leon, lies dead here; can I see the body?"

"Are you a relative of that lady?" asked Mr. Tibbetts, with a keen glance at Ruth.

"No," replied Ruth, "but she was very dear to me. The last time I saw her, not many months since, she was in tolerable health. Has she been long with you, Sir?"

"About two months," replied Mr. Tibbetts; "she was hopelessly crazy, refused food entirely, so that we were obliged to force it. Her husband, who is an intimate friend of mine, left her under my care, and went to the Continent. A very fine man, Mr. Leon."

Ruth did not feel inclined to respond to this remark, but repeated her request to see Mary.

"It is against the rules of our establishment to permit this to any but relatives," said Mr. Tibbetts.

"I should esteem it a great favor if you would break through your rules in my case," replied Ruth; "it will be a great consolation to me to have seen her once more;" and her voice faltered.

The appeal was made so gently, yet so firmly, that Mr. Tibbetts reluctantly yielded.

The matron of the establishment, Mrs. Bunce, (whose advent was heralded by the clinking of a huge bunch of keys at her waist,) soon after came in. Mrs. Bunce was gaunt, sallow and bony, with restless, yellowish, glaring black eyes, very much resembling those of a cat in the dark; her motions were quick, brisk, and angular; her voice loud, harsh, and wiry. Ruth felt an instantaneous aversion to her; which was not lessened by Mrs. Bunce asking, as they passed through the parlor-door:

"Fond of looking at corpses, ma'am? I 've seen a great many in my day; I 've laid out more 'n twenty people, first and last, with my own hands. Relation of Mrs. Leon's, perhaps?" said she, curiously peering under Ruth's bonnet. "Ah, only a friend?"

"This way, if you please, ma'am;" and on they went, through one corridor, then another, the massive doors swinging heavily to on their hinges, and fastening behind them as they closed.

"Hark!" said Ruth, with a quick, terrified look, "what 's that?"

"Oh, nothing," replied the matron, "only a crazy woman in that room yonder, screaming for her child. Her husband ran away from her and carried off her child with him, to spite her, and now she fancies every footstep she hears is his. Visitors always thinks she screams awful. She can't harm you, ma'am," said the matron, mistaking the cause of Ruth's shudder, "for she is chained. She went to law about the child, and the law, you see, as it generally is, was on the man's side; and it just upset her. She 's a sight of trouble to manage. If she was to catch sight of your little girl out there in the garden, she 'd spring at her through them bars like a panther; but we don't have to whip her *very* often."

"Down here," said the matron, taking the shuddering Ruth by the hand, and descending a flight of stone steps, into a dark passage-way. "Tired ar n't you?"

"Wait a bit, please," said Ruth, leaning against the stone wall, for her limbs were trembling so violently that she could scarcely bear her weight.

"Now," said she, (after a pause,) with a firmer voice and step.

"This way," said Mrs. Bunce, advancing towards a rough deal box which stood on a table in a niche of the cellar, and setting a small lamp upon it; "she did n't look no better than that, ma'am, for a long while before she died."

Ruth gave one hurried glance at the corpse, and buried her face in her hands. Well might she fail to recognize in that emaciated form, those sunken eyes and hollow cheeks, the beautiful Mary Leon. Well might she shudder, as the gibbering screams of the maniacs over head echoed through the stillness of that cold, gloomy vault.

"Were you with her at the last?" asked Ruth of the matron, wiping away her tears.

"No," replied she; "the afternoon she died she said, 'I want to be alone,' and, not thinking her near her end, I took my work and sat just outside the door. I looked in once, about half an hour after, but she lay quietly asleep, with her cheek in her hand,—so. By-and-by I thought I would speak to her, so I went in, and saw her lying just as she did when I looked at her before. I spoke to her, but she did not answer me; she was dead, ma'am."

O, how mournfully sounded in Ruth's ears those plaintive words, "I want to be alone." Poor Mary! aye, better even in death 'alone,' than gazed at by careless, hireling eyes, since he who should have closed those drooping lids, had wearied of their faded light.

"Did she speak of no one?" asked Ruth; "mention no one?"

"No—yes; I recollect now that she said something about calling Ruth; I did n't pay any attention, for they don't know what they are saying, you know. She scribbled something, too, on a bit of paper; I found it under her pillow, when I laid her out. I should n't wonder if it was in my pocket now; I have n't thought of it since. Ah! here it is," said Mrs. Bunce, as she handed the slip of paper to Ruth.

It ran thus:—"I am not crazy, Ruth, no, no—but I shall be; the air of this place stifles me; I grow weaker—weaker. I cannot die here; for the love of heaven, dear Ruth, come and take me away."

"Only three mourners,—a woman and two little girls," exclaimed a by-stander, as Ruth followed Mary Leon to her long home.

CHAPTER LV

T HE sudden change in Mrs. Skiddy's matrimonial prospects, necessitated Ruth to seek other quarters. With a view to still more rigid economy, she hired a room without board, in the lower part of the city.

Mrs. Waters, her new landlady, was one of that description of females, whose vision is bounded by a mop, scrubbing-brush, and dust-pan; who repudiate rainy washing days; whose hearth, Jowler, on the stormiest night, would never venture near without a special permit, and whose husband and children speak under their breath on baking and cleaning days. Mrs. Waters styled herself a female physician. She kept a sort of witch's cauldron constantly boiling over the fire, in which seethed all sorts of "mints" and "yarbs," and from which issued what she called a "potecary odor." Mrs. Waters, when not engaged in stirring this cauldron, or in her various housekeeping duties, alternated her leisure in reading medical books, attending medical lectures, and fondling a pet skull, which lay on the kitchen-dresser.

Various little boxes of brown-bread-looking pills ornamented the upper shelf, beside a row of little dropsical chunky junk bottles, whose labels would have puzzled the most erudite M.D. who ever received a diploma. Mrs. Waters felicitated herself on knowing how the outer and inner man of every son of Adam was put together, and considered the times decidedly "out of joint;" inasmuch that she, Mrs. Waters, had not been called upon by her country to fill some medical professorship.

In person Mrs. Waters was barber-pole-ish and ram-rod-y, and her taste in dress running mostly to stringy fabrics, assisted the bolster-y impression she created; her hands and wrists bore

a strong resemblance to the yellow claws of defunct ch
which children play "scare" with about Thanksgiving time; her
feet were of turtle flatness, and her eyes—if you ever provoked
a cat up to the bristling and scratching point, you may possibly
form an idea of them.

Mrs. Waters condescended to allow Ruth to keep the quart
of milk and loaf of bread, (which was to serve for her bill of fare
for every day's three meals,) on a swing shelf in a corner of the
cellar. As Ruth's room was at the top of the house, it was somewhat of a journey to travel up and down, and the weather was
too warm to keep it up stairs; to her dismay she soon found that
the cellar-floor was generally more or less flooded with water,
and the sudden change from the heated air of her attic to the
dampness of the cellar, brought on a racking cough, which soon
told upon her health. Upon the first symptom of it, Mrs. Waters
seized a box of pills and hurried to her room, assuring her that
it was "a sure cure, and only three shillings a box."

"Thank you," said Ruth; "but it is my rule never to take
medicine unless—"

"Oh, oh," said Mrs. Waters, bridling up; "I see—unless it is
ordered by a physician, you were going to say; perhaps you don't
know that *I* am a physician—none the worse for being a female.
I have investigated things; I have dissected several cats, and sent
in an analysis of them to the Medical Journal; it has never been
published, owing, probably, to the editor being out of town. If
you will take six of these pills every other night," said the doc-
tress, laying the box on the table, "it will cure your cough; it is
only three shillings. I will take the money now, or charge it in
your bill."

"Three shillings!" Ruth was aghast; she might as well have
asked her three dollars. If there was anything Ruth was afraid
of, it was Mrs. Waters' style of woman; a loaded cannon, or a
regiment of dragoons, would have had few terrors in compari-

son. But the music must be faced; so, hoping to avoid treading on her landlady's professional toes, Ruth said, "I think I 'll try first what dieting will do, Mrs. Waters."

The door instantly banged to with a crash, as the owner and vender of the pills passed out. The next day Mrs. Waters drew off a little superfluous feminine bile, by announcing to Ruth, with a malignity worthy of her sex, "that she forgot to mention when she let her lodgings, that she should expect her to scour the stairs she traveled over, at least once a week."

CHAPTER LVI

IT was a sultry morning in July. Ruth had risen early, for her cough seemed more troublesome in a reclining posture. "I wonder what that noise can be?" said she to herself; whir—whir—whir, it went, all day long in the attic overhead. She knew that Mrs. Waters had one other lodger beside herself, an elderly gentleman by the name of Bond, who cooked his own food, and whom she often met on the stairs, coming up with a pitcher of water, or a few eggs in a paper bag, or a pie that he had bought of Mr. Flake, at the little black grocery-shop at the corner. On these occasions he always stepped aside, and with a deferential bow waited for Ruth to pass. He was a thin, spare man, slightly bent; his hair and whiskers curiously striped like a zebra, one lock being jet black, while the neighboring one was as distinct a white. His dress was plain, but very neat and tidy. He never seemed to have any business out-doors, as he staid in his room all day, never leaving it at all till dark, when he paced up and down, with his hands behind him, before the house. "Whir—whir—whir." It was early sunrise; but Ruth had heard that odd noise for two hours at least. What *could* it mean? Just then a carrier passed on the other side of the street with the morning papers, and slipped one under the crack of the house door opposite.

A thought! why could not Ruth write for the papers? How very odd it had never occurred to her before? Yes, write for the papers—why not? She remembered that while at boarding-school, an editor of a paper in the same town used often to come in and take down her compositions in short-hand as she read them aloud, and transfer them to the columns of his paper. She certainly *ought* to write better now than she did when an inex-

145

perienced girl. She would begin that very night; but where to make a beginning? who would publish her articles? how much would they pay her? to whom should she apply first? There was her brother Hyacinth, now the prosperous editor of the Irving Magazine; oh, if he would only employ her? Ruth was quite sure she could write as well as some of his correspondents, whom he had praised with no niggardly pen. She would prepare samples to send immediately, announcing her intention, and offering them for his acceptance. This means of support would be so congenial, so absorbing. At the needle one's mind could still be brooding over sorrowful thoughts.

Ruth counted the days and hours impatiently, as she waited for an answer. Hyacinth surely would not refuse *her* when in almost every number of his magazine he was announcing some new contributor; or, if *he* could not employ her *himself,* he surely would be brotherly enough to point out to her some one of the many avenues so accessible to a man of extensive newspaperial and literary acquaintance. She would so gladly support herself, so cheerfully toil day and night, if need be, could she only win an independence; and Ruth recalled with a sigh Katy's last visit to her father, and then she rose and walked the floor in her impatience; and then, her restless spirit urging her on to her fate, she went again to the post office to see if there were no letter. How long the clerk made her wait! Yes, there *was* a letter for her, and in her brother's hand-writing too. Oh, how long since she had seen it!

Ruth heeded neither the jostling of office-boys, porters, or draymen, as she held out her eager hand for the letter. Thrusting it hastily in her pocket, she hurried in breathless haste back to her lodgings. The contents were as follows:

"I have looked over the pieces you sent me, Ruth. It is very evident that writing never can be *your* forte; you have no talent that way. You may possibly be employed by some inferior newspapers, but be assured your articles never will be heard of your own little provincial city. For myself I have plenty of contributors, nor do I know of any of my literary acquaintances who would employ you. I would advise you, therefore, to seek some *unobtrusive* employment. Your brother,

"HYACINTH ELLET."

A bitter smile struggled with the hot tear that fell upon Ruth's cheek. "I have tried the unobtrusive employment," said Ruth; "the wages are six cents a day, Hyacinth;" and again the bitter smile disfigured her gentle lip.

"No talent!"

"At another tribunal than his will I appeal."

"Never be heard of out of my own little provincial city!" The cold, contemptuous tone stung her.

"But they shall be heard of;" and Ruth leaped to her feet. "Sooner than he dreams of, too. I *can* do it, I *feel* it, I *will* do it," and she closed her lips firmly; "but there will be a desperate struggle first," and she clasped her hands over her heart as if it had already commenced; "there will be scant meals, and sleepless nights, and weary days, and a throbbing brow, and an aching heart; there will be the chilling tone, the rude repulse; there will be ten backward steps to one forward. *Pride* must sleep! but—" and Ruth glanced at her children—"it shall be *done*. They shall be proud of their mother. *Hyacinth shall yet be proud to claim his sister.*"

"What is it, mamma?" asked Katy, looking wonderingly at the strange expression of her mother's face.

"What is it, my darling?" and Ruth caught up the child with convulsive energy; "what is it? only that when you are a woman you shall remember this day, my little pet;" and as she kissed Katy's upturned brow a bright spot burned on her cheek, and her eye glowed like a star.

CHAPTER LVII

"D OCTOR?" said Mrs. Hall, "put down that book, will you?
I want to talk to you a bit; there you 've sat these three
hours, without stirring, except to brush the flies off your nose,
and my tongue actually aches keeping still."

"Sh-sh-sh," said the doctor, running his forefinger along
to guide his purblind eyes safely to the end of the paragraph.
"Sh-sh. 'It—is es-ti-ma-ted by Captain Smith—that—there—
are—up'ards—of—ten—hundred—human—critters—in—the
—Nor-West—sett-le-ment.' Well—Mis. Hall—well—" said
the doctor, laying a faded ribbon mark between the leaves of the
book, and pushing his spectacles back on his forehead, "what 's
to pay now? what do you want of me?"

"I 've a great mind as ever I had to eat," said the old lady,
pettishly, "to knit twice round the heel of this stocking, before
I answer you; what do you think I care about Captain Smith?
Travelers always lie; it is a part of their trade, and if they don't
it 's neither here nor there to me. I wish that book was in the
Red Sea."

"I thought you did n't want it *read,*" retorted the irritating
old doctor.

"Now I suppose you call that funny," said the old lady. "I
call it simply ridiculous for a man of your years to play on words
in such a frivolous manner. What I was going to say was this, *i. e.*
if I can get a chance to say it, if *you* have given up all idea of
getting Harry's children, *I* have n't, and now is the time to apply
for Katy again; for, according to all accounts, Ruth is getting
along poorly enough."

"How did you hear?" asked the doctor.

"Why, my milliner, Miss Tiffkins, has a nephew who tends

in a little grocery-shop near where Ruth boards, and he says that she buys a smaller loaf every time she comes to the store, and that the milkman told him that she only took a pint of milk a day of him now; then Katy has not been well, and what she did for doctors and medicines is best known to herself; she 's so independent that she never would complain if she had to eat paving stones. The best way to get the child will be to ask her here on a visit, and say we want to cure her up a little with country air. You understand? that will throw dust in Ruth's eyes, and then we will take our own time about letting her go back you know. Miss Tiffkins says her nephew says that people who come into the grocery-shop are very curious to know who Ruth is; and old Mr. Flake, who keeps it, says that it would n't hurt her any, if she is a lady, to stop and talk a little, like the rest of his customers; he says, too, that her children are as close-mouthed as their mother, for when he just asked Katy what business her father used to do, and what supported them now he was dead, and if they lived all the time on bread and milk, and a few such little questions, Katy answered, 'Mamma does not allow me to talk to strangers,' and went out of the shop, with her loaf of bread, as dignified as a little duchess.''

"Like mother, like child," said the doctor; "proud and poor, proud and poor; that tells the whole story. Well, shall I write to Ruth, Mis. Hall, about Katy?"

"No," said the old lady, "let me manage that; you will upset the whole business if you do. I 've a plan in my head, and to-morrow, after breakfast, I 'll take the old chaise, and go in after Katy."

In pursuance of this plan, the old lady, on the following day, climbed up into an old-fashioned chaise, and turned the steady old horse's nose in the direction of the city; jerking at the reins, and clucking and gee-ing him up, after the usual awkward fashion of sexagenarian female drivers. Using Miss Tiffkin's land-mark, the little black grocery-shop, for a guide-board, she soon discovered Ruth's abode; and so well did she play her part in commiserating Ruth's misfortunes, and Katy's sickly appearance, that the widow's kind heart was immediately tortured with the most unnecessary self-reproaches, which prepared the way for an acceptance of her invitation for Katy "for a week or two;" great promises, meanwhile being held out to the child of "a little pony to ride," and various other tempting lures of the same kind. Still little Katy hesitated, clinging tightly to her mother's dress, and looking, with her clear, searching eyes, into her grandmother's face, in a way that would have embarrassed a less artful maneuverer. The old lady understood the glance, and put it on file, to be attended to at her leisure; it being no part of her present errand to play the unamiable. Little Katy, finally won over, consented to make the visit, and the old chaise was again set in motion for home.

CHAPTER LVIII

"How d' ye do, Ruth?" asked Mr. Ellet, the next morning, as he ran against Ruth in the street; "glad you have taken my advice, and done a sensible thing at last."

"I don't know what you mean," answered Ruth.

"Why, the doctor told me yesterday that you had given Katy up to them, to bring up; you would have done better if you sent off Nettie too."

"I have not 'given Katy up,' " said Ruth, starting and blushing deeply; "and they could not have understood it so; she has only gone on a visit of a fortnight, to recruit a little."

"Pooh—pooh!" replied Mr. Ellet. "The thing is quietly over with; now don't make a fuss. The old folks expect to keep her. They wrote to me about it, and I approved of it. It 's the best thing all round; and, as I just said, it would have been better still if Nettie had gone, too. Now don't make a fool of yourself; you can go once in awhile, I suppose, to see the child."

"*How* can I go?" asked Ruth, looking her father calmly in the face; "it costs fifty cents every trip, by railroad, and you know I have not the money."

"That 's for you to decide," answered the father coldly; "I can't be bothered about such trifles. It is the way you always do, Ruth, whenever I see you; but it is time I was at my office. Don't make a fool of yourself, now; mind what I tell you, and let well alone."

"Father," said Ruth; "father—"

"Can't stop—can't stop," said Mr. Ellet, moving rapidly down street, to get out of his daughter's way.

"Can it be possible," thought Ruth, looking after him, "that he could connive at such duplicity? Was the old lady's sympathy a mere stratagem to work upon my feelings? How unnecessarily I reproached myself with my supposed injustice to her? Can *good* people do such things? Is religion only a fable? No, no; 'let God be true, and every man a liar.' "

CHAPTER LIX

"Is this 'The Daily Type' office?" asked Ruth of a printer's boy, who was rushing down five steps at a time, with an empty pail in his hand.

"All you have to do is to ask, mem. You 've got a tongue in your head, have n't ye? women folks generally has," said the little ruffian.

Ruth, obeying this civil invitation, knocked gently at the office door. A whir of machinery, and a bad odor of damp paper and cigar smoke, issued through the half-open crack.

"I shall have to walk in," said Ruth, "they never will hear my feeble knock amid all this racket and bustle;" and pushing the door ajar, she found herself in the midst of a group of smokers, who, in slippered feet, and with heels higher than their heads, were whiffing and laughing, amid the pauses of conversation, most uproariously. Ruth's face crimsoned as heels and cigars remained in *statu quo,* and her glance was met by a rude stare.

"I called to see if you would like a new contributor to your paper," said Ruth; "if so, I will leave a few samples of my articles for your inspection."

"What do you say, Bill?" said the person addressed; "drawer full as usual, I suppose, is n't it? more chaff than wheat, too, I 'll swear; don't want any, ma'am; come now, Jo, let 's hear the rest of that story; shut the door, ma'am, if you please."

"Are you the editor of the 'Parental Guide'?" said Ruth, to a thin, cadaverous-looking gentleman, in a white neck-cloth, and green spectacles, whose editorial sanctum was not far from the office she had just left.

"I am."

"Do you employ contributors for your paper?"

"Sometimes."

"Shall I leave you this MS. for your inspection, sir?"

"Just as you please."

"Have you a copy of your paper here, sir, from which I could judge what style of articles you prefer?"

At this, the gentleman addressed raised his eyes for the first time, wheeled his editorial arm-chair round, facing Ruth, and peering over his green spectacles, remarked:

"Our paper, madam, is most em-phat-i-cal-ly a paper devoted to the interests of religion; no frivolous jests, no love-sick ditties, no fashionable sentimentalism, finds a place in its columns. This is a serious world, madam, and it ill becomes those who are born to die, to go dancing through it. Josephus remarks that the Saviour of the world was never known to smile. *I* seldom smile. Are you a religious woman, madam?"

"I endeavor to become so," answered Ruth.

"V-e-r-y good; what sect?"

"Presbyterian."

At this the white neck-clothed gentleman moved back his chair; "Wrong, madam, all wrong; I was educated by the best of fathers, but he was *not* a Presbyterian; his son is not a Presbyterian; his son's paper sets its face like a flint against that heresy; no, madam, we shall have no occasion for your contributions; a hope built on a Presbyterian foundation, is built on the sand. Good morning, madam."

Did Ruth despair? No! but the weary little feet which for so many hours had kept pace with hers, needed a reprieve. Little Nettie must go home, and Ruth must read the office signs as she went along, to prepare for new attempts on the morrow.

To-morrow? Would a brighter morrow *ever* come? Ruth thought of her children, and said again with a strong heart—*it will;* and taking little Nettie upon her lap she divided with her their frugal supper—a scanty bowl of bread and milk.

Ruth could not but acknowledge to herself that she had thus far met with but poor encouragement, but she knew that to climb, she must begin at the lowest round of the ladder. It were useless to apply to a long-established leading paper for employment, unless indorsed by some influential name. Her brother had coolly, almost contemptuously, set her aside; and yet in the very last number of his Magazine, which accident threw in her way, he pleaded for public favor for a young actress, whom he said had been driven by fortune from the sheltered privacy of home, to earn her subsistence upon the stage, and whose earnest, strong-souled nature, he thought, should meet with a better welcome than mere curiosity. "Oh, why not one word for me?" thought Ruth; "and how can I ask of strangers a favor which a brother's heart has so coldly refused?"

It was very disagreeable applying to the small papers, many of the editors of which, accustomed to dealing with hoydenish contributors, were incapable of comprehending that their manner towards Ruth had been marked by any want of that respectful courtesy due to a dignified woman. From all such contact Ruth shrank sensitively; their free-and-easy tone fell upon her ear so painfully, as often to bring the tears to her eyes. Oh, if Harry— but she must not think of him.

The next day Ruth wandered about the business streets, looking into office-entries, reading signs, and trying to gather from their "know-nothing" hieroglyphics, some light to illumine her darkened pathway. Day after day chronicled only repeated failures, and now, notwithstanding she had reduced their already meager fare, her purse was nearly empty.

CHAPTER LX

IT was a warm, sultry Sabbath morning; not a breath of air played over the heated roofs of the great, swarming city. Ruth sat in her little, close attic, leaning her head upon her hand, weary, languid and dejected. Life seemed to her scarce worth the pains to keep its little flame flickering. A dull pain was in her temples, a heavy weight upon her heart. Other Sabbaths, *happy* Sabbaths, came up to her remembrance; earth looked so dark to her now, heaven so distant, God's ways so inscrutable.

Hark to the Sabbath-bell!

Ruth took little Nettie by the hand, and led her slowly to church. Other families, *unbroken* families, passed her on their way; families whose sunny thresholds the destroying angel had never crossed. Oh why the joy to them, the pain to her? Sadly she entered the church, and took her accustomed seat amid the worshipers. The man of God opened the holy book. Sweet and clear fell upon Ruth's troubled ear these blessed words: "There remaineth, therefore, a rest for the people of God."

The bliss, the joy of heaven was pictured; life,—mysterious, crooked, unfathomable life, made clear to the eye of faith; sorrow, pain, suffering, ignominy even, made sweet for His sake, who suffered all for us.

Ruth weeps! weeps that her faith was for an instant o'erclouded; weeps that she shrank from breasting the foaming waves at the bidding of Him who said, "It is I, be not afraid." And she, who came there fluttering with a broken wing, went away singing, soaring.

Oh man of God! pressed down with many cares, anxious and

troubled, sowing but not reaping, fearing to bring in no sheaves for the harvest, be of good courage. The arrow shot at a venture may to thine eye fall aimless; but in the Book of Life shalt thou road many an answer to the wrestling prayer, heard in thy closet by God alone.

CHAPTER LXI

"FINE day, Mr. Ellet," said a country clergyman to Ruth's father, as he sat comfortably ensconced in his counting-room. "I don't see but you look as young as you did when I saw you five years ago. Life has gone smoothly with you; you have been remarkably prospered in business, Mr. Ellet."

"Yes, yes," said the old gentleman, who was inordinately fond of talking of himself; yes, yes, I may say that, though I came into Massachusetts a-foot, with a loaf of bread and a sixpence, and now,—well, not to boast, I own this house, and the land attached, beside my country-seat, and have a nice little sum stowed away in the bank for a rainy day; yes, Providence has smiled on my enterprise; my affairs are, as you say, in a *very* prosperous condition. I hope religion flourishes in your church, brother Clark."

"Dead—dead—dead, as the valley of dry bones," replied Mr. Clark with a groan. "I have been trying to 'get us a revival;' but Satan reigns—Satan reigns, and the right arm of the church seems paralyzed. Sometimes I think the stumbling-block is the avaricious and money-grabbing spirit of its professors."

"Very likely," answered Mr. Ellet; "there is a great deal too much of that in the church. I alluded to it myself, in my remarks at the last church-meeting. I called it the accursed thing, the Achan in the camp, the Jonah which was to hazard the Lord's Bethel, and I humbly hope my remarks were blessed. I understand from the last Monthly Concert, brother Clark, that there are good accounts from the Sandwich Islands; twenty heathen admitted to the church in one day; good news that."

"Yes," groaned brother Clark, to whose blurred vision the Sun of Righteousness was always clouded; "yes, but think how many more are still, and always will be, worshiping idols; think how long it takes a missionary to acquire a knowledge of the language; and think how many, just as they become perfected in it, die of the climate, or are killed by the natives, leaving their helpless young families to burden the 'American Board.' Very sad, brother Ellet; sometimes, when I think of all this outlay of money and human lives, and so little accomplished, I—" (here a succession of protracted sneezes prevented Mr. Clark from finishing the sentence.)

"Yes," replied Mr. Ellet, coming to the rescue; "but if only *one* heathen had been saved, there would be joy forever in heaven. He who saveth a soul from death, you know, hideth a multitude of sins. I think I spoke a word in season, the other day, which has resulted in one admission, at least, to our church."

"It is to be hoped the new member will prove steadfast," said the well-meaning but hypochondriac brother Clark, with another groan. "Many a hopeful convert goes back to the world, and the last state of that soul is worse than the first. Dreadful, dreadful. I am heartsick, brother Ellet."

"Come," said Ruth's father, tapping him on the shoulder; "dinner is ready, will you sit down with us? First salmon of the season, green peas, boiled fowl, oysters, &c.; your country parishioners don't feed you that way, I suppose."

"N—o," said brother Clark, "no; there is no verse in the whole Bible truer, or more dishonored in the observance, than this, 'The laborer is worthy of his hire.' I 'll stay to dinner, brother Ellet. You have, I bless God, a warm heart and a liberal one; your praise is in all the churches."

A self-satisfied smile played round the lips of Ruth's father, at this tribute to his superior sanctity; and, seating himself at the well-spread table, he uttered an unusually lengthy grace.

———

"Some more supper, please, Mamma," vainly pleaded little Nettie.

CHAPTER LXII

RUTH had found employment. Ruth's MSS. had been accepted at the office of "The Standard." Yes, an article of hers was to be published in the very next issue. The remuneration was not what Ruth had hoped, but it was at least a *beginning,* a stepping-stone. What a pity that Mr. Lescom's (the editor's) rule was, not to pay a contributor, even after a piece was accepted, until it was printed—and Ruth so short of funds. Could she hold out to work so hard, and fare so rigidly? for often there was only a crust left at night; but, God be thanked, she should now *earn* that crust! It was a pity that oil was so dear, too, because most of her writing must be done at night, when Nettie's little prattling voice was hushed, and her innumerable little wants forgotten in sleep. Yes, it *was* a pity that good oil was so dear, for the cheaper kind crusted so soon on the wick, and Ruth's eyes, from excessive weeping, had become quite tender, and often very painful. Then it would be so mortifying should a mistake occur in one of her articles. She must write very legibly, for type-setters were sometimes sad bunglers, making people accountable for words that would set Worcester's or Webster's hair on end; but, poor things, *they* worked hard too —they had *their* sorrows, thinking, long into the still night, as they scattered the types, more of their dependent wives and children, than of the orthography of a word, or the rhetoric of a sentence.

Scratch—scratch—scratch, went Ruth's pen; the dim lamp flickering in the night breeze, while the deep breathing of the little sleepers was the watchword, *On!* to her throbbing brow and weary fingers. One o'clock—two o'clock—three o'clock—the lamp burns low in the socket. Ruth lays down her pen, and pushing back the hair from her forehead, leans faint and exhausted against the window-sill, that the cool night-air may fan her heated temples. How impressive the stillness! Ruth can almost hear her own heart beat. She looks upward, and the watchful stars seem to her like the eyes of gentle friends. No, God would *not* forsake her! A sweet peace steals into her troubled heart, and the overtasked lids droop heavily over the weary eyes.

Ruth sleeps.

————

Daylight! Morning *so* soon? All night Ruth has leaned with her head on the window-sill, and now she wakes unrefreshed from the constrained posture; but she has no time to heed *that,* for little Nettie lies moaning in her bed with pain; she lifts the little creature in her lap, rocks her gently, and kisses her cheek; but still little Nettie moans. Ruth goes to the drawer and looks in her small purse (Harry's gift); it is empty! then she clasps her hands and looks again at little Nettie. Must Nettie die for want of care? Oh, if Mr. Lescom would *only* advance her the money for the contributions he had accepted, but he said so decidedly that "it was a rule he *never* departed from;" and there were yet five long days before the next paper would be out. Five days! what might not happen to Nettie in five days? There was her cousin, Mrs. Millet, but she had muffled her furniture in linen wrappers, and gone to the springs with her family, for the summer months; there was her father, but had he not said "Remember, if you *will* burden yourself with your children, you must not look to me for help." Kissing little Nettie's cheek she lays her gently on the bed, whispering in a husky voice, "only a few moments, Nettie; mamma will be back soon." She closes

the door upon the sick child, and stands with her hand upon
her bewildered brow, thinking.

"I beg your pardon, madam; the entry is so very dark I did not
see you," said Mr. Bond; "you are as early a riser as myself."

"My child is sick," answered Ruth, tremulously, "I was just
going out for medicine."

"If you approve of Homeopathy," said Mr. Bond, "and will
trust me to prescribe, there will be no necessity for your putting
yourself to that trouble; I always treat myself homeopathically in
sickness, and happen to have a small supply of those medicines
by me."

Ruth's natural independence revolted at the idea of receiving
a favor from a stranger.

"Perhaps you disapprove of Homeopathy," said Mr. Bond,
mistaking the cause of her momentary hesitation; "it works like
a charm with children; but if you prefer not to try it, allow me
to go out and procure you whatever you desire in the way of
medicine; you will not then be obliged to leave your child."

Here was another dilemma—what *should* Ruth do? Why,
clearly accept his first offer; there was an air of goodness and
sincerity about him, which, added to his years, seemed to invite
her confidence.

Mr. Bond stepped in, looked at Nettie, and felt her pulse.
"Ah, little one, we will soon have you better," said he, as he
left the room to obtain his little package of medicines.

"Thank you," said Ruth, with a grateful smile, as he administered to Nettie some infinitesimal pills.

"Not in the least," said Mr. Bond. "I learned two years since
to doctor myself in this way, and I have often had the pleasure of relieving others in emergencies like this, from my little
Homeopathic stores. You will find that your little girl will soon
fall into a sweet sleep, and awake much relieved; if you are
careful with her, she will, I think, need nothing more in the

way of medicine, or if she should, my advice is quite at your service;" and, taking his pitcher of water in his hand, he bowed respectfully, and wished Ruth good morning.

Who was he? what was he? Whir—whir—there was the noise again! That he was man of refined and courteous manners, was very certain. Ruth felt glad he was so much her senior; he seemed so like what Ruth had sometimes dreamed a kind father might be, that it lessened the weight of the obligation. Already little Nettie had ceased moaning; her little lids began to droop, and her skin, which had been hot and feverish, became moist and cool. "May God reward him, whoever he may be," said Ruth. "Surely it *is* blessed to *trust!*"

CHAPTER LXIII

IT was four o'clock of a hot August afternoon. The sun had crept round to the front piazza of the doctor's cottage. No friendly trees warded off his burning rays, for the doctor "liked a prospect;" *i. e.* he liked to sit at the window and count the different trains which whizzed past in the course of the day; the number of wagons, and gigs, and carriages, that rolled lazily up the hill; to see the village engine, the "Cataract," drawn out on the green for its weekly ablutions, and to count the bundles of shingles that it took to roof over Squire Ruggles' new barn. No drooping vines, therefore, or creepers, intruded between him and this pleasant "prospect." The doctor was an utilitarian; he could see "no use" in such things, save to rot timber and harbor vermin. So a wondrous glare of white paint, (carefully renewed every spring) blinded the traveler whose misfortune it was to pass the road by the doctor's house. As I said, it was now four o'clock. The twelve o'clock dinner was long since over. The Irish girl had rinsed out her dish-towels, hung them out the back door to dry, and gone down to the village store to buy some new ribbons advertised as selling at an "immense sacrifice" by the disinterested village shopkeeper.

Let us peep into the doctor's sitting room; the air of this room is close and stifled, for the windows must be tightly closed, lest some audacious fly should make his mark on the old lady's immaculate walls. A center table stands in the middle of the floor, with a copy of "The Religious Pilot," last year's Almanac, A Directory, and "The remarkable Escape of Eliza Cook, who was partially scalped by the Indians." On one side of the room hangs a piece of framed needle-work, by the virgin fingers of the old lady, representing an unhappy female, weeping over a very high and very perpendicular tombstone, which is hieroglyphicked over with untranslatable characters in red worsted, while a few herbs, not mentioned by botanists, are struggling for existence at its base. A friendly willow-tree, of a most extraordinary shade of blue green, droops in sympathy over the afflicted female, while a nondescript looking bird, resembling a dropsical bull-frog, suspends his song and one leg, in the foreground. It was principally to preserve this chef-d'œuvre of art, that the windows were hermetically sealed to the entrance of vagrant flies.

The old doctor, with his spectacles awry and his hands drooping listlessly at his side, snored from the depths of his arm-chair, while opposite him the old lady, peering out from behind a very stifly-starched cap border, was "seaming," "widening," and "narrowing," with a precision and perseverance most painful to witness. Outside, the bee hummed, the robin twittered, the shining leaves of the village trees danced and whispered to the shifting clouds; the free, glad breeze swept the tall meadow-grass, and the village children, as free and fetterless, danced and shouted at their sports; but there sat little Katy, with her hands crossed in her lap, as she *had* sat for many an hour, listening to the never-ceasing click of her grandmother's needles, and the sonorous breathings of the doctor's rubicund nose. Sometimes she moved uneasily in her chair, but the old lady's uplifted finger would immediately remind her that "little girls must be seen and not heard." It was a great thing for Katy when a mouse scratched on the wainscot, or her grandmother's ball rolled out of her lap, giving her a chance to stretch her little cramped limbs. And now the village bell began to toll, with a low, booming, funereal sound, sending a cold shudder through the child's nervous and excited frame. What if *her* mother should die way off in the city? What if she should *always* live in this terrible way at her grandmother's? with nobody to love her, or kiss her, or pat her little head kindly, and say, "Katy, dear;" and again the bell boomed out its mournful sound, and little Katy, unable longer to bear the torturing thoughts it called up, sobbed aloud.

It was all in vain, that the frowning old lady held up her warning finger; the flood-gates were opened, and Katy could not have stopped her tears had her life depended on it.

Hark! a knock at the door! a strange footstep!

"Mother!" shrieked the child hysterically, "mother!" and flew into Ruth's sheltering arms.

"What *shall* we do, doctor?" asked the old lady, the day after Ruth's visit. "I trusted to her not being able to get the money to come out here, and her father, I knew, would n't give it to her, and now here she has walked the whole distance, with Nettie in her arms, except a lift a wagoner or two gave her on the road; and I verily believe she would have done it, had it been twice the distance it is. I never shall be able to bring up that child according to my notions, while *she* is round. I 'd forbid her the house, (she deserves it,) only that it won't sound well if she tells of it. And to think of that ungrateful little thing's flying into her mother's arms as if she was in the last extremity, after all we have done for her. I don't suppose Ruth would have left her with us, as it is, if she had the bread to put in her mouth. She might as well give her up, though, first as last, for she never will be able to support her."

"She 's fit for nothing but a parlor ornament," said the doctor, "never was. No more business talent in Ruth Ellet, than there is in that chany image of yours on the mantel-tree, Mis. Hall. That tells the whole story."

CHAPTER LXIV

"I HAVE good news for you," said Mr. Lescom to Ruth, at her next weekly visit; "your very first articles are copied, I see, into many of my exchanges, even into the ——, which seldom contains anything but politics. A good sign for you Mrs. Hall; a good test of your popularity."

Ruth's eyes sparkled, and her whole face glowed.

"Ladies *like* to be praised," said Mr. Lescom, good-humoredly, with a mischievous smile.

"Oh, it is not that—not that, sir," said Ruth, with a sudden moistening of the eye, "it is because it will be bread for my children."

Mr. Lescom checked his mirthful mood, and said, "Well, here is something good for me, too; a letter from Missouri, in which the writer says, that if "Floy" (a pretty *nom-de-plume* that of yours, Mrs. Hall) is to be a contributor for the coming year, I may put him down as a subscriber, as well as S. Jones, E. May, and J. Noyes, all of the same place. That 's good news for *me,* you see," said Mr. Lescom, with one of his pleasant, beaming smiles.

"Yes," replied Ruth, abstractedly. She was wondering if her articles were to be the means of swelling Mr. Lescom's subscription list, whether *she* ought not to profit by it as well as himself, and whether she should not ask him to increase her pay. She pulled her gloves off and on, and finally mustered courage to clothe her thought in words.

"Now that 's just *like* a woman," replied Mr. Lescom, turning it off with a joke; "give them the least foot-hold, and they will want the whole territory. Had I not shown you that letter, you would have been quite contented with your present pay. Ah!

I see it won't do to talk so unprofessionally to you; and you need n't expect," said he, smiling, "that I shall ever speak of letters containing new subscribers on your account. I could easily get you the offer of a handsome salary by publishing such things. No—no, I have been foolish enough to lose two or three valuable contributors in that way; I have learned better than that, 'Floy';" and taking out his purse, he paid Ruth the usual sum for her articles.

Ruth bowed courteously, and put the money in her purse; but she sighed as she went down the office stairs. Mr. Lescom's view of the case was a business one, undoubtedly; and the same view that almost any other business man would have taken, viz.: to retain her at her present low rate of compensation, till he was necessitated to raise it by a higher bid from a rival quarter. And so she must plod wearily on till that time came, and poor Katy must still be an exile; for she had not enough to feed her, her landlady having raised the rent of her room two shillings, and Ruth being unable to find cheaper accommodations. It *was* hard, but what could be done? Ruth believed she had exhausted all the offices she knew of. Oh! there was one, "The Pilgrim;" she had not tried there. She would call at the office on her way home.

The editor of "The Pilgrim" talked largely. He had, now, plenty of contributors; he did n't know about employing a new one. Had she ever written? and *what* had she written? Ruth showed him her article in the last number of "The Standard."

"Oh—hum—hum!" said Mr. Tibbetts, changing his tone; "so you are 'Floy,' are you?" (casting his eyes on her.) "What pay do they give you over there?"

Ruth was a novice in business-matters, but she had strong common sense, and that common sense said, he has no right to ask you that question; don't you tell him; so she replied with dignity, "My bargain, sir, with Mr. Lescom was a private one, I believe."

"Hum," said the foiled Mr. Tibbetts; adding in an undertone to his partner, "sharp that!"

"Well, if I conclude to engage you," said Mr. Tibbetts, "I should prefer you would write for me over a different signature than the one by which your pieces are indicated at The Standard office, or you can write exclusively for my paper."

"With regard to your first proposal," said Ruth, "if I have gained any reputation by my first efforts, it appears to me that I should be foolish to throw it away by the adoption of another signature; and with regard to the last, I have no objection to writing exclusively for you, if you will make it worth my while."

"Sharp again," whispered Tibbetts to his partner.

The two editors then withdrawing into a further corner of the office, a whispered consultation followed, during which Ruth heard the words, "Can't afford it, Tom; hang it! we are head over ears in debt now to that paper man; good articles though—deuced good—must have her if we dispense with some of our other contributors. We had better begin low though, as to terms, for she 'll go up now like a rocket, and when she finds out her value we shall have to increase her pay, you know."

(Thank you, gentlemen; thought Ruth, when the cards change hands, I 'll take care to return the compliment.)

In pursuance of Mr. Tibbetts' shrewd resolution, he made known his "exclusive" terms to Ruth, which were no advance upon her present rate of pay at The Standard. This offer being declined, they made her another, in which, since she would not consent to do otherwise, they agreed she should write over her old signature, "Floy," furnishing them with two articles a week.

Ruth accepted the terms, poor as they were, because she could at present do no better, and because every pebble serves to swell the current.

★ ★ ★

Months passed away, while Ruth hoped and toiled, "Floy's" fame as a writer increasing much faster than her remuneration. There was rent-room to pay, little shoes and stockings to buy, oil, paper, pens, and ink to find; and now autumn had come, she could not write with stiffened fingers, and wood and coal were ruinously high, so that even with this new addition to her labor, Ruth seemed to retrograde pecuniarily, instead of advancing; and Katy still away! She must work harder—harder. Good, brave little Katy; she, too, was bearing and hoping on— mamma had promised, if she would stay there, patiently, she would certainly take her away just as soon as she had earned money enough; and mamma *never* broke her promise—*never;* and Katy prayed to God every night, with childish trust, to help her mother to earn money, that she might soon go home again.

And so, while Ruth scribbled away in her garret, the public were busying themselves in conjecturing who "Floy" might be. Letters poured in upon Mr. Lescom, with inquiries, even bribing him with the offer to procure a certain number of subscribers, if he would divulge her real name; to all of which the old man, true to his promise to Ruth, to keep her secret inviolate, turned a deaf ear. All sorts of rumors became rife about "Floy," some maintaining her to be a man, because she had the courage to call things by their right names, and the independence to express herself boldly on subjects which to the timid and clique-serving, were tabooed. Some said she was a disappointed old maid; some said she was a designing widow; some said she was a moon-struck girl; and all said she was a nondescript. Some tried to imitate her, and failing in this, abused and maligned her; the outwardly strait-laced and inwardly corrupt, puckered up their mouths and "blushed for her;" the hypocritical denounced the sacrilegious fingers which had dared to touch the Ark; the fash-ionist voted her a vulgar, plebeian thing; and the earnest and sorrowing, to whose burdened hearts she had given voice, cried God speed her. And still "Floy" scribbled on, thinking only of

bread for her children, laughing and crying behind her mask,—
laughing all the more when her heart was heaviest; but of this
her readers knew little and would have cared less. Still her little
bark breasted the billows, now rising high on the topmost wave,
now merged in the shadows, but still steering with straining
sides, and a heart of oak, for the nearing port of Independence.

Ruth's brother, Hyacinth, saw "Floy's" articles floating
through his exchanges with marked dissatisfaction and uneasi-
ness. That she should have succeeded in any degree without his
assistance, was a puzzle, and the premonitory symptoms of her
popularity, which his weekly exchanges furnished, in the shape
of commendatory notices, were gall and wormwood to him.
Something must be done, and that immediately. Seizing his pen,
he dispatched a letter to Mrs. Millet, which he requested her to
read to Ruth, alluding very contemptuously to Ruth's articles,
and begging her to use her influence with Ruth to desist from
scribbling, and seek some other employment. *What* employment,
he did not condescend to state; in fact, it was a matter of entire
indifference to him, provided she did not cross his track. Ruth
listened to the contents of the letter, with the old bitter smile,
and went on writing.

CHAPTER LXV

A DULL, drizzling rain spattered perseveringly against Ruth's windows, making her little dark room tenfold gloomier and darker than ever. Little Nettie had exhausted her slender stock of toys, and creeping up to her mother's side, laid her head wearily in her lap.

"Wait just a moment, Nettie, till mamma finishes this page," said Ruth, dipping her pen again in the old stone inkstand.

The child crept back again to the window, and watched the little pools of water in the streets, as the rain-drops dimpled them, and saw, for the hundredth time, the grocer's boy carrying home a brown-paper parcel for some customers, and eating something from it as he went along; and listened to the milkman, who thumped so loudly on the back gates, and seemed always in such a tearing hurry; and saw the baker open the lid of his boxes, and let the steam escape from the smoking hot cakes and pies. Nettie wished she could have some of them, but she had long since learned *only to wish;* and then she saw the two little sisters who went by to school every morning, and who were now cuddling, laughingly together, under a great big umbrella, which the naughty wind was trying to turn inside out, and to get away from them; and then Nettie thought of Katy, and wished she had Katy to play with her, when mamma wrote such a long, long time; and then little Nettie drew such a heavy sigh, that Ruth dashed down her pen, and taking her in her arms and kissing her, told her about,

"Mistress McShuttle,
Who lived in a coal-scuttle,
Along with her dog and her cat,

What she did there, I can't tell,
But I know very well,
   That none of the party were fat."

And then she narrated the exciting adventures of "The Wise Men of Gotham," who went to sea in that rudderless bowl, and suffered shipwreck and "total *lass* of life," as the newsboys (God bless their rough-and-ready faces) call it; and then little Nettie's snowy lids drooped over her violet eyes, and she was far away in the land of dreams, where there are no little hungry girls, or tired, scribbling mammas.

Ruth laid the child gently on her little bed, and resumed her pen; but the spell was broken, and "careful and troubled about many things" she laid it down again, and her thoughts ran riot.

Pushing aside her papers, she discovered two unopened letters which Mr. Lescom had handed her, and which she had in the hurry of finishing her next article, quite forgotten. Breaking the seal of the first, she read as follows:

"TO 'FLOY.'

"I am a rough old man, Miss, and not used to writing or talking to ladies. I don't know who you are, and I don't ask; but I take 'The Standard,' and I like your pieces. I have a family of bouncing girls and boys; and when we 've all done work, we get round the fire of an evening, while one of us reads your pieces aloud. It may not make much difference to you what an old man thinks, but I tell you those pieces have got the real stuff in 'em, and so I told my son John the other night; and *he* says, and *I* say, and neighbor Smith, who comes in to hear 'em, says, that you ought to make a book of them, so that your readers may keep them. You can put me down for three copies, to begin with; and if every subscriber to 'The Standard' feels as I do, you might make a plum by the operation. Suppose, now, you think of it?

"N. B.—John says, maybe you 'll be offended at my writing
to you, but I say you 've got too much common sense.
                    "Yours to command,
                              JOHN STOKES."

"Well, well," said Ruth, laughing, "that 's a thought that
never entered this busy head of mine, John Stokes. *I* publish a
book? Why, John, are you aware that those articles were written
for bread and butter, not fame; and tossed to the printer before
the ink was dry, or I had time for a second reading? And yet,
perhaps, there is more freshness about them than there would
have been, had I leisure to have pruned and polished them—
who knows? I 'll put your suggestion on file, friend Stokes, to
be turned over at my leisure. It strikes me, though, that it will
keep awhile. Thank you, honest John. It is just such readers as
you whom I like to secure. Well, what have we here?" and Ruth
broke the seal of the second letter. It was in a delicate, beautiful,
female hand; just such an one as you, dear Reader, might trace,
whose sweet, soft eyes, and long, drooping tresses, are now
bending over this page. It said:

"DEAR 'FLOY':
"For you *are* 'dear' to me, dear as a sister on whose loving
breast I have leaned, though I never saw your face. I know not
whether you are young and fair, or old and wrinkled, but I know
that your heart is fresh, and guileless, and warm as childhood's;
and that every week your printed words come to me, in my sick
chamber, like the ministrations of some gentle friend, sometimes
stirring to its very depths the fountain of tears, sometimes, by
odd and quaint conceits, provoking the mirthful smile. But
'Floy,' I love you best in your serious moods; for as earth recedes,
and eternity draws near, it is the real and tangible, my soul yearns
after. And sure I am, 'Floy,' that I am not mistaken in thinking
that we both lean on the same Rock of Ages; both discern,
through the mists and clouds of time, the Sun of Righteousness.
I shall never see you, 'Floy,' on earth;—mysterious voices, au-

dible only to the dying ear, are calling me away; and yet, before I go, I would send you this token of my love, for all the sweet and soul-strengthening words you have unconsciously sent to my sick chamber, to wing the weary, waiting hours. We shall *meet*, 'Floy'; but it will be where 'tears are wiped away.'

"God bless you, my unknown sister.

"MARY R.——."

Ruth's head bowed low upon the table, and her lips moved; but He to whom the secrets of all hearts are known, alone heard that grateful prayer.

CHAPTER LXVI

T HAT first miserable day at school! Who that has known it —even with a mother's kiss burning on the cheek, a big orange bumping in the new satchel, and a promise of apple-dumplings for dinner, can review it without a shudder? Torturing—even when you can run home and "tell mother" all your little griefs; when every member of the home circle votes it *"a shame"* that Johnny Oakes laughed because you did not take your alphabet the natural way, instead of receiving it by inoculation, (just as he forgets that *he* did;) torturing—when Bill Smith, and Tom Simms, with whom you have "swapped alleys," and played "hockey," are there with their familiar faces, to take off the chill of the new schoolroom; torturing—to the sensitive child, even when the teacher is a sunny-faced young girl, instead of a prim old ogre. Poor little Katy! her book was before her; but the lines blurred into one indistinct haze, and her throat seemed filling to suffocation with long-suppressed sobs. The teacher, if he thought anything about it, thought she had the tooth-ache, or ear-ache, or head-ache; and Katy kept her own secret, for she had read his face correctly, and with a child's quick instinct, stifled down her throbbing little heart.

To the doctor, and "Mis. Hall," with their anti-progressive notions, a school was a school. The committee had passed judgment on it, and I would like to know who would be insane enough to question the decision of a School Committee? What did the committee care, that the consumptive teacher, for his own personal convenience, madly excluded all ventilation, and heated the little sheet-iron stove hotter than Shadrach's furnace, till little heads snapped, and cheeks crimsoned, and croup stood ready at the threshold to seize the first little bare throat that presented its perspiring surface to the keen frosty air? What did *they* care that the desks were so constructed, as to crook spines, and turn in toes, and round shoulders? What did they care that the funnel smoked week after week, till the curse of "weak eyes" was entailed on their victims for a lifetime? They had other irons in the fire, to which this was a cipher. For instance: the village pump was out of repair, and town-meeting after town-meeting had been called, to see who *should n't* make its handle fly. North Gotham said it was the business of East Gotham; East Gotham said the pump might rer before they 'd bear the expense; not that the East Gothamites cared for expense—no; they scorned the insinuation, but they 'd have North Gotham to know that East Gotham was n't to be put upon. Jeremiah Stubbs, a staunch North Gothamite, stopped buying molasses and calico at "Ezekial Tibbs' East Gotham Finding Store;" and Ezekial Tibbs forbade, under penalty of losing his custom, the carpenter who was repairing his pig-sty, from buying nails any more of Jeremiah Stubbs, of North Gotham; matches were broken up; "own cousins" ceased to know one another, and the old women had a millenial time of it over their bohea, discussing and settling matters; no marvel that such a trifle as a child's school should be overlooked. Meantime there stood the pump, with its impotent handle, high and dry; "a gone sucker," as Mr. Tibbs facetiously expressed it.

"You can't go to school to-day, Katy, it is washing-day," said old Mrs. Hall; "go get that stool, now sit down on it, at my feet, and let me cut off those foolish dangling curls."

"Mamma likes them," said the child.

"I know it," replied the old lady, with a malicious smile, as she gathered a cluster of them in one hand and seized the scissors with the other.

"*Papa* liked them," said Katy, shrinking back.

"No, he did n't," replied the old lady; "or, if he did, 'twas only to please your foolish mother; any way they are coming

off; if I don't like them, that 's enough; you are always to live
with me now, Katy; it makes no difference what your mother
thinks or says about anything, so you need n't quote *her;* I 'm
going to try to make a good girl of you, *i. e.* if she will let you
alone; you are full of faults, just as she is, and I shall have to take
a great deal of pains with you. You ought to love me very much
for it, better than anybody else in the world—don't you?"

(No response from Katy.)

"I say, Katy, you ought to love me better than anybody else
in the world," repeated the old lady, tossing a handful of the
severed ringlets down on the carpet. "Do you, Katy?"

"No, ma'am," answered the truthful child.

"That tells the whole story," said the doctor, as he started up
and boxed Katy's ears; "now go up and stay in your room till I
send for you, for being disrespectful to your grandmother."

"Like mother—like child," said the old lady, as Katy, half
shorn, moved like a culprit out of the room; then gathering up
in her apron the shining curls, she looked on with a malicious
smile, while they crisped and blackened in the glowing Lehigh
fire.

But miserable as were the week-days—Sunday, after all, was
the dreadful day for Katy; the long—long—long Sunday, when
every book in the house was put under lock and key; when even
religious newspapers, tracts, and memoirs, were tabooed; when
the old people, who fancied they could not go to church, sat
from sunrise to sunset in their best clothes, with their hands
folded, looking speechlessly into the fire; when there was no
dinner; when the Irish girl and the cat, equally lawless and he-
retical, went to see their friends; when not a sound was heard
in the house, save the ticking of the old claw-footed-clock, that
stood in the entry; when Katy crept up to her little room, and
crouching in a corner, wondered if God *was* good—why he let
her papa *die,* and why he did not help her mamma, who tried
so hard to earn money to bring her home.

The last bright golden beam of the Sabbath sun had slowly faded away. One by one the stars came gliding out. He who held them all in their places, listening ever to the ceaseless music of their motion, yet bent a pitying ear to the stifled sob of a troubled child. Softly—sweetly—fell the gentle dew of slumber on weary eyelids, while angels came to minister. Tears glittered still on Katy's long lashes, but the little lips parted with a smile, murmuring "Papa." Sleep on—dream on—little Katy. He who noteth the sparrow's fall, hath given his angels charge to keep thee.

CHAPTER LXVII

IN one of the thousand business offices, in one of the thousand crowded streets of a neighboring city, sat Mr. John Walter, with his legs crossed, his right finger pressed against the right lobe of his organ of causality, his right elbow resting on his right knee, and the fingers of his left hand beating a sort of tattoo on a fresh copy of The Standard, which lay upon the table by his side. His attitude was one of profound meditation.

"Who *can* she be?" exclaimed Mr. Walter, in a tone of blended interest and vexation; "who can she be?" Mr. Walter raised his head, uncrossed his legs, took up The Standard, and re-read 'Floy's' last article slowly; often pausing to analyze the sentences, as though he would extort from them some hidden meaning, to serve as a clue to the identity of the author. After he had perused the article thus searchingly, he laid down The Standard, and again exclaimed, "Who *can* she be? she is a genius certainly, whoever she is," continued he, soliloquizingly; "a bitter life experience she has had too; she did not draw upon her imagination for this article. Like the very first production of her pen that I read, it is a wail from her inmost soul; so are many of her pieces. A few dozen of them taken consecutively, would form a whole history of wrong, and suffering, and bitter sorrow. What a singular being she must be, if I have formed a correct opinion of her; what powers of endurance! What an elastic, strong, brave, loving, fiery, yet soft and winning nature! A bundle of contradictions! and how famously she has got on too! it is only a little more than a year since her first piece was published, and now her articles flood the whole country; I seldom take up an exchange, which does not contain one or more of them. That first piece of hers was a stroke of genius—a real gem, although not very smoothly polished; ever since I read it, I have been trying to find out the author's name, and have watched her career with eager interest; *her* career, I say, for I suppose 'Floy' to be a woman, notwithstanding the rumors to the contrary. At any rate, my wife says so, and women have an instinct about such things. I wish I knew whether she gets well paid for her writings. Probably not. Inexperienced writers seldom get more than a mere pittance. There are so many ready to write (poor fools!) for the honor and glory of the thing, and there are so many ready to take advantage of this fact, and withhold from needy talent the moral right to a deserved remuneration. Thank heaven, I have never practiced this. The 'Household Messenger' does not yield me a very large income, but what it does yield is fairly earned. Why, bless me!" exclaimed Mr. Walter, suddenly starting up, and as suddenly sitting down again; "why has not this idea occurred to me before? yes, why not engage 'Floy' to write for the Household Messenger? How I wish I were rich, that I might give her such a price as she really deserves. Let me see; she now writes for The Standard, and The Pilgrim, four pieces a week for each; eight pieces in all; that is too much work for her to begin with; she cannot do herself justice; she ought not to write, at the outside, more than two pieces a week; then she could polish them up, and strengthen them, and render them as nearly perfect in execution as they are in conception. One piece a week would be as much as I should wish; could I possibly afford to pay her as much, or more for that one piece, as she now gets for eight? Her name is a tower of strength, but its influence would be frittered away, were she to write for more than one paper. If I could secure her pen all to myself, the advertising that such a connection would give The Messenger would be worth something. Ah me, were my purse only commensurate with my feelings. If I only knew who 'Floy' is, and

could have an interview with her, I might perhaps arrange matters so as to benefit us both; and I *will* know," exclaimed Mr.
Walter, jumping up and pacing the room rapidly; "I 'll know
before I 'm a month older;" and the matter was settled; for when
John Walter paced the floor rapidly, and said "I will," Fate
folded her hands.

CHAPTER LXVIII

"A LETTER for 'Floy!' " said Mr. Lescom, smiling. "Another lover, I suppose. Ah! when you get to be my age," continued the old man, stroking his silver hair, "you will treat their communications with more attention." As he finished his remark, he held the letter up playfully for a moment, and then tossed it into Ruth's lap.

Ruth thrust it unread into her apron pocket. She was thinking of her book, and many other things of far more interest to her than lovers, if lover the writer were. After correcting the proof of her articles for the next week's paper, and looking over a few exchanges, she asked for and received the wages due her for the last articles published, and went home.

Ruth was wearied out; her walk home tired her more than usual. Climbing to her room, she sat down without removing her bonnet and leaning her head upon her hand, tried to look hopefully into the future. She was soon disturbed by Nettie, who exploring her mother's pockets, and finding the letter, exclaimed, pointing to the three cent stamp, "May I have this pretty picture, mamma?"

Ruth drew forth the letter, opened the envelope, cut out the stamp for Nettie, who soon suspended it around her doll's neck for a medal, and then read the epistle, which ran as follows:

"TO 'FLOY':

"Madam,—I have long wished to communicate with you, long wished to know who you are. Since the appearance of your first article, I have watched your course with deep interest, and have witnessed your success with the most unfeigned pleasure. My reasons for wishing to make your acquaintance at this particular juncture, are partly business and partly friendly reasons. As you will see by a copy of the Household Messenger, which I herewith send you, I am its Editor. I know something about the prices paid contributors for the periodical press, and have often wondered whether you were receiving anything like such a remuneration as your genius and practical newspaperial talent entitle you to. I have also often wished to write you on the subject, and tell you what I think is your market-value—to speak in business phrase—as a writer; so that in case you are *not* receiving a just compensation, as things go, you might know it, and act accordingly. In meditating upon the subject, it has occurred to me that I might benefit you and myself at the same time, and in a perfectly legitimate manner, by engaging you to write solely for my paper. I have made a calculation as to what I can afford to give you, or rather what I *will* give you, for writing one article a week for me, the article to be on any subject, and of any length you please. Such an arrangement would of course give you time to take more pains with your writing, and also afford you such leisure for relaxation, as every writer needs.

"Now what I wish you to do is this: I want you first to inform me what you get for writing for The Standard, and The Pilgrim, and if I find that I can afford to give you more, I will make you an offer. If I cannot give you more, I will not trouble you further on that subject; as I seek your benefit more than my own. In case you should accept any offer which I should find it proper to make, it would be necessary for you to tell me your *real* name; as I should wish for a written contract, in order to prevent any possibility of a misunderstanding.

"In conclusion, I beg that you will permit me to say, that whether or not arrangements are made for you to write for me, I shall be most happy to serve you in any way in my power. I have some experience in literary matters, which I will gladly place at your disposal. In short, madam, I feel a warm, brotherly interest in your welfare, as well as a high admiration for your genius, and it will afford me much pleasure to aid you, whenever my services can be made profitable.

"Very truly yours,
JOHN WALTER."

Ruth sat with the letter in her hand. The time *had* been when not a doubt would have arisen in her mind as to the sincerity

of the writer; but, alas! adversity is so rough a teacher! eve~
the cold finger of caution on the warm heart of trust! Ruth
sighed, and tossed the letter on the table, half ashamed of herself
for her cowardice, and wishing that she *could* have faith in the
writer. Then she picked up the letter again. She examined the
hand-writing; it was bold and manly. She thought it would be
treating it too shabbily to throw it aside among the love-sick
trash she was in the habit of receiving. She would read it again.
The tone was respectful; *that won her.* The "Household
Messenger"—"John Walter?"—she certainly had heard those
names before. The letter stated that a copy of the paper had been
sent her, but she had not yet received it. She recollected now
that she had seen the "Household Messenger" among the exchanges at "The Standard" office, and remembered that she always liked its appearance, and admired its editorials; they were
fearless and honest, and always on the side of the weak, and on
the side of truth. Ruth also had an indistinct remembrance of
having heard Mr. Walter spoken of by somebody, at some time,
as a most energetic young man, who had wrung success from an
unwilling world, and fought his way, single-handed, from obscurity to an honorable position in society, against, what would
have been to many, overwhelming odds. "Hence the reason,"
thought Ruth, "his heart so readily vibrates to the chord of
sorrow which I have struck. His experienced heart has detected
in my writings the flutterings and desolation of his own." Ruth
wanted to believe in Mr. Walter. She glanced at his letter again
with increased interest and attention. It seemed so frank and
kind; but then it was bold and exacting, too. The writer wished
to know how much she received from the "Pilgrim," and "Standard," and what was her real name. Would it be prudent to
intrust so much to an entire stranger? and the very first time he
asked, too? Even granting he was actuated by the best of motives,
would he not think if she told him all, without requiring some
further guaranty on his part, that her confidence was too easily

won? Would he not think her too indiscreet to be intrusted with his confidence? Would he not be apt to believe that she had not even sufficient discretion on which to base a business arrangement? And then, if his letter *had been* dictated by idle curiosity only, how unfortunate such an *exposé* of her affairs might be. No—she—could—not—do—it! But then, if Mr. Walter *were* honest, if he *really* felt such a brotherly interest in her, how sweet it would be to have him for a brother; a—*real, warm-hearted, brotherly brother,* such as she had never known. Ruth took up her pen to write to Mr. Walter, but as quickly laid it down. "Oh —I—cannot!" she said; "no, not to a stranger!" Then, again she seized her pen, and with a quick flush, and a warm tear, said, half pettishly, half mournfully, "Away with these ungenerous doubts! Am I never again to put faith in human nature?"

Ruth answered Mr. Walter's letter. She answered it frankly and unreservedly. She stated what wages she was then receiving. She told him her name. As she went on, she felt a peace to which she had long been a stranger. She often paused to wipe the tears—tears of happiness—from her eyes. It was so sweet to believe in *somebody* once more. She wrote a long letter—a sweet, sisterly letter—pouring out her long pent-up feelings, as though Mr. Walter had indeed been her brother, who, having been away ever since before Harry's death, had just returned, and, consequently, had known nothing about her cruel sufferings. After she had sealed and superscribed the letter, she became excessively frightened at what she had done, and thought she never could send it to Mr. Walter; but another perusal of his letter reassured her. She rose to go to the post-office, and then became conscious that she had not removed her bonnet and shawl, but had sat all this while in walking costume! "Well," said she, laughing, "this *is* rather blue-stocking-y; however, it is all the better, as I am now ready for my walk." Ruth carried her letter to the post-office; dropping it into the letter-box with more hopeful feelings than Noah probably experienced when he sent forth the dove from the ark for the third time.

CHAPTER LXIX

M R. WALTER sat in his office, looking over the morning mail. "I wonder is this from 'Floy'?" he said, as he examined a compact little package. "It bears the right postmark, and the handwriting is a lady's. A splendid hand it is, too. There 's character in that hand; I hope 'tis 'Floy's.' "

Mr. Walter broke the seal, and glancing at a few sentences, turned to the signature. "Yes, it is 'Floy'! now for a revelation." He then commenced perusing the letter with the most intense interest. After reading the first page his eye began to flash, and his lip to quiver. "Poor girl—poor girl—heartless creatures—too bad—too bad," and other exclamations rather too warm for publication; finishing the letter and refolding it, he paced the room with a short, quick step, indicative of deep interest, and determined purpose. "It is too bad," he exclaimed; "shameful! the whole of it; and how hard she has worked! and what a pitiful sum those fellows pay her! it is contemptible. She has about made The Standard; it never was heard of to any extent before she commenced writing for it. It is perfectly outrageous; she shall not write for them another day, if I can help it! I will make her an offer at once. She will accept it; and then those Jews will be brought to their senses. Ha! ha! I know them! They will want to get her back; they will write to me about it, or at least Lescom will. That will give me a chance at him; and if I don't tell him a few truths in plain English, my name is not John Walter." Then seating himself at his desk, Mr. Walter wrote the following letter to 'Floy':

"DEAR SISTER RUTH,—If you will permit me to be so brotherly. I have received, read, and digested your letter; how it has affected

me I will not now tell you. I wish to say, however, that on
reading that portion of it which relates to the compensation you
are now receiving, my indignation exhausted the dictionary!
Why, you poor, dear little genius! what you write for those two
papers is worth, to the proprietors, ten times what they pay you.
But I will not bore you with compliments; I wish to engage you
to write for the Household Messenger, and here is my offer: you
to write one article a week, length, matter and manner, to your
own fancy; I to pay you ——, the engagement to continue one
year, during which time you are not to write for any other periodical, without my consent. My reason for placing a limitation
to our engagement is, that you may be able to take advantage at
that time of better offers, which you will undoubtedly have.

"I inclose duplicates of a contract, which, if the terms suit,
you will please sign and return one copy *by the next mail;* the
other copy you will keep. Unless you accept my offer by return
of mail it will be withdrawn. You may think this exacting; I will
explain it in my next to your satisfaction. Most truly your friend,
                                        "JOHN WALTER."

This letter being dispatched, thanks to the post-office depart-
ment, arrived promptly at its destination the next morning.

Ruth sat with Mr. Walter's letter in her hand, thinking. " 'If
you do not accept my offer by return of mail, it will be withdrawn.' How exacting! 'the explanation of this to be given in
my next letter,' ah, Mr. John Walter, I shall not have to wait
till then," soliloquized Ruth; "I can jump at your reason; you
think I shall mention it to Mr. Lescom, and that then he will
interfere, and offer something by way of an equivalent to tempt
me to reject it; that 's it, Mr. John Walter! This bumping round
the world has at least sharpened my wits!" and Ruth sat beating
a tattoo with the toe of her slipper on the carpet, and looking
very profound and wise. Then she took up the contract and
examined it; it was brief, plain and easily understood, *even by a
woman,* as the men say. "It is a good offer," said Ruth, "he is
in earnest, so am I; it 's a bargain." Ruth signed the document.

CHAPTER LXX

"GOOD afternoon, 'Floy.' " said Mr. Lescom to Ruth, as she entered the Standard office, the day after she had signed the contract with Mr. Walter. "I was just thinking of you, and wishing for an opportunity to have a little private chat. Your articles are not as long as they used to be; you must be more liberal."

"I was not aware," replied Ruth, "that my articles had grown any shorter. However, with me, an article is an article, some of my shorter pieces being the most valuable I have written. If you would like more matter, Mr. Lescom, I wonder you have not offered me more pay."

"There it is," said Mr. Lescom, smiling; "women are never satisfied. The more they get, the more grasping they become. I have always paid you more than you could get anywhere else."

"Perhaps so," replied Ruth. "I believe I have never troubled you with complaints; but I *have* looked at my children some-times, and thought that I must try somehow to get more; and I have sometimes thought that if my articles, as you have told me, were constantly bringing you new subscribers, friendship, if not justice, would induce you to raise my salary."

"*Friendship* has nothing to do with business," replied Mr. Lescom; "a bargain is a bargain. The law of supply and demand regulates prices in all cases. In literature, at present, the supply greatly exceeds the demand, consequently the prices are low. Of course, I have to regulate my arrangements according to my own interests, and not according to the interests of others. You, of course, must regulate your arrangements according to *your* interests; and if anybody else will give you more than I do, you are at liberty to take it. As I said before, *business* is one thing—

189

friendship is another. Each is good in its way, but they are quite distinct."

As Mr. Lescom finished this business–like and logical speech, he looked smilingly at Ruth, with an air which might be called one of tyrannical benevolence; as if he would say, "Well, now, I 'd like to know what you can find to say to that?"

"I am glad," replied Ruth, "that you think so, for I have already acted in accordance with your sentiments. I have had, and accepted, an offer of a better salary than you pay me. My object in calling this afternoon was to inform you of this; and to say, that I shall not be able to write any more for 'The Standard.' "

Mr. Lescom looked astonished, and gazed at Ruth without speaking, probably because he did not know exactly what to say. He had argued Ruth's case so well, while he supposed he was arguing his own, that nothing more could be said. Mr. Lescom, in reality, valued Ruth's services more than those of all his other contributors combined, and the loss of them was a bitter thing to him. And then, what would his subscribers say? The reason of Ruth's leaving might become known; it would not sound well to have it said that she quit writing for him because he did not, or could not, or would not pay her as much as others. Just then it occurred to him that engaging to write for another jour- nal, did not necessarily preclude the possibility of her continuing to write for "The Standard." Catching eagerly at the idea, he said:

"Well, 'Floy,' I am really glad that you have been so fortunate. Of course I wish you to make as much as you can, and should be glad, did my circumstances admit, to give you a salary equal to what you can command elsewhere; but as I cannot give you more than I have been paying, I am glad somebody else will. Still, I see no reason why you should stop writing for 'The Standard.' Your articles will just be as valuable to me, as though you had made no new engagement."

"I am sorry to disappoint you, Mr. Lescom," replied Ruth, "but I cannot meet your wishes in this respect, as the contract I have signed will not permit me to write for any paper but 'The Household Messenger.' "

At this announcement Mr. Lescom's veil of good nature was rent in twain. " 'The Household Messenger!' Ah! it 's John Walter, then, who has found you out? I don't wish to boast, but I must say, that I think you have made but a poor exchange. The whole thing is very unfortunate for you. I was just making arrangements to club with two other editors, and to offer you a handsome yearly salary for writing exclusively for our three papers; but of course that arrangement is all knocked in the head now. It seems to me that you might have made an exception in favor of 'The Standard.' I have no doubt that Mr. Walter would have consented to let you write for it, as it was the first paper for which you ever wrote. He would probably do so now if you would ask him. He is an editor, and would understand the matter at once. He would see that I had more than ordinary claims upon you. What do you say to writing him on the subject?"

"I have no objection to doing so," replied Ruth, "if you think it will avail anything, though if I succeed in getting Mr. Walter's permission to write for *you,* I suppose Mr. Tibbetts, of The Pilgrim, will wish me to do the same for him, when he returns. I called at the Pilgrim office this morning, and his partner, Mr. Elder, said that he was out of town, and would not be home for several days, and that he would be greatly incensed when he heard I was going to leave, as I was getting very popular with his subscribers. Mr. Elder was very sorry himself, but he treated me courteously. By the way, Mr. Lescom, I think you had better write to Mr. Walter, as well as myself; you understand such matters, and can probably write more to the point than I can."

"Very well," said Mr. Lescom, "I will write to him at once,

and you had better write now by the same mail, and have the letters both enclosed in one envelope."

Ruth took a seat at the editorial table, and wrote to Mr. Walter. The letters were sent at once to the post-office, so as to catch the afternoon mail, and Ruth took her leave, promising to call on the morning of the second day after, to see Mr. Walter's reply, which, judging by his usual promptness, would arrive by that time.

CHAPTER LXXI

"A H! another letter from 'Floy,' " said Mr. Walter, as he seated himself in his office; "now I shall hear how Lescom and Tibbetts & Co., feel about losing her. 'Floy' had probably told them by the time she wrote, and they have probably told her that she owes her reputation to them, called her ungrateful, and all that sort of thing; let us see what she says."

After reading 'Floy's' letter, Mr. Walter laid it down and began muttering out his thoughts after his usual fashion. "Just as I expected; Lescom has worked on 'Floy's' kind heart till she really feels a sort of necessity not to leave him so abruptly, and requests me as a personal favor to grant his request, at least for a time; no, no, 'Floy'—not unless he will pay you five times as much as he pays you now, and allow you, besides, to write much, or little, as you please; but where is Lescom's communication? Ruth says he wrote by the same mail—ah, here it is:

"MR. WALTER:

SIR,—Mrs. Hall, 'Floy,' informs me that you have engaged her to write exclusively for the Household Messenger, and that you will not consent to her writing for any other publication. Perhaps you are not aware that *I* was the first to introduce 'Floy' to the public, and that I have made her reputation what it is. This being the case, you will not think it strange that I feel as if I had some claim on her, so long as I pay her as much as she can get elsewhere. I need not say to you that The Standard is in a very flourishing condition; its circulation having nearly doubled during the past year, and that my resources are such as to enable me to outbid all competitors for 'Floy's' services, if I choose to take such a course; but I trust you will at once perceive that the

Standard should be made an exception to your contract, and
permit 'Floy' still to write for it.

> "Respectfully yours,
>
> F. LESCOM."

"Well, upon my word," exclaimed Mr. Walter, when he had
finished Mr. Lescom's letter; "if this is not the coolest piece of
egotism and impudence that I ever saw, but it is no use wasting
vitality about it. I will just answer the letter, and let things take
their course; I have the weather-gage of him now, and I 'll keep
it; he shall have my reply to digest the first thing in the morning;
I 'll write to 'Floy' first, though."

On the designated Thursday, Ruth, according to her promise,
called at the Standard office; something had occurred to detain
Mr. Lescom, so she sat down and opened Mr. Walter's letter,
which lay on the table waiting for her, and read as follows:

"DEAR RUTH:

"I have just finished reading yours and Lescom's letters. Yours
has touched me deeply. It was just like you, but you know little
of the selfishness and humbuggery of some newspaper publishers;
you seem really to think that you ought to write for Mr. Lescom,
if he so much desires it. This is very good of you, and very
amiable, but (forgive my want of gallantry) very foolish. You can
now understand, if you did not before, why I desired you to sign
the contract by return mail. I was afraid if you went to Mr.
Lescom, or Mr. Tibbetts of the Pilgrim, *before signing it,* that they
would impose upon your good womanly heart, and thereby gain
an unfair advantage over you. I wished to surprise you into signing the contract, that I might have a fair and righteous advantage
over them. And now, 'Floy,' please to leave the whole matter
to me. I shall not consent to your writing for any paper, unless
the proprietors will give you the full value of your articles—
what they are really worth to them. If things turn out as I con-
fidently expect they will, from your present popularity, you will

soon be in a state of comparative independence. On the next page you will find a copy of my answer to Mr. Lescom's letter. Please keep me informed of the happenings at your end of the route.

"Yours most truly,

JOHN WALTER."

Ruth then read Mr. Walter's letter to Mr. Lescom, as follows:

"F. LESCOM, Esq.

"SIR,—Your letter in regard to 'Floy,' &c., is at hand. You say, that perhaps I am not aware that *you* were the first to introduce 'Floy' to the public, and that *you* have made her reputation. It is fortunate for *you* that she made The Standard the channel of her first communications to the public. I know this very well, but I am not aware, nor do I believe, that *you* have made her reputation; neither do I think that you believe this yourself. The truth is simply this; 'Floy' is a genius; her writings, wherever published, would have attracted attention, and stamped the writer as a person of extraordinary talent; hence her fame and success, the fruits of which *you* have principally reaped. As to 'Floy's' being under any obligations to you, I repudiate the idea entirely; the 'obligation' is all on the other side. *She* has made 'The Standard,' instead of you making *her* reputation. Her genius has borne its name to England, Scotland, Ireland,—wherever the English language is spoken,—and raised it from an obscure provincial paper to a widely-known journal. You say that you are wealthy, and can pay as much as any body for 'Floy's' services; I wonder this has never occurred to you before, especially as she has informed you frequently how necessitous were her circumstances. You also inform me that the circulation of The Standard has nearly doubled the past year. This I can readily believe, since it is something more than a year since 'Floy' commenced writing for it. In reply to your declaration, 'that in case you are driven to compete for 'Floy's' services, you can outbid all competitors,' I have only to say that my contract with her is for one year; on its expiration, 'Floy' will be at liberty to decide for herself; you will then have an opportunity to compete for her pen, and enjoy the privilege of exhibiting your enterprise and liberality.

          "Your ob't servant,

                JOHN WALTER."

Ruth waited some time after reading these letters, for Mr. Lescom to come in; but, finding he was still unexpectedly detained, she took a handful of letters, which the clerk had just received by mail for her, and bent her steps homeward.

CHAPTER LXXII

THE first letter Ruth opened on her return, was a request from a Professor of some College for her autograph for himself and some friends; the second, an offer of marriage from a Southerner, who confessed to one hundred negroes, "but hoped that the strength and ardor of the attachment with which the perusal of her articles had inspired him, would be deemed sufficient atonement for this in her Northern eyes. The frozen North," he said, "had no claim on such a nature as hers; the sunny South, the land of magnolias and orange blossoms, the land of love, *should* be her chosen home. Would she not smile on him? She should have a box at the opera, a carriage, and servants in livery, and the whole heart and soul of Victor Le Pont."

The next was more interesting. It was an offer to "Floy" from a publishing house, to collect her newspaper articles into a volume. They offered to give her so much on a copy, or $800 for the copyright. An answer was requested immediately. In the same mail came another letter of the same kind from a distant State, also offering to publish a volume of her articles.

"Well, well," soliloquized Ruth, "business is accumulating. I don't see but I shall have to make a book in spite of myself; and yet those articles were written under such disadvantages, would it be *wise* in me to publish so soon? But Katy? and $800 copyright money?" Ruth glanced round her miserable, dark room, and at the little stereotyped bowl of bread and milk that stood waiting on the table for her supper and Nettie's; $800 *copyright money!* it *was* a temptation; but supposing her book should prove a hit? and bring double, treble, fourfold that sum, to go into her publisher's pockets instead of hers? how provoking! Ruth straightened up, and putting on a very resolute air, said, "No, gentlemen, I will *not* sell you my copyright; these autograph letters, and all the other letters of friendship, love, and business, I am constantly receiving from strangers, are so many proofs that I have won the public ear. No, I will not sell my copyright; I will rather deny myself a while longer, and accept the percentage;" and so she sat down and wrote her publishers; but then caution whispered, what if her book should *not* sell? "Oh, pshaw," said Ruth, "it *shall!*" and she brought her little fist down on the table till the old stone inkstand seemed to rattle out *"it shall!"*

"Ah, here is another letter, which I have overlooked," said Ruth.

"TO THE DISTINGUISHED AND POPULAR WRITER, 'FLOY':

"MADAM,—I trust you will excuse the liberty I take in writing you, when you get through with my letter. I am thus confident of your leniency, because it seems to me that my case is not only a plain, but an interesting one. To come to the point, without any circumlocutory delay, I am a young man with aspirations far above my station in life. This declaration is perfectly true in some senses, but not in every sense. My parents and my ancestors are and were highly respectable people. My name, as you will see when you come to my signature, is Reginald Danby. The Danby family, Madam, was founded by Sir Reginald Danby, who was knighted for certain gallant exploits on the field of Hastings, in the year 1066, by William the Conqueror. Sir Reginald afterward married a Saxon dame, named Edith, the daughter of a powerful land-owner; hence the Danby family. All this is of very little consequence, and I only mention it in a sort of incidental way, to show you that my declaration in regard to the respectability of my family is true, and fortified by unimpeachable historical evidence; and I will here remark, that you will always find any assertion of mine as well sustained, by copious and irrefragable proof.

"The respectability of our family being thus settled, I come back to an explanation of what I mean by my 'having aspirations above my station in life.' It is this: I am poor. My family, though once wealthy, is now impoverished. The way this state of things came about, was substantially as follows: My grandfather, who was a strong-minded, thrifty gentleman, married into a poetical family. His wife was the most poetical member of said family; much of her poetry is still extant; it never was published, because in those days publishers were not as enterprising as they are now. We value these manuscripts very highly; still I should be willing to send you some of them for perusal, in case you will return them and pay the postage both ways, my limited means not permitting me to share that pleasure with you. As I have intimated, my grandmother reveled in poetry. She doated on Shakspeare, and about three months before my father's birth, she went to a theater to witness the performance of 'The Midsummer Night's Dream.' She was enchanted! and, with characteristic decision, resolved to commit the entire play to memory. This resolution she executed with characteristic pertinacity, notwithstanding frequent and annoying interruptions, from various causes entirely beyond her control. She finished committing this immortal poem to memory, the very night my father was born. Time rolled on; my father, as he grew up exhibited great flightiness of character, and instability of purpose, the result, undoubtedly, of his mother's committing 'The Midsummer Night's Dream' to memory under the circumstances which I have detailed. My father, owing to this unfortunate development of character, proved inadequate to the management of his estate, or, indeed, of any business whatever, and hence our present pecuniary embarrassments. Before quitting this painful branch of my subject, it will doubtless gratify you to have me state, that, inasmuch as my father married a woman of phlegmatic temperament, and entirely unpoetical mind, the balance of character has been happily restored to our family, so there is no fear for me. I am thus particular in my statements, because I have a high regard for truth, and for veracity, for accuracy in the *minutest* things; a phase of character which may be accounted for from the fact, that I have just gone through a severe and protracted course of mathematics. These preliminaries being thus fairly before you, I now come to the immediate topic of my letter, viz.: I wish to go through College; I have not the means. I wish you to help me. You are probably rich; I hope you are with all my heart. You must be able to command a high salary, and a great deal of influence. I don't ask you to lend me the money out of hand. What I propose is this: I will furnish you the subject for a splendid and thrilling story, founded on facts in the history of our family; the Danby family. In this book, my grandmother's poetry would probably read to advantage; if so, it would be a great saving, as her writings are voluminous. Your book would be sure to have a large sale, and the profits would pay my expenses at College, and perhaps leave a large surplus. This surplus should be yours, and I would also agree to pay back the sum used by me from my first earnings after graduation. I have thought over this matter a great deal, and the foregoing strikes me as the only way in which this thing can be done. If you can devise a better plan, I will of course gladly adopt it. I am not at all opinionated, but am always glad to listen to anything reasonable. Please let me hear from you as soon as possible, and believe me truly your friend and admirer,

"REGINALD DANBY."

CHAPTER LXXIII

M R. TIBBETTS, the editor of "The Pilgrim," having returned from the country, Ruth went to the Pilgrim office to get copies of several of her articles, which she had taken no pains to keep, never dreaming of republishing them in book form.

Mr. Tibbetts was sitting at his editorial desk, looking over a pile of manuscript. Ruth made known her errand, and also the fact of her being about to publish her book. He handed her a chair, and drawing another in front of her, said very stiffly, "My partner, Mr. Elder, Mrs. Hall, has astonished me by the information that you have very suddenly decided to withdraw from us, who first patronized you, and to write for the 'Household Messenger.' "

"Yes," replied Ruth, "I considered it my duty to avail myself of that increase of salary. My circumstances have been exceedingly straitened. I have two little ones dependent on my exertions, and *their* future, as well as my own, to look to. You have often told me that you already paid me all you could afford, so it was useless to ask you for more; beside, the contract I have accepted, obliged me to decline or accept it by return of mail, without communicating its contents."

"Ah! I see—I see," said Mr. Tibbetts, growing very red in the face, and pushing back his chair; "it is always the way young writers treat those who have made their reputation."

"Perhaps *your* making my reputation, may be a question open to debate," answered Ruth, stung by his tone; "I feel this morning, however; disinclined to discuss the question; so, if you please, we will waive it. You have always told me that you were constantly beset by the most talented contributors for patronage,

urse you will not find it difficult to supply my place,
you."

shall *not* leave," said Mr. Tibbetts, turning very pale
about the mouth, and closing his lips firmly.

"*Shall not!*" repeated Ruth, rising, and standing erect before
him. "*Shall* not, Mr. Tibbetts? I have yet to learn that I am not
free to go, if I choose."

"Well, you are *not*," said Mr. Tibbetts; "that is a little mistake
of yours, as I will soon convince you. Discontinue writing for
'The Pilgrim,' and I will immediately get out a cheap edition of
your articles, and spoil the sale of your book;" and he folded his
arms, and faced Ruth as if he would say, "Now writhe if you
like; I have you."

Ruth smiled derisively, then answered in a tone so low that
it was scarcely audible, "Mr. Tibbetts, you have mistaken your
auditor. I am not to be frightened, or threatened, or *insulted*,"
said she, turning toward the door. "Even had I not myself the
spirit to defy you, as I now do, for I will never touch pen to
paper again for 'The Pilgrim,' you could not accomplish your
threat; for think you my publishers will tamely fold their arms,
and see *their* rights infringed? No, sir, you have mistaken both
them and me;" and Ruth moved toward the door.

"Stay!" exclaimed Mr. Tibbetts, placing his hand on the latch;
"when you see a paragraph in print that will sting your proud
soul to the quick, know that John Tibbetts has more ways than
one of humbling so imperious a dame."

"That will be hardly consistent," replied Ruth, in the same
calm tone, "with the thousand-and-one commendatory notices
of 'Floy'—the boasts you have made of the almost exclusive
right to the *valuable services of so bright a literary star.*"

"Of course you will not see such a paragraph in *my* paper,"
replied Mr. Tibbetts. "I am aware, most logical of women, that
I stand committed before the public *there;* but I have many an

editorial friend, scattered over the country, who would loan me *their* columns for this purpose."

"As you please," said Ruth. "It were a *manly* act; but your threat does not move *me*."

"I 'll have my revenge!" exclaimed Tibbetts, as the last fold of Ruth's dress fluttered out the door.

CHAPTER LXXIV

THOSE of my readers who are well acquainted with journalism, know that some of our newspapers, nominally edited by the persons whose names appear as responsible in that capacity, *seldom,* perhaps *never* contain an article from their pen, the whole paper being "made up" by some obscure individual, with more brains than pennies, whose brilliant paragraphs, metaphysical essays, and racy book reviews, are attributed (and tacitly fathered) by the comfortably-fed gentlemen who keep these, their factotums, in some garret, just one degree above starving point. In the city, where board is expensive, and single gentlemen are "taken in and done for," under many a sloping attic roof are born thoughts which should win for their originators fame and independence.

Mr. Horace Gates, a gentlemanly, slender, scholar-like-looking person, held this nondescript, and unrecognized relation to the Irving Magazine; the nominal editor, Ruth's brother Hyacinth, furnishing but one article a week, to deduct from the immense amount of labor necessary to their weekly issue.

"Heigho," said Mr. Gates, dashing down his pen; "four columns yet to make up; I am getting tired of this drudgery. My friend Seaten told me that he was dining at a restaurant the other day, when my employer, Mr. Hyacinth Ellet, came in, and that a gentleman took occasion to say to Mr. E., how much he admired *his* article in the last Irving Magazine, on 'City Life.' *His* article! it took me one of the hottest days this season, in this furnace of a garret, with the beaded drops standing on my suffering forehead, to write that article, which, by the way, has been copied far and wide. His article! and the best of the joke is (Seaten says) the cool way in which Ellet thanked him, and pocketed all the credit of it! But what 's this? here 's a note from the very gentleman himself:

"MR. GATES:

"SIR,—I have noticed that you have several times scissorized from the exchanges, articles over the signature of 'Floy,' and inserted them in our paper. It is my wish that all articles bearing that signature should be excluded from our paper, and that no allusion be made to her, in any way or shape, in the columns of the Irving Magazine. As you are in our business confidence, I may say, that the writer is a sister of mine, and that it would annoy and mortify me exceedingly to have the fact known; and it is my express wish that you should not, hereafter, in any way, aid in circulating her articles.

"Yours, &c.,

HYACINTH ELLET."

"What does that mean?" said Gates; "*his* sister? why don't he want her to write? I have cut out every article of hers as fast as they appeared; confounded good they are, too, and I call myself a judge; they are better, at any rate, than half our paper is filled with. This is all very odd—it stimulates my curiosity amazingly—*his* sister? married or unmarried, maid, wife, or widow? She can't be poor when he 's so well off; (gave $100 for a vase which struck his fancy yesterday, at Martini's.) I don't understand it. 'Annoy and mortify him exceedingly;' what *can* he mean? I must get at the bottom of that; she is becoming very popular, at any rate; her pieces are traveling all over the country—and here is one, to my mind, as good as anything *he* ever wrote. Ha! ha! perhaps that 's the very idea now—perhaps he wants to be the only genius in the family. Let him! if he can; if she don't win an enviable name, and in a very short time too, I shall be mistaken. I wish I knew something about her. Hyacinth is a heartless dog—pays me principally in fine speeches; and because I am not in a position just now to speak my mind about it, I suppose he takes me for the pliant tool I appear, By Jupiter! it makes my blood boil; but let me get another and better offer, Mr. Ellet, and see how long I will write articles for you to father, in this confounded hot garret. '*His* sister!' I will inquire into that. I 'll bet a box of cigars she writes for daily bread—Heaven help her, if she does, poor thing!—it 's hard enough, as I know, for a *man* to be jostled and snubbed round in printing-offices. Well, well, it 's no use wondering, I must go to work; what a pile of books here is to be reviewed! wonder who reads all the books? Here is Uncle Sam's Log House. Mr. Ellet writes me that I must simply announce the book without comment, for fear of offending southern subscribers. The word 'slave' I know has been tabooed in our columns this long while, for the same reason. Here are poems by Lina Lintney—weak as diluted water, but the authoress once paid Mr. Ellet a compliment in a newspaper article, and here is her 'reward of merit,' (in a memorandum attached to the book, and just sent down by Mr. Ellet;) 'give this volume a first-rate notice.' Bah! what 's the use of criticism when a man's opinion can be bought and sold that way? it is an imposition on the public. There is 'The Barolds' too; I am to 'give that a capital notice,' because the authoress introduced Mr. Ellet into fashionable society when a young man. The grammar in that book would give Lindley Murray convulsions, and the construction of the sentences drive Blair to a madhouse. Well, a great deal the dear public know what a book is, by the reviews of it in this paper. Heaven forgive me the lies I tell this way on compulsion.

"The humbuggery of this establishment is only equaled by the gullibility of the dear public. Once a month, now, I am ordered to puff every 'influential paper in the Union,' to ward off attacks on the Irving Magazine, and the bait takes, too, by Jove. That little 'Tea-Table Tri-Mountain Mercury,' has not muttered or peeped about Hyacinth's 'toadyism when abroad,' since Mr. Ellet gave me orders to praise 'the typographical and literary excellence of that widely-circulated paper.' Then, there is the editor of 'The Bugbear,' a cut-and-thrust-bludgeon-pen-and-ink-desperado, who makes the mincing, aristocratic Hyacinth quake in his patent-leather boots. I have orders to toss him a sugar-plum occasionally, to keep his plebeian mouth shut; something after the French maxim, 'always to praise a person for what they *are not;*'—for instance, 'our very *gentlemanly* neighbor and contemporary, the discriminating and refined editor of The Bugbear, whose very readable and spicy paper,' &c., &c. Then, there is the *religious* press. Hyacinth, having rather a damaged reputation, is anxious to enlist them on his side, particularly the editor of 'The Religious Platform.' I am to copy at least one of his editorials once a fortnight, or in some way call attention to his paper. Then, if Hyacinth chooses to puff actresses, and call Mme. ———— a 'splendid personation of womanhood,' and praise her equivocal writings in his paper, which lies on many a family table to be read by innocent young girls, he knows the caustic pen of that religious editor will never be dipped in ink to reprove him. That is the way it is done. Mutual admiration-society—bah! I wish *I* had a paper. Would n't I call things by their right names? Would I know any sex in books? Would I praise a book because a woman wrote it? Would I abuse it for the same reason? Would I say, as one of our most able editors said not long since to his reviewer, 'cut it up root and branch; what right have these women to set themselves up for authors, and reap literary laurels?' Would I unfairly insert all the adverse notices of a book, and never copy one in its praise? Would I pass over the wholesale swindling of some aristocratic scoundrel, and trumpet in my police report, with heartless comments, the name of some poor, tempted, starving wretch, far less deserving of censure, in God's eye, than myself? Would I have my tongue or my pen tied in any way by policy, or interest, or clique-ism? No—sir! The world never will see a paper till mine is started. Would I write long descriptions of the wardrobe of foreign *prima donnas,* who bring their cracked voices, and reputations to our

American market, and 'occupy suites of rooms lined with satin, and damask, and velvet,' and goodness knows what, and give their reception-soirees, at which they *affably notice* our toadying first citizens? By Jupiter! why *should n't* they be 'affable'? Don't they come over here for our money and patronage? Who cares how many 'bracelets' Signora ——— had on, or whose 'arm she leaned gracefully upon,' or whether her 'hair was braided or curled'? If, because a lord or a duke once 'honored her' by insulting her with infamous proposals, some few brainless Americans choose to deify her as a goddess, in the name of George Washington and common sense, let it not be taken as a national exponent. There are some few Americans left, who prefer ipecac in homeopathic doses."

CHAPTER LXXV

"HARK! Nettie. Go to the door, dear," said Ruth, "some one knocked."

"It is a strange gentleman, mamma," whispered Nettie, "and he wants to see you."

Ruth bowed as the stranger entered. She could not recollect that she had ever seen him before, but he looked very knowing, and, what was very provoking, seemed to enjoy her embarrassment hugely. He regarded Nettie, too, with a very scrutinizing look, and seemed to devour everything with the first glance of his keen, searching eye. He even seemed to listen to the whir —whir—whir of the odd strange lodger in the garret overhead.

"I don't recollect you," said Ruth, hesitating, and blushing slightly; "you have the advantage of me, sir?"

"And yet you and I have been writing to each other, for a week or more," replied the gentleman, with a good-humored smile; "you have even signed a contract, entitling me to your pen-and-ink services."

"Mr. Walter?" said Ruth, holding out her hand.

"Yes," replied Mr. Walter, "I had business this way, and I could not come here without finding you out."

"Oh, thank you," said Ruth, "I was just wishing that I had some head wiser than mine, to help me decide on a business matter which came up two or three days ago. Somehow I don't feel the least reluctance to bore you with it, or a doubt that your advice will not be just the thing; but I shall not stop to dissect the philosophy of that feeling, lest in grasping at the shadow, I should lose the substance," said she, smiling.

While Ruth was talking, Mr. Walter's keen eye glanced about the room, noting its general comfortless appearance, and the little bowl of bread and milk that stood waiting for their supper. Ruth observed this, and blushed deeply. When she looked again at Mr. Walter, his eyes were glistening with tears.

"Come here, my darling," said he to Nettie, trying to hide his emotion.

"I don't know you," answered Nettie.

"But you will, my dear, because I am your mamma's friend."

"Are you Katy's friend?" asked Nettie.

"Katy?" repeated Mr. Walter.

"Yes, my *sister* Katy; she can't live here, because we don't have supper enough; pretty soon mamma will earn more supper, won't you mamma? Shan't you be glad when Katy comes home, and we all have enough to eat?" said the child to Mr. Walter.

Mr. Walter pressed his lips to the child's forehead with a low "Yes, my darling;" and then placed his watch chain and seals at her disposal, fearing Ruth might be painfully affected by her artless prattle.

Ruth then produced the different publishers' offers she had received for her book, and handed them to Mr. Walter.

"Well," said he, with a gratified smile, "I am not at all surprised; but what are you going to reply?"

"Here is my answer," said Ruth, "*i. e.,* provided your judgment indorses it. I am a novice in such matters, you know, but I cannot help thinking, Mr. Walter, that my book will be a success. You will see that I have acted upon that impression, and refused to sell my copyright."

"You don't approve it?" said she, looking a little confused, as Mr. Walter bent his keen eyes on her, without replying.

"But I do though," said he; "I was only thinking how excellent a substitute strong common-sense may be for experience. Your answer is brief, concise, sagacious, and business-like; I indorse it unhesitatingly. It is just what I should have advised you to write. You are correct in thinking that your book will be popular, and wise in keeping the copyright in your own hands.

In how incredibly short a time you have gained a literary reputation, Floy."

"Yes," answered Ruth, smiling, "it is all like a dream to
me;" and then the smile faded away, and she shuddered involuntarily as the recollection of all her struggles and sufferings came
vividly up to her remembrance.

Swiftly the hours fled away as Mr. Walter, with a brother's
freedom, questioned Ruth as to her past life, and drew from her
the details of her eventful history.

"Thank God, the morning dawneth," said he in a subdued
tone, as he pressed Ruth's hand, and bade her a parting good-
night.

Ruth closed the door upon Mr. Walter's retreating figure,
and sat down to peruse the following letters, which had been
sent her to Mr. Walter's care, at the Household Messenger office.

"MRS. OR MISS 'FLOY:'

"Permit me to address you on a subject which lies near my
heart, which is, in fact, a subject of pecuniary importance to the
person now addressing you. My story is to me a painful one; it
would doubtless interest you; were it written and published, it
would be a thrilling tale.

"Some months since I had a lover whom I adored, and who
said he adored me. But as Shakspeare has said, 'The course of
true love never did run smooth,' ours soon became an up-hill
affair, my lover proved false, ceased his visits, and sat on the other
side of the meeting-house. On my writing to him and desiring
an explanation, he insultingly replied, that I was not what his
fancy had painted me. Was that *my* fault? false, fickle, ungenerous
man! But I was not thus to be deceived and shuffled off. No, I
employed the best counsel in the State and commenced an action
for damages, determined to get some balm for my wounded feelings; but owing to the premature death of my principal witness,
I lost the case and the costs were heavy. The excitement and
worry of the trial brought on a fever, and I found myself on my
recovery, five hundred dollars in debt; I intend to pay every cent

of this, but how am I to pay it? My salary for teaching school is
small and it will take me many years. I want you, therefore, to
assist me by writing out my story and giving me the book. I will
furnish all the facts, and the story, written out by your magic
pen, would be a certain success. A publisher in this city has
agreed to publish it for me if you will write it. I could then
triumph over the villain who so basely deceived me.

"Please send me an early answer, as the publisher referred to
is in a great hurry.

"Very respectfully yours,

"SARAH JARMESIN."

"Well," said Ruth, laughing, "my bump of invention will be
entirely useless, if my kind friends keep on furnishing me with
subjects at this rate. Here is letter No. 2."

"DEAR 'FLOY':

"My dog Fido is dead. He was a splendid Newfoundland,
black and shaggy; father gave $10 for him when he was a pup.
We all loved him dearly. He was a prime dog, could swim like
a fish. The other morning we found him lying motionless on the
door-step. Somebody had poisoned poor Fido. I cried all that
day, and did n't play marbles for a whole week. He is buried in
the garden, and I want you to write an epithalamium about him.
My brother John, who is looking over my shoulder, is laughing
like everything; he says 't is an epitaph, not an epithalamium that
I want, just as if *I* did n't know what I want? John is just home
from college, and thinks he knows everything. It is my dog, and
I 'll fix his tombstone just as I like. Fellows in round jackets are
not always fools. Send it along quick, please, 'Floy'; the stone-
cutter is at work now. What a funny way they cut marble, don't
they? (with sand and water.) Johnny Weld and I go there every
recess, to see how they get on with the tombstone. Don't stick
in any Latin or Greek, now, in your epithalamium. Our John
cannot call for a glass of water without lugging in one or the
other of them; I 'm sick as death of it. I wonder if I shall be such
a fool when I go to college. You ought to be glad you are a

woman, and don't have to go. Don't forget Fido, now. Remember, he was six years old, black, shaggy, with a white spot on his forehead, and rather a short-ish tail—a prime dog, I tell *you*.

"BILLY SANDS."

"It is a harrowing case, Billy," said Ruth, "but I shall have to let Fido pass; now for letter No. 3."

"DEAR MADAM:

"I address a stranger, and yet *not* a stranger, for I have read your heart in your many writings. In them I see sympathy for the poor, the sorrowing, and the dependent; I see a tender love for helpless childhood. Dear 'Floy,' I am an orphan, and that most wretched of all beings, a loving, but unloved wife. The hour so dreaded by all maternity draws near to me. It has been revealed to me in dreams that I shall not survive it. 'Floy,' will you be a mother to my babe? I cannot tell you why I put this trust in one whom I have only known through her writings, but something assures me it will be safe with you; that you only can fill my place in the little heart that this moment is pulsating beneath my own. Oh, do not refuse me. There are none in the wide world to dispute the claim I would thus transfer to you. Its father—but of him I will not speak; the wine-cup is my rival. Write me speedily. I shall die content if your arms receive my babe.

"Yours affectionately,
MARY ANDREWS."

"Poor Mary! that letter must be answered," said Ruth, with a sigh;—"ah, here is one more letter."

"MISS, OR MRS., OR MADAM FLOY:

"I suppose by this time you have become so inflated that the honest truth would be rather unpalatable to you; nevertheless, I am going to send you a few plain words. The rest of the world flatters you—I shall do no such thing. You have written tolerably, all things considered, but you violate all established rules of composition, and are as lawless and erratic as a comet. You may startle and dazzle, but you are fit only to throw people out of their orbits. Now and then, there 's a gleam of something like reason in your writings, but for the most part they are unmitigated trash—false in sentiment—unrhetorical in expression; in short, were you my daughter, which I thank a good Providence you are not, I should box your ears, and keep you on a bread and water diet till you improved. That you *can* do better, if you will, I am very sure, and that is why I take the pains to find fault, and tell you what none of your fawning friends will.

"You are not a genius—no, madam, not by many removes; Shakspeare was a genius—Milton was a genius—the author of 'History of the Dark Ages,' which has reached its fifteenth edition, was a genius—(you may not know you have now the honor of being addressed by him;) no, madam, you are not a genius, nor have I yet seen a just criticism of your writings; they are all either over-praised, or over-abused; you have a certain sort of talent, and that talent, I grant you, is peculiar; but a genius—no, no, Mrs., or Miss, or Madam Floy—you don't approach genius, though I am not without a hope that, if you are not spoiled by injudicious, sycophantic admirers, you may yet produce something creditable; although I candidly confess, that it is my opinion, that the *female* mind is incapable of producing anything which may be strictly termed *literature*.

"Your honest friend,
WILLIAM STEARNS.

"Prof. of Greek, Hebrew, and Mathematics, in Hopetown College, and author of 'History of the Dark Ages.' "

"Oh vanity! thy name is William Stearns," said Ruth.

CHAPTER LXXVI

"HAVE you ever submitted your head to a phrenological examination?" asked Mr. Walter, as he made a call on Ruth,
the next morning. *begins in her space*

"No," said Ruth; "I believe that much more is to be told by
the expression of people's faces than by the bumps upon their
heads."

"And you a woman of sense!" replied Mr. Walter. "Will you
have your head examined to please me? I should like to know
what Prof. Finman would say of you, before I leave town."

"Well—yes—I don't mind going," said Ruth, "provided the
Professor does not know his subject, and I see that there 's fair
play," said she, laughing; "but I warn you, beforehand, that I
have not the slightest faith in the science."

Ruth tied on her bonnet, and was soon demurely seated in *sexual*
the Professor's office, with her hair about her shoulders. Mr.
Walter sat at a table near, prepared to take notes in short-hand.

"You have an unusually even head, madam," said the Professor. "Most of the faculties are fully developed. There are not
necessarily any extremes in your character, and when you man-
ifest them, they are more the result of circumstances than the
natural tendency of the mind. You are of a family where there
was more than ordinary unity in the connubial relations; certainly in the marriage, if not in the after-life of your parents.

"Your physiology indicates a predominance of the nervous
temperament; this gives unusual activity of mind, and furnishes
the capacity for a great amount of enjoyment or suffering. Few
enjoy or suffer with such intensity as you do. Your happiness or
misery depends very much on surrounding influences and
circumstances.

"You have, next, a predominance of the vital temperament, which gives great warmth and ardor to your mind, and enables you to enjoy physical comfort and the luxuries of life in a high degree. Your muscular system is rather defective; there not being enough to furnish real strength and stamina of constitution. Although you may live to be aged, you will not be able to put forth such vigorous efforts as you could do, were the motive or muscular temperament developed in a higher degree. You may think I am mistaken on this point, but I am not. You have an immense power of will, are energetic and forcible in overcoming obstacles, would display more than ordinary fortitude in going through trials and difficulties, and possess a tenacity of purpose and perseverance in action, which enable you to do whatever you are determined upon doing; but these are *mental* characteristics not *physical,* and your mind often tires out your body, and leaves you in a state of muscular prostration.

"Your phrenology indicates an unusual degree of respect and regard for whatever you value as superior. You never trifle with superiority. I do not mean conventional superiority or bombastic assumption, but what you really believe to be good and noble. As a child, you were very obedient, unless your sense of justice (which is very strong) was violated. In such a case, it was somewhat difficult for you to yield either ready or implicit obedience. You are religiously disposed. You are also characterized by a strong belief in Divine influences, providences, and special interpositions from on high. You are more than ordinarily spiritual in the tone of your mind. You see, or think you see, the hand of Providence in things as they transpire. You are also very conscientious, and this, combined with your firmness, which is quite strong, and supported by your faith in Providence, gives you a striking degree of what is called moral courage. When you believe you are right, there is no moving you; and your friends probably think that you are sometimes very obstinate; but let them convince your intellect and satisfy your conscience, and

you will be quite tractable, more especially as you are characterized by unusual sympathy and tenderness of feeling. You too
easily catch the spirit of others,—of those you love and are interested in, and feel as they feel, and enjoy or suffer as they do.
You have very strong hope with reference to immortality and
future happiness. When a young girl, you were remarkably
abounding in your spiritual anticipations of what you were going
to be as a woman.

"You possess an extraordinary degree of perseverance, but
have not a marked degree of prompt decision. After you have
decided, you act energetically, and are more sure to finish what
you commence, than you are ready to begin a new enterprise.
You are decidedly cautious, anxious, mindful of results, and desire to avoid difficulty and danger. You take all necessary care,
and provide well for the future. Your cautiousness is, in fact, too
active.

"You place a very high value on your character; are particularly sensitive to reproach; cannot tolerate scolding, or being
found fault with. You can be quite reserved, dignified, and even
haughty. You are usually kind and affable, but are capable of
strong feelings of resentment. You make few enemies by your
manner of speaking and acting. You are uniform in the mani-
festation of your affections. You do not form attachments readily,
or frequently; on the contrary, you are quite particular in the
choice of your friends, and are very devoted to those to whom
you become attached. You manifested these same traits when a
child, in the selection of playmates.

"Your love is a mental love—a regard for the mind, rather
than the person of the individual. You appreciate the masculine
mind as such, rather than the physical form. You have a high
regard for chivalry, manliness, and intellectuality in man, but you
also demand goodness, and religious devotion. It would give you
pain to hear a friend speak lightly of what you consider sacred
things; and I hardly think you would ever love a man whom

you *knew* to be irreligious. Your maternal feelings are very strong. You are much interested in children. You sympathize with and understand them perfectly. You are, yourself, quite youthful in the tone of your mind; much younger than many not half your age. This, taken in connection with your sympathy with, and appreciation of, the character of children, enables you to entertain them, and win them to your wishes; but, at times, you are too anxious about their welfare. You are strongly attached to place, and are intensely patriotic. You believe in Plymouth Rock and Bunker Hill. You are not content without a home of your own; and yet, in a home of your own, you would not be happy without pleasant surroundings and associations, scenery, and such things as would facilitate improvement and enjoyment.

"You are very fond of poetry and beauty, wherever you see it,—of oratory, sculpture, painting, scenery, flowers, and beautiful sentiments. You must have everything nice; you cannot tolerate anything coarse or gross. The world is hardly finished nice enough for you. You are too exacting in this respect. The fact is, you are made of finer clay than most of us. You are particular with reference to your food, and not easily suited. You must have that which is clean and nice, or none. Whatever you do, such as embroidery, drawing, painting, needlework, or any artistic performance, is very nicely done. Your constructiveness is very large. You can plan well; can lay out work for others to advantage; can cut out things, and invent new and tasteful fashions. Your appreciation of colors is very nice; you can arrange and blend them harmoniously, in dress, in decoration of rooms, &c. You could make a slim wardrobe, and a small stock of furniture, go a great way, and get up a better looking parlor with a few hundred dollars, than some could with as many thousands.

"You exhibit a predominance of the reflective intellect over the perceptive, and are characterized for thought, judgment, and the power to comprehend ideas, more than for your knowledge

of things, facts, circumstances or conditions of things.
member and understand what you read, better than
see and hear; still, you are more than ordinarily observant. In
passing along the street, you would see much more than people
in general, and would be able to describe very accurately the
style, execution and quality of whatever you saw. You have a
pliable mind. You love acting, and would excel as an actress.
You have great powers of sarcasm. You enjoy fun highly, but it
must be of the right kind. You will tolerate nothing low. You
are precise in the use of language, and are a good verbal critic.
You ought to be a good conversationist, and a forcible and spicy
writer. In depicting character and describing scenes, you would
be apt to display many of the characteristics which Dickens exhibits. Your aptness in setting-forth, your keen sense of the lu-
dicrous, your great powers of amplification, and the intensity of
your feelings, would enable you to produce a finely wrought
out, and exquisitely colored picture. You have also an active
sense of music; are almost passionately fond of that kind which
is agreeable to you.

"You have more than ordinary fortitude, but are lacking in
the influences of combativeness. Your temper comes to a crisis
too soon; you cannot keep angry long enough to scold. You
dislike contention. You read the minds of others almost instantaneously; and at once form a favorable or unfavorable impression of a person. You are secretive, and disposed to conceal your
feelings; are anxious to avoid unnecessary exposure of your faults,
and know how to appear to the best advantage. You have a
good faculty of entertaining others, but can be with persons a
long time without their becoming acquainted with you.

"You dream things true; truth comes to you in dreams, fore-
warnings, admonitions, &c.

"You are liable to be a very happy, or very unhappy, woman.
The worst feature of your whole character, or tone of mind,
arises from the influence of your education. Too much attention

was paid to your mind, and not enough to your body. You were brought forward too early, and made a woman of too soon. Ideas too big for you were put into your mind, and it was not occupied enough about the ordinary affairs of life. This renders your mind too morbid and sensitive, and unfits you for encountering the disagreeable phases of life. You can endure disagreeable things with martyr-like firmness, but not with martyr-like resignation. They prey both on your mind and body, and wear heavily upon your spirit. You feel as though some one must go forward and clear the way for you to enjoy yourself; and if by any reverse of fortune, you have ever been thrown on your own resources, and forced to take care of yourself, you had to learn some lessons, which should have been taught you before you were sixteen years old. But in the general tone of your mind, in elevation of thought, feeling, sympathy, sentiment, and religious devotion, you rank far above most of us, above many who are, perhaps, better prepared to discharge the ordinary duties of life. In conclusion, I will remark, that very much might be said with reference to the operations of your mind, for we seldom find the faculties so fully developed, or the powers so versatile as in your case."

"Well," said Mr. Walter, with a triumphant air, as they left the Professor's office, "well, 'Floy,' what do you think?"

"I think we have received our $2 worth in flattery," replied Ruth, laughing.

"There is not a whit of exaggeration in it," said Mr. Walter. "The Professor has hit you off to the life."

"Well, I suppose it would be wasting breath to discuss the point with you," said Ruth, "so I will merely remark that I was highly amused when he said I should make a good actress. I have so often been told that."

"True; Comedy would be your forte, though. How is it that when looking about for employment, you never contemplated the stage?"

"Well, you know, Mr. Walter, that we May-Flower descendants hold the theater in abhorrence. For my self, however, I can speak from observation, being determined not to take that doctrine on hearsay; I have witnessed many theatrical performances, and they only served to confirm my prejudices against the institution. I never should dream of such a means of support. Your Professor made one great mistake; for instance," said Ruth, "he thinks my physique is feeble. Do you know that I can walk longer and faster than any six women in the United States?"

"Yes," replied Mr. Walter, "I know all about that; I have known you, under a strong impetus, do six days' work in one, and I have known you after it prostrated with a nervous headache which defied every attempt at mitigation. He is right, Ruth, your mind often tires your body completely out."

"Another thing, your Professor says I do not like to be found fault with; now this is not quite true. I do not object, for instance, to *fair* criticism. I quarrel with no one who denies to my writings literary merit; they have a right to hold such an opinion, a right to express it. But to have one's book reviewed on hearsay, by persons who never looked between the covers, or to have isolated paragraphs circulated, with words italicized, so that gross constructions might be forced upon the reader, which the author never could dream of; then to have paragraphs taken up in that state, credited to you, and commented upon by horrified moralists,—that is what I call unfair play, Mr. Walter. When my sense of justice is thus wounded, I do feel keenly, and I have sometimes thought such persons knew the suffering that such thoughtlessness to baptize it by the most charitable name, may cause a woman, who must either weep in silence over such injustice, or do violence to her womanly nature by a public contention for her rights, such outrages would be much less frequent. It seems to me," said she earnestly, "were I a man, it would be so sweet to use my powers to defend the defenseless. It would seem to me so impossible to use that power to echo

the faintest rumor adverse to a woman, or to keep cowardly silence in the shrugging, sneering, slanderer's presence, when a bold
word of mine for the cause of right, might close his dastard lips."

"Bravo, Ruth, you speak like an oracle. Your sentiments are
excellent, but I hope you are not so unsophisticated as to expect
ever to see them put in universal practice. Editors are but men,
and in the editorial profession, as in all other professions, may
be found very shabby specimens of humanity. A petty, mean-
spirited fellow, is seldom improved by being made an editor of;
on the contrary, his pettiness, and meanness, are generally
intensified. It is a pity that such unscrupulous fellows should be
able to bring discredit on so intelligent and honorable a class of
the community. However," said Mr. Walter, "we all are more
or less responsible, for if the better class of editors refrained from
copying abusive paragraphs, their circulation would be confined
to a kennel class whose opinion is a matter of very little consequence."

"By the way, Ruth," said Mr. Walter, after walking on in
silence a few rods, "how is it, in these days of female preachers,
that you never contemplated the pulpit or lecture-room?"

"As for the lecture-room," replied Ruth, "I had as great a
horror of that, as far as I myself am concerned, as the profession
of an actress; but not long since I heard the eloquent Miss Lucy
Stone one evening, when it really did appear to me that those
Bloomers of hers had a mission! Still, I never could put them
on. And as to the pulpit, I have too much reverence for that to
think of putting my profane foot in it. It is part of my creed that
a congregation can no more repay a conscientious, God-fearing,
devoted minister, than—"

"*You* can help 'expressing your *real* sentiments,' " said Mr.
Walter, laughing.

"As you please," replied Ruth; "but people who live in glass
houses should not throw stones. But here we are at home; don't
you hear the 'whir—whir'?"

CHAPTER LXXVII

A ND now our heroine had become a regular business woman. She did not even hear the whir—whir of the odd lodger in the attic. The little room was littered with newspapers, envelopes, letters opened and unopened, answered and waiting to be answered. One minute she might be seen sitting, pen in hand, trying, with knit brows, to decipher some horrible cabalistic printer's mark on the margin of her proof; then writing an article for Mr. Walter, then scribbling a business letter to her publishers, stopping occasionally to administer a sedative to Nettie, in the shape of a timely quotation from Mother Goose, or to heal a fracture in a doll's leg or arm. Now she was washing a little soiled face, or smoothing little rumpled ringlets, replacing a missing shoe-string or pinafore button, then wading through the streets while Boreas contested stoutly for her umbrella, with parcels and letters to the post-office, (for Ruth must be her own servant,) regardless of gutters or thermometers, regardless of jostling or crowding. What cared she for all these, when Katy would soon be back—poor little patient, suffering Katy? Ruth felt as if wings were growing from her shoulders. She never was weary, or sleepy, or hungry. She had not the slightest idea, till long after, what an incredible amount of labor she accomplished, or how her *mother's heart* was goading her on.

"Pressing business that Mis. Hall must have," said her landlady, with a sneer, as Ruth stood her dripping umbrella in the kitchen sink. "Pressing business, running round to offices and the like of that, in such a storm as this. You would n't catch *me* doing it if I was a widder. I hope I 'd have more regard for appearances. I don't understand all this flying in and out, one minute up in her room, the next in the street, forty times a day,

and letters by the wholesale. It will take me to inquire into it.
It may be all right, hope it is; but of course I like to know what
is going on in my house. This Mis. Hall is so terrible close-
mouthed, I don't like it. I 've thought a dozen times I 'd like
to ask her right straight out who and what she is, and done with
it; but I have not forgotten that little matter about the pills, and
when I see her, there 's something about her, she 's civil enough
too, that seems to say, 'don't you cross that chalk-mark, Sally
Waters.' I never had lodgers afore like her and that old Bond,
up in the garret. They are as much alike as two peas. *She* goes
scratch—scratch—scratch; *he* goes whir—whir—whir. They
haint spoke a word to one another since that child was sick.
It 's enough to drive anybody mad, to have such a mystery in
the house. I can't make head nor tail on't. John, now, he don't
care a rush-light about it; no more he would n't, if the top of
the house was to blow off; but there 's nothing plagues *me* like
it, and yet I aint a bit curous nuther. Well, neither she nor Bond
make me any trouble, there 's that in it; if they did I would n't
stand it. And as long as they both pay their bills so reg'lar, I
shan't make a fuss; I *should* like to know though what Mis. Hall
is about all the time.

———

Publication day came at last. There was *the* book. Ruth's book!
Oh, how few of its readers, if it were fortunate enough to find
readers, would know how much of her own heart's history was
there laid bare. Yes, there was the book. She could recall the
circumstances under which each separate article was written. Little shoeless feet were covered with the proceeds of this; a little
medicine, or a warmer shawl was bought with that. This was
written, faint and fasting, late into the long night; that composed
while walking wearily to or from the offices where she was employed. One was written with little Nettie sleeping in her lap;

another still, a mirthful, merry piece, as an escape-v
wretched heartache. Each had its own little history. Ea
serve, in after-days, for a land-mark to some thorny p... ... ..-
gone trouble. Oh, if the sun of prosperity, after all, should gild
these rugged paths! Some virtues—many faults—the book had
—but God speed it, for little Katy's sake!

"Let me see, please," said little Nettie, attracted by the gilt
covers, as she reached out her hand for the book.

"Did you make those pretty pictures, mamma?"

"No, my dear—a gentleman, an artist, made those for me—
I make pictures with a-b-c's."

"Show me one of your pictures, mamma," said Nettie.

Ruth took the child upon her lap, and read her the story of
Gertrude. Nettie listened with her clear eyes fixed upon her
mother's face.

"Don't make her die—oh, please don't make her die,
mamma," exclaimed the sensitive child, laying her little hand
over her mother's mouth.

Ruth smiled, and improvised a favorable termination to her
story, more suitable to her tender-hearted audience.

"That is nice," said Nettie, kissing her mother; "when I get
to be a woman shall I write books, mamma?"

"God forbid," murmured Ruth, kissing the child's changeful
cheek; "God forbid," murmured she, musingly, as she turned
over the leaves of her book; "no happy woman ever writes.
From Harry's grave sprang 'Floy.'"

CHAPTER LXXVIII

"YOU have a noble place here," said a gentleman to Ruth's brother, Hyacinth, as he seated himself on the piazza, and his eye lingered first upon the velvet lawn, (with its little clumps of trees) sloping down to the river, then upon the feathery willows now dipping their light green branches playfully into the water, then tossing them gleefully up to the sunlight; "a noble place," said he, as he marked the hazy outline of the cliffs on the opposite side, and the blue river which laved their base, flecked with many a snowy sail; "it were treason not to be poetical here; I should catch the infection myself, matter-of-fact as I am."

"Do you see that steamer yonder, floating down the river, Lewis?" said Hyacinth. "Do you know her? No? well she is named 'Floy,' after my sister, by one of her literary admirers."

"The————! *your* sister? *'Floy'*—your *sister!* why, everybody is going mad to know who she is."

"Exactly," replied Hyacinth, running his white fingers through his curls; " 'Floy' is my sister."

"Why the deuce did n't you tell a fellow before? I have wasted more pens, ink, and breath, trying to find her out, than I can stop to tell you about now, and here you have kept as mum as a mouse all the time. What did you do it for?"

"Oh, well," said Hyacinth, coloring a little, " 'Floy' had an odd fancy for being *incog.,* and I, being in her confidence, you know, was on honor to keep her secret."

"But she *still wishes it kept,*" said Lewis; "so her publishers, whom I have vainly pumped, tell me. So, as far as that goes, I don't see why you could not have told me before just as well as now."

Hyacinth very suddenly became aware of "an odd craft in the river," and was apparently intensely absorbed looking at it through his spy-glass.

"Hyacinth! I say, Hyacinth!" said the pertinacious Lewis, "I believe, after all, you are humbugging me. How *can* she be your sister? Here 's a paragraph in ———— Sentinel, saying—" and Lewis drew the paper from his pocket, unfolded it, and put on his glasses with distressing deliberation: " 'We understand that "Floy," the new literary star, was in very destitute circumstances when she first solicited the patronage of the public; often wandering from one editorial office to another in search of employment, while wanting the commonest necessaries of life.' There, now, how can that be if she is 'your sister'? and you an editor, too, always patronizing some new contributor with a flourish of trumpets? Pooh, man! you are hoaxing;" and Lewis jogged him again by the elbow.

"Beg your pardon, my dear boy," said Hyacinth, blandly, "but 'pon my honor, I have n't heard a word you were saying, I was so intent upon making out that craft down the river. I 'm a little afraid of that fog coming up, Lewis; suppose we join Mrs. Ellet in the drawing-room."

"Odd—very odd," soliloquized Lewis. "I 'll try him again.—

"Did you read the panegyric on 'Floy' in 'The Inquisitor' of this morning?" said Lewis. "That paper, you know, is decidedly the highest literary authority in the country. It pronounces 'Floy's' book to be an 'unquestionable work of genius.' "

"Yes," replied Hyacinth, "I saw it. It is a great thing, Lewis, for a young writer to be *literarily connected;*" and Hyacinth pulled up his shirt-collar.

"But I understood you just now that nobody knew she *was* your sister, when she first published the pieces that are now collected in that book," said Lewis, with his characteristic pertinacity.

"There 's that craft again," said Hyacinth; "can't you make
her out, Lewis?"

"No—by Jove," replied Lewis, sarcastically; "I can't make
anything out. I never was so be-fogged in my life;" and he bent
a penetrating glance on the masked face before him. "It is past
my finding out, at least just now; but I 've a Yankee tongue in
my head, so I don't despair, with time and perseverance;" and
Lewis followed Hyacinth into the house.

"Confounded disagreeable fellow," soliloquized Hyacinth, as
he handed him over to a knot of ladies in the drawing-room;
"very awkward that paragraph; I wish I had the fellow who
wrote it, at pistol-shot distance just now; well, if I am badgered
on the subject of 'Floy's' poverty, I shall start a paragraph saying,
that the story is only a publisher's trick to make her book sell;
by Jove, they don't corner me; I have got out of worse scrapes
than that before now, by the help of my wits and the lawyers,
but I don't think a paper of any influence would attack me on
that point; I have taken care to secure all the more prominent
ones, long ago, by judicious puffs of their editors in the Irving
Magazine. The only one I fear is the ———, and I will lay an
anchor to windward there this very week, by praising the editor's
last stupid editorial. What an unmitigated donkey that fellow is."

CHAPTER LXXIX

"How are you, Walter," said Mr. Lewis, extending his hand; "fine day; how goes the world with you? They say *you* are a man who dares to 'hew to the line, let the chips fly in whose face they will.' Now, I want you to tell me if 'Floy' is *really* a sister of Hyacinth Ellet, the editor of 'The Irving Magazine.' I cannot believe it, though he boasted of it to me the other day, I hear such accounts of her struggles and her poverty. I cannot see into it."

"It is very easily understood," said Mr. Walter, with a dark frown on his face; "Mr. Hyacinth Ellet has always had one hobby, namely—social position. For that he would sacrifice the dearest friend or nearest relative he had on earth. His sister was once in affluent circumstances, beloved and admired by all who knew her. Hyacinth, at that time, was very friendly, of course; her husband's wine and horses, and his name on change, were things which the extravagant Hyacinth knew how to appreciate.

"Hall ('Floy's' husband) was a generous-hearted, impulsive fellow, too noble himself to see through the specious, flimsy veil which covered so corrupt a heart as Hyacinth's. Had he been less trusting, less generous to him, 'Floy' might not have been left so destitute at his death. When that event occurred, Hyacinth's regard for his sister evaporated in a lachrymose obituary notice of Hall in the Irving Magazine. The very day after his death, Hyacinth married Julia Grey, or rather married her fortune. His sister, after seeking in vain to get employment, driven to despair, at last resorted to her pen, and applied to Hyacinth, then the prosperous editor of the Irving Magazine, either to give her employment as a writer, or show her some way to obtain it. At that time Hyacinth was constantly boasting of the helping

hand he had extended to young writers in their extremity,
(whom, by the way, he paid in compliments after securing their
articles,) and whom, he was constantly asserting, had been raised
by him from obscurity to fame."

"Well," said Lewis, bending eagerly forward; "well, he helped
his sister, of course?"

"He did no such thing, sir," said Mr. Walter, bringing his
hand down on the table; "he did no such thing, sir; but he wrote
her a cool, contemptuous, insulting letter, denying her all claim
to talent, (she had sent him some specimen articles,) and advising
her to seek some unobtrusive employment, (*what* employment
he did not trouble himself to name,) and then ignored her existence; and this, too, when he was squandering money on 'distressed' actresses, etc."

"Well?" said Mr. Lewis, inquiringly.

"Well, sir, she struggled on bravely and single-handed, with
the skeleton Starvation standing by her hearth-stone—she who
had never known a wish ungratified during her married life,
whose husband's pride in her was only equaled by his love. She
has sunk fainting to the floor with hunger, that her children
might not go supperless to bed. And now, when the battle is
fought and the victory won, *he* comes in for a share of the spoils.
It is 'my sister "Floy," ' and 'tis *his* 'literary reputation which
was the stepping-stone to her celebrity as a writer.'

"To show you how much 'his reputation has helped her,' I
will just state that, not long since, I was dining at a restaurant
near two young men, who were discussing 'Floy.' One says,
'Have you read her book?' 'No,' said the other, with a sneer,
'nor do I want to; it is enough for me that Hyacinth Ellet claims
her as a sister; *that* is enough to damn any woman.' Then,"
continued Mr. Walter, "there was an English paper, the editor
of which, disgusted with Hyacinth's toadyisms, fopperies, and
impudence while abroad, took occasion to cut up her book (as

he acknowledged) because the writer was said to be Ellet's sister. That is the way *his* reputation has helped her."

"No wonder she is at sword's-point with him," remarked Mr. Lewis.

"She is not at sword's-point with him," replied Mr. Walter. "She simply chooses to retain the position her family assigned her when she was poor and obscure. They would not notice her then; she will not accept their notice now."

"Where was the old man, her father, all this time?" said Mr. Lewis, "was he alive and in good circumstances?"

"Certainly," said Mr. Walter; "and once in awhile he threw her a dollar, just as one would throw a bone to a hungry dog, with a 'begone!' "

"By Jove!" exclaimed Mr. Lewis, as he passed by, "what a heartless set."

CHAPTER LXXX

R UTH returned from her daily walk to the Post Office, one morning, with a bundle of letters, among which was one from Mr. Walter. Its contents were as follows:

"DEAR SISTER RUTH:

"I wonder if you are enjoying your triumph half as much as I? But how should you, since you do not know of it? Your publishers inform me that orders are pouring in for your book faster than they can supply them. What do you think of that? 'Floy,' you have made a decided hit; how lucky that you had the foresight to hold on to your copyright. $800 will not be a circumstance to the little fortune you are going to make. Your success is glorious; but I don't believe you are half as proud of it as I am.

"And now, I know of what you are thinking as well as if I were by your side. 'Tis of the little exile, 'tis of Katy. You would fly directly to bring her home. Can I be of any service to you in doing this? Business takes me your way day after to-morrow. Can you curb your impatience to see her till then? If so, I will accompany you. Please write me immediately.

"Yours truly,
            JOHN WALTER."

"P. S.—I send you a batch of letters, which came by this morning's mail, directed to 'Floy,' office of the Household Messenger."

Ruth tossed the "batch of letters" down unopened, and sprang to her feet; she tossed up Nettie; she kissed the astonished child till she was half strangled; she laughed, she cried, and then

she sat down with her forehead in both her hands, for a prolonged reverie.

What *good* news about the book! How could she wait two
days before she brought back Katy! And yet it would be a happy
thing, that Mr. Walter, whose name was synonymous with good
tidings, should be associated with her in the return of the child.
Yes, she would wait. And when Katy *was* secured, what then?
Why, she would leave forever a city fraught with such painful
associations; she would make her a new home. Home? Her heart
leaped!—comforts for Nettie and Katy,—clothes—food,—
earned by her own hands!—Tears trickled through Ruth's fingers, and her heart went out in a murmured prayer to the "God
of the widow and fatherless."

"May I play house with these?" said Nettie, touching Ruth's
elbow, and pointing to the unopened letters.

"No, little puss," said Ruth, "not yet. Wait a bit till I have
glanced at them;" and she broke the seal of one.

It was an offer of marriage from a widower. He had read an
article of hers on "Step-Mothers," and was "very sure that a
woman with *such* views could not fail to make a good mother
for his children." He was thirty-five—good-looking, (every man
who had written her a love-letter *was!*) good disposition —
warm-hearted—would love her just as well as if he had never
bent an adoring knee to Mrs. Dorrance No. 1—was not at all
set in his ways—in fact preferred she should, in everything, save
him the trouble of *choice;* would live in any part of the Union
she desired, provided she would only consent to *the union.* These
last two words Mr. Dorrance had italicised, as indicating, probably, that he considered it a pun fit even for the critical eye of
an authoress.

"Oh, pshaw!" said Ruth, throwing the letter to Nettie,
"make anything you like of it, pussy; it is of no value to me."
The next letter ran as follows:

"MADAM:

"I have the honor to be guardian to a young Southern lady (an orphan) of large fortune, who has just completed her education. She has taken a suite of apartments, and given me orders to furnish them without regard to expense, according to her fancy. I have directions to procure busts of Mrs. Hemans, Miss Landon, and several other distinguished female writers, among whom Miss Le Roy includes 'Floy,' (I have not the pleasure, madam, of knowing your true name,) with whose writings she has become familiar, and who is as great a favorite with her as she is with the multitude who have paid tribute to her genius.

"Please send me a line, (my address as below,) allowing me to inform my ward how her favorite wish can be best carried out.

"Yours truly,
THOMAS PEARCE."

Ruth glanced around her little dark room and smiled. "I would rather, instead, that an artist would take a sketch of my room, now," said she; "that little black stove, where I have so often tried in vain to thaw my frozen fingers—that rickety old bed—the old deal table, with its yellow bowl of milk—that home-made carpet—those time-worn chairs—and then you, my little bright fairy, in the foreground;" and she pushed back the soft, glossy curls from Nettie's fair brow.

"No, no," said Ruth, "better reserve the niche destined for 'Floy' for some writer to whom ambition is not the hollow thing it is to me.

"Well, what have we here? Another letter?" Ruth broke the seal of letter No. 3, and read:

"DEAR MADAM:

"I am a poor devil, and worse editor; nevertheless, I have started a paper. If you will but allow me to put your name on it as Assistant Editress, I am sure it will go like a locomotive. If, in addition to this little favor, you could also advance me the sum of one hundred dollars, it would be an immense relief to your admirer,

"JOHN K. STAPLES.

"P. S.—Be sure you direct to John *K.* Staples, as there is another John Staples in this place, who is a great rascal.

J. K. S."

"Well!" exclaimed Ruth, "I did not believe I should ever be astonished again, but then—I had not heard from Mr. Staples. But here is another letter. Let us see what the contents of No. 4 are."

Letter No. 4 ran as follows:

"DEAR 'FLOY':

"I am a better son, a better brother, a better husband, and a better father, than I was before I commenced reading your articles. May God bless you for the words you have spoken (though unintentionally) so directly to me. May you be rewarded by Him to whom the secrets of all hearts are known.

"Your grateful friend,

M. J. D."

"This will repay many a weary hour," said Ruth, as her tears fell upon the page.

CHAPTER LXXXI

THE rain had poured down without mitigation for seven consecutive days; the roads were in a very plaster-y state; dissevered branches of trees lay scattered upon the ground; tubs and hogsheads, which careful housewives had placed under dripping spouts, were full to overflowing; the soaked hides of the cattle looked sleek as their owners' pomatum'd heads of a Sunday; the old hen stood poised on one leg at the barn-door, till even her patience had given out; the farmers had mended all the old hoe and rake handles, read the Almanac through and through, and worn all the newspapers and village topics threadbare, when the welcome sun at last broke through the clouds, and every little and big puddle in the road hastened joyfully to reflect his beams.

Old Doctor Hall started down cellar for his "eleven o'clock mug of cider;" to his dismay he found his slippered pedestals immersed in water, which had risen above the last step of the cellar-stairs.

"A pretty piece of work this rain has made, Mis. Hall," said the doctor, stamping his wet feet and blowing his nose, as he returned from his visit to the lower regions; "the water has overflowed the cellar, and got most up to those hams that you set such store by. You 'd better tell Bridget to climb over the heads of those barrels, and get the hams out before they are clean sp'iled."

Before the last words had fairly left the doctor's mouth the old lady's cap-strings were seen flying towards the kitchen.

"I shan't do it, for anybody," exclaimed the new help, as she placed her red arms a-kimbo. "I 'm not going to risk my neck going over those tittlish barrels in that dark cellar, for all the hams that was ever cured."

"You can carry a lamp with you," suggested the old lady.

"I shan't do it, I tell you," said the vixen; "help is skerse out here in the country, and I can get a new place before sundown, if I like."

"Katy!" screamed the old lady, with a shrill voice, "Katy!"

Katy started from her corner and came out into the entry, in obedience to the summons.

"Come here, Katy; Bridget is as contrary as a mule, and won't go into the cellar to get those hams. I cannot go in after 'em, nor the doctor either, so you must go in and bring them out yourself. Climb up on those barrels heads, and then feel your way along to the further corner; go right down the cellar-stairs now, quick."

"Oh, I cannot! I *dare* not!" said Katy, trembling and shrinking back, as the old lady pushed her along toward the cellar-door.

"I 'm *so* afraid," said the child, peeping down the cellar-stairs, with distended eyes, "oh, *don't* make me go down in that dark place, grandma."

"Dark, pooh!" said the old lady; "what are you afraid of? rats? There are not more than half-a-dozen in the whole cellar."

"Can't Bridget go?" asked Katy; "oh, I 'm *so* afraid."

"Bridget *won't,* so there 's an end of that, and I 'm not going to lose a new girl I 've just got, for your obstinacy; so go right down this minute, rats or no rats."

"Oh, I can't! if you kill me I can't," said Katy, with white lips, and clinging to the side of the cellar door.

"But I say you shall," said the old lady, unclinching Katy's hands; "don't you belong to me, I 'd like to know? and can't I do with you as I like?"

"No!" said Ruth, receiving the fainting form of her frightened child; "no!"

"Doctor! doctor!" said the old lady, trembling with rage; "are you master in this house or not?"

"Yes—when *you* are out of it," growled the doctor; "what 's to pay now?"

"Why, matter enough. Here 's Ruth," said the old lady, not noticing the doctor's taunt; "Ruth interfering between me and Katy. If you will order her out of the house, I will be obliged to you. I 've put up with enough of this meddling, and it is the last time she shall cross this threshold."

"You never spoke a truer word," said Ruth, "and my child shall cross it for the last time with me."

"Humph!" said the doctor, "and you no better than a beggar! The law says if the mother can't support her children, the grandparents shall do it."

"The mother *can*—the mother *will*," said Ruth. "I have already earned enough for their support."

"Well, if you have, which I doubt, I hope *you earned it honestly,*" said the old lady.

Ruth's heightened color was the only reply to this taunt. Tying her handkerchief over Katy's bare head, and wrapping the trembling child in a shawl she had provided, she bore her to a carriage, where Mr. Walter and his brother-in-law, (Mr. Grey,) with little Nettie, awaited them; the door was quickly closed, and the carriage whirled off. The two gentlemen alternately wiped their eyes, and looked out the window as Katy, trembling, crying, and laughing, clung first to her mother, and then to little Nettie, casting anxious, frightened glances toward the prison she had left, as the carriage receded.

Weeping seemed to be infectious. Ruth cried and laughed, and Mr. Grey and Mr. Walter seemed both to have lost the power of speech. Little Nettie was the first to break the spell by offering to lend Katy her bonnet.

"We will do better than that," said Ruth, smiling through her tears; "we will get one for Katy when we stop. See here, Katy;" and Ruth tossed a purse full of money into Katy's lap.

"You know, mother said she would come for you as soon as she earned the money."

"Yes, and I *knew* you would, mother; but—it was so very—" and the child's lips began to quiver again.

"She is so excited, poor thing," said Ruth, drawing her to her bosom; "don't talk about it now, Katy; lean your head on me and take a nice nap;" and the weary child nestled up to her mother, while Nettie put one finger on her lip, with a sagacious look at Mr. Walter, as much as to say, "*I* will keep still if *you* will."

"She does not resemble you as much as Nettie does," said Mr. Grey to Ruth, in a whisper.

"She is like her father," said Ruth; the "resemblance is quite startling when she is sleeping; the same breadth of forehead, the same straight nose, and full lips.

"Yes, it has often been a great solace to me," said Ruth, after a pause, "to sit at Katy's bedside, and aid memory by gazing at features which recalled so vividly the loved and lost;" and she kissed the little nestler.

"Nettie," said Mr. Walter, "is Ruth second, in face, form and feature."

"I wish the resemblance ended there," whispered Ruth, with a sigh. "These rose-tinted dawns too often foreshadow the storm-cloud."

CHAPTER LXXXII

A N hour after the conversation narrated in the last chapter, the driver stopped at a fine-looking hotel.

"This is the place, then, where you are going to stay for a few weeks, before you leave this part of the country for ———," said Mr. Walter; "allow me to speak for a dinner for us all; such a day as this does not dawn on us often in this world;" and he glanced affectionately at little Katy.

The party was soon seated round a plentifully-furnished table. Nettie stopped at every other mouthful to look into Katy's eyes, or to kiss her, while little Katy gazed about bewilderingly, and grasped her mother's hand tightly whenever her ear caught the sound of a strange voice or footstep.

"Will you have some soup, little puss?" said Mr. Walter, after they were seated at the table, pulling one of Nettie's long curls.

"Ask my mother," replied the child, with a quizzical look; "she 's the *soup*-erintendent."

Mr. Walter threw up his hands, and a general shout followed this precocious sally.

"Come, come," said Mr. Walter, when he had done laughing; "you have begun too early, little puss; come here and let me feel your head. I must take a phrenological look at you. Bless me! what an affectionate little creature you must be," said he, passing his hand over her head; "stick a pin there now, while I examine the rest of your bumps."

"You must not stick a pin in my head," said Nettie; "I don't like that way of expressing an o-*pin*-ion."

"No further examination is necessary," said the extinguished Mr. Walter; "I have done with *you*, Miss Nettie. What do you mean?" whispered he to Ruth, "by having such a child as that? Are we going to have another genius in the family?"

"I don't know about that," said Ruth, laughing; "she often says such things when she gets excited and hilarious, but I never encourage it by notice, and you must not; my physician told me not to teach her anything, and by all means not to let her see the inside of a schoolroom at present."

"Well, well," said Mr. Walter, "Miss Nettie and I must have a tilt at punning some day. You had better engage, Ruth, to furnish the Knickerbocker with smart repartees for his 'Children's Table,' from your own fireside."

"Prenez garde," whispered Ruth, "don't spoil her. Such a child needs careful training; she is high-spirited, warm-hearted, and sensitive;" and Ruth sighed.

"I interpret your thoughts," said Mr. Walter; "but we must have no backward glances to-day. Those children will never suffer what you have suffered; few women ever did. Ruth, for the thousandth time I tell you, you are a brave woman!"

"—Upon my word," said Mr. Walter, suddenly, blushing and thrusting his hand in his pocket, "I have committed the sin so common to all *man*-kind; carried letters for you round in my pocket all this time, without delivering them: here they are. I never saw a woman have so many letters as you do, 'Floy;' you 'll need a private secretary before long."

Ruth broke the seal of one, saying, "You 'll excuse me a few moments," and read:

"TO 'FLOY':

"DEAR MADAM,—We have established a very successful Infant School in our neighborhood, numbering about fifty pupils. Our first anniversary occurs next month. It is our intention to gather together the parents and children, and have a sort of jubilee; hymns will be sung, and short pieces spoken. We should be very much obliged to you if you would write us a little dialogue to be repeated by two little girls, of the age of six; something sweet and simple, such as you know how to write. We make no apology for thus intruding on your time, because we know your heart is with the children.

"Yours respectfully,

JOHN DEAN.

"Secretary of the Leftbow Infant School."

"Patience, gentlemen, while I read No. 2," said Ruth. No. 2 ran as follows:

"DEAR 'FLOY':

"Old Guardy has sent me up to this academy. I hate academies. I hate Guardy's. I hate everything but snipe shooting and boating. Just now I am in a horrid fix. Every fellow in this academy has to write a composition once a week. I cannot do it. I never could. My talents don't lie in that way. I don't know where they do lie. What I want of you is to write those compositions for me. You can do it just as easy as water runs down hill. You could scratch one off while I am nibbing my pen. Old Phillips will think they are uncommon smart for me; but never mind, I shall keep dark, and you are such a good soul I know you can't refuse. My cigars have been out two whole days; so you may know that I have no funds, else I would send you a present.

"Yours truly,

HAL. HUNNEWELL."

After glancing over this letter Ruth broke into a merry laugh, and saying, "This is too good to keep," read it aloud for the amusement of the company, who unanimously voted Hal. Hunnewell a composition every week, for his precocious impudence.

"Come, now," said Mr. Walter, as Ruth took up No. 3, "if you have another of the same sort, let us hear it, unless it be of a confidential nature."

Ruth looked over the letter a moment, and then read:

"DEAR 'FLOY':

"Mamma has read me some of your stories. I like them very much. You say you love little children. Don't you think we 've got a bran new baby! It came last night when I was asleep in my trundle-bed. It is a little pink baby. Mamma says it will grow white by-and-by. It has got such funny little fingers; they look all wrinkled, just like our maid's when she has been at the wash-tub. Mother has to stay in bed with him to keep him warm, he 's such a little cold, shaky thing. He has n't a bit of hair, and he scowls like everything, but I guess he 'll be pretty by-and-by. Anyhow I love him. I asked mother if I might not write and tell you about him, and she laughed and said, I don't know who 'Floy' is, nor where she lives; but Uncle Jack (he gives me lots of candy and dolls) said that I must send it to 'Floy's' publishers! I don't know what a publisher is, and so I told Uncle Jack; and he laughed and said he would lose *his* guess if I did n't have something to do with them one of these days. I don't know what that meant either, and when I asked him, he said 'go away, Puss.' I think it is very nice to have an Uncle Jack at Christmas and New Year's, but other times they only plague little children. I wish I could see you. How do you look? I guess you look like mamma; mamma has got blue eyes, and soft brown hair, and her mouth looks very pleasant when she smiles. Mamma's voice is as sweet as a robin's, so papa says. Papa is a great big man, so big that nobody could ever hurt me, or mamma. Papa wants to see you too. Won't you write me a letter, a little letter all to myself? I 've got a box made of rosewood, with a lock and key on it, where I 'd hide it from Uncle Jack, (that would tease him!) Uncle Jack wants to see you too, but I hope you never will let him, for he 's such a terrible tease, he 'd plague you dreadfully. I guess our baby would send his love to you if he only knew you. Please write me soon, and send it to Kitty Mills, care of Uncle Jack Mills, and please seal it up all tight, so he cannot peep into it.

"P. S.—I want you to write a book of stories for little girls, and don't make them end bad, because it makes me cry; nor put

; in them, because it scares me; or have any 'moral'
he bottom, because Uncle Jack always asks me if I
. Write something funny, won't you? I like funny
things, and fairy stories. Oh, I like fairy stories so *much!* Was n't
it nice about the mice and the pumpkin, in Cinderella? Make
them all end well, won't you?

"Your affectionate little

KITTY."

"I suppose you do not feel any curiosity to know what the
papers say about your book," said Mr. Walter, as Ruth refolded
her letters. "I have quite a stock of notices in my pocket, which
I have saved up. You seem to have taken the public heart by
storm. You could not desire better notices; and the best of it is,
they are spontaneous—neither begged nor in a measure de-
manded, by a personal call upon the editors."

"What on earth do you mean?" asked Ruth.

"Look at 'the spirit of '76' flashing from her eyes," said Mr.
Grey, laughing, as he pointed at Ruth.

"I mean this," said Mr. Walter, "that not long since I expressed my surprise to an able critic and reviewer, that he could
praise a certain book, which he must have known was entirely
deficient in merit of any kind. His answer was: 'The authoress
of that book made a call on me at my office, deprecated in the
strongest terms any adverse criticism in the paper with which I
am connected; said that other papers would take their tone from
mine, that it was her first book, and that her pen was her only
means of support, &c., &c. What can a man do under such
circumstances?' said my informant."

"How *could* she?" said Ruth. "Of what ultimate advantage
could it be? It might have procured the sale of a few copies at
first, but a book, like water, will find its level. But what astonishes me most of all is, that any able reviewer should be willing
to risk his reputation as a critic by such promiscuous puffery.
How are the people to know when he speaks his *real* sentiments?

It strikes me," said Ruth, laughing, "that such a critic should have some cabalistic mark by which the initiated may understand when he speaks truthfully. It is such a pity!" continued Ruth thoughtfully; "it so neutralizes criticism. It is such a pity, too, that an authoress could be found so devoid of self-respect as to do such a thing. It is such an injury to those women who would disdain so to fetter criticism; who would launch their book like a gallant ship, prepared for adverse gales, not sneaking near the shore, or lowering their flag for fear of a stray shot."

"Do you know, Ruth," said Mr. Walter, "when I hear you talk, I no longer wonder at Hyacinth's lack of independence and common sense; his share must, by some unaccountable mistake, have been given to you in addition to your own. But where are the children?"

They looked around; Katy and Nettie, taking advantage of this prolonged discussion, had slid from the table, in company with a plate of nuts and raisins, and were holding an animated conversation in a further corner.

"Why! what a great, big mark on your arm, Katy," exclaimed Nettie; "how *did* it come?"

"Hush!" replied Katy; "grandma did it. She talked very bad about mamma to grandpa, and I started to go up into my little room, because, you know, I *would n't* bear to hear it; and she called to me, and said, 'Katy, what are you leaving the room for?' and you know, Nettie, mamma teaches us always to tell the truth, so I said, 'because I cannot bear to stay and hear you say what is not true about my mamma.' And then grandma threw down her knitting, seized me by the arm, and set me down, oh, *so* hard, on a chair; and said, 'but you *shall* hear it.' Then, oh, Nettie, I *could not* hear it, so I put my fingers in both ears; and then she beat me, and left that place on my arm, and held both my hands while she made me listen."

During this recital, Nettie's eyes glowed like living coals. When Katy concluded, she clenched her little fists, and said:

"Katy, why did n't you strike her?"

Katy shook her head, and said in a low tone, "Oh, Nettie, she would have killed me! When she got angry she looked just like that picture of Satan we saw once in the shop window."

"Katy, I *must* do something to her," said Nettie, closing her teeth together, and planting her tiny foot firmly upon the floor; "she *shan't* talk so about mamma. Oh, if I was only a big woman!"

"I suppose we must *forgive* her," said Katy thoughtfully.

"*I* won't," said the impulsive little Nettie, "never—never—never."

"Then you cannot say your prayers," said the wise little Katy; " 'forgive us, as we forgive those who have trespassed against us.' "

"What a pity!" exclaimed the orthodox Nettie; "don't you wish that had n't been put in? What *shall* we do, Katy?"

"Nettie," said her mother, who had approached unnoticed, "what did you mean when you said just now, that you wished you were a big woman?"

Nettie hung her head for a minute, and twisted the corner of her apron irresolutely; at last she replied with a sudden effort, "you won't love me, mamma, but I will tell you; I wanted to cut grandma's head off."

Little Katy laughed outright, as the idea of this Lilliputian combatant presented itself. Ruth looked serious. "That is not right, Nettie," said she; "your grandmother is an unhappy, miserable old woman. She has punished herself worse than anybody else could punish her. She is more miserable than ever now, because I have earned money to support you and Katy. She *might* have made us all love her, and help to make her old age cheerful; but now, unless she repents, she will live miserably, and die forsaken, for nobody can love her with such a temper. This is a dreadful old age, Nettie!"

"I *think* I 'll forgive her," said Nettie, jumping into her mother's lap; "but I hope I shan't ever hear her say anything against you, mother. I'm glad I was n't Katy. Did n't you ever wish, Katy, that she might fall down stairs and break her neck, or catch a fever, or something?"

"Oh, mother, what a funny girl Nettie is!" said Katy, laughing till the tears came; "I had almost forgotten her queer ways! Oh, how grandmother *would* have boxed your ears, Nettie!"

The incorrigible Nettie cut one of her pirouettes across the room, and snapped her fingers by way of answer to this assertion.

While Ruth and her children were conversing, the two gentle-men were quite as absorbed in another corner of the apartment.

"It astonishes me," said Mr. Grey to Mr. Walter, "that 'Floy' should be so little elated by her wonderful success."

"It will cease to do so when you know her better," said Mr. Walter; "the map of life has been spread out before her; she has stood singing on its breezy heights—she has lain weeping in its gloomy valleys. Flowers have strewn her pathway—and thorns have pierced her tender feet. The clusters of the promised land have moistened her laughing lip—the Dead Sea apple has mocked her wasted fingers. Rainbows have spanned her sky like a glory, and storms have beat pitilessly on her defenseless head. Eyes have beamed upon her smiling welcome. When wounded and smitten, she fainted by the way, the priest and the Levite have passed by on the other side. 'Floy' knows every phase of the human heart; she knows that she was none the less worthy because poor and unrecognized; she knows how much of the homage now paid her is due to the *showy setting* of the gem; therefore, she takes all these things at their true valuation. Then, my friend," and Mr. Walter's voice became tremulous, "amid all these 'well done' plaudits, *the loved voice is silent.* The laurel crown indeed is won, but the feet at which she fain would cast it have finished their toilsome earth-march."

★   ★   ★

"It is time we gentlemen were going; let us talk business now," said Mr. Walter, as Ruth returned from her conversation with the children. "How long did you propose remaining here, Ruth?"

"For a month or so," she replied. "I have several matters I wish to arrange before bidding adieu to this part of the country, I shall try to get through as soon as possible, for I long to be settled in a permanent and comfortable home."

"I shall return this way in a month or six weeks," said Mr. Walter, "and if you are ready at that time, I shall be most happy to escort you and your children to your new residence."

"Thank you," said Ruth. "Good-by, good-by," shouted both the children, as the two gentlemen left the room.

CHAPTER LXXXIII

"I DON'T know about holding you *both* in my lap at once," said Ruth smiling, as Nettie climbed up after Katy.

"Do, please," said Nettie, "and now let us have a nice talk; tell us where we are going to live, mamma, and if we can have a kitty or a rabbit, or some live thing to play with, and if we are going to school, and if you are going to leave off writing now, and play with Katy and me, and go to walk with us, and ride with us. Shan't we have some rides? What is the matter, mamma?" said the little chatterbox, noticing a tear in her mother's eye.

"I was thinking, dear, how happy we are."

"Is n't that funny?" said Nettie to Katy, "that mamma should cry when she is happy? I never heard of such a thing. *I* don't cry when I 'm happy. Did n't we have a good dinner, Katy? Oh, I like this house. It was such an old dark room we used to live in, and there was nothing pretty to look at, and mamma kept on writing, and I had nothing to play with, except a little mouse, who used to peep out of his hole, when it came dark, for some supper. I liked him, he was so cunning, but I could n't give him any supper, because—" here the little chatterbox glanced at her mother, and then placing her mouth to Katy's ear, whispered, with a look the gravity of which was irresistible, "because mamma could n't support a mouse."

Ruth laughed heartily as she overheard the remark, and Nettie thought her mother more of a puzzle than ever, that she should keep laughing and crying so in the wrong place.

"What have you there, Nettie?" asked Katy.

"Something," said Nettie, looking very wise, as she hid her chubby hands under her pinafore. "It is a secret. Mamma and I know," said she with a very important air, "don't we, mamma? Would you tell Katy, mother, if you were me?"

"Certainly," said Ruth; "you know it would not be pleasant to keep such a great secret from Katy."

Nettie looked very searchingly into her mother's eyes, but she saw nothing there but sincerity.

"Won't you *ever* tell, Katy ever? it is a terrible secret."

"No," replied Katy, laughing.

"Not even to Mr. Walter?" asked Nettie, who had learned to consider Mr. Walter as their best friend, and the impersonation of all that was manly and chivalrous.

Katy shook her head negatively.

"Well, then," said Nettie, hanging her head with a pretty shame, *"I 'm in love!"*

Katy burst into an uncontrollable fit of laughter, rocking herself to and fro, and ejaculating, "Oh! mamma! oh! did you ever? Oh, how funny!"

"Funny?" said Nettie, with the greatest naïvete, "it was n't funny at all; it was very nice. I 'll tell you all how it happened, Katy. You see I used to get so tired when you were away, when I had nobody to play with, and mamma kept up such a thinking. So mamma said I might go to a little free school opposite, half-a-day, when I felt like it, and perhaps that would amuse me. Mamma told the teacher not to trouble herself about teaching me much. Well, I sat on a little low bench, and right opposite me, across the room, was such a *pretty* little boy! his name was Neddy. He had on a blue jacket, with twelve bright buttons on it; I counted them; and little plaid pants and drab gaiters; and his cheeks were so rosy, and his hair so curly, and his eyes so bright, oh, Katy!" and Nettie clasped her little hands together in a paroxysm of admiration. "Well, Katy, he kept smiling at me, and in recess he used to give me half his apple, and once, when nobody was looking,—*would* you tell her mamma?" said Nettie, doubtfully, as she ran up to her mother. "Won't you tell, now, Katy, certainly?" again asked Nettie.

"No," promised Katy.

"Not even to Mr. Walter?"

"No."

"Well, once, when the teacher was n't looking, Katy, he took a piece of chalk and wrote 'Nettie' on the palm of his hand, and held it up to me and then kissed it;" and Nettie hid her glowing face on Katy's neck, whispering, "was n't it beautiful, Katy?"

"Yes," replied Katy, trying to keep from laughing.

"Well," said Nettie, "I felt most ashamed to tell mamma, I don't know why, though. I believe I was afraid that she would call it 'silly,' or something; and I felt just as if I should cry if she did. But, Katy, she did not think it silly a bit. She said it was beautiful to be loved, and that it made everything on earth look brighter; and that she was glad little Neddy loved me, and that I might love him just as much as ever I liked—just the same as if he were a little girl. Was n't *that* nice?" asked Nettie. "I always mean to tell mamma everything; don't you, Katy?"

"But you have not told Katy, yet, what you have hidden under your apron, there," said Ruth.

"Sure enough," said Nettie, producing a little picture. "Well, Neddy whispered to me one day in recess, that he had drawn a pretty picture on purpose for me, and that he was going to have a lottery; I don't know what a lottery is; but he cut a great many slips of paper, some long and some short, and the one who got the longest was to have the picture. Then he put a little tiny mark on the end of the longest, so that I should know it; and then I got the picture, you know."

"Why did he take all that trouble?" asked the practical Katy. "Why did n't he give it to you right out, if he wanted to?"

"Because—because," said Nettie, twirling her thumbs, and blushing with a little feminine shame at her boy-lover's want of

independence, "he said—he—was—afraid—the—boys—would
—laugh at him if they found it out."

"Well, then, I would n't have taken it, if I had been you,"
said the phlegmatic Katy.

"But, you know, I *loved* him so," said Nettie naïvely.

CHAPTER LXXXIV

DAYS and weeks flew by. Katy and Nettie were never weary of comparing notes, and relating experiences. Nettie thought gloomy attics, scant fare and cross landladies, the climax of misery; and Katy considered a score of mile-stones, with Nettie and a loving mother at one end, and herself and a cross grandmother at the other, infinitely worse.

"Why, you can't tell anything about it," said Katy. "Grandma took away a little kitty because I loved it, and burned up a story-book mamma brought me, and tore up a letter which mamma printed in big capitals on a piece of paper for me to read when I was lonesome; and she would n't let me feed the little snow-birds when they came shivering round the door; and she made me eat turnips when they made me sick; and she said I must not run when I went to school, for fear it would wear my shoes out; and she put me to bed *so* early; and I used to lie and count the stars (I liked the seven little stars all cuddled up together best); and sometimes I looked at the moon and thought I saw faces and mountains in it, and I wondered if it was shining into mamma's window; and then I thought of you all snug in mamma's bed; and then I cried and cried, and got up and looked out into the road, and wondered if I could not run away in the night, when grandmother was asleep. Oh, Nettie, she was a *dreadful* grandmother! She tried to make me stop loving mother. She told me that she loved you better than she did me; and then I wanted to die. I thought of it every night. I knew it was not true, but it kept troubling me. And then she said that very likely mamma would go off somewhere without letting me know anything about it, and never see me again. And she always said such things just as I was going to bed; and then you know I could not get to sleep till almost morning, and when I did, I dreamed such dreadful dreams."

"You poor little thing!" exclaimed Nettie, with patronizing sympathy, to her elder sister, and laying her cheek against hers, "you poor little thing! Well, mamma and I had a horrid time, too. You can't imagine! The wind blew into the cracks of the room *so* cold; and the stove smoked; and I was afraid to eat when we *had* any supper, for fear mamma would not have enough. She always said 'I am not hungry, dear,' but I think she did it to make me eat more. And one night mamma had no money to buy candles, and she wrote by moonlight; and I often heard her cry when she thought I was asleep; and I was so afraid of mamma's landladies, they screamed so loud, and scowled at me so; and the grocer's boy made faces at me when I went in for a loaf of bread, and said 'Oh, ain't we a fine lady, ain't we?' And the wheel was off my old tin cart—and—oh—dear—Katy—" and Nettie's little voice grew fainter and fainter, and the little chatterbox and her listener both fell asleep.

Ruth, as she listened in the shadow of the further corner, thanked God that they who had had so brief an acquaintance with life's joys, so early an introduction to life's cares, were again blithe, free, and joyous, as childhood ever should be. How sweet to have it in her power to hedge them in with comforts, to surround them with pleasures, to make up to them for every tear of sorrow they had shed,—to repay them for the mute glance of sympathy—the silent caress—given, they scarce knew why, (but, oh, how touching! how priceless!) when her own heart was breaking.

And there they lay, in their pretty little bed, sleeping cheek to cheek, with arms thrown around each other. Nettie—courageous, impulsive, independent, irrepressible, but loving, generous, sensitive, and noble-hearted. Katy—with veins through which the life-blood flowed more evenly, thoughtful, discriminating, diffident, reserved, (so proud of those magnetic qualities in her little sister, in which she was lacking, as to do injustice to her own solid but less showy traits;) needing ever the kind word of encouragement, and judicious praise, to stimulate into life the dormant seeds of self-reliance. Ruth kissed them both, and left their future with Him who doeth all things well.

Twelve o'clock at night! Ruth lies dreaming by the side of her children.

She dreams that she roves with them through lovely gardens, odorous with sweets; she plucks for their parched lips the luscious fruits; she garlands them with flowers, and smiles in her sleep, as their beaming eyes sparkle, and the rosy flush of happiness mantles their cheeks. But look! there are three of them! Another has joined the band—a little shadowy form, with lambent eyes, and the smile of a seraph. Blessed little trio. Follows another! He has the same shadowy outline—the same sweet, holy, yet familiar eyes. Ruth's face grows radiant. The broken links are gathered up; the family circle is complete!

With the sudden revulsion of dream-land, the scene changes. She dreams that the cry of "fire! fire!" resounds through the streets; bells ring—dogs howl—watchmen spring their rattles— boys shout—men whoop, and halloo, as they drag the engine over the stony pavements. "Fire! fire!" through street after street, she dreams the watch-word flies! Windows are thrown up, and many a night-capped head is thrust hastily out, and as hastily withdrawn, when satisfied of the distant danger. Still, on rush the crowd; the heavens are one broad glare, and still the wreathed smoke curls over the distant houses. From the doors and windows of the doomed building, the forked flame, fanned by the fury of the wind, darts out its thousand fiery tongues. Women with disheveled locks, and snow-white vestments, rush franticly out, bearing, in their tightened clasp, the sick, maimed, and helpless; while the noble firemen, heedless of risk and danger, plunge fearlessly into the heated air of the burning building.

★　★　★

Now Ruth moves uneasily on her pillow; she becomes conscious of a stifling, choking sensation; she slowly opens her eyes. God in heaven! it is not all a dream! With a wild shriek she springs from the bed, and snatching from it her bewildered children, flies to the stairway. It has fallen in! She rushes to the window, her long hair floating out on the night-breeze.

A smothered groan from the crowd below. "They are lost!" The showering cinders, and falling rafters, have shut out the dreadful tableau! No—the smoke clears away! That portion of the building still remains, and Ruth and her children are clinging to it with the energy of despair. Who shall save them? for it were death to mount that tottering wall. Men hold their breath, and women shriek in terror. See! a ladder is raised; a gallant fireman scales it. Katy and Nettie are dropped into the out-stretched arms of the crowd below; the strong, brave arm of Johnny Galt is thrown around Ruth, and in an instant she lies fainting in the arms of a by-stander.

The butchering, ambitious conqueror, impudently issues his bulletins of killed and wounded, quenching the sunlight in many a happy home. The world shouts bravo! bravo! Telegraph wires and printing-presses are put in requisition to do him honor. Men unharness the steeds from his triumphal car, and draw him in triumph through the flower-garlanded streets. Woman—gentle woman, tosses the slaughtering hero wreaths and chaplets; but who turned twice to look at brave Johnny Galt, as, with pallid face, and smoky, discolored garments, he crawled to his obscure home, and stretched his weary limbs on his miserable couch? And yet the clinging grasp of rescued helplessness was still warm about his neck, the thrilling cry, "save us!" yet rang in the ears of the heedless crowd. God bless our gallant, noble, but *unhonored* firemen.

CHAPTER LXXXV

"STRANGE we do not hear from John," said Mrs. Millet to her wooden husband, as he sat leisurely sipping his last cup of tea, and chewing the cud of his reflections; "I want to hear how he gets on; whether he is likely to get any practice, and if his office is located to suit him. I hope Hyacinth will speak a good word for him; it is very hard for a young man in a strange place to get employment. I really pity John; it must be so disagreeable to put up with the initiatory humiliations of a young physician without fortune in a great city."

"Can't he go round and ask people to give him work, just like cousin Ruth?" asked a sharp little Millet, who was playing marbles in the corner.

"It is time you were in bed, Willy," said his disconcerted mother, as she pointed to the door; "go tell Nancy to put you to bed.

"As I was saying, Mr. Millet, it is very hard for poor John— he is so sensitive. I hope he has a nice boarding-house among refined people, and a pleasant room with everything comfortable and convenient about it; he is so fastidious, so easily disgusted with disagreeable surroundings. I hope he will not get low-spirited. If he gets practice I hope he will not have to *walk* to see his patients; he ought to have a nice chaise, and a fine horse, and some trusty little boy to sit in the chaise and hold the reins, while he makes his calls. I hope he has curtains to his sleeping-room windows, and a nice carpet on the floor, and plenty of bed-clothes, and gas-light to read by, and a soft lounge to throw himself on when he is weary. Poor John—I wonder why we do not hear from him. Suppose you write to-day, Mr. Millet?"

Mr. Millet wiped his mouth on his napkin, stroked his chin,

pushed back his cup two degrees, crossed his knife and fork transversely over his plate, moved back his chair two feet and a half, hemmed six consecutive times, and was then safely delivered of the following remark:

"My—over-coat."

The overcoat was brought in from its peg in the entry; the left pocket was disemboweled, and from it was ferreted out a letter from "John," (warranted to keep!) which had lain there unopened three days. Mrs. Millet made no remark;—that day had gone by;—she had ate, drank, and slept, with that petrifaction too long to be guilty of any such nonsense. She sat down with a resignation worthy of Socrates, and perused the following epistle:

"DEAR MOTHER:

"Well, my sign hangs out my office-door, 'Doctor John Millet,' and here I sit day after day, waiting for patients—I should spell it *patience*. This is a great city, and there are plenty of accidents happening every hour in the twenty-four, but unluckily for me there are more than plenty of doctors to attend to them, as every other door has one of their signs swinging out. Hyacinth has been sick, and I ran up there the other day, thinking, as he is a public man, it might be some professional advantage to me to have my name mentioned in connection with his sickness; he has a splendid place, six or eight servants, and everything on a corresponding scale.

"To think of Ruth's astonishing success! I was in hopes it might help me a little in the way of business, to say that she was my cousin; but she has cut me dead. How could *I* tell she was going to be so famous, when I requested her not to allow her children to call me 'cousin John' in the street? I tell you, mother, we all missed a figure in turning the cold shoulder to her; and how much money she has made! I might sit in my office a month, and not earn so much as she can by her pen in one forenoon. Yes—there 's no denying it, we 've all made a great mistake. Brother Tom writes me from college that at a party the other night, he happened to mention (incidentally, of course) that 'Floy' was his cousin, when some one near him remarked, 'I should think the less said about that, by 'Floy's' relatives, the better.' It frets Hyacinth to a frenzy to have her poverty alluded to. He told me that he had taken the most incredible pains to conciliate editors whom he despised, merely to prevent any allusion to it in their columns. I, myself, have sent several anonymous paragraphs to the papers for insertion, contradicting the current reports, and saying that 'Floy' lost her self-respect before she lost her friends. I don't suppose that was quite right, but I must have an eye to my practice, you know, and it might injure me if the truth were known. I find it very difficult, too, to get any adverse paragraph in, she is getting to be such a favorite (*i. e.* anywhere where it will *tell;*) the little scurrilous papers, you know, have no influence.

"It is very expensive living here; I am quite out of pocket. If you can get anything from father, I wish you would. Hyacinth says I must marry a rich wife as he did, when I get cornered by duns. Perhaps I may, but your rich girls are invariably homely, and I have an eye for beauty. Still there 's no knowing what gilded pill I may be tempted to swallow if I don't get into practice pretty soon. Hyacinth's wife makes too many allusions to 'her family' to suit me (or Hyacinth either, if the truth must be told, but he hates a dun worse, so that squares it, I suppose). Love to Leila.

> "Your affectionate son,
>
> JOHN MILLET."

CHAPTER LXXXVI

"GOOD afternoon, Mrs. Hall," said one of the old lady's neighbors; "here is the book you lent me. I am much obliged to you for it. I like it better than any book I have read for a long while. You said truly that if I once began it, I should not lay it down till I had finished it."

"Yes," said the old lady, "I don't often read a book now-a-days; my eyes are not very strong, (blue eyes seldom are, I believe," said she, fearing lest her visitor should suspect old Time had been blurring them;) "but that book, now, just suits me; there is common-sense in it. Whoever wrote that book is a good writer, and I hope she will give us another just like it. 'Floy' is a queer name; I don't recollect ever hearing it before. I wonder who she is."

"So do I," said the visitor; "and what is more, I mean to find out. Oh, here comes Squire Dana's son; he knows everything. I 'll ask *him*. Yes, there he comes into the gate; fine young man Mr. Dana. They *do* say he 's making up to Sarah Jilson, the lawyer's daughter; good match, too."

"Good afternoon," said both the ladies in a breath; "glad to see you, Mr. Dana; folks well? That 's right. We have just been saying that you could tell us who 'Floy,' the author of that charming book, 'Life Sketches,' really is."

"You are inclined to quiz me," said Mr. Dana. "I think it should be *you* who should give *me* that information."

"Us?" exclaimed both the old ladies; "us? we have not the slightest idea who she is; we only admire her book."

"Well, then, I have an unexpected pleasure to bestow," said Mr. Dana, rubbing his hands in great glee. "Allow me to inform you, Mrs. Hall, that 'Floy' is no more, nor less, than your daughter-in-law,—Ruth."

"*Im*possible!" screamed the old lady, growing very red in the face, and clearing her throat most vigorously.

"I assure you it is true. My informant is quite reliable. I am glad you admire your daughter-in-law's book, Mrs. Hall; I quite share the feeling with you."

"But I don't admire it," said the old lady, growing every moment more confused; "there are several things in it, now I think of them, which I consider highly immoral. I think I mentioned them to you, Mrs. Spear," said she, (trusting to that lady's defective memory,) "at the time I lent it to you."

"Oh no, you did n't," replied Mrs. Spear; "you said it was one of the best and most interesting books you ever read, else I should not have borrowed it. I am very particular what I put in my children's way."

"Well, I could n't have been thinking of what I was saying," said the old lady; "the book is very silly, a great part of it, beside being very bold, for a woman, and as I said before, really immoral."

"It is highly recommended by the religious press," said Mr. Dana, infinitely amused at the old lady's sudden change of opinion.

"You can't tell," said the old lady; "I have no doubt she wrote those notices herself."

"She has made an ample fortune, at any rate," said the young man; "more than I ever expect to make, if I should scribble till dooms-day."

"Don't believe it," said the old lady, fidgeting in her chair; "or, if she has, it won't last long."

"In that case she has only to write another book," said the persistent Mr. Dana; "her books will always find a ready market."

"We shall see," said the old lady bridling; "it is my opinion she 'll go out like the wick of a candle. People won't read a second edition of such trash. Ruth Hall 'Floy'? Humph! that accounts,—humph! Well, anyhow, if she *has* made money, she had her nose held to the grindstone pretty well first; that 's one comfort. *She* 'Floy'? Humph! That accounts. Well, some times money is given for a curse; I 've heern tell of such things.

"—Yes, yes, I 've heern tell of such things," muttered the old lady, patting her foot, as her two visitors left. "Dreadful grand, Ruth—'Floy' feels now, I suppose. A sight of money she 's made, has she? A great deal she knows how to invest it. Invest it! What 's the use of talking about that? It will be invested on her back, in silk gowns, laces, frumpery, and such things. I have n't a silk gown in the world. The least she could do, would be to send me one, for the care of that child.

"—Yes, laces and feathers, feathers and laces. The children, too, all tricked out like little monkeys, with long ostrich legs, and short, bob-tailed skirts standing out like opery girls, and whole yards of ribbin streaming from their hair, I 'll warrant. The Catechize clean driven out of Katy's head. Should n't be at all astonished if they went to dancing school, or any other im- moral place.

"—Wonder where they 'll live? In some grand hotel, of course; dinner at six o'clock, black servants, gold salt-cellars and finger-glasses; nothing short of that 'll suit now; humph. Should n't be astonished any day to hear Ruth kept a carriage and servants in livery, or had been to Victory's Court in lappets and diamonds. She 's just impudent enough to do it. She isn't afraid of anybody nor anything. Dare say she will marry some Count or Duke; she has no more principle.

"—Humph! I suppose she is crowing well over me. V-e-r-y w-e-l-l; the wheel may turn round again, who knows? In fact, I am sure of it. How glad I *should* be! Well, I must say, I did n't think she had so much perseverance. I expected she 'd just sit down, after awhile, and fret herself to death, and be well out of the way.

"—'Floy'! humph. I suppose I sha n't take up a newspaper now without getting a dose about her. I dare say that spiteful young Dana will call here again just to rile me up by praising her. What a fool I was to get taken in so about that book. But how should I know it was hers? I should as soon have thought of her turning out Mrs. Bonaparte, as an authoress. Authoress! Humph! Wonder how the heels of her stockings look? S'pose she wears silk ones now, and French shoes; she was always as proud as Lucifer of her foot.

"—Well, I must say, (as long as there 's nobody here to hear me,) that she *beats all.* Humph! She 'll collapse, though; there 's no doubt of *that.* I 've heard of balloons that alighted in mud-puddles."

CHAPTER LXXXVII

"GOOD morning, Mr. Ellet!" said Mr. Jones, making an attempt at a bow, which the stiffness of his shirt-collar rendered entirely abortive; "how d' ye do?"

"Oh, how are you, Mr. Jones? I was just looking over the Household Messenger here, reading my daughter 'Floy's' pieces, and thinking what a great thing it is for a child to have a good father. 'Floy' was carefully brought up and instructed, and this, you see, is the result. I have been reading several of her pieces to a clergyman, who was in here just now. I keep them on hand in my pocket-book, to exhibit as a proof of what early parental education and guidance may do in developing latent talent, and giving the mind a right direction."

"I was not aware 'Floy' *was* your daughter," replied Mr. Jones; "do you know what time she commenced writing? what was the title of her first article and what was her remuneration?"

"Sir?" said Mr. Ellet, wishing to gain a little time, and looking very confused.

"Perhaps I should not ask such questions," said the innocent Mr. Jones, mistaking the cause of Mr. Ellet's hesitation; "but I felt a little curiosity to know something of her early progress. What a strong desire you must have felt for her ultimate success; and how much your influence and sympathy must have assisted her. Do you know whether her remuneration at the commencement of her career as a writer, was above the ordinary average of pay?"

"Yes—no—really, Mr. Jones, I will not venture to say, lest I should make a mistake; my memory is apt to be so treacherous."

"She wrote merely for amusement, I suppose; there could be

no *necessity* in *your* daughter's case," said the blundering Mr. Jones.

"Certainly not," replied Mr. Ellet.

"It is astonishing how she can write so feelingly about the poor," said Mr. Jones; "it is so seldom that an author succeeds in depicting truthfully those scenes for which he draws solely upon the imagination."

"My daughter, 'Floy,' has a very vivid imagination," replied Mr. Ellet, nervously. "Women generally have, I believe; they are said to excel our sex in word-painting."

"I don't know but it may be so," said Jones. " 'Floy' certainly possesses it in an uncommon degree. It is difficult else to imagine, as I said before, how a person, who has always been surrounded with comfort and luxury, could describe so feelingly the other side of the picture. It is remarkable. Do you know how much she has realized by her writings?"

"There, again," said the disturbed Mr. Ellet, "my memory is at fault; I am not good at statistics."

"Some thousands, I suppose," replied Mr. Jones. "Well, how true it is, that 'to him who hath shall be given!' Now, here is your literary daughter, who has no need of money, realizes a fortune by her books, while many a destitute and talented writer starves on a crust."

"Yes," replied Mr. Ellet, "the ways of Providence are inscrutable."

CHAPTER LXXXVIII

"FEMALE literature seems to be all the rage now," remarked
a gentleman, who was turning over the volumes in Mr.
Develin's book store, No. 6 Literary Row. "Who are your most
successful lady authors?"

"Miss Pyne," said Mr. Develin, "authoress of 'Shadows,' Miss
Taft, authoress of 'Sunbeams,' and Miss Bitman, authoress of
'Fairyland.'"

"I have been told," said the gentleman, "that 'Life Sketches,'
by 'Floy,' has had an immense sale—a larger one, in fact, than
any of the others; is that so?"

"It has had a *tolerable* sale," answered Mr. Develin, coldly. "I
might have published it, I suppose, had I applied; but I had a
very indifferent opinion of the literary talent of the authoress.
The little popularity it *has* had, is undoubtedly owing to the
writer being a sister of Hyacinth Ellet, the Editor of 'The Irving
Magazine.'"

"But *is* she his sister," said the gentleman; "there are many
rumors afloat; one hardly knows what to believe."

"No doubt of it," said Mr. Develin; "in fact, I, myself, *know*
it to be true. 'Floy' is his sister; and it is altogether owing to the
transferring of her articles, by him, to the columns of his paper,
and his liberal indorsement of them, that she has had any
success."

"Indeed," said the gentleman; "why I was a subscriber both
for 'The Standard,' when her first article appeared in it, and also
for 'The Irving Magazine,' and I am very sure that nothing of
hers was copied in the latter until she had acquired an enviable
popularity all over the Union. No, sir," said Mr. Walter, (for it
was he,) "I know a great deal more about 'Floy' and her writings

than *you* can tell me, and some little about yourself. I have often heard of the version you give of this matter, and I came in to satisfy myself if it had been correctly reported to me. Now, allow me to set you right, sir," said he, with a stern look. "The Editor of 'The Irving Magazine' never recognized 'Floy' as his sister, till the universal popular voice had pronounced its verdict in her favor. Then, when the steam was up, and the locomotive whizzing past, he jumps on, and says, 'how fast *we* go!' "

"I think you are mistaken, sir," replied Mr. Develin, with a faint attempt to retain his position.

"I am not mistaken, sir; I know, personally, that in the commencement of her literary career, when one or two articles of hers were copied into his paper by an assistant in the office, he positively forbade her *nom de plume* being again mentioned, or another of her articles copied into the Irving Magazine. He is a miserable time-server, sir. Fashion is his God; he recognizes only the drawing-room side of human nature. Sorrow in satin he can sympathize with, but sorrow in rags is too plebeian for his exquisite organization.

"Good morning, Mr. Develin; good morning, sir. The next time I hear of your giving a version of this matter, I trust it will be a correct one," added he with a stern look.

"Well," exclaimed Mr. Walter, as he walked down street, "of all mean meanness of which a man can be guilty, the meanest, in my estimation, is to rob a woman of her justly-earned literary fame, and I wish, for the credit of human nature, it were confined to persons of as limited mental endowments and influence as the one I have just left."

CHAPTER LXXXIX

"OH, how frightened I was!" exclaimed Nettie, as her mother applied some healing salve to a slight burn on her arm; "how frightened I was, at that fire!"

"You mean, how frightened you were *after* the fire," replied her mother, smiling; "you were so bewildered, waking up out of that sound sleep, that I fancy you did not understand much about the danger till after good Johnny Galt saved you."

"If I did not love Neddy so much, I should certainly give Johnny Galt my picture," said Nettie, with a sudden outburst of enthusiasm.

"I will see that Johnny Galt is rewarded," replied Ruth. "But this is the day Mr. Walter was to have come. I hope Johnny Galt will meet him at the Dépôt as he promised, else he will be so alarmed about our safety when he learns of the fire. Dear me! how the rain comes down, it looks as though it meant to persevere."

"Yes, and *pour-severe* too," said Nettie, with an arch look at her mother.

Katy and Ruth had not finished laughing at this sally, when Mr. Walter was announced.

His greeting was grave, for he trembled to think of the danger they had escaped. After mutual congratulations had been exchanged, a detailed account of their escape given, and Johnny Galt's heroism duly extolled, Mr. Walter said:

"Well, I am glad to find you so comfortably housed after the fire; but the sooner I take all of you under my charge, the better, I think. What do you say to starting for ———— to-morrow? Are you sufficiently recovered from your fright and fatigue?"

"Oh, yes," replied Ruth, laughing; "do we not look as good

as new? Our wardrobe, to be sure, is in rather a slender condition; but that is much easier remedied than a slender purse, as I
have good reason to know."

"Very well, then," said Mr. Walter; "it is understood that we
go to-morrow. I have some business to look after in the morning; shall you object to waiting till after dinner?"

"Not at all," replied Ruth. "In my opinion, nothing can equal
the forlornness of forsaking a warm bed, to start breakfastless on
a journey, with one's eyes half open."

" 'Floy,' " said Mr. Walter, taking a package from his pocket,
"I have obeyed your directions, and here is something which you
may well be proud of;" and he handed Ruth a paper. It ran thus:

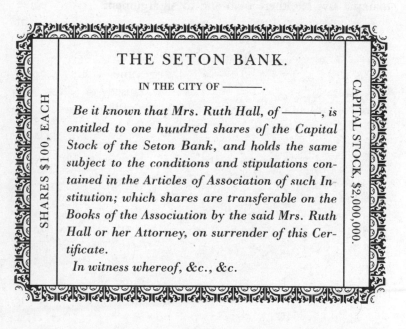

THE SETON BANK.

IN THE CITY OF ———.

*Be it known that Mrs. Ruth Hall, of ———, is
entitled to one hundred shares of the Capital
Stock of the Seton Bank, and holds the same
subject to the conditions and stipulations con-
tained in the Articles of Association of such Institution; which shares are transferable on the
Books of the Association by the said Mrs. Ruth
Hall or her Attorney, on surrender of this Certificate.*

In witness whereof, &c., &c.

SHARES $100, EACH

CAPITAL STOCK, $2,000,000.

"There," said Mr. Walter, laughing, "imagine yourself, if you
can, in that dismal attic one year ago, a bank-stock holder! Now
confess that you are proud of yourself."

"We are proud of her," said the talkative Nettie; "if she is not proud of herself. Don't you think it is too bad, Mr. Walter, that mamma won't let Katy and me tell that 'Floy' is our mother? A little girl who lived at the hotel that was burnt up, said to Katy, that her uncle had just given her Life Sketches for a birthday present, and told her that she must try and write as well as 'Floy' one of these days; and Katy looked at me, and I looked at Katy; and oh, is n't it *too bad,* Mr. Walter, that mamma won't let us tell, when we want to so much?"

"Well," said Mr. Walter, laughing, "I have only one little remark to make about that, namely, I have no doubt you two young ladies discovered some time before I did, that when your mamma says *No,* there is an end to all argument."

CHAPTER XC

THE morning of the next day was bright and fair. After dinner our traveling party entered the carriage in waiting, and proceeded on their way; the children chattering as usual, like little magpies, and Ruth and Mr. Walter occupied with their own solitary reflections.

One of the greatest luxuries of *true* friendship is the perfect freedom one feels, irrespective of the presence of another, to indulge in the mood of the moment—whether that mood be grave or gay, taciturn or loquacious, the unspeakable deliciousness of being reprieved from talking at a mark, hampered by no fear of incivility or discourtesy. Ruth had found this a great charm in the society of Mr. Walter, who seemed perfectly to understand and sympathize with her varied moods. On the present occasion she particularly felt its value—oppressed as she was by the rush of thoughts, retrospective and anticipatory—standing as it were on the threshold of a new epoch in her changing existence.

"Where are we going, mother?" asked Katy, as the carriage passed through a stone-gateway, and down a dim avenue of ancient trees.

"To dear papa's grave," replied Ruth, "before we leave this part of the country."

"Yes!" murmured Katy, in a low whisper.

———

It was very beautiful, that old avenue of pine trees, through which the setting sun was struggling faintly, now resting like a halo on some moss-grown grave-stone, now gilding some more ambitious monument of Mammon's raising. The winding cemetery paths, thronged by day with careless feet, were silent now. No lightsome laughter echoed through those leafy dells, grating upon the ear which almost listened for the loved voice. No strange eye, with curious gaze, followed the thoughtful group, speculating upon their heart's hidden history; but, now and then, a little loitering bird, tempted beyond its mate to lengthen its evening flight, flitted, with a brief gush of song, across their pathway. Hushed, holy, and unprofaned, was this Sabbath of the dead! Aching hearts here throbbed with pain no longer; weary feet were still; busy hands lay idly crossed over tired breasts; babes, who had poised one tiny foot on life's turbid ocean brink, then shrank back affrighted at its surging waves, here slept their peaceful sleep.

The moon had silvered the old chapel turrets, and the little nodding flowers glistened with dew-drops, but still Ruth lingered. Old memories were thronging, thick and fast, upon her;—past joys—past sorrows—past sufferings;—and yet the heart, which felt them all so keenly, would soon lie pulseless amid these mouldering thousands. There was a vacant place left by the side of Harry. Ruth's eye rested on it—then on her children—then on Mr. Walter.

"So help me God," reverently murmured the latter, interpreting the mute appeal.

As the carriage rolled from under the old stone gateway, a little bird, startled from out its leafy nest, trilled forth a song as sweet and clear as the lark's at heaven's own blessed gate.

"Accept the omen, dear Ruth," said Mr. Walter. "Life has much of harmony yet in store for you."

EXPLANATORY NOTES

4 [Hyacinth] "Apollo Hyacinth" was the title of an article Fanny Fern published in the *Musical World and Times*, June 18, 1853. This satiric and often bitter portrayal of Fern's brother, Nathaniel P. Willis, as a fashionable journalist oblivious to the needs of his family and friends, was the origin for Ruth Hall's unsympathetic brother, who was, like Willis, a successful editor and poet.

5 [duenna] A chaperon or a companion for a young woman.

5 [flounces] Pleated or gathered strips of material attached along the upper edge to form a flowing, lower skirt.

6 [bugbear] An object of dread such as a mischievous elf or hobgoblin.

7 [beaver] A man's top hat, made of a beaver's underfur.

7 [Terpsichore ally] Terpsichore was one of the nine Greek Muses; she was devoted to dancing and choral singing.

10 [jackanapes] A vain, impudent person.

11 [de laines] French for fine woolen fabrics.

14 [a very select little library] Mrs. Hall refers to commonplace reading material in the nineteenth century, manuals on health for women and printed sermons.

16 [Esculapius] A variant spelling of Aesculapius, the Roman god of medicine and healing.

16 ["When he opened his mouth, no dog must bark"] A rephrasing of "When I ope my lips let no dogs bark," William Shakespeare, *The Merchant of Venice* I, i, 94, a part of a character description of the conceit and arrogance some individuals assume in positions of authority.

19 [Aesculapian experiments] Medical tests or simple experiments undertaken by a doctor.

21 ["to comb out her 'false front' "] A suggestion that Mrs. Jiff had a hairpiece of a type worn by older women to cover thinning hair at the top of the head.

26 ["The rose that sweetest doth awake, / Will soonest go to rest"] Probably lines from one of dozens of popular poems expressing the fairly conventional sentiment that suggests the fleeting beauty of roses.

27 [brick-bat] A piece of brick used as a missile or weapon.

29 [Dinah] Evidently a free black woman who is happy to work "if she don't work to the tune of a lash," suggesting the frequent whippings to which black slaves were subject.

34 [crouching "Venus"] Mrs. Hall has discovered a reproduction of a statue of Venus, the Roman goddess of love and beauty.

42 [brazen tube] A brass tube that produces a loud, resonant sound like a trumpet.

45 [croup] A pathological condition that affects the larynx in children; it is usually accompanied by respiratory difficulties and a loud, harsh cough.

47 [seven sleepers] An allusion to a legend about seven youths of Ephesus who hid in a cave from pagan persecutors and slept for 187 years. They awoke to find that the world had become Christian while they slept.

48 [leeches] Chiefly aquatic bloodsucking or carnivorous annelid worms of the class Hirudinea, of which one species (*Hirudo medicinalis*) was formerly used by physicians to bleed patients. In the mid-nineteenth century, the efficacy of the practice was beginning to be questioned.

55 [magnetism] Franz Anton Mesmer (1734–1815) was an Austrian physician who believed that "magnetism" emanated from people, animals, and stars. He developed a theory of attractions and repulsions that formed the basis of what was often called mesmerism. Associated with spiritualism, hypnotic experiments, "cures," and other pseudosciences such as phrenology, mesmerism attracted a great deal of interest in the nineteenth century; some prominent people were fascinated by the possibilities—Nathaniel Hawthorne, Margaret Fuller, Harriet Martineau, and Horace Greeley.

56 [David's harp] David, the second king of Israel (1 Samuel 16–31; 2 Samuel; 1 Kings 1; 2 Chronicles 11–29), was a strong king who was a tireless warrior and a good statesman. His weaknesses, sexual temptation and pride, resulted in multiple marriages and numerous children, which eventually caused great rivalries and difficulties in deciding his succession. David was also well known for his many artistic accomplishments. He was a fine musician and is often represented in manuscripts and paintings as playing a harp. Ruth is no doubt thinking of David's musical abilities (he composed many of the Psalms) as she sings to Mrs. Leon to help ease her pain.

58 [ague chill] A fever that causes often uncontrollable shaking or shivering.

59 [typhus fever] A severe disease characterized by high fever, stupor, delirium, headache, and a dark rash.

60 [the sad plaint of Gethsemane's Lord] Ruth paraphrases Jesus' accusing question of his disciple Peter, "Could ye not watch with me one hour" (Matthew 26:40) and keeps the promise that Peter was unable to when she says, "I will never leave thee, nor forsake thee" (Matthew 26:33–34, 69–75).

61 [demi-john] A narrow-necked bottle of glass or stoneware enclosed in a wickerwork; its one or two handles for carrying make it easily portable.

69 [physic] An obsolete term for medicine.

72 ["May the Lord be your support, and let the light of His countenance shine upon you"] A paraphrase of Numbers 6: 24–26.

80 ["Leave thy fatherless children with me"] A verse that does not appear in exactly this sense in the Bible. However, the exhortation to provide for the safekeeping of children is a frequent motif in both the Old and New Testaments, and Ruth is paraphrasing this idea to suggest that her own father does indeed have some responsibility for helping to provide for her children.

83 ["They made a great fuss about his writings"] The Halls are commenting on the popularity of Ruth's brother's writings, which mirror the popularity of Nathaniel P. Willis's essays and sketches for the *Home Journal*. Specifically designed for light reading, the *Home Journal* included articles about fashion, social news and events, theatrical performances, generally laudatory reviews of popular poets, brief articles on writers such as Washington Irving or Henry Wadsworth Longfellow, travel sketches, and stories and poems by a variety of men and women who could be depended upon to entertain and amuse.

87 [milliner] One who designs, makes, and sells women's hats.

87 [delf] Jim refers to the difference between two kinds of pottery in common use in the nineteenth century: "delf" (delft), which characteristically had a dark-blue-and-white glaze and was used frequently in tableware; and "porcelain," generally much paler in shade than delft and more often used in ornamental ware. He is suggesting that Ruth Hall is a more delicate woman than Susan Gill, the milliner.

88 ["rough-dry"] The practice of shaking out clothes after washing and letting them air dry rather than pressing them dry and smooth with hot irons.

89 [limpsey] Weak, lacking in energy or strength.

90 [new publications] Mr. Develin is wary of the complex negotiations required in the exploding marketplace for periodicals and books. See my introduction for a discussion of the economic, technological, and social forces that changed the nature of publishing in the early and mid-nineteenth century.

102 [castor] A small sifter for serving condiments (such as pepper) at a table.

102 ["de parabola of Dives and Lazarus"] Gatty refers to the miracle of Jesus' restoration of Lazarus from the dead, John 11–12.

104 [Golconda's mines] Diamond mines in Hyderabad, India, a source of great wealth.

111 ["griping" rents] An allusion to the controversy in the mid-nineteenth century about the high cost of rents and whether there should be governmental regulations to protect tenants from the practice of avaricious landlords of continually raising rents.

113 [bark] A small sailing ship.

114 ["go to Californy"] The discovery of gold in California in 1848–1849 initiated a "gold rush," and men from all over the world, and especially from the eastern part of the United States, traveled there by wagon train or by boat to seek their fortunes.

115 [limpsey dicky] Mr. Skiddy is wearing a "dickey," a detachable shirtfront commonly worn by working-class men in the nineteenth century; both his dickey and shirt are limp and soiled after his exertions with the baby.

118 [Dickens' young hero] In Charles Dickens's *Oliver Twist* (1837–1838), Oliver asks for more gruel at dinner in the dismal workhouse where he is being brought up following the death of his mother.

126 [Examination day] Ruth Hall is quizzed about a series of educational methods and texts during the course of this examination. This entire passage alludes to competing theories about the way children might best be taught in the nineteenth century, which can roughly be divided into those who generally followed John Locke (1632–1704), who maintained an empirical view of knowledge consistent with the findings of Newtonian physics, and those who followed Jean Jacques Rousseau (1712–1778), the philosopher and social critic who held the view that intuition and individual conscience were the ways toward understanding human nature. In this view, the role of childhood in shaping the adult personality and the developmental education of children are very important. In part, Fern's presentation of Ruth's examination is a commentary on the competing systems that arise from these different views. For example, Dana Pond Colburn (1823–1859) was the author of *The First Steps in Numbers* (1849) and *The Decimal System of Numbers* (1852), as well as a variety of early texts for schools in arithmetic instruction. In the meantime, Frederick Emerson (1788–1857) published *The North American Arithmetic* (1830) and *A Key to the North American Arithmetic* (1833); all these books went through numerous editions in the nineteenth century. The central difference between the two approaches to arithmetic is that Emerson's system depended more on memorization, while Colburn's system attempted to introduce reasoning and analysis into a child's study, more along the lines of a Rousseauean approach to allowing children's experience and intuition to guide them. The other methods used to teach geography and handwriting mentioned in *Ruth Hall* demonstrate similar differences in approach.

127 ["Pollok's Course of Time"] Robert Pollok (1798–1827) wrote *The Course of Time, a Poem*, first published in the early 1820s. An enormously popular volume, it was republished in dozens of editions in both England and America through the first half of the century.

127 [Fanny Kemble] A British actress from a distinguished theatrical family. Equally well known in America, Fanny Kemble (1809–1893) appeared in a variety of plays as a young woman. From 1848 to 1874, she made a second, highly successful career for herself by reading selections from Shakespeare's plays in one-woman shows.

129 ["Webster" was used instead of "Worcester"] Fanny Fern alludes to the war of the dictionaries, another dimension of the controversy over the proper way to educate children in the nineteenth century. Noah Webster (1758–1843) first published his elementary spelling book *A Grammatical Institute of the English Language* (1782) and followed this volume with a grammar and a reader. Feeling that language instruction books neglected the national experience, he tried to incorporate American materials into all of his books. His *American Dictionary of the English Language* (1828) was among the most ambitious publications undertaken in the United States. Joseph Emerson Worcester (1784–1865) published an edition of Samuel Johnson's English dictionary in 1828, and followed it with an abridgment of Webster's in the same year. In 1830, Worcester published his *Comprehensive Pronouncing and Explanatory Dictionary of the English Language*. Webster was outraged and accused Worcester of plagiarism. But the central difference between the two dictionaries is that Webster was trying to write an innovative *American* dictionary, while Worcester, much more of a traditionalist, promoted conventional British pronunciations and usages. In general, Worcester's works appealed to the more fastidious, and Ruth's commentary that the most powerful man on the examining committee was a Worcesterite also suggests her position as outside the traditional and conventional.

131 ["Panorama of Niagara"] Large paintings and murals of Niagara Falls had become popular exhibitions and sources of entertainment in many eastern cities. The "Panorama of Niagara" mentioned here probably refers to the one-thousand-foot painting composed of nearly 200 single canvases of various illustrations of the Falls, completed by Godfrey N. Frankenstein in 1852–1853. Frankenstein showed his painting by unrolling it and providing musical accompaniment and commentary. He toured with this exhibit in all the major eastern cities from 1853 to 1859.

134 [Daguerreotype] The name of the first permanent photographic image, invented in 1837 by Louis J. M. Daguerre (1787–1851). Developed by Daguerre and Joseph Niépce, this process used a camera obscura to expose a specially treated silver-plated sheet of copper which was then treated with mercury vapors. The result was an original image or picture that formed on the plate. Often the plate was placed in a frame, as Mrs. Skiddy describes here.

136 [Uriah Heep] In Charles Dickens's *David Copperfield* (1849–1850), Uriah Heep is Mr. Wickfield's law clerk whose humility is a mask for his mean, malicious, and vengeful character.

139 ["her husband left her here for her health"] Throughout *Ruth Hall*, Fanny Fern suggests that marriage provides few real protections for women, and the marriage of the Leons is her most poignant and painful example. Mr. Leon, as he was well within his legal right to do, pays to have his wife consigned to an "insane hospital," and simply leaves her there, where she

dies. Although the women's rights movement of the nineteenth century was certainly devoted to obtain a woman's right to vote, it is important to remember that women were vitally interested in the equality of the sexes and the reform of marriage laws. Fern devoted many of her columns for the *Ledger* to discussions of ways to change the laws governing marriage to make partnerships more equal. In the Declaration of Sentiments and Resolutions of the Seneca Falls Convention of 1848, two of the principal statements that summarized the history of mankind's injuries to women are: "He has made her, if married, in the eye of the law, civilly dead," and "He has taken from her all right in property, even to the wages she earns." The passage of the Married Women's Property Act in New York in 1848 (advocated by Elizabeth Cady Stanton and others) was only the beginning of changing this system. In Fanny Fern's own life, she had suffered when her first husband died, leaving her without resources. Then she fell victim to an obsessively jealous second husband. When Fanny Fern married James Parton on January 5, 1856, they signed an unusual pre-nuptial agreement, giving Fern complete authority over her own income and property.

146 [Irving Magazine] By calling Hyacinth Ellet's journal the *Irving Magazine*, Fanny Fern suggests the close ties between her brother, Nathaniel P. Willis, and Washington Irving (1783–1859), who was at this time the most successful professional literary man of the day. Willis wrote many articles that praised his works and even lived near him on the Hudson River during the last years of Irving's life. Given Irving's considerable international reputation and influence, Willis had good reason to treat him well. But Fern may have felt that Willis was baldly catering to Irving's tastes.

155 ["know-nothing" hieroglyphics] The flood of immigration from Germany and Ireland in the 1840s alarmed many Americans who blamed many social ills on the influx of newcomers. The Native American Party was established in 1845 for the purpose of limiting the right to vote to native-born Americans. In the early 1850s, the members were often called "know-nothings" because of their secretive manner. Ruth Hall feels that the newspaper offices were operated in a conspiracy of silence, in that she, as an outsider, is having difficulty in determining how to enter into the business.

158 ["the accursed thing . . . Bethel"] Mr. Ellet refers to two Old Testament figures who attempted to thwart God's plans. In Joshua 6: 17–19 and 7: 1–8; 24, Achan, a member of the tribe of Judah, stole plunder from Jericho, which greatly angered God. As a result, the Israelites suffered a defeat in their next battle. Significantly, the alternate form of Achan's name is Alchar, meaning trouble. Jonah, the recalcitrant prophet, was ordered by God to preach at Nineveh. Instead he escaped in a boat and was swallowed by a whale, only to be rescued later by God. Both of these figures might be said to have tried to "hazard the Lord's Bethel," which

was a prominent center of worship in ancient times. Mr. Ellet is more cheered by the news from the Sandwich Islands, a name given to present-day Hawaii in 1778 by Captain James Cook to honor the fourth earl of Sandwich. From 1820 throughout the nineteenth century, a steady stream of New England missionaries went to Hawaii to introduce Christianity and Western education to the natives.

160 [Worcester's or Webster's] See note for page 129. This time, Ruth Hall reverses the order of the names, as though her bitter experience has made her feel that the war of the dictionaries was a quite trivial affair.

162 [Homeopathy] The system of medical treatment established by Samuel Hahnemann (1755–1843) based on the premise that the symptoms of a disease are evidence of the curative process at work in the body responding to the disease. Homeopathic practitioners promote the development of the symptoms in order to accelerate the body's ability to cure itself.

167 ["your very first articles are copied"] Because of the absence of copyright laws, articles published in a newspaper were often copied into others, without attribution. Although it was flattering, authors did not, of course, receive payment for such articles from the newspapers who pirated them.

176 [Shadrach's furnace] An allusion to one of the several court tales in the Book of Daniel. In chapters 1–5, a group of Jewish noblemen, Shadrach, Meshach, and Abednego, are ordered by King Nebuchadnezzar to worship his golden image. The punishment for disobedience is being thrown into a fiery furnace to be burned alive. Shadrach, Meshach, and Abednego refuse to worship the image and are made to stoke the furnace to its hottest level. But they are miraculously saved by God.

186 ["this *is* rather blue-stocking-y"] Ruth fears that she is developing the characteristics of a "blue-stocking," a denigrating term in common use in the nineteenth century to indicate a woman with literary or intellectual interests. The term was probably coined in the mid-1700s when a group of society women who gathered at Montague House in London were known to prefer discussing literature to the usual evening entertainment of playing cards. The men who joined them often did not wear formal dress (as one would for a more social evening) but instead wore their everyday blue worsted wool stockings rather than the black silk stockings that signified full evening attire. The gatherings began to be known informally as the Blue Stocking Society and those who attended were bluestockings. The name survived into the nineteenth century as a term for women with affected literary tastes.

187 ["those Jews will be brought to their senses"] The stereotype of Jews as sharp-dealing and penurious was common in the nineteenth century, and here Fanny Fern uses the formulaic conception to suggest Mr. Walter's opinion of the ungenerous dealings that Ruth Hall has had with Mr. Lescom.

204 [Horace Gates] A thinly disguised portrayal of James Parton, who worked for Fanny Fern's brother Nathaniel P. Willis in a similar position and resigned when Willis ordered him not to publish any more pieces by Fanny Fern in the *Home Journal*.

206 ["Uncle Sam's Log House"] A play on the title of Harriet Beecher Stowe's *Uncle Tom's Cabin*, the best-selling novel of the nineteenth century, published in the spring of 1852. In this passage and through the end of this chapter, Gates rails against the self-serving policies of the *Irving Magazine*, particularly the editorial decision not to publish any articles or comments that would offend southern readers. Nathaniel P. Willis had a similar policy for the *Home Journal* and attempted to refrain entirely from political commentary. Despite the tumultuous years leading up to the Civil War, Willis devoted his magazine to the contemporary social scene, and nothing was said about slavery or sectionalism in the *Home Journal* until June 15, 1861, when the Confederacy became a fact.

208 [Ipecac] A tropical South American plant, the roots of which are dried and used to induce vomiting.

215 [phrenological examination] An aspect of a popular pseudoscience, phrenology, that stressed the physiology of the brain as the key to health. Founded by the German physician and anatomist of the brain Franz Joseph Gall and his student Johann Gaspar Spurzheim, phrenology achieved its greatest popularity during the early part of the nineteenth century. Convinced that the brain was the center of investigation, phrenologists took elaborate measurements of the skull and conducted lengthy examinations of the bumps and contours of the head. Many of their investigations were conducted as public performances and audiences were often highly entertained by the character analyses that were made on the basis of the examinations. Lorenzo and Orson Fowler, two brothers who were responsible for the popularity of phrenology in the United States, published *Phrenology, Proved, Illustrated, and Applied* in 1837 as well as numerous charts and maps of the skull. When Professor Finman tells Ruth Hall that most of her faculties are "fully developed," his evidence is that he believes he can detect enlarged brain areas by touching places on her skull.

222 [Lucy Stone] Lucy Stone (1818–1893), an abolitionist and pioneer in the women's rights movement, graduated from Oberlin College in 1847. Opposed to the legal restrictions of marriage for women, she finally agreed to marry Henry Brown Blackwell in 1855 and prepared with him an unprecedented statement of protest against the laws governing marriage, which was read at their marriage ceremony. Lucy Stone retained, as did Fanny Fern when she married James Parton, her separate property and the control of her own earnings. She also took the unusual step of retaining her name and was known as Mrs. Stone. Stone was an eloquent orator who spoke frequently for the American Anti-Slavery Society; although Ruth Hall seems to admire her bravery, she clearly could not imagine

such a public career for herself. Bloomers, a comfortable outfit of a short skirt worn over baggy trousers, were designed by Amelia Jenks Bloomer (1818–1894), who founded the *Lily* in 1849, the first American magazine edited by and published for women.

231 [he passed by] This phrase appeared in the original edition as "he passed but"; I have corrected the probable typographical error.

240 ["a phrenological look"] See my note for page 215. Mr. Walter entertains Nettie by performing a phrenological examination on the shape of her head.

241 [the Knickerbocker] The *Knickerbocker Magazine* was the actual title of a successful periodical, similar in style and substance to the *New York Mirror*, established in 1833 and continuing publication throughout the 1850s. Regular contributors included James Fenimore Cooper, William Cullen Bryant, James Kirke Paulding, Henry Wadsworth Longfellow, James Greenleaf Whittier, and Nathaniel Hawthorne. It was conventional, Anglophile, and fashionable; it is not likely that Ruth Hall (or Fanny Fern) would have written for the *Knickerbocker* at any time.

266 ["Female literature seems to be all the rage now"] As Susan Geary and other scholars have demonstrated, women writers did in fact dominate the literary marketplace in the 1850s. See my introduction for a discussion of the success of women writers.

FOR THE BEST IN PAPERBACKS, LOOK FOR THE 🐧

In every corner of the world, on every subject under the sun, Penguin represents quality and variety—the very best in publishing today.

For complete information about books available from Penguin—including Penguin Classics, Penguin Compass, and Puffins—and how to order them, write to us at the appropriate address below. Please note that for copyright reasons the selection of books varies from country to country.

In the United States: Please write to *Penguin Group (USA), P.O. Box 12289 Dept. B, Newark, New Jersey 07101-5289* or call 1-800-788-6262.

In the United Kingdom: Please write to *Dept. EP, Penguin Books Ltd, Bath Road, Harmondsworth, West Drayton, Middlesex UB7 0DA.*

In Canada: Please write to *Penguin Books Canada Ltd, 10 Alcorn Avenue, Suite 300, Toronto, Ontario M4V 3B2.*

In Australia: Please write to *Penguin Books Australia Ltd, P.O. Box 257, Ringwood, Victoria 3134.*

In New Zealand: Please write to *Penguin Books (NZ) Ltd, Private Bag 102902, North Shore Mail Centre, Auckland 10.*

In India: Please write to *Penguin Books India Pvt Ltd, 11 Panchsheel Shopping Centre, Panchsheel Park, New Delhi 110 017.*

In the Netherlands: Please write to *Penguin Books Netherlands bv, Postbus 3507, NL-1001 AH Amsterdam.*

In Germany: Please write to *Penguin Books Deutschland GmbH, Metzlerstrasse 26, 60594 Frankfurt am Main.*

In Spain: Please write to *Penguin Books S. A., Bravo Murillo 19, 1° B, 28015 Madrid.*

In Italy: Please write to *Penguin Italia s.r.l., Via Benedetto Croce 2, 20094 Corsico, Milano.*

In France: Please write to *Penguin France, Le Carré Wilson, 62 rue Benjamin Baillaud, 31500 Toulouse.*

In Japan: Please write to *Penguin Books Japan Ltd, Kaneko Building, 2-3-25 Koraku, Bunkyo-Ku, Tokyo 112.*

In South Africa: Please write to *Penguin Books South Africa (Pty) Ltd, Private Bag X14, Parkview, 2122 Johannesburg.*